SUFFER THE CHILDREN

Looking down at the child, he reached out and tore open the filmy material of her gown. Without a word, he pushed the point of the blade into her soft flesh, bearing down with the full weight of his upper body as the blade met the resistance of delicate young bones. Oblivious to the sound of their snapping, he worked the stone blade in a crude semicircle, tearing a crescent-shaped hole in her flesh.

Throughout the agony of her own dying flesh, she uttered not a sound. As his thick fingers probed under the flap he had cut, her mouth dropped open, but if there were any sounds of protest they were lost in the snapping of gristle and bone as he tore open the grisly doorway. At the touch of his cold hand on her heart her eyelids fluttered, then all movement ceased as his hand wrenched the still beating organ from her chest.

MORGAN DRAKE

SACRIFICE

LEISURE BOOKS   NEW YORK CITY

J.D. "Fergy" Ferguson
Who believes I can do anything and refuses
to allow me to prove him wrong.

A LEISURE BOOK ®

May 1990

Published by

Dorchester Publishing Co., Inc.
276 Fifth Avenue
New York, NY 10001

Printed in the United States of America.

"Everyone should have a hobby—
mine is doing evil."

James Thurber—*The 13 Clocks*

Lord of the Night Hammer

SMOKE FROM THE INCENSE BRAZIERS HUNG OVER THE SCENE like a malevolent fog. With each movement on the floor below, it curled, serpentlike, enfolding and mingling with the unseen presence of gathering forces.

She was small, barely three feet tall. The skin of her soft brown face glistened with sweat, mixing the yellow and blue paint she wore. Her thick, long black hair, clean and combed for perhaps only the second time in her young life, swirled about her rounded shoulders. Her small feet, still swaddled in a cushion of baby fat, slapped in time to the rhythms of the Teponaxtle against the stone floor.

With the coquettishness of young females, her chubby little fingers flipped up the hem of her long white gown exposing thick stubby legs. Like a puppet under the hand of a master puppeteer, she instinctively moved to the complicated rhythms.

The primeval call of the conch shell trumpet cut through the rhythms of the Silbahtoes and Omitzicahaushtli, stilling their haunting tones. Silence filled the room, yet the child, lost to her surroundings, whirled on. At the second sounding of the trumpet her movements turned toward the black-stained Techatl stone.

From behind the sacrificial stone, attention fixed on the young dancer, he lifted the conch shell to his lips sounding its melancholy tone for the third and last time.

The child's movements stopped so abruptly that for an instant she swayed unsteadily on her feet. Regaining her balance, she turned toward the dark form awaiting her behind the altar stone. The childish smile that had filled her plump young face during the dance melted from her visage, draining down her body as she looked to the figure with heavy-lidded eyes and drug-dulled features.

The muted tapping of the sacred skin drum began once more, the driving rhythms of the dance replaced by a somber cadence. With sluggish movements, eyes locked on the looming figure, she moved forward. As she approached the stone the ethereal tones of the pan flute added its many voices to the lyric poem.

He lifted his arms at her approach as one would in welcome. The ancient skin of his cape crinkled under the weight of hundreds of once brilliant Quetzal feathers. The flickering light of the braziers reflected dully off the broad cuffs of hammered gold circling his forearms and from the bits of mica trapped in the hand-chipped blade of the knife.

Like a sleepy child stretching out for a nap she spread herself out upon the surface of the cold stone.

Lifting his gaze to the smoke-shrouded ceiling his voice swelled with the long dead language of his ancestors. He chanted words last uttered in this world at the time of Christ, their complex pronunciations singing from his lips, their translation ringing in his mind as clearly as the crude words of his adopted language, English.

Looking down at the child, he reached out and tore open the filmy material of her gown. The sound of the Teponaxtle rose as he lowered the tip of his blade over the center of her chest. Without a word, his face registering nothing, he pushed the point of the blade into her soft flesh, bearing down with the full weight of his upper body as the blade met the resistance of delicate young bones. Oblivious to the sound of their snapping, he worked the stone blade in a crude semicircle, tearing a crescent-shaped hole in her flesh.

Throughout the agony of her own dying flesh, she uttered not a sound. As his thick fingers probed under the flap he had cut, her mouth dropped open, but if there were any sounds of protest they were lost in the snapping of gristle and bone as he tore open the grisly doorway. At the touch of his cold hand on her heart her eyelids fluttered, then all movement ceased as his hand wrenched the still beating organ from her chest.

With all the casual indifference to his victim of the common rapist, he turned away from her, lifting his prize toward the ceiling. Only the smoke witnessed the last movements of her small life as the nerves of her body, confused at the sudden abandonment of the stolen heart, twitched and spasmed.

For several seconds the startled heart continued to function. Held gently in the palm of his hand he watched it, entranced by its last futile movements. As its palpitations began to slow he held it over the center of a terra cotta bowl, the interior surface designs blotched under a reddish black coating. With the supple movements of a constrictor, his fingers closed around the organ and slowly began to squeeze, draining its fluids into the center of the bowl. The blood dribbled silently into the container, adding its deep red color to the dark stain.

He then lifted the heart away from the bowl and, throwing back his head, thrust the organ into his mouth. Strong white teeth cut into the soft organ quickly reducing it to swallowing size. With a gulp it vanished down his gullet. Quickly licking the blood from his hand, he reached down and pulled open the front of his cape.

A wide, heavy gold collar studded with bits of jade and turquoise covered his chest to the breastbone. Below this his hairless chest glistened under a series of painted figures, each representing the lords his prayers called into service.

Discarding the stone knife he reached to a golden plate placed beside the bowl. On its surface lay a number of long, black, needle like objects, stinging spines of stingrays dead a thousand years before the birth of Napoleon.

Silently mouthing the names of his lords, he picked up a spine and drove it through the center of the first of the nine drawings decorating his chest. When a spine protruded from each of the drawings he paused for a moment, watching as his blood mixed with the bright colors of the figures. Pulling back the fringed loincloth that covered his abdomen he drew forth his penis and drove three of the sharp spines into its length and a fourth into the penal opening.

He paused, his black eyes glittering. A tight smile turned up the corners of his thick lips. For that moment, he gloried in the torture, his spirit soaring as the pain washed over him. Each spasm brought him spiritually closer to those who had come before him. Slowly breaking from his ecstasy, he raised the bowl to his chest and withdrew each spine, one at a time. As he did so, a small jet of dark blood was added to the bowl's contents.

Setting the bowl down, he quickly removed the three spines from his penis. Clenching his teeth, he thrust the fourth into the canal again and again; with each thrust the member spasmed until it filled with blood and stood erect. Removing the final spine, he stroked the ravaged organ, pumping semen and blood into the bowl. Draining the last drops of precious liquid into the bowl he allowed a whisper of a sigh to slip from his lips.

Composing himself, he picked up a white silk scarf and, holding it over the bowl for a moment, lowered it into the blood. Within seconds the bloody mixture soaked the scarf. A smile flickered across his face then vanished as the blood soaked into the embroidered initials WDM on the edge of the scarf.

Wiping up the last drops of blood, he lifted the sopping scarf and placed it in the center of the brazier. At first the red coals hissed and turned dark. Taking up a small cup, he sprinkled a glittering white powder onto the scarf. A bright flare issued from the brazier, and the scarf burst into flame. He watched as the fire consumed the material.

Suddenly his face contorted in a rictus of pain. His knees buckled, and he pitched forward. He clutched the edge of the table to steady himself, but the pain was swallowing him. His hands trembled as he slid down, landing hard on his knees. Balanced there, he lowered his head to the altar and wept. His large thick hands curled into fists, and he pushed his fists against his mouth and bit down. Slowly the tears stopped and with the gasping breaths of an hysterical child, he forced himself to stand and watch as the last of the bloodied scarf turned into ash.

An hour later he watched as the final traces of red-stained water vanished down the shower drain. Carefully blotting the drain dry, he looked over the bathroom. Satisfied that no telltale stains marred its gleaming white tile, he turned and walked stiffly into the bedroom.

Picking up his briefcase from the bed he looked around the immaculate room one last time then descended the spiral staircase to the suite's living room. Next to the door sat two large suitcases, one rich, expensive, leather valise holding the artifacts of his obsession. The other, a cheap, scuffed vinyl, contained the dismembered remains of the child.

With a glance around the room he settled himself on the couch facing the windows looking out over the city. From the 30th floor, Los Angeles spread out below him like a jeweler's display on gray velvet.

As he waited for the bellman to fetch his luggage he allowed himself to luxuriate in his success at removing yet another of the annoying hindrances on the pathway to his destiny. On the street below a police car raced through the sparse traffic, its siren echoing off the steel and glass towers. He smiled at the faint sound. Was it possible they had discovered the latest evidence of his powers? He had no doubt that the punishment had been delivered. If they had yet to discover it, that was of no immediate importance. Discover it they would, and in time—a very short time now—they would come to understand and obey.

January 23rd—7:15 p.m.

WITH THE ONSET OF DARKNESS THE RAIN DRIBBLED TO A halt. Los Angeles was settling in for another typical winter's evening, the kind the Chamber of Commerce denied any knowledge of.

Along Santa Monica's equally celebrated and decaying pier, the last of the out-of-towners, clutching their wallets and their Nikons, hurried to the parking lot, eager for the sanctity of their rented automobiles. They averted their gaze from the city's less celebrated inhabitants now drifting in with the tide.

On those areas of Santa Monica Boulevard never mentioned in the travel brochures, charter members of the "sidewalk sorority" began pacing off the boundaries of their territories.

Raven St. James, formerly Richard Kentner of Seattle, Washington, considered his reflection grinning back at him from the thrift store window. The street around him was deserted, but throbbing just under the city sounds, he could feel the pounding beat of music rolling out the open doors of a gay bar two blocks away.

Stepping away from the window he moved with quick mincing steps to the curb—the best he could manage in his too-tight spandex pants. Craning his neck, he searched the sparse approaching traffic.

The blare of a horn sent Raven's heart into overdrive. Wheeling around, he glared at the driver of the glittering black Mercedes, but his anger quickly defused as he recognized William, Sir's driver.

"Where were you? You're late," Raven said, pouting and climbing into the back and draping himself over the front seat.

"Never," William said haughtily.

William clearly showed his disdain for Sir's current paramour.

Raven slumped down in the seat.

"Bitch," he muttered under his breath when he was certain William's attention had returned to the road.

The Mercedes turned off the boulevard and nosed its way through the dark narrow hillside roads of the older, monied section of Pacific Palisades.

The Mercedes finally pulled up to an old house, well into its prime when Raven's mother had been a girl. It filled the center of the street on the Pacific side on a lot nearly three times that of its nearest neighbor. It was the last of its kind on the street, perhaps even the last in this area, and its newer neighbors were pressing the old girl hard.

The Mercedes eased past the crescent-shaped drive around to the side of the house and stopped beside a lighted doorway. Beyond, the dim lights from the carriage house marked the boundaries of the garage. William watched as Raven slipped out of the car and entered the house.

Raven waited until the Mercedes disappeared into the darkness, then turned the light out over the porch. Turning, he paused, staring into the darkened kitchen to his left.

In the small half-bath adjacent to the kitchen Raven found the accoutrements of his service to Sir—a white dinner jacket with wide padded shoulders and even wider lapels, a pale gray silk shirt, a black cumberbund and matching pleated pants. Four thick black towels waited for him on the john beside the small shower. On a narrow shelf over the sink sat a collection of bottles, a razor, and in a small blue bud vase, one tiny, perfect white orchid for his lapel. Everything according to routine.

Once Raven had considered the possibility of cutting out the elaborate costuming and dramatics, but he quickly learned that Sir was a man addicted to routine.

Nothing out of place, nothing left to chance, everything neatly following its prescribed patterns. At no time was Sir more adamant about this addiction than when he was paying the bill.

Showered, perfumed and costumed, his pale lemon-yellow hair slicked straight back from his forehead and the orchid nestled in his lapel, Raven's mind turned fully to the scene Sir required him to play.

Stepping out of the overheated bathroom, the air in the hallway seemed cold. Succumbing to a shiver he moved quickly through the butler's pantry and out into the front foyer. There, as in the remainder of the house, time quite literally had ceased to exist, locked forever somewhere in the early forties.

The soles of his black, patent leather slippers whispering over the thick dark carpeting, Raven moved quickly up the stairs. At the top of the stairs he stepped onto the landing and paused, listening for what was obvious by its absence. Raven frowned.

Until tonight, at this place in the scenario, music could be heard coming from the sitting room adjacent to Sir's bedroom. The music altered from time to time depending on his moods. One night it might be Claire De Lune or something similar, but never had the scene started without appropriate music.

While he pondered over the mystery of the missing music his nose detected an odor that had bedeviled him earlier.

Raven sniffed the air as he moved cautiously up to the doors to Sir's bedroom suite. His frown deepening, Raven sniffed at the doors. There was little doubt in his mind. Whatever the strange scent was it was coming from behind those doors. Leaning closer he listened, holding his breath, searching vainly for a sound, something to indicate the altering of their routine, but no clue readily presented itself.

Raven took a half-step away from the door and swallowed considering the dull brass doorknobs. The evening had started out lousy, and he had a sinking feeling things were about to take a turn for the worse.

Raven began to start a long list of reasons why he should get the hell out of there. At the same time his practical side was reminding him of the small blue envelope that would be waiting for him in the foyer table at the end of tonight's performance.

"Why run?" he chided mentally. "So the old queen forgot to put on the record, and he's got a new after shave. For this I should blow five hundred bucks?"

With a derisive snort he reached out, taking a firm hold on the door handles. He paused for a moment before turning them. Silently he promised himself that if the doors were locked or anything else funny happened, he'd be out of there like a shot.

Pressing down on the handles a sigh of relief softened the tension in his body. He was saved from keeping his promise; the doors were unlocked.

Straightening he made to push through them when he met resistance. Frowning at the recalcitrant doors he pushed harder.

Downstairs, in the foyer, William entered quietly. Looking up, he caught sight of Raven moving quickly down the stairs. The driver's crisp blue eyes narrowed as Raven crossed hurriedly toward him.

Raven shoved the onyx and gold studs, his cummerbund and the orchid toward William. "Here, take this stuff. I don't know what he's up to, but I don't want to play."

William stared at him dumbly as if he were speaking a foreign language.

"Look, you can keep the money. I don't give a shit. This whole thing stinks." Raven frowned, remembering the strange scent emanating from Sir's room. His attention was drawn rudely back to the present as strong fingers clamped themselves around his wrist. "What're you doing? Let go of me."

"What's happened? Why aren't you upstairs with Sir?"

Raven swallowed. "He won't let me in. I mean, the

doors are always unlocked . . . well, they are now only I can't get in, and he won't answer when I call him." Taking a furtive glance in the direction of the stairs he added, "And it stinks up there like . . ."

Before he could finish the sentence William began pulling on his arm, dragging him toward the stairs. Realizing William meant to take him back upstairs, Raven dug in his heels and clawed at the man's hairy fingers, like a recalcitrant child.

"Let go of me. I'm not going back up there. Something's gone wrong, and I don't want any part of it. Keep the fuckin money!"

"Shut up, you silly queer," William snarled, dragging Raven nearer the stairs. Raven swung out wildly, landing a glancing blow on the side of William's temple. William stopped abruptly.

Raven was no stranger to blows. Over the years the blows had been so many he would have needed a computer to have kept track, but when William turned on him and Raven saw the look of anger on the man's face he knew all the others would pale in comparison.

By the time the pair stepped onto the upper landing all feeling in the lower three-quarters of Raven's face had vanished. At least two of his teeth were loose, he was fairly certain his nose was broken, and his jaw seemed totally disconnected from his face. Every few steps he would reach up and trace his jaw's sticky outline with his free hand, taking comfort from the impression, at least, that it was still attached.

William stopped in front of the doors to Sir's suite and, scowling briefly in Raven's direction, ordered, "Stay put or I'll break your legs."

Raven, too scared to run, took root while William turned his attention on the impassive doors. With an almost feminine knock William put his broad face close to the doors and called softly, "Sir, you have a guest." He waited. "Sir?" He called a little louder, "Sir, is there a problem?"

When his third call did no better than the first two, he

took hold of the door handles. They turned but did not open. William called loudly, "Sir, this is William. Answer me, Sir!"

William battered at the doors with his shoulder. Their top halves seemed willing enough to part, but something heavy and solid, pressing against their lower half, held its ground. Taking several steps backward, William rushed forward, hitting them with such force that Raven jumped. The doors splintered, the top halves pulling free of their hinges, and they and William spilled into the room, riding over the obstruction at their base like a surfer on a wave.

The sound of William and the doors hitting the floor made Raven wince. From where he stood, it was impossible to see into the room, a fact that Raven considered a plus. At any moment he expected to see William's brooding face reappear and announce that Sir had died. He wasn't certain just how he knew, but he knew. Sir was in there, all stiff and pale; he probably had the heart attack he was always threatening to have whenever Raven became the least bit creative. Sir, at his age, wasn't an attractive sight at the best of times. Raven was positive seeing Sir dead was an experience he would gladly pass on.

Standing there, waiting for William to return with the inevitable report, Raven's overactive imagination began playing out the scene where the cops arrived and asked him to explain his presence here.

Raven inched closer to the open doorway. Squinting, so as not to see too much, he eased his head past the doorjamb and stopped.

The first sight that captured his attention was William who lay unconscious across the doors, his feet elevated slightly by whatever had held the doors closed. His gaze took in the room beyond.

Always a little nearsighted, he squinted in a futile effort to straighten out the images his eyes were relaying to his confused brain. When the room began to take on a clarity of its own, Raven's eyes widened.

Later, much later, the doctors would say that Raven's jaw was broken and it would have been impossible for him to have been the source of the screams that Mr. and Mrs. Gerrimandy claimed to have heard while walking their Schnauzer—but he was.

January 24th—12:05 a.m.

THE PLYMOUTH RELIANT SWAYED AND SWERVED AROUND THE curves in the road like a drunk with D.T.'s. Inside the car, Det. Sgt. Hyiam Chang clutched the dash in a desperate effort to avoid being tossed to the floorboard among his partner's discarded cigarette packs and Big Mac wrappers.

"Jesus fucking Chrysler, would you slow the hell down? The fucking stiff ain't goin nowhere till we get there," Hy groaned.

"They oughta widen these goddamn streets," Duncan muttered as he let the rear end of the car slide around a curve.

Hyiam ground his big buck teeth and pressed his size 12 Brogans into the car's meager floorboard, a habit he had acquired after five years of riding with Forbes. Fourteen years of piloting LA's streets had done little to soften Duncan's brand of Kamikaze driving, and cases like this one only served to put a keener edge on it.

The house was lit up, inside and out, like a demented Christmas tree.

"Will you look at this shit?" Duncan groaned, slowing slightly as he cut a second driveway into the yard. Wrenching on the parking brake with sufficient force to rein in a team of runaway horses, he pushed his six foot one, 200 pound frame out from behind the wheel and slammed the door, causing the Reliant to echo like the tin can he always swore it was.

Three steps ahead of Chang, Duncan shouldered his way through a covey of patrolmen.

The front doors stood wide open, with lights blazing in the foyer. Cordoned off in one corner were the early birds from the local stations, mini-cams at the ready. Daniel Marks, city hall's answer to Gary Speaks, was smiling into the cameras and explaining he was still in the dark about everything.

Hyiam caught up with Duncan in the foyer where he was searching his pockets for the pack of cigarettes he always seemed to be out of. Hyiam handed over the last of his Salems and nodded toward the stairway.

If there was ever an individual who looked like a character out of *Nicholas Nickleby* it had to be Jasper Heep, Chief Coroner's Investigator. At slightly under six foot six and 140 pounds soaking wet, all he needed was a stovepipe hat and a black hearse and four. Heep spotted the two detectives and headed in their direction.

Hyiam shuddered and suddenly developed a fascination for the wallpaper. He didn't like Heep, not that the poor bastard had ever been anything but nice to him, but Hy just couldn't warm up to the guy.

"If you guys don't catch this creep pretty soon I'm gonna be the first man in the history of the department to go over budget on industrial size spatulas," Heep said without preamble.

Duncan chewed the filter on his cigarette. "Our boy's MO, is it?"

"If you call shovin' a full-grown man into a blender, putting it on puree and leaving the top off, then that's as close to a description of this as I can get."

Grinding out his half-smoked cigarette on the tile, Duncan said, "Give me the good news."

Jasper sighed like a dying whale and shoved his bony hands into the pockets of his shiny polyester suit. "Well, from the bigger pieces I'd say it's as close to a match as we're likely to get. I've got two tech's up there scraping the walls, floor and ceilings on the off chance we might find something that didn't belong to the victim. They should finish within the next half hour provided they can stop barfin' long enough. Unless you boys have any objections I'd like to shovel the deceased into a baggie or two and get him down to the plant before he gets any gamier than he already is."

Duncan's dinner began rising toward his windpipe at the prospect of inspecting another human being that had been skinned then turned inside out. Lighting another smoke, just to give his mouth something else to occupy itself, he muttered, "Give it a few minutes and then you can haul him away."

A commotion from the press section drew the men's attention. Two attendants who looked like they should have been playing for the Raiders were manhandling a stretcher down the stairs.

"What the fuck?" Duncan grumbled looking to Heep. "Who's this?"

Jasper tried to look innocent and failed. "The motor boys wanted to save it for a surprise, but I guess . . ."

"Yeah, yeah, cut the shit."

"You've got two almost witnesses and both alive."

"No shit." Duncan frowned wondering how he got so lucky.

"One is the old man's driver who's upstairs with a bump on his head from knockin down the door."

"Shoulda used his foot. So who's this?"

Jasper favored Duncan with one of his rare almost smiles. Easing toward the front door he purred, "Mary, Queen of Scots."

Before either of the detectives could question Heeps cryptic reference he was heading through the front door.

The news hounds were giving the beat boys a run for their money. Mini-cams, sound men and blue serge collided in a clump as the news teams rushed the stretcher bearers. A second wave of serge checked the flood but just barely, allowing the linebackers and their pale charge to make a dash up the middle.

Holding up his hand like a crossing guard in a busy intersection Chang rumbled, in his best riot control bass, "Hold on a minute. Let's have a look."

"Wonderful—fucking wonderful!"

Chang looked over his shoulder to his partner then down at the bandaged face shining purple and blue against the sharp whiteness of the stretcher.

"Of all the faggots in the world why does it have to be her?" Duncan groaned, his face contorted in a look of genuine pain.

Hy wanted to laugh. He could feel a giggle crawling up the back of his throat and it was only with a supreme force of will that it came out as a cough. Duncan and he were more than familiar with the infamous Raven St. James. In at least one judge's mind Duncan was still the prime suspect when the Hollywood fixture, Raven, was found with his bare ass superglued to a bus stop bench outside the entrance to the Santa Monica pier.

Duncan waved the stretcher on and moved toward the stairway, shaking his head and leaving a trail of ashes on the already grimy tiles. Chang fell into step behind him, trying to think of something solicitous to say when an all too familiar voice drove all constructive thoughts from his head.

"Detective Forbes, can you tell us what progress you've made in capturing the Bel Air Butcher?"

Hyiam stopped, but Duncan continued slowly plodding up the stairs.

As Duncan crossed the landing it hit him—that God-awful smell. It made a slaughterhouse smell like a day at the beach. Swallowing his dinner for the second time that day, he crossed the threshold.

Heep's queasy techs were spread out along the boundaries of the room, each engrossed in some piece of furniture or section of wall with their backs turned to what must have been the epicenter of the crime.

Duncan surveyed the scene slowly. It was the kind of room that time had no effect on. It, like its owner, had been protected, sheltered and nurtured, but in the end they had both fallen victim to the one force no living thing on the face of this planet could protect itself from—random violence.

"All right to bag this one now, Sergeant?"

Duncan wished he could say yes and have it done with, but the game didn't work that way. Sooner or later he'd have to pay the deceased the respect of at least looking at his remains, not that it was going to help either of them or for that matter tell him anything new and startling that was likely to bring him closer to the perpetrator. Still there was a routine to these things and he was too old a dog to start changing the rules at this stage of the game.

"Let's see what'cha got."

"Which piece you interested in?"

Duncan looked up at the man's face for the first time. The graying lab coat marked him as one of Heep's boys, but the face was unfamiliar. Forbes considered a number of responses but suddenly felt too tired to make the effort.

He settled for, "Give me the one with the head on top." As he followed the tech toward the shattered doors he noticed Chang closeted in the corner with a pair of Santa Monica motor cops.

Just beyond the trio sat a man with half a roll of gauze, holding a bandage against his forehead. He was Duncan's age but with a build, even under the cheap black suit, that spoke of years of conditioning. His posture was rigid and his face an unreadable mask, but his eyes glittered under the burden of unshed tears. Duncan knew that to speak to him now would break the barrier and release the flood. The rules said he had to, but he'd say when. Duncan turned sharply at the tech's cough. The tech inclined his head toward the floor. Without thinking Duncan looked down.

It stared up at him. Like some ghastly joke the upper third of the torso lay cushioned on a film of its own fluids. Lips denuded of skin pulled back in the rictus of a smile. Only the rigor of the jaw held the gleaming white dentures in place. A white glob of fatty tissue clung to the bridge of the nose while the dangling left eyeball lay against what had once been a cheek. The right eye, covered by the thin transparent veil of the remaining lid, gave the face the look of an obscene wink.

"Male Caucasian." The sound of Chang's voice pulled

Duncan's gaze away with abrupt suddenness. "Seventy-three years of age. One Mr. Wilfred Daniel Mangrove . . . " Chang paused for a moment, watching his partner.

Duncan expelled a deep breath. "What else?"

Returning to his notes Chang continued giving Duncan the condensed version. "The motor boys got a disturbing the peace call around eleven. Upon arrival they found Raven out in the hallway making like a piece of the furniture. The guy with the bandage is William Martin, the old guy's driver. They found him out cold. Mr. Mangrove they found in various places around the room. That half," Hyiam nodded toward it, "was under the doors that Mr. Martin broke getting inside. Raven's got a broken jaw, so his side of the story is up in the air."

"We got any idea how that happened?"

Chang glanced in Martin's direction. "Seems Raven was a little hysterical so William slapped him."

"Some slap. Do we know if either of them saw anything?"

"Look, if you guys are through with me . . ."

Duncan swung around glaring at the young tech. "The county pays you thirteen bucks an hour. Most nights you sit on your ass at the morgue and play cards or smoke dope. So tonight you earn your keep. When we're through with ya you'll be the first one to know. Until then keep your trap shut until somebody asks you something. You got all that, or am I goin' too fast for you?"

"Actually it's closer to fifteen and I don't play cards," the tech said indolently.

Duncan turned toward the bedroom. Stranded in the doorway, the two coroner's assistants stared down at the black-bagged lump that represented the upper third of Mr. Mangrove. In their rush to load the stretcher, they had lost their grip on the bag and sent that portion of Mr. Mangrove toppling over onto the floor.

A thick, heavy silence filled the room, leaking out into the hall. It wasn't that such an occurrence had never happened before. Such topplings happened with surprising frequency, but under the circumstances it seemed an unnecessary affront to an already severely affronted human being.

The bearers reclaimed their burden, crossed to the stairs and descended.

Duncan watched until they disappeared out into the foyer. All that concerned him now was putting a stop to the maniac responsible for this bloody havoc.

January 24th—3:50 p.m.

"WOULD YOU PLEASE GIVE ME A FUCKING BREAK."

Unaffected by Duncan's request, Chang regaled his partner with yet another news flash. "The woman has a file with the fucking CIA. Can you believe this shit? She did some kind of work for them under the classification. Get this—Field Consultant. What do you think that means? This stuff is unfucking real," he added quickly.

Duncan took the Hollywood Way/Burbank Airport exit off the Golden State freeway at a speed that would have made Mario Andretti nervous. One side of his face twisted up into a satisfied grin as Hy lost his battle with gravity and slid against the door handle with a grunt.

"Did you read this stuff about the boat vanishing with twelve people on board in the middle of the marina while a hundred witnesses . . ."

Duncan threw the gear shift into park. His head snapped around in Hy's direction, his eyes set on kill. "Enough is fucking enough. I've heard a belly full of this broad, her file and her bloody case record."

"Did you read about the priest who caught fire right in the middle of Mass? Incredible. This woman has lived through some serious shit."

Oblivious to Duncan's groans and only faintly aware of the car door slamming with sufficient force to rock the vehicle, Chang closed the manila file and pushed it under the other debris on the front seat.

Duncan stormed toward the front steps of the passenger terminal, his jaw working furiously.

Chang scrambled out of the car, and caught up with Duncan about 15 seconds before he would have passed through the metal detectors. Hy slipped in front of him, quickly flashing his badge at the dull-eyed black woman behind the x-ray machine. This didn't stop the detectors from screeching their little metal lungs out, but it did add a couple of years to the guard's life span, having been spared the shock of such a rude awakening.

At Burbank Airport all planes, both arriving and departing, were reached off one long concourse. Flight 19 out of San Francisco was arriving at Gate 6. A loose gaggle of would-be passengers and impatient loved ones had begun to press against the doors leading out onto the tarmac, and the plane hadn't even rolled to a stop yet.

Duncan settled into a vacant chair, his bulk casting a shadow over the whiny six year old in the chair next to his. If the youngster became apprehensive at Duncan's appearance he went rigid at Chang's arrival. Chang tried to look at ease and even smiled down at the small boy, a fact that only served to send the boy scurrying into his mothers lap. With a quiet sigh he gave up and took the child's vacated seat.

Hy leaned toward Duncan and whispered, "You realize we haven't any idea what this Morgan woman looks like. How the hell are we suppose to . . ." His train of thought was temporarily derailed as a tall platinum blonde glided through the crowd. Dressed in complimentary shades of pale gray and trailing enough silver fox to set off a Green Peace demonstration, he quickly decided she was either a call girl or a reformed madame with a best seller in her briefcase. Hy's nose detected a hint of her perfume as she passed. "Serious money."

"What is?" Duncan asked.

"Her." Hy pointed, but the fox lady had already glided out of sight. "Nothing."

Duncan flickered a frown in Hy's direction and

pushed himself to his feet. "As to Mrs. Morgan . . ."

"I think it's Ms."

"Whatever. Unless I miss my guess, this should be her now." Duncan stepped forward into the path of a squat, elderly woman who bore a striking resemblance to a midwestern version of Agatha Christie's Miss Marple. With a smile he reserved for white-haired, little old ladies and attractive young widows, Duncan said, "Excuse me, Ms. Morgan, but I believe you're looking . . ."

The smile left Duncan's face as an extremely rotund young woman rushed forward to rescue Miss Marple, showering Forbes and Chang with looks clearly announcing that she considered them would-be rapists. The two women wasted little time in putting distance between themselves and the two detectives. Duncan felt the grin spreading across Hy's face.

"Not a word," he muttered menacingly, causing Hy's grin to double geometrically. Ignoring his grinning partner, Duncan rumbled up to the passenger check-in desk and, flashing his badge, snapped, "We were suppose to meet a passenger off this flight. Check and see if our party was on board."

The stewardess asked, "And what would your party's name be, detective?"

"Morgan, Maxine—"

"Montgomery."

The voice was deep and soft but loud enough to be heard over the noise around them. Hy's nose told him his fox lady had returned.

"You would be Detective Sergeant Forbes?" she asked Duncan, offering a slender hand.

Duncan cleared his throat. "Mrs. Morgan? You were suppose to meet us at—"

"Please, it's Max. The only Mrs. Morgan I know is my father's mother."

"Can I take that for you?" Hy stepped in-between Duncan and Max. He glanced over his shoulder at Duncan. The expression on Forbes' face wasn't quite as good as the one he'd worn the night he had busted the D.A.'s wife for shoplifting, but it was close. "Hyiam

Chang. Just call me Hy." Max accepted his outstretched hand, but at the touch of his skin she was startled by a queer sensation. Her first reaction was to look to her hand, but seeing the man's broad, innocent smile, she forced her own wilting smile to bloom once more.

"Is this all of your luggage?" Hy asked, unaware of Max's rather hasty removal of her hand from his.

"I tend to travel light."

"Wish my wife could get the hang of that. We go to Vegas overnight, and she packs a trunk." Hefting the single, large, gray shoulder case he winced. "Whew, what've you got in this thing?" Hy frowned, surprised at the weight of the bag the woman had appeared to carry so easily.

"We're parked out front if you're ready," Duncan announced firmly. Without waiting for an answer, he began moving away down the aisle, leaving Max and Hy to bring up the rear.

Chang noticed the small frown Max aimed at Duncan's departing back. When she looked to him he shrugged innocently. "We're double-parked."

At the curb Forbes climbed behind the wheel leaving Chang to struggle with the weighty bag and Max to fend for herself.

"We'll stop at the Task Force Command center first so you can check in," Duncan said, starting the engine.

"I would prefer to settle into my accommodations first. When I spoke to your Chief Merchinson I asked that whoever he sent to the airport bring with them a copy of the case file to date. I trust you have that?"

"Right here, at least a synopsis. The more in-depth stuff you can get at Central." Hy handed her a thick manila file.

"Good. I'd like to look this over tonight. Tomorrow will be time enough to visit the Task Force." Max smiled. Her manner was polite enough, but it was obvious she would not be swayed in her decision.

Duncan divided his attention between the traffic around him and studying Morgan in the rearview mirror. As she leafed through the material in the folder she began questioning Chang on various points of the investigation to date. The pair chatted as if they'd known each other for years, and that only served to increase Duncan's general aggravation.

"Not being the mind reader in this car, would somebody mind telling me where I'm going?" Duncan cut in abruptly.

Max looked out at the traffic then smiled tightly. "Frightfully sorry. I got rather carried away. Charrington Towers, Marina Del Rey."

"Wonderful," Duncan groaned.

"Traffic still as bad as ever, I assume. You might find it easier going if you took—"

"I'll manage, unless of course you'd like to—"

Hy cut Duncan off. "Forbes here is a whiz when it comes to freeway driving. Don't worry, it's no problem for him." With a hasty frown in Forbes' general direction he turned a toothy grin to Max. "That's right. I read where you used to live in L.A. In the Marina, wasn't it?"

"Actually down the coast a bit. South Bay. The Marina apartment belongs to a friend. I'll be using it while he's out of town. Tomorrow I'll rent a car so you boys don't have to dash all the way across town to pick me up every time I'm needed somewhere."

"Well, that's up to you, but it's no problem. Diehl said we were to stick pretty close to you in case you needed anything." Draping his arm over the back of the seat, Hy said hesitantly, "Listen, I've read your file and . . . well, I was just wondering . . . well, the file said you worked with the CIA. Is that right?"

"Yes," Max said cautiously, a look of total innocence on her face.

His voice dropped to a conspiratorial level. "What exactly did you do for them?"

Max studied him for a moment then favored him with a blinding smile. "Did I mention what an absolutely stunning tie that is you're wearing?"

Hy looked down at his dull brown tie and mumbled, "Thanks . . . I think."

"About this latest victim—", Max began.

"That hardly answers the question, Ms. Morgan," Duncan grumbled in his best interrogator's voice.

Flashing him a quick reprise of her innocent look, Max smiled. "Oh, really? I rather thought it had." Turning her attention back to Chang she continued, "About Mr. Mangrove . . ."

Duncan tuned out their conversation but continued to watch Max through the rearview. This Morgan woman was nothing like he had expected. She didn't look, dress or talk like he'd figured she would. That was annoying enough to him. He was a cop, cops prided themselves on placing types, and he was no exception to the rule. He knew people. He knew how they thought and what to expect from them.

It wasn't that he didn't recognize her type. Morgan had, he thought, the unmistakable smell of that kind of money.

"Just exactly what is it you do?" Duncan snapped peevishly.

Max looked at Duncan, paused for a moment, then asked quietly, "About what, Detective Forbes?"

"Save the cute dialogue for the tourists. You know exactly what I mean."

"Me being the mind reader and all, is that what you meant?" Max asked smoothly, her voice slightly softer than before.

"Look, lady, I don't know about those other cases you're supposed to have worked on, but we've got a killer on our hands here, and if we've got to put our lives on the line covering your ass while you poke around through the muck I want to know what you're about." Duncan's blue eyes had taken on a flinty hardness.

"What you want, Detective, is for me to defend what I do. I won't do that for you or for anybody else. As for my ass, I'm of the habit of covering it all by myself, so there's one less worry for you. Come tomorrow I'll be getting on with what I do. There's nothing very secretive or hidden about my side of an investigation so if you just keep an eye on the proceedings you should get a pretty clear picture of what I'm about. Now does that cover all your questions, or is there something else I can clear up for you?"

The tension between the pair hung thick and heavy for the remainder of the drive.

The Charrington Towers complex rose above the Marina skyline, defiantly proclaiming its supremacy to the surrounding buildings. If you still had questions about the level of affluence necessary to reside in a complex of this kind one glimpse of any of the suites on the 23rd floor quickly dispelled it.

Max must have told them to make themselves comfortable at least half a dozen times.

Max dropped into an uncomfortable-looking overstuffed chair. "Please, sit down."

Hy grinned sheepishly and settled onto a divan which fitted him like an easy chair.

"We can't stay long so if you've got any other questions . . ."

"Actually, I need to know our schedule for tomorrow. Oh, and by the way, my friend Michael who owns this place left a note for me. Seems he's taken care of my transport problem. He's left a car for my use while I'm here."

Before Duncan could get in a word Hy jumped in. "Our schedule pretty much depends on you. Where do you want to start?"

"First I want to see each of the crime scenes. That is possible, isn't it?"

"I can get the clearances first thing in the morning. What time do you want to start?"

"As soon as possible. I would like to see the sites in chronological order, finishing with the most recent. After that I think a visit with the coroner's investigator would be in order."

"That would be Heep." Hy nodded.

"The remains of the last victim . . . ah, Mangrove, was it?"

"Yeah, Wilfred Daniel . . ." Hy paused, looking quickly to Duncan then back to Max. "Are you sure you want . . . ?"

"Yes, I'm sure." Max said quietly but firmly.

Duncan leaned forward. "You realize this isn't gonna be like a trip to the local undertaker. There's no powder and paint on this one. In fact there's damn little . . ."

"In order for me to do my job it will be necessary not only for me to see the corpse but see it at close range. I appreciate your concern for my sensibilities, but it goes with the territory."

Duncan studied her for a moment longer then leaned back into the couch, the beginning of the tiniest smile shadowing the corners of his mouth. "Suit yourself," he added evenly.

Hy leaned forward quickly, blocking Max's line of sight. He was more than familiar with that Cheshire grin, and he didn't want Max to see it on the off chance it's portent might be clear to her as well. "What else?"

"If we make it to the coroner's office I'll want a complete copy of his reports on the other victims."

"And then?" Hy smiled eagerly.

Max suppressed a grin. "If—and that's a big if—we get through with that much I'll consider it a good day."

"O.K. How about we pick you up at say ten?"

"Nine would be all right, too. Eight if you're feeling perky." Max smiled genuinely. "Now I'm going to make a good strong pot of coffee. Can I interest either of you?"

Duncan pushed to his feet. "That settles it then. We'll be downstairs at eight, if you're sure that won't be too early for you."

"I'll be ready," Max responded evenly. "Thank you for driving me home."

She shook his hand. Though her long slender fingers were engulfed in his wide paw the shake was firm. Hy smiled sheepishly. "No problem." He fished one of his cards out of his pocket. "If you need to get in touch, that's the number."

"Good, I would have forgotten. Thanks."

She walked with him to the door. Duncan was already standing out in the hallway, impatient to be out of there and making damn certain everyone involved was well-aware of his feelings.

"See you in the morning," Hy grinned.

"Good night."

Locking the door she paused, eyes narrowed, as she considered the curious reaction she had experienced at Detective Chang's touch. What was it she was sensing?

Still sorting through the possibilities Max crossed to the kitchen. Startled by the brilliance of the overhead lighting she suppressed a giggle as she beheld a kitchen that would make any homemaker swoon with ecstasy. "Michael," she sighed quietly, as she headed for the coffeemaker.

January 25th—7:03 a.m.

THE SUN CLIMBED OVER THE EASTERN HORIZON AND SMILED down on the city the Indians called the Valley of Smoke. By 7:35 a.m., every photographer who made his or her living producing postcards was busily exercising their shutter fingers. It was the kind of weather that made the Chamber of Commerce ecstatic.

In her borrowed penthouse high atop Charrington Towers, Max cupped both hands around the comfortable ceramic mug, sipping her coffee. She stood in front of the glass wall looking out to sea. The hills above Malibu glittered from the morning sunlight reflected off the windows of the all but invisible homes there. The sky was an innocent shade of blue, complementing the slate gray of the ocean below, and the air was so clear she could see all the way to the horizon. It was one of those mornings that made you believe the world was a clean white canvas and you could create it anew in a more pleasing aspect. Unfortunately, the canvas she would paint today would certainly be far from pleasant.

Even knowing this, there was no foreboding, no apprehension, no dread, just a kind of tension deep in her stomach.

There were certain immutable laws that made the universe and its inhabitants revolve. They were simple things, for the most part, so simple most never had cause to question or even think about them. One of the basics said human beings shouldn't willingly play with dead things. Max was, always had been and always would be eager to do just that.

By the ripe old age of eight, Maxine Montgomery Morgan was on a first name basis with death. In that short span of years she had come in close physical contact with one victim of a shotgun suicide, a hanging, one drowning and the assorted body parts resulting from a natural gas explosion in a crowded restaurant. Max was hardly a street orphan in one of the globe's current war zones but was in fact the only child of an extremely wealthy elderly couple living in the serene country environs of the English countryside.

Shortly before the onset of puberty, Max had discovered the world of the occult, not that surprising an occurrence for any child living within spitting distance of the Salisbury Plain and Stonehenge. Over the years she had tried, at the insistence of her parents, teachers and peers, to suppress her interest in the arcane sciences, but no matter how hard she tried she never succeeded for very long. With the death of her parents, shortly before her 18th birthday, finding herself financially secure but absolutely alone, she tried to make peace with the modern world only to find that once the old powers recognized your presence their claim on you was not to be broken.

Turning away from the window Max crossed to the couch and fished a pack of cigarettes and lighter out of her jacket pocket. Before she could open the pack the doorbell chimed. "Just a minute," she called, snatching up her jacket and leather tote.

She opened the door.

"Good morning," she piped. Noticing Detective Chang staring at her, she gave him a worried smile and asked, "Is there something wrong?"

With a kind of half-shrug Hy said, "No, I guess not." He crossed to the elevator, trying not to stare too openly and not having much success. In the end he gave up, saying, "You sure look different than you did last night."

"Is that good or bad?"

"I didn't mean . . ."

She grinned. "Couldn't hardly work in that rig, could I?"

Hy nodded. "Nope I guess you couldn't, but you sure look different." Giving her boots, levi's, and worn aviator's jacket one last furtive glance, he fixed his attention on the elevator doors, trying hard to identify the lady in fox last night with the youthful-looking tomboy standing beside him.

Waiting in the car, Duncan heard the rear door open. In the back seat he saw a familiar blonde head as Hy got behind the wheel.

"We're off." Hy grinned as he started the car. Duncan muttered something, but it was lost in the sound of the car's engine.

Hancock Park, their first destination, was no more than a handful of broad, tree-lined streets wrapped neatly around the Los Angeles County Art Museum, the Paige Museum and the fabled La Brea Tar Pits.

They pulled up in front of a brick, two-story colonial. The broad front yard was covered by a thick layer of dead leaves littering the grass and driveway and giving the house an abandoned look. Parked in front of the doorway sat a dark, late model Jaguar. Max glanced inside, noting the briefcase and a copy of a court calendar sitting on top with several dates underlined. No grieving family members here.

As they reached the front steps, the door opened. "You're late," the man in the doorway snapped impatiently. He stood aside, watching Max speculatively as the trio entered. "I trust this will be the last time . . ."

"If it isn't, councilor, you'll be the first to know," Duncan drawled, pulling a fresh pack of cigarettes out of his breast pocket.

The lawyer studied Forbes through narrowed eyes. "How much longer are you going to keep that room sealed? This house is an integral part of the Worthington estate, and houses in this price range are a glut on the market. We can't even think about listing it until we can do something about the . . ." He paused searching for an appropriate word.

"Mess?" Duncan supplied an accurate if inappropriate one.

The lawyer dismissed his suggestion with a vague gesture. "How much longer?"

"I'm sorry, Mr. Laughton, but you'd have to check with the D.A.'s office on that," Hy said with a certain guarded pleasantness.

"I'll be seeing Dick this afternoon for lunch. I'll make a note to discuss that little detail with him," Laughton said arrogantly. "Now that you're here I trust my presence will no longer be necessary?"

"No sir, we'll take it from here on out," Hy said evenly.

"Do see that the doors are locked and the alarm system on before you leave." Laughton turned on his heel and marched out the door, closing it hard behind him.

"Prissy little prick," Duncan muttered loudly, sticking a cigarette in the corner of his mouth.

The crime scene was a second floor bedroom at the rear of the house. The door was closed and crisscrossed with broad yellow tape.

Duncan pulled loose the tape on one side and opened the door, but before he could enter Max squeezed past him.

"It's best I work alone. However, if you could stay nearby it would be helpful. That way if I need anything I can just shout." Without waiting for a response she switched on the lights and proceeded into the room.

The room was done in shades of rose and pink, and the furniture was just old enough to be comfortable but not so old as to be thought of as antiques. On one of the nightstands sat an impressive collection of prescription bottles. The bottles as well as the surface of the table were covered by a fine white powder, evidence of the forensic team's presence. The wallpaper behind the bed was stained by splattered blood, the bed having been the site of the actual murder. Its linen had been removed by the lab boys leaving behind the mattress, it's gold satin cover nearly invisible under the massive bloodstain.

Lowering her tote to the floor, Max quickly slipped off her aviator jacket. Reaching into the bag she withdrew a miniature tape recorder and small headset with microphone. Dropping the jacket onto the tote she clipped the recorder to her waistband and settled the headset into a comfortable position. Moving around to the head of the bed she began speaking into the recorder in a low quiet voice.

Max continued her slow perusal of the room for the next hour, maintaining a steady monologue. From time to time she would stop, examining a spot here, picking up some ceramic shard or piece of fiber from the carpeting, or simply standing in one area and staring back to the bed.

Max suddenly called out to Hy.

"What became of the dog?"

"Beg pardon?"

"Mrs. Worthington's dog. What happened to it? Was it killed during the attack?"

"What dog? There wasn't any dog," Duncan said.

"Actually, there was," Hy said firmly.

"What?" Duncan frowned.

"Yeah, there was. Old, kinda' moth-eaten poodle."

"Was it killed in the attack?"

"Yes and no."

Max rested her chin in her hand, and Duncan groaned, leaning his frame against the doorjamb.

"See, some of the lab boys found him cowering in the closet. Made an awful mess in there. Poor little bastard must have been scared outa his wits. Anyway they didn't know what to do with him so they took him to the pound." Hy paused.

"Well," Max and Duncan said in unison.

"Nobody ever claimed him, so they put him to sleep."

"Lovely," Max muttered.

"Things like that happen. The old lady didn't have any living relatives, and the dog just got lost in the paperwork. The only reason I know is 'cause I saw the guy who picked him up that night. I asked how the dog was doin', and he said it wasn't." Hy looked helplessly from Duncan to Max. "Is it important?"

Before Max could respond Duncan grumbled, "How'd you know about the dog anyway?"

Max smiled at him then disappeared behind the bed. When she reappeared her smile was even wider.

"Well, shit!" Duncan stared down at the floor. There at his feet lay a small, well-chewed, red rubber ball.

Max stood up. "Ladies of Mrs. Worthington's age rarely gnaw on things like that, so it's a safe assumption something canine did."

Max moved over to the French doors and pulled back the drapes.

"Give me about another ten minutes to shoot some tape on this place and that will about cover it."

Max pulled from the tote a small video camera. She moved the camera slowly around the room, pausing from time to time for a close-up of one section or another.

"That covers it here. Where to next?"

"Well, the next in order is in Pasadena, but I was thinking we could take care of the locations on this side of town and . . ."

"Hy, it's important that I see the locations in order. Sorry, but that's the way it has to be done." Settling the shoulder strap of her tote in place she closed the bedroom door and moved off down the hall toward the stairs.

Hy returned some of the tape to its original place while Duncan pushed his chair against the wall.

As the pair followed after her Duncan grumbled, "That's the way it has to be. Why does it have to be that way? If you ask me, it doesn't. And what's with the costume this morning? Fucking Indiana Jones in drag. If you ask me, it's nothing but bullshit."

"Don't recall anybody did," Hy said quietly, securing the front door.

Inside the car, Max looked at her sketch of the Worthington bedroom. It was little more than a floor plan noting the general layout of the room and placement of the two exits. She made a few brief notations but found her attention continually wandering. She stared at the tip of her pen. That strange tic she had experienced last night had returned.

It had not made itself readily apparent when Chang had called for her this morning, but once they'd arrived at the Worthington house it had made its presence known. At first she'd convinced herself that part of the feelings she picked up on were from Duncan. His hostility was evident enough, but surprisingly she found his negativity having little effect on her. The annoyingly distracting sensation was emanating from Hy.

The car swayed, and she looked out the window. They were turning onto a residential street. In topography it was so similar to the area they had just left that one might well believe they had driven no more than a street or two over and were still in the same neighborhood. In fact they had crossed the city and were now in one of the residential areas of Pasadena.

The home of Dr. Robert Paxon, Chief of Staff of Angels of Mercy Hospital and second of the murder victims, looked far less deserted. Signs of life were abundant here. In the driveway sat several cars including a sleek silver Porsche.

A short, overweight teenager, her dark unkempt hair framing a face of quiet pain, answered the door. She smiled shyly at Forbes and led them into a living room obviously in the throes of redecorating. The house was cool to the point of chilliness, a thick annoying kind of silence filling the air.

"Mother couldn't wait for you. She and the decorator had appointments. If you have any questions I'm to write them down, and Mother or Mr. Norton, her attorney, will get back to you."

The girl's voice held traces of bitterness, easily allowing Max's fertile mind to cultivate detailed pictures of the child's life.

The girl's clothes were expensive but hardly fashionable, falling more into that dubious category of stylishly stout. Her face was blotched by acne, and her fingernails had been bitten to the quick. Max felt a wave of pity for the child, certain that she would have to work at achieving a similar emotion for the deceased.

Dr. Paxon had been murdered, nine days after Mrs. Worthington, in his den. This room, like the Worthington bedroom, was sealed off from the rest of the house by the ubiquitous yellow tape. The young Miss Paxon, after having guided them to the den, disappeared with promises of sandwiches and coffee. Chang and Forbes took up positions in the hallway while Max entered the den alone.

Arranged before the far wall sat a large desk. It was here the doctor's rapidly cooling remains had been found. Max approached the desk slowly, allowing her unconscious mind to absorb the total scene. All papers associated with the surface of a working desk had been removed. According to the report, the desk top had been awash in the late doctor's blood. The red leather chair which had sat behind the desk had also been removed.

Max moved around behind the desk. On the carpet, under the desk's knee space, white masking tape traced the outline of a pair of men's shoes. At first she tried squatting down in a sitting position but quickly abandoned this, pulling up an ottoman. The height of her makeshift seat brought the level of the desk up to her chest, providing a worm's eye view of the surroundings. A green, glass-shaded lamp remained on the desk along with a gold framed photograph of the good doctor cutting the ribbon on what appeared to be a condominium complex and a dark wooden box, which on closer scrutiny Max discovered held a push button phone. These items seemed to have been spared the tide of blood but bore gritty evidence of the lab techs' workmanship along with the surface of the desk.

Incurably nosy, Max opened the center drawer of the desk. The pencil railing held a series of dark bloodstains attesting to the fact that the drawer had been partially open at the time of the murder.

She then pressed her hands down flat on the surface of the desk. Slowly she removed the impressions of external stimuli from her mind until her eye lids became heavy and closed. Concentrating on the simple rise and fall of her own breathing her range of vision began to widen. Impressions began to take shape, some so brief their length of duration was incalculable.

In the beginning the impressions were from a number of sources but gradually she began to focus on the surface of the wood until she was startled by a loud popping sound.

Max flinched, her eyes flashing open. She turned her head quickly from side to side, searching for a source of the sound somewhere within the room. Preparing to stand she pressed her hands hard against the wood but suddenly stopped.

She stared straight ahead but saw nothing, a fine patina of sweat beading her forehead and a nervous tic twitching in her right eye. She gagged, her eyes watering. Stomach churning, a tight, hard lump growing with alarming speed filled her chest—and then as quickly as the sensation had come, it vanished.

For several moments she sat still, breathing raggedly through her mouth. Then as her breathing began to take on a more natural rhythm she lowered her head to the desk, a great sigh shaking her body.

In the hallway Chang paused, his mouth full of dry chicken and stale white bread. He glanced in Duncan's direction, then looked away, certain the sound that had captured his attention had not been heard by Forbes. Slowly, so as not to arouse Duncan's curosity, he rose and stepped into the doorway of the den.

"Is everything all right?"

Max looked up quickly as if awakening from a nap.

"I'm sorry, did you say something?"

Hy smiled lopsidedly. "Is something wrong?"

"Ah, no, why do you ask?"

"When I saw you with your head down, I just wondered . . ." His voice trailed off. "Sorry, didn't mean to bother you."

"No problem. About another fifteen minutes or so and we should be done here. I'll yell when I'm ready." Max watched Chang until he had backed out of the doorway. When he'd gone she relaxed somewhat. It would take time to sort out the visions she had experienced, and she needed that time before she discussed it with others, if she ever did.

Collecting herself, she rose and crossed the room to her tote resting on the coffee table. As she pulled the recorder and camera from the bag something caught her attention and caused her to look in the direction of the sofa.

Behind the couch stood a long, narrow sofa table. In the center of the table sat a terra cotta figure. Settling the headset over her ears Max circled round the couch to look more closely at the figure. Over a foot in length and approximately the same in height including a polished marble base, the style of the figure was immediately recognizable as Meso-American in composition.

The figure depicted was that of a reclining male laying on his back, the weight of his upper body resting on his elbows with his knees drawn up close to his chest. Over the figure's abdomen lay a wide, flat circular tray. The figure's dress appeared to be that of a warrior wearing the traditional short leather kilt and high, laced-up sandals. On his head he wore a decorative crown. A small brass plaque in the center of the marble base read 'In appreciation of support—The Chandler Marston White Museum's Golden Circle Society—Dr. Robert Edmund Paxon.'

Speaking softly into the recorder Max lifted the heavy sculpture, surprised at its weight. Replacing it she was about to turn her attention back to the room itself when she paused and looked back at the statue. As she had turned away she had unconsciously run her hand over its surface. Looking at her fingertips, she discovered a residue of an unusual grayish dust.

Max reached for her tote and withdrew a small black leather case from which she selected a small, fan-shaped brush and plastic, pinch-mouthed bag. Brushing the sculpture carefully, she collected a tiny quantity of the gray dust in the bag. Sealing it, she attached a label, making a notation as to the contents and location of discovery. She studied the dust for a moment before carefully placing the bag into the kit. There was no way of being certain the dust was of any importance—still, you could never be too thorough. Closing the kit she turned her attention to completing the remainder of her investigation. Less than an hour after she had entered the room, Max stepped into the doorway and asked for a glass of water.

Returning with the water, Hy stumbled into the middle of a terse exchange.

". . . then would you please find out?"

"Why?" Duncan snapped.

"Because I need to know," Max said evenly. The pair stood looking at one another for a moment longer than Max turned and smiled at Hy. "Next would be—what? Pacific Palisades?"

"No, actually Brentwood, then the Palisades. Are we all done here?" Hy looked to Duncan then back at Max.

"Yes, I think that covers everything."

Max turned and moved off down the hall, leaving the two men alone.

"What were you two talking about?"

Duncan sighed dramatically. "The silly bitch asks me did I know if there was a fire in the fireplace the night of the murder."

"Why would she want to know that?"

"How the hell should I know?" Duncan grumbled.

Hy shrugged, saying simply, "Damned if I know, but I think we better find out."

Duncan climbed in behind the wheel and immediately adjusted the mirror. As he focused it he caught sight of Max bent over the small video camera. Twice he heard

her mutter something under her breath that sounded
distinctly like "shit." His curiosity was beginning to
prod him into asking her what she was doing, but before
he could Chang came bounding out the front door.

Forbes smiled slyly and started the car, certain in the
knowledge that Chang lacked the level of self-control he
did and would quickly do the asking for him.

11:25 a.m.

Adding its burden to K-Mart's already crowded parking lot a burnt orange Toyota with darkened windows
and a mud-caked license plate cruised quietly up one
lane then down the next, looking for a parking place.
Unlike the others however, the Toyota passed spot after
spot until, causing a seven car line up, it paused to allow
a family to crowd into a sleek new Ford wagon and back
out of a place almost directly across from the building's
large front doors. When the spot was vacated the Toyota
quickly filled it, the delayed drivers trailing past and
showering the small vehicle with angry looks. After
several minutes the passenger door of the Toyota opened
and a short, heavyset Hispanic woman wearing a nonde-
script housedress waddled across the drive and into the
building.

With her mother occupied little Leana grew restive,
eager to wander amidst the treasures of the toy aisle.
Employing the persistence that only an anxious five-
year-old can muster Leana tugged and pleaded and
pulled and pestered until her beleaguered mother literally chased away, not that it took much chasing. Leana ran
down the crowded aisles toward the toy department with
her mother's stern warning to remain there until she
came for her still ringing in her ears.

The heavyset woman watched Leana with an absolute
concentration that could easily be attributed to a doting
grandparent. Moving up beside the child she spoke to
her in a voice so reassuring and so soft that even
someone standing close by would have had difficulty
overhearing the conversation.

Leana smiled shyly at the woman but withdrew into herself as the woman held out a wide, brown hand, but when that hand opened, revealing thick cubes of wrapped chocolates, Leana's shell began to melt.

For hours her panicked mother searched the store from deli to garden shop. After paying for her purchases she pushed the cart out to the front of the store and waited, as if by performing this vigil Leana would magically walk out the front doors and come to her side. Only when the sun dropped below the horizon and the hard glare of the store's vapor lights filled the darkness did the mother break her long vigil and start for home. Though several times police cars came within view, the old fear never allowed her to raise her hand to stop them or seek their aid.

12:45 p.m.

Max sat on the floor directly in front of the blood-stained couch and stared at the dark red blotches on the pale gray material. Pressing her eyes tightly closed she took a deep breath, then opening them she looked at the stocky young man standing at the French windows, his back to the room.

In a voice at once quiet and firm she asked, "Then you were not in the house at the time of the attack?"

He turned toward her, quickly averting his gaze as it fell upon the couch. "No. I returned about eleven, saw the lights on in here and went directly to my room."

Max looked down at the small video camera resting in her lap. Victor Stein was a 28-year-old, unemployed model. The slight bulge around his middle stated eloquently the reason for his unemployment though his face was attractive enough. He lived in the house at 37 Sundown Way with his friend, translate lover, Dawson Gillis, art dealer, gallery owner, collector and third of the victims. She knew from the reports that several of the investigators had labeled Stein as a possible suspect, and from the nervousness he exhibited it was clear he was aware of their suspicions.

Max could feel his gaze on her as he moved quietly around the room. She looked up, catching his eye. "I'm not advising you on any professional level. Point of fact if you repeat what I'm about to tell you I'll deny it, but you're a fool if you don't tell them you and Gillis quarreled that night."

"We didn't. I don't know what you're talking about!"

"If you keep it from them and they find out, even though you had nothing to do with his murder, it'll look bad for you."

Victor's angry face lost some of its fire, but the suspicion clung on tenaciously. "Even though I had nothing to do with his murder, you said. How do you know that?"

The faint shadow of a smile drifted across Max's lips then vanished. "What you're really asking yourself is how did I know you argued, isn't that right?"

Before he could respond Duncan appeared in the entryway and glared down into the living room at the pair. "You about done in here?"

"Just about," Morgan assured him. Waiting until Duncan had made a grumbling retreat Max pushed herself up and began putting away her equipment. Victor hovered about the room, giving the couch a wide berth. Closing the bag, she crossed to the mantel and looked at the small replica of the Chac Mool, an exact duplicate of the one found at the Paxon home. "What do you know about this sculpture?"

"It was a gift from the museum. Mr. Gillis was a contributor, member of their Golden Circle Society. He was very fond of the museum and . . ."

For a moment his words faded from her ears, as did all sound. Replacing them came a very sharp, clear impression of anger. Max focused on the impression for a moment then realized it was not simply anger but fear as well. Turning, she cut him off in midsentence. "Why do you dislike this piece so much?"

The color drained out of Victors face. "Who are you? You're no cop."

"Stop playing games with me, Victor. Nobody ever

said anything about me being a cop. What I am is somebody who's trying very hard to find out how your Mr. Gillis and the others were murdered, and don't bother with that old dodge about how I know what I know. You're a very bright, intuitive young man, and for some reason, perhaps one that may be of some help to me, you are very uncomfortable about this little piece of bric-a-brac. Why?"

He glanced over his shoulder to make certain they were truly alone then moved closer. "Have you ever seen the real one? It's a nasty thing. We were at the private showing held for the society members. It was there he and the others got that thing. I couldn't stand to be in the same room with the big one. When he brought that one home and put it there instead of in his office we quarreled. He laughed at me when I said it made me feel funny. He said I was turning into an old queen and he had enough of them at the gallery. He didn't need one at home as well."

"Can you tell me how it made you feel? Anything you can remember could be helpful."

He sighed and began kneading his fingertips as if they were cold. "I don't know exactly. Just uneasy. Like . . . like . . ." He paused then looked at her and said, "You know how sometimes you get a feeling on the back of your neck like somebody's watching you, and when you turn around there's nothing there? I mean, you can't see anything but . . ." His voice trailed off again. "I can't really explain it. I'm sorry."

Max pulled a small note pad from her pack and quickly marked down her telephone number. Tearing the number off she held it out to him. "Victor, I want you to do me a favor. This is a number where I can be reached. I know that right now you've a lot on your mind, but I want you to think about the night Mr. Gillis was killed. Try and remember everything you can."

"I told the police everything I could."

"Listen to me. The kind of things I'm interested in would be of no interest to them. I want you to think about how the house felt when you came in. Was it cold or warm? How did it feel? When you were in your room, perhaps just before you went to sleep, did you have an impression of any kind? Did you dream that night, and if so can you recall any of it? No matter how unrelated or unimportant you may think it is. Can you do this for me?"

He studied her for a moment then took the scrap of paper from her hand with a quick birdlike gesture. "I'll try," he mumbled.

Max wanted to say something of a comforting nature but had found over the years there really weren't any words soothing enough. Willing herself to shut out Victor's anguish she turned abruptly, colliding with Duncan's solid bulk.

"Bloody 'ell," Max snapped.

"Something wrong, Ms. Morgan?" Duncan purred smoothly.

"Next time you sneak up on me please have the courtesy of coughing or something."

"I woulda thought somebody in your profession wouldn't spook so easy. No pun intended."

Max suppressed the urge to say something nasty and smiled quietly. "I believe our next stop is Pacific Palisades, isn't that right?"

"Not so fast. How did you know about Gillis and Victor arguing that night?"

The pleasant expression vanished from her face. Quietly and slowly she said, "For convenience sake and just to save wear and tear on your arches it will not be necessary for you to eavesdrop on any future conversations I may have. When I make out my report you'll get a copy, along with everybody else, and you can read what you need to know."

Duncan smiled smugly. "Perhaps I should refresh your memory on a little legal detail. You know the one I have in mind surely. The one about withholding information pertinent to a criminal investigation."

Max smiled sweetly. "The day they convict me of that

one you have my permission to say I told you so. Until then kindly piss off."

Hy furtively observed the other two occupants of the car. Max and Duncan obviously had some kind of a run-in. Over just what or exactly when it had occurred he hadn't a clue, but you could read it in the deafening silence. In an effort to relieve the pressure, Hy tried casual chatter, but when that received only terse mutters and grunts he decided to put his verbiage to some constructive use.

"I'm curious about something, Max."

She looked in his direction but said nothing.

"You made quite an issue out of wanting to see the crime scenes in progressive order. How come? I mean, seems to me you'd want to see the most recent one first, it being the freshest and all." He glanced into the back seat and noticed Max's posture relaxing.

"It's a lot like painting a picture, for me anyway. I prefer to start with a sketch and work up to the full painting as opposed to painting the canvas first and trying to draw in details later."

"Sure, I guess that makes sense." Hy smiled and nodded.

Max concentrated on the passing scenery and on a growing tightness at the back of her neck. She turned and stretched, as much as her position would allow, but the tension seemed to be increasing. As they turned into the driveway at the Mangrove residence Chang announced their arrival, but he could have saved himself the effort for Max knew where they were and where the tension was coming from. She climbed slowly out of the car and stood staring up at the house even as Forbes and Chang climbed the front steps, unaware Max was not with them.

Glancing over his shoulder, Chang noticed her hesitance and frowned. "Is something wrong?"

She looked at him slowly. "Is there another door?"

"Beg pardon?"

"Another entrance?" Without waiting for a response,

she began moving away from the car toward the south side of the house.

Her gaze directed at the ground, Max centered on the strong impression fixed in her mind. How that impression had come to her with such clarity and strength she did not stop to consider. Pausing, she looked to the right. There, behind a glass-topped Dutch door, stood a tall man watching her. She turned to face the man, and the pair held each other's gaze. Max felt herself moving closer to the man even though she remained stationary until his face filled her vision completely. Then even as she focused on it, it dissolved, replaced by a very different view of that entrance.

The doorway was draped in shadows. A wind, wet and cold brushed against her cheek. A small porch light over the door appeared and vanished behind a thick curtain of windblown ivy. A figure dressed in fur opened the door and stepped inside, closing the door behind him.

"Hi there, William. You remember me? Detective Chang and my partner Detective Forbes?" Hy smiled genuinely at William.

"Yes sir, I've been expecting you. Please come in."

Max blinked, and the vision vanished. She heard the voices of Chang and William, felt the presence of Forbes nearby, recognized her whereabouts, but something stronger pushed these things to the back of her awareness. Stepping quickly forward she entered the side door and paused for a moment, looking into the kitchen area. Seemingly oblivious to all else she turned and quickly moved down the adjacent hall. Her steps slowed as she approached a series of doors. Stopping, she studied the surface of each then selected one and opened the door, feeling no surprise at finding behind it the small, neat, half-bath. Giving the room a brief scan Max closed the door then proceeded on. She paused, only for a moment, before selecting the door that lead through the butler's pantry and out into the foyer.

By the time Max reached the second floor landing a pressure at her temples added a feeling of light-headedness to an overall sensation of disorientation.

The ruined doors to the bedroom lay propped against either side of the threshold leaving only three stripes of the bright yellow and black tape to bar the entrance. Climbing through the tape like a fighter entering a ring, Max entered the bedroom. The pressure in her temples shifted slightly, making itself more of a tight band encircling her entire head. An odd taste filled her mouth and a cold sensation saturated her lungs. Her gaze took in the room in quick, blinding flashes. Views of it's current condition mixed haphazardly amid strange, clouded visions of it at another time. Max blinked rapidly, her eyes watering in an effort to focus these kaleidoscope patterns, to slow them somehow, and as she strained to maintain a precarious kind of control other elements closed in, adding to the sensory mayhem.

She swayed and dropped to the floor, her knees buckling under her.

"Jesus Christ," Hy snapped, rushing forward. Squatting down beside her, Hy asked, "Max, are you all right? What's wrong? Max, can you hear me?"

Max looked at him and with a goofy smile. "See why I never wear a dress on one of these outings?"

While William drew a chair into the center of the room Chang helped Max to stand. Watching all this from a safe distance, Duncan stood quietly in the doorway. He watched Max and her two benefactors with bemused scrutiny, then crossing to the railing overlooking the foyer below he fished out a cigarette and lit it, his thoughts turned inward. He was still puffing on that cigarette as Hy descended the stairs only to return moments later carrying Max's large red tote.

Max reassured William and Chang of her well-being then turned to her equipment, allowing them to exit quietly, but when she was certain they were no longer in the room she paused. Tape recorder in hand and headset in place she settled into the chair and began speaking rapidly into the mike, trying to capture the essence of the experience before all but the most prominent of the images vanished.

Max pulled the video tape from the recorder and

noting the final entry on the label sealed it in a black plastic case. Quickly returning her equipment to her bag, she gave the room one final survey.

Max reached for the rear door of the car and found Duncan's hand already there. She watched him out of the corner of her eye as she climbed inside but suppressed a facial reaction to his unorthodox action. An even greater act of control was called for when he abruptly inquired, "You hungry? We got about an hour before Heep comes on duty?"

"Heep?"

"The coroner's investigator," Hy said.

"Oh. Well . . . yeah, a little something in the stomach wouldn't be too hard to take."

Twenty minutes later the trio settled themselves around the end of a long table in what served as a lunch room in the basement of the morgue. Four large wall vents labored mightily to remove the odor of stale cigarettes, sour milk and formaldehyde—and lost.

While Duncan and Hy worked over paper cups of bitter black coffee Max nursed a nearly empty chocolate milk carton and toyed with the remaining half of a dubious-looking egg salad sandwich.

"Food here's not real great, but it's convenient," Hy said by way of an apology.

Max nodded. Pulling a small note pad out of her bag. "Tell me about your witness."

"Not much to tell." Hy shrugged.

Duncan rubbed out his cigarette. "Not much of a witness."

"Was he an actual witness to the event?" Max persisted.

"Not as far as we can tell. See he had something of an accident, and we haven't exactly had a chance to question him yet." Discomfort showed clearly on Chang's round face.

"An accident?"

Hy took a deep breath, glancing quickly in Duncan's direction. "He broke his jaw."

Max nodded but said nothing, waiting for the rest of the story.

Duncan lit another cigarette and exhaled a cloud of blue smoke. "William, Mangrove's driver, slapped the little . . ." Hy coughed violently. Duncan grimaced in Chang's direction then, apparently having gotten the message, continued. "Slapped Mr. St. James a little too hard while trying to quiet his hysteria."

Max studied the tip of her pen. "I see. Was Mr. St. James a regular guest of Mr. Mangroves?"

"What Mr. St. James was . . ." Duncan paused, a slow smile turning up the corners of his lips. ". . . is a boy tart, if you get my drift, Ms. Morgan?"

Max made several quick notes in her pad. "When you talk to Mr. St. James I'd like to be present."

"If not you can always read our report," Duncan purred smugly.

"I'll do that as well, but I'll still need to question him myself."

"Why? What are you gonna ask him that we won't?" Duncan's smugness was slipping a bit.

"Trust me our questions won't even be in the same ball park."

"Like?"

"Like, what impressions do you remember when you first entered the house? Did you feel, hear, smell anything of an unusual nature? Did you experience any anxiety before entering the house? After the incident were you able to sleep, and if so did you dream? What can you recall about that dream? Get my drift?" Max met Duncan's even gaze with an easy confidence.

"How do questions like that help?" Hy asked with genuine curiosity.

"Every human being, to a greater or lesser degree, experiences impressions from events about to occur. It's just possible that Mr. St. James may have experienced just such impressions, and if he can recall them they might prove very helpful."

"Ha," Duncan laughed scornfully.

"And on that note I think it's time we headed upstairs," Chang said, groaning and pushing back from the table.

"Detective Chang, you're a very kind, sensitive man, and I appreciate what you've been trying to do, but do yourself and everybody else a big favor and knock it off. If Forbes and me go picking on one another from time to time, stand back and enjoy the show. We're grownups and can handle mutual ass chewing without falling apart. Spare yourself the aggravation. He's not going to say anything to me I haven't heard before." She looked at Duncan. "Are you?"

Duncan's face screwed up into a suspicious frown. "I wouldn't be too sure about that."

"Trust me." Turning back to Hy she whispered loudly, "Besides I think he kinda likes me."

"Ha!" Duncan barked.

Duncan shook his head and pushed back from the table. Standing up he looked down at the pair and with a smirk aimed in Max's direction and said, "You believe that and you're even goofier than I gave you credit for."

"If not now then later," Max purred.

"Ha!"

Max shrugged. "And if not, who cares?"

Duncan marched down the corridor toward the distant elevator with Hy and Max bringing up the rear.

Hy leaned closer to Max. "I'll tell you something if you swear never to mention where you heard it?"

"What?"

"Forbes owns a boat."

"So?"

"He hates the water. Never puts the thing in the water but just keeps it parked out behind his garage. Works on the thing all the time, keeps saying how's he's gonna take it to Catalina as soon as it's seaworthy. Had it maybe ten years now and the closest it's ever been to the ocean is Wilshire Boulevard."

Max's smile stretched her mouth to the bursting point. As she and Chang entered the elevator she looked at him and said loudly, "How very interesting." Duncan looked at the pair suspiciously but said nothing. Chang closed his eyes and prayed.

"Are you sure you really want to do this?" Jasper Heep asked, concern screwing up the corners of his weak brown eyes. "It's not that I'm sayin' you can't or anything. It's just that I think maybe it would be better if you concentrated on the photographs. They're very detailed . . ."

"Thank you, Mr. Heep, but if it's all the same to you I'd really rather like to see the remains." Max fitted the headset into place and clipped the recorder to her belt loop. Into the tiny mouthpiece she said, "Visual inspection: remains of Wilfred Daniel Mangrove, January 25th, 4:38 p.m. Looking to Jasper she announced firmly, "Ready when you are."

Jasper looked quickly to Chang and Forbes, but seeing no escape from that direction he crossed out of the room shaking his head and muttering to himself. Several minutes later he returned pushing a sheet-covered gurney. Without further comment he locked the wheels on the gurney and pulled aside the crisp white sheet. Underneath lay two long, thick, black plastic bags, metal zippers dividing the bags neatly down the center. As Heep opened the bags, Max moved up beside him.

Duncan pulled out a cigarette and was about to light it when Jasper said quietly, "Please take that outside." Turning to Max he asked softly, "Is there anything you'll need?"

"Gloves may prove useful."

"Fine, but if you wish the body repositioned please allow me to do that. Is there anything else?"

"No."

While Jasper pulled out a pair of thin rubber gloves Duncan and Hy stepped outside, content to see Mr. Mangrove again through the viewing windows.

Inside Max watched intently as Heep peeled away the open bags. When he stepped aside she slowly scanned the ragged collection of exposed tissue and bone. "The body is severed mid-thorax by a diagonal rupture. Rupture appears to be surprisingly clean in nature, lacking however the crispness of a blade cutting. It appears as if some force has literally broken the top third of the body away from the lower portion. Organs affected by this breaking exposed at bottom of rupture. Lower portion of lung sacks visible and relatively intact but remnants of torn musculature indicates tearing under extreme pressure. Condition of exposed organs similar on lower section rupture line." She pushed the small mike away from her mouth. "My medical terminology is severely limited so feel free to step in if I go too far afield."

"So far you're on the money but I'll keep an eye on you."

"Thanks. It doesn't have to be that technical. This is primarily for my own information. You ever have a body come in here like this one before the museum murders started?"

Heep twisted up his too thin face into what served him as a frown. "Not when there wasn't a very large truck and a couple hundred yards of asphalt involved. By the way you handle yourself I'd say this wasn't the first occasion you'd had to spent time with the recently deceased. Ever see one like this?"

With a shake of her head Max stood back from the gurney and considered the remains of the late Mr. Mangrove for several long minutes then made a final notation. "Research ritual significance regarding removal of victim's hands and feet, as well as skinning." Switching off the recorder she removed the headset. "That about does it for Mr. Mangrove if you want to return him to his room."

When Heep returned from the cooler he found Max leaning against the countertop pouring over the collection of photos. "If you need them I can have copies made."

She looked up slowly. "Thank you. If it becomes necessary I'll give you a call. There are a couple of questions I'd like to ask, if you have the time."

"I'm here till four a.m., after that it'll cost you." Jasper grinned tentatively. Heep was, as a rule, nervous around humans that were still warm to the touch, especially the female of the species.

"Fair enough. Each of the victims' bodies suffered similar ruptures, correct?"

Jasper leaned forward, resting his bony elbows on the counter. Pointing to the photographs he explained, "With the exception of Mrs. Worthington whose abdominal cavity was ruptured, the other three victims were quite literally torn in two. As you can see by the photos, each in different areas—Gillis severed at nearly the waist, Paxon in the hip region, and Mangrove at mid-thorax."

"Hands and feet of all victims were missing. Serrations on the legs differ from those on the wrists. Was that common to all four victims?"

"Yes. While it appeared as though the hands had been pulled off the wrist, the feet . . ." He paused and rubbed at the faint stubble on his nearly pointed chin. "I know this isn't possible, but it's almost like the feet had been . . . chewed off, not like a wolf or something but very similar to the kind of wounds seen in a . . ." He paused and looked at her. "You're gonna think I'm nuts."

Max grinned slyly. "Let me see if I can guess. A shark. Is that what you had in mind?"

Jaspers mouth sagged for a moment as his eye's took on a suspicious look. "You a mind reader or something?"

Max smiled broadly. "I saw *Jaws* four times and rooted for the shark until he ate Robert Shaw. Believe me, at this stage of things nothing you could say would sound crazy. When a solution to this case, and I do believe there is a solution, is finally discovered I'm afraid it's going to alter a lot of people idea's about what's crazy and what isn't."

Jasper considered that for a moment longer, then glancing quickly over his shoulder moved closer. "Let me ask you one."

"All right."

"How do you think these people were killed?"

Max chewed on her bottom lip and gave the photos a quick second look. "I can't say that I've formed any really concrete conclusions yet, but I can't shake the feeling that whatever caused this did so on some kind of internal level. From the way the organs are pushed outward, the musculature along the rupture lines forced out, I'd have to suspect that whatever did this came from inside their own bodies."

A small spark ignited in Heep's watery brown eyes. "Bingo—and I can go you one better. I'd be willing to bet my pension that each one of the victims remained alive for at least several minutes."

A look of disbelief twisted up Max's face. "Are you saying . . ."

"Exactly. They were alive while all of this was happening, up to and possibly including the removal of the skin."

A cool silence wrapped itself around the pair.

"If that's true then how is it possible that even in cases like Gillis, where there was someone else in the house with them at the time, no one heard them cry out?"

"If you're compiling questions how about this one . . ." Heep reached over and pulled out a particularly detailed black and white shot of what appeared to be a white-haired, little old lady with an octopus growing out of her stomach. "Rosalyn Worthington, seventy-two years of age. Cardiac patient, asthmatic, occasionally ambulatory, suffering from an advanced case of almost anything you'd care to mention. Now it's a proven medical fact no matter how physically fit an individual may be there are limits of tolerance that the human body will not ignore. The nervous system will only tolerate just so much pain before it shuts down. The patient faints, blacks out if you will. Explain to me how it is then that a woman in Mrs. Worthington's condition could have remained conscious under the kind of trauma these injuries dictate."

Max shrugged helplessly.

"If you're interested I have about another hundred such questions."

"No offense, but if it's all the same to you I'd like to chew on the ones we've already gathered before I try any new ones on."

"Well, if you get through them, just remember I've got a list."

"Moving on, I've got a favor to ask." Max reached into her tote and pulled out the black leather case.

"Shoot."

"I'd like you to run some tests on these dust samples." From the case she produced several plastic bags each marked with the location the sample were taken from.

Holding the bags up to the light Jasper studied their contents. "Am I looking for anything in particular?"

"Actually I'd be satisfied just knowing the composition."

"Simple enough. What are these samples from?"

"A piece of sculpture. Three of the four victims each had the same piece. An award of some kind from the museum."

"O.K. Provided things stay quiet tonight I can maybe have them ready for you by tomorrow. That soon enough?"

"Perfect."

The sun had dropped behind the western horizon when their car pulled into the visitors parking lot at Carrington Towers again.

"The general meeting will begin about ten but Chief Merchinson would like to have a few words with you beforehand, so I guess we'll pick you up about nine. That all right with you?"

Max pulled her tote under her arm and looked at Hy with red-rimmed eyes. The day had not been without stress, and the silent ride back to the apartment wrapped in the comforting warmth of her aviator's jacket had nearly lulled Max to sleep. Blinking back the cobwebs, she fixed a smile across her lips.

"Why don't I meet you there, say about 9:30?" Unwilling to allow any alteration to this simple plan, Max pushed open the door and stepped out. "See you in the morning. Drive carefully," she said, moving quickly into the complex.

Hy watched her disappear into the building, wondering if he should have insisted on having things his way. Merchinson wasn't a man Chang easily crossed swords with. Even if you won an argument with the chief you still lost.

"I think we deserve a treat. What say?" Duncan grinned broadly.

"What?"

"A drink. In fact a lot of drinks, and I'm buying." Duncan jumped on the gas, leaving half a steel-belted radial on the drive. The sound, sending several seagulls perched on the fence around the tennis court crying raucously into the air, drowned out the last of his offer. "At least the first."

Outside of a small pilgrimage to the kitchen for the preparation of scrambled eggs, crisp bacon, English muffins and a large pot of coffee, Max spent the remainder of the night on her bed, the tools of her craft spread out around her.

Giving the collected materials around her one final check to make certain nothing was amiss Max began a slow perusal of the video records. After a half hour she stopped the tape on a freeze-frame close-up of the Chac Mool sculpture atop the mantel in the living room of Dawson Gillis.

Selecting one of several large manila envelopes from a pile, she dumped out its contents, a large number of photocopied press clippings. Somewhat impatiently she began scanning the collection. Several were nothing more than press releases of the usual sort and held little in the way of information or interest. A short article from the *Los Angeles Times,* dated August 21st, proved more pertinent.

The article from the Mexican bureau desk recounted a statement issued by the National Museum of Mexico refuting claims made by the White as to their cooperation and cosponsorship of the nationwide tour of the Peten Chac Mool. According to the statement, the National Museum claimed neither they nor their government had ever given such permission and were operating through diplomatic channels to have the piece returned to Mexico. A brief statement from the White—one had to assume issued by Dr. Westeridge, though no credit was given—said the exact opposite, but they likewise were dealing with the issue through diplomatic agencies.

Max looked at the screen, surprised to find the five minute hold had elapsed and the video had proceeded on. Watching with only a portion of her attention she wondered aloud, "If they didn't give their permission, then how did the bloody thing get away from them?"

Before turning off the lights she crawled across the bed and pulled a small, bone-colored leather pouch from the watch pocket of her jeans. Slipping back under the covers she carefully opened the pouch, emptying its contents onto her lap. In the pile were several highly polished stones, three small feathers held together by a thin leather thong, one clear, brilliant white crystal half the size and length of her thumb, several small white bones, a worn, brownish gold claw, a small glass vial covered by a silver filigree to protect the vial and the sea water it held, three dolphin's teeth the size of a child's, and lastly, the size of an infant's nail, a pitted and scarred piece of iron from a meteorite. Clustered together on the broad plain formed by the bedspread the collection looked pitifully small and insignificant. They were faded relics of an older time, a time when mankind ritually carried such medicine pouches to deal with spirits and forces modern man no longer recognized.

Max's fingers traced the sharp, angular surface of the crystal, opening her thoughts to the stone's restful influence. As the first shadows of inner peace coiled silently around her, she centered on the scope of the investigation and the parameters thus far indicated, allowing them to fix in her mind in a proscribed fashion. When satisfied with the arrangement she began opening the doorways that would allow access to forces and abilities long forgotten in mankind's distant past.

January 26th—8:40 A.M.

WITH AN AIR OF QUIET CONFIDENCE MAX PRESSED DOWN ON the gas while releasing the clutch, praying that the two actions were done in just the right combination so the big car wouldn't lurch and buck. When the vintage 1938 Packard convertible rumbled smoothly toward the exit ramp Max sighed, "Thank you, lady," patting the large ivory-colored steering wheel affectionately.

The trip downtown went too quickly, and by the time she pulled into a space, Max had formed a genuine affection for the proud, white beauty. Walking away from the car she found herself looking back at its gleaming outline and smiling. "Yep," she thought, "it's gonna be a nice day."

The first black clouds on Max's horizon, like those rapidly encroaching on the coastline, raced toward her sunny disposition shortly after opening the door to the building. A bored young officer at the desk threatened to show her the door, physically, when he did not find her name on the visitors list, ignoring Max's requests that he contact Chief Merchinson's office. The pair argued for several minutes longer before Max struck her colors and beat a grudging retreat.

At the door Max paused to allow several men in assorted casual and uniform dress to enter. Stepping into the doorway, as if to leave, she furtively watched their progress. The group entered an unmarked door several yards south of the recalcitrant desk officer. Stepping back inside she glanced around quickly then headed purposefully for the unmarked door. Without pause for second thought she pulled it open and stepped quickly inside. Rows of gymnasium lockers formed the perimeter of the modest room. In front of a number of these lockers stood men in various stages of undress. With a broad smile fixed confidently over her lips Max chirped, "Good morning," when some of them looked up curiously at her entrance. Not waiting for any kind of response she crossed the room with long determined strides exiting through the opposite door.

Smiling at a nearby officer she said quietly, "I seem to be lost. Can you direct me to the Task Force squad room?"

The officer complied quickly enough with her request, relieved that this stranger in his midst was not another weed for his already overburdened garden.

"Chang, wait up." Max called.

"Hi there," he said with genuine surprise. Looking past her he asked, "Where's Forbes?"

Max looked behind her and with a shrug smiled innocently. "I don't know."

"He was supposed to meet you at the desk."

"I took a short cut."

"Well, as usual, things are screwed up around here. The chief is tied up with the mayor so I guess your meeting will have to be postponed."

"No problem. In the meantime I need some copies of this," Max said, pulling a small computer disk from her tote.

"Why don't we go over to the office, and I'll get Maggie onto this," Chang offered.

"Sure."

Entering a doorway marked "Task Force" Max felt the heat of a dozen eyes fixed on their entrance. Chang, playing the part of tour guide, seemed oblivious to the attention. Settling her at a deserted desk he left in search of coffee and returned minutes later with a battered mug and trailing two tall, nearly identical officers.

Over the next half hour a steady stream of Task Force members entered the squad room all of whom Hy diligently introduced to Max. In the blur of faces Max gave up all pretext of trying to remember names.

Shortly before 10:30 Hy snatched her from the midst of the crowd that had formed and ushered her into a long, narrow area separated from the main squad room by glass walls. The one solid wall of the room was covered by long, old-fashioned black boards littered with a confusing conglomeration of lists, black and white photographs and typed memos. A single, narrow table with several metal folding chairs fitted around it was the only other piece of furniture in the room. The table was covered by a profusion of paper. A number of phones sprouted up through the debris like aged black mushrooms. Seated at the table were three men. Their ages ranged from somewhere in the mid-thirties to well into the fifties. Even dressed in neatly tailored suits they appeared wrinkled and disheveled. In each man's eyes there was a look of weariness beyond the range of their earthly years.

Commanders Liebschuetz, Helmer and Diehl formed the leadership network of the Task Force. Commander Diehl, senior member of the triumvirate, fixed a pair of lopsided reading glasses on the bridge of his broad red nose and lifted a plain manila folder off the top of the clutter. Opening it he studied the material inside for several minutes, pausing occasionally to look over the edge of the folder in Max's direction.

Due to the cleanliness of the folder, its thin size and the intensity of those gazes Max surmised the folder contained a copy of her preliminary report.

Duncan slipped through the door quietly. He moved up beside Chang and looked down at her with a tight, funny kind of grimace straining the corners of his mouth. It was an almost childish expression of ire.

Commander Diehl cleared his throat and looked at her over the top of his lopsided glasses, which were now resting considerably lower on his nose. Glancing at his fellow commanders he began. "This report of yours, Ms. Morgan . . . well let's just say it wasn't exactly what we were led to expect."

"Really," Max said quietly, her gaze locked on Diehl's watery blue eyes.

The commanders waited, fully expecting Max to launch into an explanation. When this did not occur and when it became apparent this single word might well be all she planned to say on the subject, the three men exchanged a number of worried glances.

Commander Liebschuetz, youngest of the three, leaned forward and tried another approach. "I think what Commander Diehl is saying is that your report is a little confusing. Perhaps you could explain."

Max, her expression pleasant, looked at Liebschuetz and asked simply, "What part of the report do you find confusing?"

Liebschuetz opened his mouth as if to speak then quickly closed it. Picking up his copy of the report Helmer cut right to the heart of the complaint, as he saw it. "What is this shit?"

While Liebschuetz looked genuinely shocked by Helmer's approach Diehl looked content to let his subordinate have a run at it. Max didn't need to see Forbes' satisfied smile to know it was there.

Swallowing an urge to call Helmer an asshole Max asked innocently, "Exactly which part of this shit seems to be confusing you?"

There was a brief, stunned kind of silence.

"Gentlemen, I'm not clear on just what you were led to expect from my participation on this case or by whom but, that's not really relevant at this time. I am, for lack of a better definition, a kind of physic investigator. My realm of expertise lies in those areas outside of those considered in a mundane investigation. Over the past month you have experienced a series of senseless murders of an extremely bizarre nature for which you and your people have been unable to supply natural channels of exploration." A small frown tightened the wrinkles around Diehl's eyes. "Simply put, you have no clues as to the felon's identity. My presence was requested in the hope that an alternative perspective might be useful in this case. What that report says, simply put, is that the killer you're looking for falls within my realm of expertise and not yours. Does that clear things up a little for you?"

"No, it doesn't, not one damn little bit. What, exactly, does all that mean?" Helmer snapped.

"After retracing the evidence your team has already covered and working under the parameters of my speciality it is my opinion the perpetrator of these crimes is not human."

"Wonderful!" Helmer scoffed, rocking back in his chair again.

Before things had a second chance to get out of hand Commander Diehl took control. "Let me get this straight. Are you saying some kind of ghost is responsible for these murders?"

"Ghosts have a tendency to wander halls, cause cold spots and move the furniture about. Commander, let's agree on something right now. Terms such as ghosts, poltergeists, physic phenomena create different mental images for individuals outside my field then they do for me. When you say ghost your frame of reference is limited to such things as film, television and the odd Stephen King novel. Believe me when I say that these impressions are a far cry from the reality of the situation. Am I saying a ghost is responsible for these crimes? No, I am not. At this premature point of my investigation I would be quite unwilling to make an exact determination as to the direct cause. The one thing I am most certain of is that your killer isn't Jack the Ripper or the Night Stalker or a great white shark. Human beings have been known to do some incredible things to their fellow men, but nowhere in the annals of crime will you find a criminal who, without mechanical or outside aid of any kind, was able to quite literally rip his victims in half from the inside out then neatly vanish with the poor blighter's hands and feet—all without leaving either a fingerprint or sign of his coming or going. Really, gentlemen . . ."

Max broke off abruptly, realizing her little speech had become more passionate then she might have wished it to be. Taking a deep breath she settled back into her chair and waited, knowing all to clearly what to expect.

Diehl slowly took off his glasses and wiped them on an oversized white handkerchief. Without looking directly at her he spoke slowly with a tone of voice most often heard in exasperated parents. "But at this time you can't tell us exactly what is doing these killings."

"Correct."

"That being the case I trust you would not find our proceeding with this investigation in our usual manner too disruptive to yours."

A small, sly smile turned up one side of Max's mouth. Diehl may look the part of the silent senior partner but under that guise lurked a formidable elder statesman. Without saying so he had managed to make abundantly clear just what his position on her presence was.

"Then let's proceed with things status quo. I will expect reports from you on a weekly basis. If there is anything you need which either Detectives Forbes or Chang can not provide, please contact me. Now I think for the time being we'll keep the material in this report on file unless there are any instructions you'd like to give the rest of the team that would be of aid to you."

"I can't think of any at this time."

"Good, then I think that about covers it."

"There is something."

Diehl looked at her with a slight squint. "And that would be?"

"I'd like to visit the museum and speak to the director, Dr. Westeridge."

"For what reason?" Diehl's guard was suddenly up.

Max could feel the tension in his voice. Choosing her words carefully she said calmly, "Each of the victims were members of the museum's most prestigious society, each a recipient of a recent award from the museum. It is quite important to my investigation that I make myself as fully versed on the interests and concerns of those individuals involved as possible. I'm not really that familiar with Meso-American artifacts, and I thought possibly by exposing myself to the White and it's collection I may learn something." Max held her breath and hoped Diehl wouldn't poke to hard at her thin lie.

He considered her for a moment then said. "I trust you have no objection to Forbes and Chang accompanying you?"

"I shouldn't think so."

"Then I don't see any harm, provided that you limit your discussion with Dr. Westeridge to matters of art. I can hardly see any advantage in advising him of your position in this investigation at this point. Don't you agree?" The question was purely rhetorical, and Max easily recognized it as such. "Right. Forbes, tell Westeridge you'll be bringing Ms. Morgan over. When would you like to . . ."

"This afternoon would be fine."

Diehl glanced at Forbes then began burrowing in the clutter in front of him. "This afternoon," he mumbled to no one in particular. Pulling out a rumpled yellow legal pad he began making notes. "Helmer, I want you to get somebody over to see . . ."

Max felt a tap on her shoulder. Duncan crooked his finger, indicating it was time they left.

"Just how the hell did you get up here anyway?" Duncan grumbled, closing the door behind them.

"I beg your pardon?"

Conscious of the stares of several of the men in the squad room he moved closer, lowering his voice. "I waited at the desk for damn near an hour. You didn't come in that way, so how did you get in here?"

"I took a short cut." Max smiled innocently.

Duncan was warming up for a lecture when a new county was heard from.

"Ms. Morgan?"

"Yes?" The man approaching them with his hand extended looked like a network anchorman, his clothes expensive and stylish, every strand of his styled hair in place.

"I'm Daniel Marks, Public Information Officer assigned to the Butcher Task Force and personal assistant to Chief Merchinson on this case. I'm sorry I wasn't here to meet you this morning, but the meeting with the mayor took us all quite by surprise. I trust everyone in the Task Force is being helpful?"

There was the briefest of glances in Forbes direction with that last remark, a glance that was not wasted on Max. "We're all getting along swimmingly."

"Grand. Now Chief Merchinson is very anxious to discuss this case with you. He would like you to join him for lunch."

"That's, ah, very nice of him, but Detective Forbes was about to arrange an appointment for this afternoon."

"No problem. We'll have an early lunch, and I'll have you back here, oh say, one at the latest. Did you bring a jacket? It's a bit nippy out but such a beautiful day I thought lunch at the Century Club would be nice. It's one of our newest restaurants, and the view from up there is quite spectacular. A perfect introduction to the City of Angels for such a lovely visitor."

"Why not? I wouldn't think of disappointing the chief. If you'll excuse me I'll just get my jacket."

Still smiling Marks edged closer to Forbes and, without taking his eyes off Max, hissed, "Whatever that woman wants you see she gets it. One more fuck-up and you're out on your ass. I'm keeping my eye on you."

"You must be some contortionist to do that with your nose shoved so far up Merchinson's ass," Duncan hissed with equal ire.

Marks' cheeks flushed and his eyes bulged.

"Ready when you are." Max grinned, stepping up to the pair. Daniel Marks' face looked like a toad's who'd just had a run in with a semi and lost. Forbes, on the other hand, looked like the proverbial canary who'd swallowed the cat. You didn't need to be a mind reader to see that this pair hated each other's guts. For a spiteful moment Max considered asking that Forbes and Chang join the outing.

To his credit, Marks did a marvelous recovery. When he looked at Max his eyes had almost returned to their normal size and his smile only waivered for the smallest of instants. "Grand. Shall we go?" They started to move away when he paused and looking back over his shoulder purred, "Be a good lad and make Ms. Morgan's appointment for after one. There's a good boy."

Forbes smiled sweetly and said, "Right you are, Danny," all the while glaring black death at the hapless Marks. Max lost it and had to move quickly out into the corridor to hide the sound of her laughter.

The impromptu luncheon with Chief Merchinson and Daniel Marks, to Max's surprise, had turned out to be a rather pleasant one. The restaurant displayed a commanding view of the city from it's roost on the 71st floor of the Mitsubishi Bank building. Adding to the surprise was the fact that along with the view came some very good food. Merchinson had been much as her first mental impression of him had lead her to believe. Although he treated her with a kind of deference most often given to high explosives, she found him to be a fair, even-handed man. And in those instances when conversation lagged Daniel Marks filled those gaps with pleasant, mindless chatter. In comparison to other such meetings Max had experienced this was definitely one of the better ones.

Returning to the squad room Max found the area nearly deserted with the exception of Chang and Forbes.

"What's that?" Max asked frowning down at the greasy concoction on Chang's desk.

"Spareribs, why?" Chang looked at his plate then at her with a puzzled expression.

Then looking at Forbes plate she asked. "And that?"

Not taking his eyes off his lunch he asked, "What's it look like?"

"Raw fish."

"Bingo. Next question?"

Max considered the obvious anachronism and decided against comment. "When do we see the White Museum?"

Duncan leaned back in his chair and looked past her to a large wall clock. "I figure, if we leave right now, we'd be five minutes late for the appointment."

"Wonderful. Would it be all right if we left now, while we're still only five minutes late?" Max asked hopefully.

Chang took a swallow of coffee then emptied the remains into his wastebasket. Balancing his plate under his chin he turned toward the door. "O.K. by me," he grunted.

Max looked to Duncan.

"Just waitin on you," he muttered, rising slowly to his feet. Grabbing a paper napkin he dumped the contents of his plate onto it, dropped the plate into the trash, crumpled the napkin around his fish and stuffed it in his pocket.

1:40 P.M.

The Chandler Marston White Museum crouched on the cliffs overlooking the Pacific Ocean in a neighborhood filled with expensive condos, exclusive beach clubs and multimillion dollar waterfront homes. The dollar figure of the land alone on which the White stood would have housed and fed the homeless in a tristate area for several years. More than one land developer driving along the Pacific Coast Highway had been known to have shed a tear when passing that magnificent piece of real estate.

Sitting on the crest of the cliffs, surrounded by gardens designed for another era, the Museum itself had been constructed during the financial heydays of the early twenties. The kindest description of the structures architecture might well be an uncomfortable mixture of Egyptian and Aztec art as rendered through the eyes of an impressionable pupil of Erte. While originally painted in tones of flamingo and aquamarine it's last five years of financial success had made possible a pristine coating of brilliant white converting her from town whore to village dowager.

Max nodded at the guard's directions, but her attention was centered on the huge, gleaming white building ahead. A hundred yards or so inside the gate the driveway split in two, wrapping itself around a long, low reflecting pool. Rolling to the edge of that pool Max stopped the Packard and sat looking over the rim of the wheel.

Chang leaned forward resting his arms on the back of the front seat. "Something wrong?"

Max shook her head. "Just enjoyin' the view."

Easing her foot off the brake they continued on, past the front entrance, beyond the deserted visitors parking and around to the rear and lowest parking level reserved for the museum's deliveries and staff. The staff parking area was only partially filled, allowing Max to locate a space well away from the other cars in the lot.

"Museum closed today?" Max asked, stepping out of the car.

"Yeah. Getting ready for some big exhibition." Chang replied pulling himself out of the back seat. "Westeridge says he can't spare us a lot of time on account of he's got so much to do to get ready for it."

Joining the two men she asked, "Who does he think I am?"

"Diehl said to tell him you're on the mayor's payroll, kind of an observer. Westeridge and the mayor are on real good terms so we figure he might be a little more cooperative with you." Forbes grinned. "You being a female and close to the mayor."

Max ignored the jab. "Uncooperative, is he?"

"Not so's you notice. It's just that the guy is kinda . . ." Chang paused searching for the right word, and Duncan supplied one.

"Weird." The guy's weird."

They tabled their discussion while a lethargic guard searched the list on his clipboard for their names. About 30 seconds into the search, Forbes pulled out his badge, waved it under the man's nose and mumbled something unpleasant. Max wasn't quite certain if it was the sight of the badge or what he'd said; whichever, it worked.

Making sure they were out of earshot, Max took up the conversation where it had left off. "You said this Westeridge is weird. How?"

"Don't pay any attention to Forbes. He thinks everybody is weird, except him," Hy whispered.

"Well, this guy is."

"O.K., he's weird, but how weird? What does he do or say? What? Explain your version of weird," she said.

Duncan considered the question for a minute as they walked on. "It's like you're talkin to this guy—right?—and he's answering you like there's somebody inside him, somebody different pulling the strings, moving his mouth and working his face and saying the words . . ." He paused and the others stopped behind him. "And the thing that's the creepiest is you look at his eyes and it's like they belong to the guy that's inside of him, you know, the one workin' the wires and stuff. And the guy inside is laughing at what he's makin' Westeridge say and at you for bein' dumb enough to believe it."

Max looked at him and smiled. "That's really good, Duncan." His face took on a skeptical expression. "No, really, I'm serious. That's a very good observation. You'd be surprised at the number of people who would have overlooked such an impression, and had they noticed would not have been able to describe it so graphically."

A smile reached Forbes eyes if not his lips. With a glance to Hy he shrugged and continued on up the stairs. "You don't make it to my age, a detective sergeant, and live to tell about it without picking up certain skills the average guy never gets."

Hy moved up beside her. "Modest guy. Never could take a compliment."

"Thanks for telling me. Next time I'll just pat him on the head and toss him a fish."

The executive offices of the museum were located at the very top level of the structure in an area that overlooked the gardens and the Pacific Ocean beyond. The corridor outside these offices, it's white mosaic floor tiles buried under a layer of aged and yellowing wax, smelled of old wood and the scent most often associated with mildewed books.

The trio arrived at the reception area to the offices of Executive Director Dr. Malcom Westeridge, and Duncan walked briskly up to the desk of a heavyset, middle-aged, Hispanic woman. He waited almost 45 seconds, a phenomenal length of time for him, before he leaned forward, rested his palms on the desk and cleared his throat. The woman, busily pounding out correspondence on an elderly I.B.M., was either deaf, absorbed in her work or incredibly rude for she gave them no more attention than she had upon their entrance. Duncan, his eyes narrowed to slits, considered the woman then reached out to snatch the paper from the typewriter.

Max stepped forward quickly, slapped his hand in passing and reached for the doors to the inner office. Before she could open them more than a crack the woman looked up. "You can't go in there."

In a voice both calm and firm she said quietly, "Inform Dr. Westeridge that his 1:30 appointment has arrived."

"He's not in. You're late, and he could not wait."

"He's left the building then?" Max asked.

"No, he is still in the museum. He is a very busy man with much to do."

"As are we. Kindly locate him and remind him that his appointment, arranged by the mayor's office, has now arrived. We'll wait."

The woman said, "You wait here. I will see if he can be disturbed." Then she stepped out into the corridor and closed the door behind her.

Max crossed to the doors to the inner office and nudged them open with the toe of her boot. As she stepped inside Chang nervously lurched to his feet.

"Hey," he hissed sharply, "what are you doin?"

Max's disembodied voice called back, "Snooping. Want to help?"

"Jesus Christ," Chang muttered, darting to the outer doors and peeking outside. When he looked back he saw

Duncan headed for the open doors. "Where are you goin?"

"To help." Forbes smiled as he likewise vanished inside.

"Wonderful," Chang moaned.

The executive office itself was extremely long and narrow. Across from the door and directly in front of a large plate glass window sat a single wooden desk of a proportion not duplicated by modern manufacturers. The top of the desk was clear save for a bronze work lamp, a phone and a large leather-trimmed blotter that covered the working area of the desk. In front of the desk, separated by a worn and somewhat faded area rug, sat two sturdy leather chairs.

Max stepped up to the desk, casually running a finger along its wooden surface. A residue of dust clung to her finger. With a frown she brushed it away and turned her gaze to the left.

The walls bore a number of primitive prints, each encased in heavy but simple wooden frames and spotlighted by small exhibition lights. Between these prints, on tall wooden pedestals made out of the same dark wood as the paneling, sat several vases and two small pieces of sculpture. All artifacts, as would befit a museum specializing in the era, were of the Meso-American cultures of the Aztecs, Toltecs and Mayans.

The right side of the room ended in a massive fireplace with a mantel, the top of which easily reached Max's forehead. Over the mantel a small exhibition lamp still clung to the wall, but below it sat nothing more than a large rectangular spot where the wood of the paneling was noticeably lighter, indicating a picture had resided there for some considerable time but was now missing. On the mantel several small pieces of sculpture sat seemingly abandoned. A rug sat in front of the hearth, but as Max stepped forward she paused, looking down at it's fading surface. Stooping she ran a hand over the fabric near the corner furthest away from the fireplace.

"Whatcha got?" Duncan asked moving closer.

Standing slowly she shook her head. "Nothing really,

but there used to be a piece of furniture here, possibly a couch, and its been removed recently. See the indentations in the pile of the rug. Whatever did that was heavy and sat there for a long time. See the scars in the floor where it was dragged out?"

Both men looked at the marks on the old wooden floor. "So what?" Duncan frowned.

Moving up to the mantel Max said casually, "Nothing, just practicing." Craning her neck she studied one of the small pieces. Picking it up carefully she brushed the cobweb from its stubby little arm. Absent-mindedly she turned it over and noticed a small silver-toned stamp marking it as having been produced in Juarez for the White Museum gift shop. She was about to make mention of this when Chang interrupted.

"Psst, he's coming," he hissed.

Chang darted out into the waiting room. Forbes moved considerably slower, while Max carefully replaced the sculpture, then paused as a small, bright yellow string caught her attention. Pulling on the string she started as a tiny golden object jumped off the shelf, flying into her face. With a muted squeak she trapped the object in her hand and sprinted through the doorway shoving the object into her pocket.

Dr. Malcom Westeridge could not possibly have been further from the mental image his name conjured. Instead of the tall, scholarly, pale Englishman one might have expected, Westeridge was short, almost to the point of being squat, stocky and of a decidedly swarthy complexion. For a man supposedly immersed in the hectic last minute details of a major showing his attire seemed more suited to that of a Vegas pit boss—albeit one that knew the better clothiers. He wore a simple, two piece, gray flannel suit, his shirt and tie a shade of summer peach. His shoes were dove gray loafers each with a small tasseled ball resting on the instep, and the socks that peaked out from under his pants leg were the same color as his shirt and tie.

Westeridge entered the room with a look of brooding disapproval clearly stamped on his face, a look that was quickly replaced by a broad, toothy smile two steps inside the room, "Detective Forbes and Chang, how nice to see you again." He pumped their extended hands with what could pass for genuine warmth. With little more than a glance in Max's direction he said, "Please, come into my office."

Max trailed the three men into the inner office but not before she got a clear glimpse of the angry glare aimed in her direction by Westeridge's secretary as she settled her bovine rump behind her desk.

Ever-vigilant Chang stepped into the social breech. "Dr. Westeridge, this is Ms. Maxine Morgan. She is overseeing the investigation on behalf of the mayor's office."

Max stepped forward and was about to extend her hand when Westeridge sat down behind his desk. "How do you do, Dr. Westeridge."

"How do you do?" he muttered, his gaze directed more at the ceiling than her face. "Please, everyone be seated." He smiled at Chang and Forbes, obviously knowing there were only two chairs in front of his desk. Forbes dropped into one while Chang stood back allowing Max to take the other. Looking directly at her for the first time he asked, "And how is Geoffrey these days? We see far too little of him of late."

Max allowed one side of her mouth to turn up in the parody of a smile. "Busy, extremely busy, but then what can one expect of such a vital, active man?"

"Yes, so he is," he said slowly, his gaze slipping away from her. "As am I. I was led to believe there were certain questions you wished to ask."

Max pulled a small notebook from her tote. "Just a few. Standard really, but you know Geoffrey—details, details, details. This won't take long, and when we're done you can give me a quick tour of the museum." As Westeridge started to protest, Max hurried on. "It's a crime to say it, but in all the years I've lived here I've never been inside the White. Geoff insisted I see it. You know how he is." Westeridge swallowed a look of irritation and smiled at her with pale warmth.

During the questioning period Max made notes but not of Westeridges responses, as one might have believed, but of his gestures, composure, facial responses and most importantly the impressions she was gathering about the man from these things. As she neared the end of her questioning she became aware of a pattern in his responses. Westeridge was answering her not with just merely a close version of his earlier responses but, as much as she could recall, the same words. The good doctor was like an actor repeating a much studied soliloquy.

Closing her notebook Max smiled. "I think that about covers everything." She stood. "Now for that tour you promised."

Westeridge glanced first to Forbes then Chang, and finding no potential help there pushed away from his desk. "You realize that a complete tour of the museum at this time would be impossible."

"Actually I'm rather pressed for time myself but I would like to see this Chuck Mal thing," Max purred innocently, purposefully mangling the sculpture's name.

Malcom's dark eyes became flinty as he glared at her. "Certainly. I shall be happy to show you the Peten Chac Mool. It is without doubt the museum's most important piece." Softening his hard gaze he smiled tightly. "If you'll follow me to the central gallery." His politeness was pointedly for the benefit of the detectives and not Max.

Westeridge led them to the central gallery.

One end of the gallery had been stripped bare of other artifacts and a waist-high platform had been erected in the center of the floor. Resting atop this platform, its round black eyes gazing over the heads of the visitors, was the great Chac Mool of Peten. Over eight feet in length and a little over five feet at it's tallest point, the recumbent warrior presented an image of primitive power and majesty last seen on this earth nearly 2000 years ago.

The male figure—laying on his back, his upper torso supported in an upright position by the elbows, knees bent, feet flat with the heels pressed tight against the buttocks—supported across his lower abdomen a large, flat, oblong platterlike object. The expression across the warrior's square face was one of stern watchfulness. The statue itself had been originally carved from a solid block of clay and then covered by a thin coating of plaster. Onto this plaster, in shades of ochre, seneca, turquoise and red, details were painted of his elaborate breast plate, crown and short feathered skirt. Over the ages much of this outer coating had fallen away, exposing the mottled clay beneath.

Max's gaze was fixed on the statue. She centered her concentration, closing out the drone of Westeridge's boring voice as he repeated the kind of badly written speech usually delivered by equally boring tour guides.

"I'm sorry but you'll have to stay back."

Max's concentration snapped. Looking down she saw Westeridge's arm blocking her forward progress. Without being physically conscious of having done so she had moved closer to the statue until she now stood less than four feet from the foot of the platform. With a muttered apology she stepped back.

"This area will be roped off during the exhibition. In recent years, with attacks occurring on various works of art in museums around the world, such precautions unfortunately have become necessary. This platform is just another in a series of protective devices we must employ in order to protect this artifact." Westeridge directed this little speech to Chang and Forbes, but Max could sense its true direction.

"Yeah, well, there are a lot of nut cases runnin' around out there," Duncan said flatly.

"Does that include electronic devices," Max asked casually. Westeridge looked at her briefly, his dark eyes narrowing speculatively, "At the Louvre during special exhibitions I've seen—"

"This is hardly an object likely to find it's way into someone's pocket. Electronic devices will not be necessary. A guard will be present during the exhibition, and the museum is well-guarded at night. No, I can assure you, the Peten Chac Mool is in no danger of being stolen." Almost as if on cue he looked at the heavy gold watch on his wrist. "Now I'm afraid this interview really must end. I have a directors meeting shortly. Mateo."

A young Hispanic male dressed in the tan and brown uniform of a security guard stepped over. Chang swung around at the man's entrance, and a small frown of annoyance flickered across his face then quickly vanished.

"Yes sir," the guard said with almost military crispness.

"Mateo will show you out. Please do come back to the museum during our exhibition, Ms. Morgan." He smiled cooly.

"I certainly will, Doctor," Max purred with just a hint of mystery.

"Gentlemen." With a curt nod in the general direction of the two detectives Westeridge turned on his heels and moved toward the rear of the gallery to a small plain door recessed discretely within an alcove.

Max watched his departure covertly until she became aware of the guard's gaze. Smiling briefly at Mateo she followed quietly along behind the men.

When the group reached the receiving dock, where the trio had entered, Max froze. "Shit! Shit, shit, shit!" She barked loudly. The men came to an abrupt halt at her cries.

Max stood unnaturally straight, her fist pressed against her right eye. Duncan frowned, the guard glared at her apprehensively, while Chang, a puzzled look etched across his broad face, made a move in her direction. "What? What's wrong?"

"No!" she cried out. "Don't move. My contact, my goddamn contact, I lost it." Duncan groaned. Chang smiled tightly, turning his gaze toward the ceiling, and the guard's stiff posture seemed to ease. "Down. Everybody down and help me find it." Chang complied almost instantly. Duncan folded his arms across his chest, refusing to crawl around the floor on this stupid errand. Max, moving her hands over the floor like a blind man, crawled on her knees toward the still immobile guard. Tugging on his pants leg she pleaded, "Come on, help or we'll be here all night. I'm not leaving without the damn thing."

Mateo hesitated for a moment longer then dropped to his knees. Max continued to move away from the place where she had first given the alarm. Slowly she crawled toward the battered gray desk and the heavyset guard they had first encountered sitting at his post. She paused, craned her neck, then in a soft voice asked the man, "There, what's that under the desk? See it? That little shiny thing?" The guard sighed loudly then pushed his chair back and leaned down squinting under his desk. Duncan, watching this scene with undisguised amusement, suddenly turned his attention to Max. While the guard's attention was directed under his desk Max's head swung up, her gaze sweeping over the door and the surrounding wall. Duncan watched this strange action, but before he could do more than observe, Max let out a cry.

"I got it." Bent over double she popped something in her mouth, made swishing motions, then spit the object into her hand. With quick expert gestures she popped the object into her eye and stood up. "Whew, thought I'd lost another one of those damn things." She smiled at the two guards who were looking at her with expressions of exasperation. "Thanks, guys." Turning that smile on Chang and Forbes she beamed. "What's the hold up, folks?" Without a backward glance she pulled open the door and darted out into the parking lot.

Outside the sky was darkening rapidly, and a wind with the smell of distant rain was picking up strength. Duncan overtook Max.

"All right, what was all that bullshit?" he snapped, blocking her path.

"Why don't you drive? I'm tired," Max said loudly. Pulling the keys from her pocket she tossed them to him and stepped around him. Under her breath she muttered, "Shut up. We're being watched."

Duncan swallowed an urge to look back. Clutching the

keys he turned, focusing on the Packard and letting the idea of driving the object of his affection calm him.

Chang's mouth started to sag as he saw Forbes heading around to the drivers side of the vehicle. Looking to Morgan he wondered aloud, "Are you sure you want to do this?"

Max opened the passenger door and swung the front seat forward. "You carry a gun. You have my permission to shoot him first funny move he makes." Hy frowned at her. "Do please get in. We have very nosey neighbors," she urged.

"Haul it in here, Chang," Duncan called in a low hard whisper. "Little pictures got big eyes."

With a grunt Hy tucked himself into the back seat. As Max closed the door and Duncan started the engine he grumbled, "You two gonna tell me why you're both suddenly talking like Sam Spade?"

Max and Duncan exchanged frowns.

By the time the Packard pulled up to the curb in front of Division Headquarters, the trio had come to an agreement that there was a lot more to the White museum and it's director than antiquities and fund raisers, but thanks to certain directives from the mayor's office, Westeridge, the museum and it's elite subscribers were a closed file ending any avenues of interest in that direction. Most mysterious was the absence of employees and workmen.

Chang squeezed his way out of the back seat. "You coming in?"

"No, I've got some notes I need to go over. I'll call you tomorrow," Max said.

Chang excused himself then tried to two-step his way between the raindrops into the building. Duncan waited for a patrol car to pass then eased open the door. As he slid out he muttered under his breath, "Thanks for lettin' me drive." Standing in the rain he closed the door firmly but with care and said something through the glass that vaguely sounded like, "G'night." With a lumbering gait he skipped around the puddles and into the station house.

Max watched him vanish, a small smile playing over her lips. Threading her way toward the freeway through the sluggish traffic she was beginning to contemplate an early evening and a good night's sleep. Starting to get comfortable with that thought she suddenly sat up very straight and reached quickly into her jacket pocket. For several seconds she fumbled, pushing around a crumpled Kleenex and a half-pack of cigarettes when her fingers brushed against something cold and hard.

Removing the object, she suspended it from the piece of rough, yellowed yarn it was attached to. A small parking lot in front of a discount children's clothing outlet beckoned out of the drizzle a few yards ahead. Parking well away from the other two cars in the lot, she shut off the ignition and turned her attention to the swag her quick fingers had purloined from the museum.

Suspended from the yarn, the small object, no bigger than the thumbnail of an average adult, was surprisingly heavy. Squinting at the thing she scratched it with her nail, producing a deep groove. "Whew," she sighed, "make that grand theft."

Judging from the weight of the thing it was at least a good three ounces of pure gold. Turning it over in the palm of her hand she pushed thoughts of its worth to the back of her mind and concentrated on trying to decide just what it might be.

It was rounded and partially open on one end like a bloated clamshell. The side she had gouged with her nail was smooth and polished while the reverse side bore deeply carved lines. Studying the lines she tried to make a constructive pattern. It was a kind of face, swollen and irregular, with large round eyes and a thick upper lip which formed a ridge around one side of the opening in the bottom. Two small indentations formed a child's interpretation of a nose. Just above the eyes two swirling patterns represented what might possibly be ears. She stared at the strange bloated features for several moments longer, then turned her attention to the yarn fragment it was attached to.

The fiber was unbelievably coarse. The end opposite

the object was worn and frazzled. Fingering that end she decided whatever this had been a part of, this piece had worn away from the rest. Sniffing the fiber she found it to be a form of hemp. Studying the ends of the frayed fibers she was almost certain the color was a result of dyeing. Where it attached itself to the object the yard was tied in a series of knots, small and delicate. Judging by the size, number and delicacy of those knots she was certain the thing's overall construction must have been of a very special nature. This was no hurried item made for casual use but something created with particular skill.

Pressing the trinket between her palms she closed her eyes, sealing her hands together tightly. Turning her hands independently she tried to pick up some impression, some mental image as to its nature, but after several unsuccessful minutes she gave up the effort. She opened her hands and looked at the small piece. She was perplexed but not concerned by the lack of response. After all, some things spoke with voices so soft that even those willing to listen were unable to hear without assistance.

Swinging the small golden orb like a pendulum Max stared out at the rain. She thought back to the museum and the unusual quiet of the place, not the quiet she had discussed with Duncan and Hy but the deeper less obvious quiet she alone had experienced. Museums were, for those who cared to listen, seldom quiet places. The structures themselves, as well as the artifacts they housed, spoke in voices of light and color, composition and history, passion and compassion. No, museums were seldom quiet places, but to this rule the White was a rude exception. All inside the White was cold, still and lifeless, yet just under that surface something stirred, something deserving of a much closer look.

Max leaned forward abruptly and tugged the tote up onto the seat beside her. Trapping the trinket in her hand, she burrowed into the bag until she located a thick, red leather notebook. Flipping through the sections, she came to one containing names and addresses. Running her nail down the alphabetized markers, she selected the

"Mc" file. A number of pages filled with entries made up this section, some typed with great neatness, some written in pen and others scribbled hurriedly in pencil along the margins. Finding the one she wanted, she paused to consider her location and the shortest possible route. Leaving the notebook open beside her, she returned the orb to her pocket and started the car. There were just too many unanswered questions, and if she stood any chance at all of finding the answers she needed help, a very special kind of help.

4:17 P.M.

The room was bright and warm. The television, a small color set, was something Leana had never seen before outside of store windows. She sat on the edge of the bed, her big brown eyes fixed on the gaily colored cartoon figures that danced across the screen. Across her lap sat a tray on slender wicker legs. In between gulps of a thick chocolate shake Leana stuffed her small mouth with handfuls of fat, crispy french fries.

The door opened, and the woman who had brought Leana to this bright, warm room stepped inside along with two, dark, powerful-looking men. The men stood just inside the door watching Leana as the woman crossed to the bed. She looked down at Leana for a moment then reached out, laying her hand on the child's shoulder. Leana looked up, blinking slowly as though she was having difficulty focusing.

Leana did not resist when the woman took away the tray or when she lifted her to her feet. From a pocket in her faded house dress the woman produced a small phial. Selecting a pill and using her fingers like a press, she pinched the sides of Leana's face on either side of her jaw. The child's mouth opened slowly, and the woman administered the pill much in the same manner one would to a sick cat. When she was certain the pill had been swallowed, she reached into her pocket a second time and withdrew several pieces of wrapped chocolate. While Leana fumbled with the foil, the woman looked over her shoulder to the men and nodded.

The modest home sat on the end of a promontory overlooking the South Bay community of Hermosa Beach. It was separated from it's neighbors by a condo unit under construction to the north and a sheer 100-foot drop down the hillside to Artesia Boulevard on the south. Built 30 years ago before the rush to beach communities for the tidy sum of $28,000, it was now considered, even by conservative standards, to be well worth 20 times that amount. Not that anyone wanted the little blue and white bungalow; most wanted only the sand and clay it stood on. Even at that price, the view, sweeping all of the South Bay, Palos Verde and Catalina Island beyond, made it a developer's dream. The people who inhabited the small bungalow this rainy evening, quite without the knowledge or permission of the vacationing owners, had a particular interest in that view but not for a purpose that would add to the property's value.

The low ceiling, coupled with the heat and smoke from the brazier, made the air in the small living room feel close and unbearably foul, a fact that seemed to have no effect on the shadowy figures that moved in the dimness, sweat glistening on their bodies from the light of the brazier. Leana stood between the two men who had carried her to this place. Her hair was freshly washed and brushed, and she wore a clean white cotton dress that fell to the floor covering her small feet. The nearly naked men who stood on either side of her reeked of their own excrement which they had smeared over their bodies. They muttered harsh, guttural prayers, all the while piercing their arms and legs with small knives still crusted with blood and bodily waste from similar ceremonies. Her eyes were heavy, and she found herself unable to either pull her gaze from the flames of the brazier or to stop her small body from swaying to the strange music. Under the long gown her small toes curled and flexed as if they had a mind of their own. She somehow knew she could dance to that strange music, dance in a way she had never been taught, in a way she had never seen danced before, in a way that would bring her great happiness and joy.

As her eyes continued to watch the bright flickers of light from the brazier a darkness spread over that light until it was blocked completely from her sight. She tilted her small head sideways in an effort to regain the pleasant image of the bright flames then, as if unseen hands lifted her chin, she looked upward.

A great golden crown raining a shower of long, glittering, blue/green feathers rode over a face with dark compassionate eyes, eyes that looked at Leana with such a tender gaze that her small heart swelled. He spread his arms wide and without uttering a word called her to him. For an instant she stood there, too overwhelmed by the godlike image before her to move, then strong hands against her small back propelled her forward. The volume of the music rose, and Leana began to dance in a way she knew would give great pleasure and joy to the man with the dark, compassionate eyes.

4:18 P.M.

Outside the rain was coming down with steady determination. Each time the door opened a bit of the outside gloom seeped in on the heels of refugees fleeing into the welcoming warmth of the Boarshead Inn, unwilling to face that long, dreary drive home without the aid of liquid fortification. The Boarshead Inn, like its owner Riley McCall, was something of an anachronism. In a city where it was barely legal to smoke on the street, smokers were welcome here. While other chefs searched for new ways to lower calories, and owners sought new ploys to make portions served even smaller, customers of the Inn reveled in giant bowls of thick, rich Irish Stew and a near lethal concoction simply labeled Chili McCall. At the Boarshead they did not serve local beer or wine coolers. Everything that looked like wood was, muzak was blasphemy, neon was for gas stations and art nouveau was a French venereal disease. In a city that prided itself on everything that was upscale and posh, the Inn was lowdown and comfortable like old levis and worn sneakers.

Riley McCall—Da to his friends which included if not everyone who had ever entered his establishment then at least those who paid their tabs without being pestered—was squire of the manor at the Boarshead, and as he liked to tell his family and friends, he considered it the crowning jewel of his empire. According to records at City Hall, three pub-styled restaurants formed the cornerstone of McCall's own private little dynasty. Along with this went a controlling interest in a local British-style tabloid catering to the area's large English population, a healthy percentage of a Palm Springs hotel/spa and a partnership in a small commercial fishing fleet operating out of San Pedro, all of which were on stable financial footing and producing enough capital to keep the IRS interested.

Riley looked over the meager crowd with only casual dismay. Easing behind the bar, he paused with a regular long enough to share a particularly raunchy joke and refill the man's empty glass before passing on to the register and a quick count of the early take. Margie, an attractively plump 35-year-old divorcee, Riley's head barmaid, bent over to retrieve a fallen bar rag, her short costume revealing more than a little cheek. Without taking his eyes off the cash or loosing count Riley reached out and patted her behind with genuine affection. "Give us a pint and a bowl, will'ya, love?" He purred, his accent purposefully thick.

"I'll take care o'that, Margie. You go on home." Ruth Elizabeth, Riley's only daughter, moved up beside her father and growled under her breath, "You're a randy old sod, and you should be ashamed of yourself usin' Margie that way."

"That's a hard tongue you got in your head for your old Da."

"You can save that for the paying trade. Honestly, Father, when are you going to grow up and act your age?"

Riley returned the cash to the drawer and tried to look

like the stern Irish father, but when his gaze fell on Ruth Elizabeth all he could do was smile. Ruth, youngest of his three children and the only one whose mother randy Riley had paused long enough to marry, was the image of her mother. At 27 she was a prototype of everyman's vision of an Irish lass complete with long red hair and quick intelligent green eyes, and like her mother before her she had stolen Riley's heart completely. She completely ruled her father and her two older brothers, having long ago taking on the role of lady of the manor.

Riley settled himself into the corner booth and sighed contentedly. Sean, oldest of his two boys, came out of the back office and crossed directly to the register. He sat there watching Sean, his hair the same blue black Riley's had been at that age, the same blue eyes, a bit taller and his mind fixed more certainly on business than Riley's had been. He was the kind of a son a man could be proud of. Riley frowned as a shapely brunette at the bar smiled and called to Sean, only to have the boy fill her glass and pass on, polite but distant.

Ruth Elizabeth set down his tray, heavy with an oversized bowl of steaming stew, half a loaf of crispy fresh bread and a thick mug of strong black coffee. "What're you frowning about?"

"That boy needs to pull his nose outa those blasted books and loosen up. He's as prickly as a Protestant."

"You leave Sean be, just because he's not chasin after every skirt in the county like a certain McCall who shall remain—"

"Da?"

Ruth Elizabeth was just getting her teeth into the role when Conna, Riley's second son, appeared at the table his reddish hair plastered wetly across his broad forehead, water still dripping off the light cotton jacket stretched across his massive chest.

"Conna, look at ya. You're soaked to the skin. Get that jacket off before you catch your death." Ruth Elizabeth fussed, standing on her tiptoes trying to pull the sodden jacket off him.

Conna looked confused for a moment, then collecting

himself, he said, "There's a lady here to see you."

Max suddenly appeared at the table.

"You!" Riley grumbled. Elbowing his way up and past his son, Riley fixed Max with a steely glare. "You."

"Hello, Riley, it's been awhile. I wasn't sure . . ."

"Maxine Montgomery Morgan," Riley said slowly, his face twisting up like a thunderhead about to rain all over Max.

Shifting uncertainly, a grin flickered across Max's lips then disappeared while her eyes searched out a possible exit from the approaching storm. "Well, at least you got the name right."

"You icy-eyed, black-hearted witch." With each unflattering pronoun Riley took a menacing step closer.

"Right . . . well, perhaps another time." Max leaned back on one heel preparing for a speedy retreat.

"The most inconsiderate, irritating, confounding piece of baggage . . ."

"I take strong umbrage to the term baggage." Max protested edging away as Riley drew closer, his children bringing up the rear.

"Umbrage, is it? Maxine Montgomery Morgan, herself, takes umbrage, does she?"

A small frown twisted up her brows while a smile worked it's way up one side of her face. With a shrug she offered lamely, "Maybe I should have called first?"

Riley, now standing toe to toe with Max, studied her for a moment longer, then his broad face broke into a thick smile that colored his cheeks and set his eyes to sparkling wetly. "Aschula!" He flung his arms open wide capturing Max in an embrace that was at once affectionate and punishing.

". . . and it was bitter cold and black as a pit, not so much as a hint of a moon. She was late, and we was all for turnin' back, all except the good father, him sayin' how the lads was needin' them guns and all. Another hour passed and then the signal come . . ." Riley paused, everyone around the corner booth riveted on him, even Max who, having been there, knew the story as well as he. "I raised me torch to give'm the all clear, and no sooner did I turn the bloody thing on than it slipped outa my hands, them being that cold. I bent over to pick it up and the next thing I'm knowing herself here kicks me bum over tea kettle into the water." A rumbling of laughter erupted, and Riley, being the master storyteller he was, waited for it to subside before continuing. "It was a long cold swim but not, I'll warrant, as cold as the plans them government boys had for us and the lads. You may thank herself here for the fact that your dear ole father is telling you this bit of his sordid past from the comfort of his own pub and not Wormwood Scrub." Riley smiled proudly.

"And for that you have my deepest apology," Max joked, embarrassed by the attention.

Ignoring the laughter this remark roused from his offspring, Riley frowned. "There's just one thing I've never understood about that night."

"Only one, fortunate man." Max smiled.

"The truth now—how did you know the priest was a government grass?"

"I didn't, not right away, but if you'll recall I never liked the man from the beginning."

Riley laughed and looked to the others. "As she told us all repeatedly. We all put it down to him bein' a man of the cloth and herself nothing more than an unrepentant pagan."

"Could well have been, but it was this pagan's sharp little eyes that saved us all."

"But how, girl, how?"

"Brown shoes," Max said simply.

A series of almost identical frowns sprang up around the table. Max laughed. "When Riley dropped the torch I noticed the good father's shoes. They were brown." When the frowns failed to dissolve Max got one of her own. "Look, I may be a heathen, but I've yet to see a Catholic priest wear brown shoes with a black suit."

When the last of the frowns vanished from the table, Ruth Elizabeth having explained everything to Conna, a serious rehashing of old times threatened to erupt with the younger McCalls, eager for more stories. Riley allowed them a few more questions then drove them from the table with promises Max would not run away.

"That's some family you've got yourself, Riley." Max smiled.

"That they are." Riley's beaming face spoke volumes about his pride in his children.

"Apologize to Conan for me. I didn't mean to startle him outside."

"Ah, it's not you. It's those damn silly movies they made a few years back, and what with him lookin' the way he does, well, the boy took some serious ribbin'. I tried tellin' him about his namesake but . . ." Riley paused.

A shadow past over Max's face. Unable to meet his gaze she studied the coffee in her cup with false intensity.

Riley watched her for a moment longer then turned his gaze to the glass in his own hand. He said quietly, "You still think about him, don't ya, girl?" He waited for a moment longer then glanced in her direction. Her gaze was still riveted on the cup. Looking away he cursed himself for bringing up such a tender subject. Quickly swallowing the last of his drink he cleared his throat. "But you didn't come here to talk over old times, did ya?"

Max sighed. "No, not really."

"You're here on a case." Max nodded. "The butcher." She nodded again. "I wondered how long it would take those fools to come to their senses." Riley was all business now, losing a noticeable portion of his brogue.

Max smiled. "What can you tell me about a Malcom Westeridge, Director of the White Museum?"

Riley shrugged. "Big money, big contacts. What's to tell?"

"That's one of the things I hoped you'd be able to help me with."

"I could do some poking around. I have a few friends with an interest in his type. What are you looking for exactly?"

"Exactly? Exactly anything. I met Mr. Westeridge this

afternoon, and like our friend with the brown shoes he seems an odd piece of work. Anything you could dig up would be of help. My employers don't seem very anxious to have me bothering him. Also I'd be curious to see what you can dig up on the museum's latest acquisition, the Peten Chac Mool."

"All right." Riley nodded, making several notes on a handy napkin. "I'll see what I can come up with. It'll take me a day or two. I may be a little out of practice these days."

"I seriously doubt that."

"Ta. Now you said that was one thing. You've got another?"

"I'm in needs of some tools."

Riley's thick eyebrows jumped for his hairline, and a smile turned up one corner of his mouth. Leaning closer he asked quietly, "A job, is it?"

"Hmmm, something suitable for a cracksman," Max said slyly.

"Well, we *are* in fast company. Keys or a straight away haul?"

"Commercial locks on the fly."

The pair looked at one another.

"Ahhhh." Riley smiled.

"Ahhhh." Max laughed.

"I get my hands on that little faggot I'm gonna rip off his head, scoop it out and give it to his mother as a vase."

Hy considered that image for a moment then turned away.

Duncan muttered something else ugly under his breath then pounded the horn as an overburdened city bus lumbered out into the lane their car was currently occupying. Hy looked up into the windows of the bus as they passed, his gaze careening over the unfamiliar faces behind the dirty glass.

The rain had settled itself into a thick, steady drizzle, giving all appearances of being up to the task of staying the entire night. Rush hour traffic, which for Los Angeles meant any time of the day when it was physically impossible to get from point A to point B without having to wait in line for the privilege, had stuttered to an absolute halt on the downtown freeways and was only marginally better on the surface streets. The usual ten minute ride to Chang's father-in-law's restaurant, The Black Pearl, in Chinatown was well into the 20 minute plus range and counting.

Not that Hy was in any hurry. Those nights he volunteered to play part-time bartender, part-time security guard at the restaurant wasn't one of his favorite chores.

The front tire collided with the curb, and the car shuddered to a stop. Hy looked through the rain-streaked window at the neon bright entrance of the Black Pearl and groaned behind his teeth. He shifted his big body around, laying a hand tentatively on the door handle. Like a child trying to ease the pain of a visit to the dentist he looked at Duncan. "Why don't you come in and have a drink? The old man won't be down until the dinner rush. That gives us at least an hour. The drinks are on me."

Duncan went through the gestures of looking like he was thinking over the offer. He wasn't, and Chang knew he wasn't. They'd played this game too many times, but Hy was his friend and this little charade made this part of the ritual go down a little smoother. The truth of the problem was that no matter how much Chang swore to the contrary the drinks always came out of his pay, because the old man could smell a free drink crossing his bar at 50 yards.

"Naw, not tonight. I got something I got to do."

"Yeah, like what? Gonna work on your boat?" It was the closest to pouting Hy ever came.

"Matter'a'fact, smart ass, I'm gonna take a ride past the little dirt bag's apartment and see if he's holed up there."

"And do what? Far as I know ain't no law against a man checking himself outa the hospital. You go over there and kick down his door and his lawyer is gonna be all over you."

"So who said anything about kickin' in any doors anyway? All I'm gonna do is drive by, and if I see a light I'll stop in for a little chat." A tight, little smile twisted up the corners of his mouth then vanished as quickly as it had appeared.

"And if you don't see a light? Maybe a little solo stake-out in his drive way, a little cruise of the neighborhood to chat with his friends? You know, whether you like it or not, so far he's just a witness."

"You want to loan me a pair of your kid gloves, or should I stop and buy a pair of my own on the way?"

Hy waggled a warning finger. "Don't get cute over there."

"Give me credit for some smarts, will ya?"

"If I could I wouldn't let you outa my sight tonight."

"But you can't, so haul your big ass outa here before some snot-nosed rookie rolls up and gives me a ticket for blockin' traffic."

Hy opened the door then looked back hesitantly. "You remember what I said."

"Yes, Mother, and I got clean underwear on, too." Duncan nodded wearily.

"Good, 'cause it wouldn't do to have dirty ones on when Diehl chews you a new asshole."

"Out!"

Hy stood on the curb, the rain dripping off his closely cropped hair and running down the back of his neck. Watching the car as it picked it's way through traffic he muttered, "He's gonna get into trouble. I just know it."

No matter what the city fathers said, Cable wasn't a street; it was an alley. Until people started living in the small apartments made out of converted garages and storage buildings it didn't even have a name. By the time Duncan reached Santa Monica most of the residents of Cable were home, their cars parked haphazardly along the narrow alley making driving down it nearly impossible.

Parking a block away he pulled the collar of his raincoat up around his ears and did his best impression of a man out for a casual evening's stroll. Duncan hunched his shoulders and shoved his hands into the pockets of his raincoat. His gaze followed a line of dark cracks in the pavement, allowing him the luxury of weaving his way around the larger puddles.

Raven's apartment, number 8, was one of three in what had once been a five car garage for an older apartment building. Even in the darkness the haphazard conversion left numerous clues to the structure's former life. The door to number 8 was at the side of the building, part of the original construction.

Giving up all pretenses of subtlety Duncan rapped loudly, frowning as the door slide open at his touch.

The interior of the apartment was dark. He eased the door open a little further then stepped inside and closed it behind him. In the blackness he fumbled for a light, finally locating a wall switch on the wrong side of the door.

From the instant he'd found the door unlocked, he'd known what he would find inside. The single fixture in the middle of the ceiling shed no light on any surprise here. The room was long and narrow and at the rear was what realtors liked to call a half bath. On that same wall, clustered around a small sink, hung four mismatched kitchen cabinets. Beside the sink sat a two burner hot plate and below that, shoved into a space that had once been a cabinet, sat a tiny refrigerator. A single bed, a battered end table, a large green vinyl recliner, a floor lamp and a tall metal cabinet with two doors was the sum total of the room's meager furnishings. On the end table sat a dirty white phone and above it on the wall a small grouping of pictures torn from magazines.

Duncan looked at the room for several minutes then sat down in the vinyl recliner, sighing deeply. The bed was unmade and littered with wire coat hangers, plastic bags and one forlorn brown sock. The tall metal cabinet had apparently served as a closet for it, too, was littered with empty hangers. A pair of rundown sneakers huddled in the corner beside an impressive stack of phone books.

Duncan knew he should be searching through the debris, picking through the contents of the kitchen and bathroom, sifting for some telltale indication that would lead him to his witness' whereabouts, but somehow he just couldn't rouse himself to do that. He'd known, almost from the moment he first heard of Raven's unexpected departure from the hospital, they had seen the last of Raven St. James. He'd known it even on the drive over, and through all of the other wasted steps he'd taken on this little jaunt, but he'd gone along with it anyway, the same way he'd been going along with any number of wasted efforts in the last month. At first he'd done it simply because it was that kind of a case, one of those bastards that no matter how many right moves you made you never came up with the right answers. You kept doing the same thing over and over because you knew sooner or later you'd stumble over something stupid and there'd be all the answers you hadn't been able to find in the first place, but recently a new factor had been added to the equation. Part and parcel of this new element was Maxine Montgomery Morgan.

Morgan was on to something, but just what that something was he hadn't a clue, just a small itch around that area of his brain where his intuition hung out. To his considerable annoyance, since the disappearance of St. James that itch was rapidly becoming a rash.

Applying a healthy kick to the mental seat of his pants, Forbes hauled himself out of the chair and pawed his way through the apartment's pitiful remains. He did this because it was part of the ritual, and right now he had a sinking feeling he needed all the rituals he could lay his hands on. The search took a grand total of half an hour and for his trouble he found a stack of overdue bills and some porn.

He pulled the door to the apartment closed and made a dash for the car. By the time he reached the car his shoes squished and the front of his suit was soaked. He sat there behind the wheel, puffing and wheezing like a faulty tea kettle. He stuffed his collection of goodies into the glove box, stuck the key in the ignition and made a mental note to burn his new running shoes.

The car's heater was doing a fine job of steaming up the windows but a bad one of warming his feet. Sitting at the intersection while waiting for the light, he promised himself a leisurely drive home with a stop at his favorite Mexican restaurant for some take-out. He'd even begun considering the possibility of eating his dinner while soaking in a hot tub, something Rachel would have found just unbearably decadent enough to have joined him in. He was reminding himself to let the past rest when a big white and chrome specter of his present cruised through the intersection. The Packard and the all too familiar platinum-haired driver were heading in the opposite direction of the Marina. Suddenly all thoughts of home and food were forgotten. Slipping into the slow lane about a quarter of a block behind the Packard his itch began working itself into a lather.

The storm had cleared the streets of most traffic, but Max drove slowly toward her destination, her mind centering on the task ahead. After the pleasant reunion with Riley her state of mind was far too content for such an adventurous undertaking. Unconsciously her grip on the huge old steering wheel began to tighten. Slowly she pushed aside the restraints of civilization and allowed a low level hum of hostile aggression to settle over her. Ever so gradually she allowed the darker side of her nature to come into dominance.

On the ocean side of Pacific Coast Highway sat a large restaurant, a long time favorite of the locals. Pulling up to the front door, Max waited until a parking attendant opened her door before giving him stern instructions as to the parking of the Packard.

Forbes pulled into the lot and paused long enough to see Max go inside. For a moment he considered the possibility of following her then slowly turned around and pulled back out onto the highway. As he headed back toward the city, his itch started complaining again. He managed to ignore it for nearly a mile before veering into the left hand lane and turning back toward the restaurant. This time he stopped across the street just out of the circle of brightness thrown by the lights of the parking lot.

He eased back on the cold plastic seat and pulled the last cigarette out of his pack. With a grunt of displeasure he tossed the crumpled pack into the back seat and reached for the lighter. He leaned against the recalcitrant lighter, willing it to hurry. Then unwilling to wait any longer he pulled it out of the dash and plugged it's faint redness against the end of his cigarette.

It was only by accident he noticed the flicker of white moving up off the beach a few hundred yards further down the road. Replacing the lighter he leaned forward, straining his eyes against the darkness, and for this effort he was rewarded.

"Those damn boots," he said aloud, smacking the steering wheel gleefully. Max had worn them the last two days—tall, knee-high boots, like cowboy boots but similar only in the shape of the toe and the height of the heel. Forbes had noticed them because of their strange color, not unlike that of bleached bones you sometimes find in the desert. He'd thought it somehow apropos at the time. He stopped congratulating himself long enough to watch as she proceeded across the highway then disappeared into the road leading up to the museum.

"What the hell," he muttered. He then started the car and without turning on the lights drove down the shoulder cautiously to give her sufficient time to move further up into the hills before he approached the road. Pulling into the center of the small two-lane blacktop he leaned into the passenger seat and looked up the road. Once he thought he detected movement but could not be sure. Turning the car around he backed a few yards up onto the road then shut off the ignition. Getting out he pulled his light-colored raincoat off and tossed it in the back seat before locking the door. Sticking to the thick shadows at the side of the road he began climbing up the hill.

Max turned her head from side to side like a frustrated pointer trying to pick up a lost scent, but the sound had escaped her. With one last glance back toward the highway, she quickened her pace, leaning even further into the shadows. Around the next bend the floodlights from the museum's parking lot filtered dimly out onto the roadway. Leaving the road she stepped into the fringe of trees that marked the outer boundary of the museum property. Using them as cover she approached the broad grassy slope leading up to the front gate.

The small guard shanty at the front gate was dark and deserted. The heavy main gates stood open, a thick chain with a metal placard and the museum's hours stenciled on it hanging from its center. Max sighed a thank you to the gods of arrogance and complacency then crossed the lawn at a quick pace. As she neared the booth her posture took on a decidedly different pose; suddenly she became agitated and anxious. She made a great show of searching the darkened glass of the shanty giving, to all outward appearances, a neat imitation of a stranded motorist looking for a phone. Continuing this guise she stepped over the chain and proceeded onto the main drive, but as the bright lights at the gate faded into the darkness beyond so did Max's performance. Ducking into the shadows provided by a cluster of large palms she paused for a moment, and when nothing stirred she moved on.

Several minutes later Duncan stepped over the chain. He listened for a moment but could hear nothing. He'd been too far back to witness Max's performance or see her enter the grounds, but he knew she was in here somewhere—only where? The answer flashed into his mind as he got a vivid picture of the missing contact lens stunt earlier this afternoon.

"Jesus friggin' Chrysler," he muttered under his breath. "She's gonna break into the goddamned place."

Max pressed back against the side of the building then leaned toward the door, looking quickly inside. A small desk lamp burned at the guard's station, but the guard was nowhere in sight. Lifting her watch toward the light Max strained to make out the time. Five after the hour. "Great," she thought. "He's either just left or is on his way back. Shit!"

Turning to the door she opened the small case Riley

had given her, selected a pick and thrust it up into the lock mechanism. Working as quickly as she dared she ground her teeth unconsciously as the lock proved to be more stubborn than she might have hoped. Adding what should have been unnecessary force to the equation she felt the tumblers at last fall into place.

Opening the door she pulled a piece of silver tape off the leather face of the kit and covered the door's plate in preparation for a speedy exit. Crossing the dock area she paused long enough to call to mind the general layout of the museum then, hugging the shadowed recesses of the outer corridors, headed for the main gallery.

Duncan looked at the silver tape plastered over the locking bolt. For a moment he considered retracing his path, getting into his car and going home; it wasn't too late, not yet anyway. But if he continued on, and God forbid, they both got caught . . . He shook off that thought, telling himself he had to go on now if for no other reason then to make damn certain nobody did get caught.

Max climbed the stairs to the main gallery and ducked into the shadows at the sound of approaching footsteps. Burrowing into the darkness she held her breath as the guard passed within feet of where she stood. Waiting until the sounds of the man's shoes on the marble floor faded away, she sighed quietly at having been spared the nuisance of having to face the man.

The great dark work curtain still stretched across the mouth of the central gallery, the illumination of a single work light glowing faintly out from underneath it. Parting the opening a bit, she peered in, took a deep breath and stepped through the curtain.

Four metal standards holding a thick velvet rope stood in place about five feet out from the foot of the platform. Standing there, in the deep almost tangible silence of the museum, Max looked slowly up into the face of the great brooding statue, allowing a smile that had nothing to do with humor slip quietly over her lips. Stepping up to the velvet barrier she whispered to the Chac Mool.

"Hello, old one. I've come tonight so you and I may

speak in private. I have the ears to hear you, old one. Do you have the voice to speak?" Stepping over the rope without taking her gaze from the statue's face she crossed to the foot of the platform. Stretching one arm over her head she lifted up on her toes, the tips on her fingers barely brushing the throat of the statue. "Speak with all your voices, old one. I bring the ears to hear you."

Moving around the platform she studied its surface until she found what she sought.

Duncan pushed back a corner of the work curtain, and his breath caught in his throat. Swallowing hard he watched as Max climbed up onto the platform with the statue. Standing behind the sculpture, she threw back her head and for several heart beats stared up into the dark recesses of the ceiling several stories above. Duncan tried following the line of her gaze but finding nothing quickly abandoned the effort. When he looked back Max was pressing her hands tightly together, rubbing them in a gesture similar to one he had once seen a distraught junkie make. She continued this for a moment or two longer then, leaning forward, laid both hands on the statue's tall crown.

For the next 15 minutes Forbes watched, in growing impatience, while she repeated this gesture over the sculpture, pausing in first one spot then another, eyes pressed tightly closed, turning her head from side to side, sometimes leaning down until it appeared as if she were listening to some sound coming from within the piece itself. Only once did he look away when a sound from the far end of the long gallery caught his attention. He listened but decided it was nothing more than a ventilating system coming on.

When Max finally stood erect, Duncan sighed quietly, certain the show was over for the evening and sure she would depart, but his relief was short-lived. Standing over the statue Max glared down at the thing with an anger he could feel, forcing the hairs on his arms to stand on end.

In a voice unbearably loud for the still of the museum she growled down at the thing. "Speak to me, damn you.

I have the ears!" With this she slapped the palms of her hands down hard onto the center of the platterlike object the sculpture held across it's abdomen.

Duncan patted himself on the back for suppressing the urge to shout at her to keep it down. He froze, listening for any sounds of an approaching guard. Hearing nothing he quickly made up his mind to put an end to this insanity.

He pushed through the curtain and crossed quickly to the base of the statue. At the rope barrier he looked up at Max and hissed, "Get down from there—now!"

Max increased the pressure of her palms against the clay, oblivious to all else. Almost immediately a numbing, burning sensation raced along the muscles of her arms, her fingertips throbbing. Her head suddenly became incredibly heavy and dropped forward, her chin resting on her chest. The silence around her faded, only to be replaced by a strange, muted, rushing sound not unlike the sound of the ocean when heard in the distance. A blackness so thick and so tangible that it could be tasted on the surface of the tongue washed over her. Unlike the simple absence of light blackness represents, this black had weight and density pressing down on her, fitting close round her body, pushing itself up into the openings of her nostrils and ears, trying even to insinuate itself between her closed lips. The electrical impulses from her brain signaled her hands to lift themselves away, releasing contact with the sculpture, but the blackness encased them so completely as to make even this simple act of self-control impossible.

The brain sent out order after useless order to its once obedient appendages only to be thwarted in each and every turn by the oppressive blackness. Thus thwarted, the mind began to turn in upon itself, folding and compressing not unlike the celestial phenomenon of the black hole.

"Goddamn you," Duncan grumbled. For the past five minutes he had used nearly every expletive in his vocabulary as well as several originals all to no avail. He might as well have spoken to the statue which Max now gave every sign of having become a part of. Moving around to the rear of the platform and taking a firm hold on one of her ankles, he yanked.

The concussion of Duncan's behind hitting the cold marble floor was sufficient to send the breath rushing from his lungs. For nearly a minute he sat there, first trying to return oxygen to his lungs then checking to see if he still had fingerprints. He could feel his fingertips turning a bright cherry red from the friction generated when his grip on Max's booted ankle had given way.

His head snapped up, and at the sight of the woman still standing upright his fingertips weren't the only thing that turned red. Pushing himself into an upright position he rubbed his injured hands on the sides of his trousers. Prepared now to climb up onto the platform and take Max off bodily, he promised himself, "I don't know how you managed that little trick, but if you want to play rough, you got it." He reached out, preparing to haul himself up beside her.

The muscles of his broad shoulders were bunching for the effort of pulling himself up onto the platform when his brain suddenly canceled that action.

The movement was so slight, a change so subtle in Max's posture, that he sensed rather than saw it. He swung his gaze upward in time to see her upper body flinch then straighten as if jerked into position by unseen hands. He gaped as Max rose several inches off the platform then hurtled toward the rear wall of the gallery. The sound of her body striking the floor put him in motion. Squatting down beside her he paused for a fraction of second, long enough for his practiced eye to scan for physical signs of damage. Finding nothing obvious but suspecting there must be, he layed his fingers against the carotid artery. To his relief there was a strong pulse.

Max's body gave a small twitch causing Duncan to pull his hand away as though he'd been stung. He watched as suddenly her mouth dropped open and she gulped in great, gasping breaths like a drowning swimmer. Her eyelids fluttered, then her head jerked violently from side to side. Small, feeble mewing sounds escaped her lips, and suddenly her hands and arms began to move in strangely static striking motions.

The blackness had all but completely receded. The only thing that remained between herself and the light of consciousness was a thick swimming gray void. Moving, pushing, clawing her way through it's layers she grew panicky as the gray clung to her and threatened to draw her back down into the deeper darkness. Increasing her efforts she strove toward the surface. With a will she forced her leaden eyes to open.

"Stop it!" Duncan snarled under his breath. Clamping his hand firmly over her mouth he glanced over his shoulder, certain at any minute now the curtain would fly open and the guards would arrive putting an end to this farce. Feeling her struggles abate Duncan looked down.

Max's eyes bulged from her head, her face was flushed, but her body no longer twitched. All striking motions of her hands and feet had ceased, and she was breathing through her nose in a manner much closer to normal. He opened his mouth to speak but froze as the sound of hard leather soles moving across the marble flooring echoed through the gallery.

"Shit!"

Pushing his face close to hers he whispered, "Can you stand up?" Unable to speak thanks to the presence of Duncan's hand across her mouth Max nodded. He pulled her to her feet. The sound of the guard's footsteps were growing louder with each passing second. "Come on," he hissed, pulling her toward the curtain.

Max's knees were understandably wobbly. In the first few steps she nearly fell twice. Their start again, stop again progress would put them at the curtain approximately the same instant as the guard's arrival, a conclusion both Max and Duncan arrived at in unison. Duncan looked for an alternative direction when Max settled the dilemma.

"This way. The door," she whispered urgently.

"What door?"

"Back there. Come on," Max hissed, tugging on Duncan's arm and drawing him back past the Chac Mool toward the recessed doorway she had seen Malcom enter earlier. With each step she found the fog clearing from her mind and the strength returning to her muscles. As her fingers closed around the doorknob she held her breath for a split second until she could feel it turn.

Duncan was still easing the door shut behind them when the sound of voices could be heard from the other side. The pair stood frozen, barely breathing, listening, straining to hear snatches of the guards' conversation in Spanish.

His lips close to her ear, Duncan whispered, "Can you make out what they're saying?"

"No, but I get the nasty feeling it's not 'see, I told you it was nothing.'" She craned her neck and looked back over Duncan's shoulder. "Up there. Go on," she urged, giving him a little shove.

They had entered a narrow access way between the first and second floor. Above them, at the top of a steep set of stairs, a fixture with a single bulb burning shed a feeble light over the area. Reaching the landing Duncan eased open the door and made to step out when he sensed Max was no longer behind him. He turned around angrily. He looked back down the stairs but could not see her. A second flight of stairs led upward into darkness. Closing the door gently he crossed to them and looked up. Max tiptoed down out of the darkness.

"What the hell are you doing?"

"There's another door up there, but it's locked."

"Screw the other door. This one's open." He latched onto the shoulder of her jacket and jerked her ahead of him. "Get your ass through there," he hissed.

Out on the balcony they kept to the shadows along the wall, stealthily moving along. Reaching the gilded elevator Max hazarded a glance over the rail. Something solid poked against her spine. She looked over her shoulder to see Forbes' angry glare. Silently he mouthed the words. "Get back here!"

As she stepped away from the railing he took a firm

grip on the collar of her jacket and yanked her to him. Millimeters from her face he hissed, "I want you in front of me. You stop for any other reason than I tell you to before we get out of here and I'll break your knees. You get that?"

Max nodded, a small smile twisting up one side of her face and making her appear faintly demented.

Duncan's eyes narrowed. "Move," he grumbled pushing her ahead of him. She took a few steps forward then stopped abruptly, causing him to bump up against her back. "Why're you stopping?" he growled in her ear.

"I thought you might like to know the guards have split up."

"Fucking wonderful."

"I only saw the one, but he's headed back toward the dock."

"Shit!"

"Follow me. I've got an idea."

Before he could mount a protest she was moving away from him toward the broad marble stairs leading down to the central gallery. Reaching the staircase Max quickly surveyed the area below then climbed up onto the thick, polished banister and slid down like a child. Duncan groaned behind his teeth until it dawned on him that her move wasn't as nutty as it appeared on the surface. She had managed to decend without making a sound, climbing off quietly at the other end. It would have been far more time-consuming and risky had she tried to walk down the stairs in those boots. He considered his own hard-soled shoes for a moment and then with only a trace of embarrassment mimicked her actions.

Crouched but with quick strides, Max led the way out past the deserted information desk and into the wide corridor running directly in front of the long bank of doors at the front of the museum. She continued to move down the corridor, ignoring the doors when Duncan grabbed her elbow.

"Why not go out the front?" he whispered irritably.

"Can't. Most likely locked. This way." She tried to pull away from him but he held fast.

"Bullshit," he grumbled. "We go out this way. Now!"

With Max in tow Duncan crossed down to the foyer and through to the long bank of glass and wooden doors. Across the center of each door rested a long metal bar that served as an opening device. Carefully he reached out to the nearest door and pushed against the bar. It depressed easily enough, but the door did not budge. He tried a second time then moved to another with similar results. After five such failures he looked back at her.

Shaking her head theatrically she turned back in the direction they had come. Duncan hesitated for a moment longer then reluctantly followed, listing the possible disastrous outcomes to this course of action under his breath.

"Come on. I found one," she whispered, gesturing him inside.

Their route had taken them into the section of the lower wing that housed the museum's small research/ lending library and the rest rooms. So far they had been spared the indignity of running into the second guard. However they had been forced twice to duck for cover at the sound of his harried footsteps coming from somewhere nearby. While Max rushed into the ladies' room Duncan tried the library door and was not terribly surprised to find it locked. Max came out of the rest room very quickly and moved on into the men's room. Duncan's first reaction was to regard her actions with skepticism, but recalling the banister sliding incident he decided to reserve judgement—a wise decision considering what awaited him behind that door.

Max smiled. "I knew there had to be one."

Wasting little time she pulled the lid off a round trash receptacle. Turning it upside down she climbed up onto it and worked the catch holding the window closed. With a small squeak from the swollen wood the window opened, the pane swinging down to the wall. Over the outside of the window hung a metal screen which Max made short work of by balancing on one leg and attacking with her booted heel.

The window opened about seven feet above ground level at the rear of the museum to one side of the formal gardens. Max scooted out, dropping to the ground, and Duncan followed quickly behind.

As she moved toward the gardens he latched onto her arm. "Where do you think you're going now?"

"Down the hill, where else?" She grinned. "I think it's safe to say the boys are now of the opinion they've had visitors other than the museum mice. No sense walking into their arms when we've gone to this much trouble to avoid it."

Duncan dropped his hold and silently fell into step behind her, glancing anxiously back over his shoulder every few minutes. The gardens were dark, the only illumination coming from small area lights high up on the museum roof. Still the pair kept close to the tall hedges bordering the walkways. Even though both were experiencing a certain relief at being out of the building they maintained a brisk pace, knowing they were far from safe. Despite their caution dark eyes watched their retreat from the high windows overlooking the gardens.

"What exactly happened in there?" Duncan finally asked.

"Well, I would have thought that was apparent."

"Really?"

"Yes, really. I wasn't expecting company so naturally when you showed up things got a little messy. Hadn't been for you I could have made it out of there with the boys being none the wiser. What are you doing here anyway? Or is breaking and entry a hobby of yours?"

"Damn!"

"What?"

"I'm amazed they don't clank when you walk?"

"They who?"

"Balls, the big brass ones you got, lady. I put my ass in a sling . . ."

"So who asked you?"

". . . save your silly hide . . ."

"Ha!"

". . . should have left you laying there. Stood back and watched you turn . . ."

"Damn near smothered me with that big ham of yours across my mouth."

". . . and this is the thanks I get."

They scrambled over a fence at the rear of the gardens and dropped down into a vacant lot filled with scrub plants, detritus from the recent storms and assorted stones ranging in size from toe breaker to the slipped disc variety. Slipping and sliding, clinging to one another for support, they worried their way through the tangle, eventually sliding down an embankment a few hundred feet from Pacific Coast Highway. During the entire trip not once did the pair cease their bickering.

Max started across the road toward the restaurant, but at Duncan's insistence and a firm hold on the collar of her jacket they walked to his car and drove across. Duncan wanted to park himself, but Max chided him into allowing the attendant to do so.

Inside only Duncan seemed to notice the stares their disheveled appearance aroused from the maître d'. The man made a half-hearted attempt to stop her from entering the dining room, but with a few quick words whispered in his ear not only did the man perk up considerably but even escorted them both to a window booth.

"We'll both be having coffee, and give him a whiskey. Make it a double. Thanks." Max smiled then turned her attention to Duncan. "You look like a whiskey sort of guy, right?"

"What did you say to him?"

"Didn't you hear? I ordered coffee."

"Don't get cute with me. That guy looked at us like we were a couple of derelicts washed up on his patio, but two words outa you and we get a table the Queen would've had to cool her heels twenty minutes at the bar for. What did you tell him?"

"Spielberg." Duncan frowned. "I told him you were Spielberg's brother, and you were expecting a call from Steven." Duncan's frown dissolved into a look of total disbelief. "Okay, so it wasn't great, but I'm tired. Besides I know everybody says he's washed up, but he could be staging a comeback."

A bright crimson ring was forming around Duncan's collar and moving rapidly up his face. He looked like a thermometer about to burst.

The redness vanished almost instantly when Max added quietly. "When I get a bad scare I always react this way. Bad jokes, talking fast, general smart ass routine— sorry."

A silence dropped over the table and remained there for sometime. A waiter brought their order, and though the whiskey looked tempting, Duncan pushed it toward her.

"You could use this."

She refused with a tight little shake of her head.

"Drink it. It'll do you good."

"No doubt it would, but I can't. A blood thing. I can't take alcohol of any kind."

"No shit?" Duncan was genuinely amazed.

A little smile twisted up one side of her face. "No shit."

"Geez, that's a shame." Without having to be prompted he downed the double shot, baring his teeth as a sign of his approval. Taking a swallow of the coffee he settled back in the booth and studied her for a moment then quickly leaned forward and whispered urgently, "What the hell happened back there?"

"I'm not quite certain."

"One minute you're standing there like a rock and the next you're flying across the room like something out of the damned *Exorcist*. You telling me you don't remember any of that?"

"From the time I placed my hands on the bowl until I woke up with your hand over my mouth there was nothing." Max sipped at her coffee, eyes refusing to meet his for more than a moment at a time.

"What were you doing up there anyway? For that matter what did you think you were up to breaking in like that? Do you know what you can get for a little stunt like that?"

"Is this a multiple choice?" Duncan glared at her. "Sorry, I can't help myself. I've run into Westeridge and his lot before. It's always the same—big money, big contacts, hands off. Sorry, Mac, you'll have to scrub round this one, solve it at someone else's expense. Just don't bother Mr. Big, thank you very much. I've learned from sorry experience to forget the front door at times like this and look for an open window. After that farce this afternoon, I felt a pressing need for some serious one on one with the Chac Mool, and I had a pretty accurate notion of what my chances were of getting there working through channels. So I went looking for windows."

"Teach you that in the CIA, did they?"

"Plumbers School of San Clemente, actually."

"And what did you get for your trouble?"

"You mean besides an abused tail bone, battered elbow and a blinding headache?" Duncan left eyebrow flew up to his hairline and perched there like a warning beacon. "All right, Forbes, if you want the down and dirties here they are. Only get this straight up front. I gave up caring a long time ago whether guys like you believed in the kind of things I deal with or not, so don't worry about offending my sensibilities when you feel a smirk coming on. Tonight I was trying to communicate with that thing by a method known as psychometry. Well, I made contact with something but not in the way I'm accustomed to. Truth be told, I'm going to have to open a whole new chapter to cover this little experience. The only thing that's got me baffled is what to call the chapter. If you say I flew across the room I'll have to take your word for it. You were there and I did wind up on my ass, so your explanation is as good as any I can come up with. The only thing I know for certain, and don't ask me to explain how, but that thing is a very big part of what's been happening to the Golden Circle members." Leaning back in the booth she crossed her arms over her chest, the fingers of her left hand massaging her throbbing elbow as discretely as possible. "All right, you've been a good boy. You can smirk now."

To Duncan's amazement, as much as hers, he didn't smirk. He didn't confess any conversion of faith either but at least he didn't smirk. Over the next two hours they kicked the incident back and forth, in the end reaching separate but marginally compatible opinions. Duncan agreed to keep any mention of tonight's incident out of his paperwork as long as she agreed to curtail her window work if not indefinitely then at least until they mutually felt a need for the service. The restaurant closed and the maître d' seemed genuinely depressed about not getting a call from Mr. Spielberg but quickly lost his depression when Max tipped him rather heavily. Duncan offered to drive her home and come back for his car later but she declined, seeing no problem if he followed her as far as the freeway which seemed to make him somewhat happier.

Later, as Duncan drove homeward, he found himself feeling more at ease about the case than he had in weeks, a feeling he could not rationalize but sensed all the same.

Equally distracted but for a far different reason Max drove slowly toward the Marina, unaware of the battered orange Toyota shadowing the Packard.

January 27th—12:31 a.m.

BERNARD "BERNIE" CALDICOTT, SENIOR PARTNER OF Caldicott, Winslow & Moore, shifted his posterior, trying vainly to relieve the pressure on a complaining sciatic nerve. He rubbed the two craters on either side of his nose left by nearly 50 years of wearing glasses while simultaneously smothering a belch inspired by the rebellious remains of a rich, hurried dinner that was certain to reveal itself on the cholesterol test at his insurance physical next week. A weary sigh slipped through his thick ruddy lips. Glancing at the small, lucite, digital clock sitting next to his desk lamp he sniffled irritably. 12:31. Shuffling the assortment of papers strewn across his desk into a rough approximation of order he turned his attention back to his work, losing himself in the comforting confusion of the stock market.

The fragile clicking of high heels on polished wood drifted into his consciousness before her light touch brushed his shoulder.

"Nightie night, hon." Claire, Bernie's second wife, kissed the air just above his left ear.

Bernie blinked up at her, startled and confused by her sudden appearance. "Home already? What time is it?" he stuttered, knowing the answer to both questions equally well.

"Don't get up, hon. I'm bushed. The opening was a complete farce. I'll give you all the gruesome details at breakfast. Nightie night." She smiled from the doorway blowing him another kiss.

He watched her slip out of the room over the top of his glasses. His red-rimmed eyes narrowed as the little voice in the back of his head shouted all of the things he always wanted to say at times like this, but he knew that a man with a wife half his age who looked the way Claire did never would. Grudgingly he tore his gaze from the vacant door and his mind from the even more vacant imaginary confrontation and turned his attention back to the one area of his life at which he had ever really been successful.

By 1:15 the bottom line on the Henderson portfolio was beginning to show sufficient promise, affording him the possibility of at least slowing down if not postponing indefinitely the departure of one of his firm's oldest and richest clients. Removing a small tape recorder from his briefcase he replaced the tiny cassette with a blank.

Pushing back from the desk he stretched his legs, loosened the collar of his shirt and settled back in his chair, tilting it to a more comfortable angle. Eyes staring at the ceiling he pressed the record button lifting the small machine to his lips.

"Gertrude, I want the usual copies of this letter with additional copies to Willetts at Bank of America . . ." He shut off the machine and sat listening as a small sound tugged at his attention. For a moment he thought he'd heard footsteps, but the house was quiet. They were alone tonight. Ho Peng, their only resident employee, was in San Francisco for his daughter's wedding and would not be returning until Monday. Claire was in her bedroom on the other side of the house, leaving only himself in this wing, yet he had heard the unmistakable sound of movement from the hallway beyond. He leaned forward and looked out into the darken hall.

"Claire?" he called softly.

He waited for a response, but when none came and no repeat of the small sound was heard again he settled back. He lifted the recorder and was fumbling for the record button when a brittle scratching drew his attention to the windows on the north wall of his office.

On clear nights those windows offered a glittering panoramic view of the Los Angeles coastline below. Tonight, thanks to the rain and cloud cover, little of that million dollar view was visible. Eyes narrowing, he squinted, trying to pierce the darkness beyond. The scratching sound repeated itself somewhat louder than before, and Bernie flinched. A fine patina of sweat broke out across his forehead. Lowering the recorder to the desk, he slowly rose from the chair. For a moment he considered the small revolver laying in the right-hand drawer of his desk but quickly abandoned the thought, having no desire to further perpetuate the image of an old fool if the disturbance proved to be illusionary.

With a stiff, shuffling gait, he crossed the room and came to a stop with his nose close to the fabric of the drapes bound at either side of the window by silken draw cords. Cautiously he leaned to his right, keeping the majority of his body hidden behind the drape until one eye could see around their obstruction and out into the darkness.

The truncated back garden stretched from the north wall of the house four feet to a broad flagstone patio. A large, square eight person spa, its underwater lights reflecting palely, marked the end of the patio. Beyond a great blackness stretched, covering the remaining portion of the rear property all the way to the edge of the cliff.

Seeing nothing Bernie stepped into the center of the window and, cupping his hands around his face, continued his search. After a few moments he lowered his hands and was about to step away when his gaze dropped toward the ground, his attention drawn by movement there. As he watched a large, thick bush shivered in the wind's gusts, causing its sharp leaves to brush against the windowpane.

"Christ," he sighed loudly. He gave the exterior one last glance and returned to his desk.

Shucking off his wrinkled vest, Bernie settled himself behind the desk and returned to his recorder.

"Today's date. Mrs. Wilcox Henderson, number 23 Rue da . . . Gertie, check Helen's Paris address—I can never remember that damn silly street—and make certain I send a copy of this letter to her daughter-in-law at the Santa Barbara address so she'll get off my . . ."

Bernie paused, sniffing at the air.

A small frown twisted up one side of his puffy face. He sniffed a second then a third time. It was there, just under the artificial pine scent, a smell not unlike that of burning electrical circuitry. He sniffed at the small recorder in his hand then lowered it. Swiveling round he surveyed the small, cluttered office, unable to locate anything which might produce such an odor, yet the scent persisted, growing stronger and more pungent. Perhaps the odor was coming from another part of the house. He considered this for a moment wondering why, if this were true and he could smell it all the way into his office, why none of the numerous smoke detectors dotting the house had sounded an alarm.

Torn by several emotions at once, not the least of which was a pressing desire to finish his work and go to bed, Bernie gave in to the paranoia of the homeowner and opted for a quick search. He pushed the chair back from the desk and stood up, freezing abruptly as the room swung crazily before his eyes and his knees threatened to buckle under him.

Stretching out a cautionary hand to the desk he lowered himself back into the chair. Breathing raggedly through his mouth like a winded runner, he reminded himself not to try getting up that fast again when a pressure began to make its presence known in a region alarmingly close to his heart.

Like a vast number of men his age Bernie had schooled himself on the symptoms of a heart attack. Quickly he ran over the check list and felt immediate relief that the most ominous of signs, a pain in his left arm, did not accompany the pressure. Still, taking no chances, he clutched his left wrist for a pulse. Even as he forced his whirring brain to concentrate on the steady, rhythmic pulse there the pressure increased until he abandoned the count and rubbed the center of his diaphragm. His stiff, stubby fingers kneaded the flaccid rise of paunch just below his bottom rib, yet for all of his manipulations the pressure only increased.

Slumping into the chair, his head thrown back, jaw slack, eyes watering, Bernie whimpered against the growing pain like a child. Swallowing the dryness that filled his gasping mouth, his lips moved. In his mind he heard his own voice calling, rising and falling over the vowels and consonants of the only source of aid available to him. Over and over again he heard himself call that single name. "Claire . . . Claire."

Abruptly the muscles in his legs began to cramp. The sciatic nerves in both hips began to spasm, and a torturous piercing pain lanced through his bladder. The pressure below his diaphragm had, within a matter of minutes, grown to a sharp, expanding pain a thousand times more cutting than any gastric pain he had ever experienced. His hands flew to the arms of the chair, locking themselves into positions of such tension the knuckles turned an almost iridescent white.

His head whipped back and forth, his lungs hammering out the cries that to his punished mind no longer resembled the sound of a name but simply a long tortured howl of excruciating pain. His eyes bulged from their sockets, tears streaming down his wrinkle twisted face.

It began as a roiling sensation deep within the pit of his stomach. For several moments this additional torture warred with the pain in his diaphragm for dominance; then by the sheer magnitude of its presence it won sway. His hands flew from the arms of the chair, clutching his abdomen. The gag impulse tore at the back of his throat, forcing his tongue out across his teeth and stretching it to the farthest limits of extension. The thick padding of fat across his abdomen flexed and rippled under his fingers, exhibiting a life force of it's own. The undulations became so violent in nature that his hands became incapable of hindering or slowing their movements.

As quickly as the torture had come upon him it vanished. The pressure in his diaphragm disappeared, leaving in its wake only a pale soreness. The undulations of his abdomen ceased completely, and the desire to gag abated, returning his tongue to a more normal position. Gasping for breath, sweat dripping from his chin, he whimpered, as frightened by the cessation as by the attack itself. For the span of a dozen, ragged heartbeats, the world threatened to return to normal, and his worn body reveled at the prospect.

A wave of nausea swept over him. He belched, filling his mouth and nostrils with a stench of unbelievable foulness. Slumping forward he opened his mouth and felt a rush of vomit climbing up out of his stomach and racing through his esophagus with all the abandon of a runaway freight train, but reaching the depot of his larynx it slammed on the brakes, unable or unwilling to pass through into the station. Like a demented thirsty bird Bernie slammed back against the chair then forward, bent double over his quaking knees again and again. With each pounding the chair was driven further from the desk until it collided with the wall and sent several books and a small silk fern tumbling to the floor.

On the center of that wall, nestled between two book shelves crowded with heavy volumes, sat a small neat shelf bearing a number of plaques, a tennis trophy and a heavy, engraved silver bowl. Holding the center of this display was a replica of the giant Chac Mool resting on a black onyx slab, a golden bronze plaque proudly announcing Mr. Bernard Caldicott as an outstanding member of the Golden Circle Society. As Bernie's chair slammed into the wall below, a bit of the thick layer of dust that was growing thicker over its surface with each moment clumped off, falling wetly onto the shelf.

Bernie rebounded off the back of the chair one final time then lay back exhausted, splayed out like a spring lamb in a butcher shop window. The material of his fine linen shirt was saturated with sweat and clung to his trembling skin. The material immediately over the area of the first pain began to move again. It thrust itself outward stretching the skin and the material as one.

Like a sheet of thin latex the flesh just under Bernie's bottom rib expanded, pushing and thrusting outward in a macabre parody of the birth spasm.

Bernie's bulging eyes glazed over but continued to register and record the sight of his body's metamorphosis. Barely noticeable under the contortions of his lower body, a trembling encased him. The first brittle snapping of bone, popping of gristle and rending of his flesh reached his ears as if from some far-off distance. His embattled mind had abandoned the further recognition of pain, having been burdened beyond its own endurance, leaving itself surprisingly free to observe and contemplate the agony of its host dispassionately.

The skin of Bernie's abdomen ruptured like the linen of his shirt, fraying along the rent. A gout of blood washed across his lap, mixing with the fluids released from his blatter and rinsing down over the tops of his sox and shoes and onto the pale beige carpeting. The spleen, gall bladder and left lobe of the liver crowded toward the opening and pushed the stomach forward ahead of them. The thin layer of the aorta tissue ruptured outward, freeing hundreds of tiny blood vessels to empty their fluids into the flood. Twenty feet of small intestine convulsed outward and slithered onto his lap, adding pancreatic juices, bile and other secretions to the already heady concoction there.

The skin on both sides of the rupture began to roll back away from the opening even as the tear widened. The epidermal layer peeled away from the body leaving its brother, the dermis with all its blood vessels, nerves, sweat glands, hair follicles and fat cells exposed. In some places the two skin layers refused to be separated, causing the outer skin to tear out small divots of flesh, exposing the muscle groupings below. Abruptly, as his left hand tore itself free of his arm, Bernie's glazed eyes ceased their movements, and his shattered body sighed as his soul slipped its earthly restraints.

Outside the wind abated as abruptly as it had arisen, while in the small office the last drop of blood joined its brothers on the stained carpet. The small bulb in the desk lamp flared and swelled beyond its meager capacity then blinked out. Several minutes later, in the cool, calm silence that had settled over the room a small metallic click echoed with unnatural loudness as the miniature tape recorder, oblivious to all else, completed its assigned task and shut itself off.

January 27th—8:15 a.m.

RING.

Flinging out an arm Max groped for the phone. Wedging it against her ear, she brushed the hair back from her eyes.

"Yes, hello?"

"Max? That you?"

"Don't press me. Who's this?"

"Hy."

"Uh? . . . Oh, hi, Hy."

"You all right?"

"Yeah, just having a little trouble shaking the cobwebs. What time is it?"

"We've got another one."

The cobwebs vanished. Kicking free of the sheets, she swung her legs over the side of the bed and sat up. "Where? When?"

"Sometime last night. Look, I'm sending a car for you. I'd come myself, but we're already on site."

"I'm dressing now. Be in the lobby when he gets here," she said, hanging up and reaching for her clothes and a cigarette all in one movement.

By the time the black and white pulled into the lot, Max was pacing out the dimensions of the walkway for the 30th time. Tossing her cigarette away she reached out for the passenger door when it popped open. Max stared up at what she was certain must be the tallest female cop in the tristate area, possibly further. The woman stepped out of the car and just kept standing up. "Ms. Morgan?"

"Yes." Max scolded herself for staring.

"Detective Forbes sent us to deliver you to the crime scene," the woman said with a stiffness that clearly announced the academy wasn't too far behind her. "If you don't mind, ma'am, you'll have to ride in the back."

Max looked inside, trying hard not to show how much she would have rather walked. Tossing the tote in ahead of her she climbed in. The door slammed closed behind her, and the amazon climbed into the front seat. Max looked at the heavy metal grill dividing the front seat from the rear, noticing a number of dark scuff marks on its beige surface. Fidgeting in an attempt to find a place on the cold vinyl seat where the springs didn't poke through, Max purposefully kept her gaze away from the blank rear doors. The idea of being locked inside was a disconcerting one, even when you knew all you had to do to get out was ask. Lighting a cigarette, she exhaled deeply, forcing herself to relax.

"Sorry, ma'am, but you can't smoke back there." The tall cop looked back over her shoulder. Her long face twisted up into the semblance of a sympathetic smile. At least Max hoped it was sympathetic.

"Sorry." Max looked around for a way to get rid of the thing. "Maybe you could toss it . . ."

"Sure, shove it through the screen."

"You're workin' with the mayor's office, right?"

Max leaned forward and with a start realized the driver was a woman as well. "Ah, yeah, sort of."

The driver, a dark-haired copy of the other cop, looked at her partner, then adjusted the mirror to gain a clearer view of the rear seat. "Talk is the Task Force brought in a physic. You . . ."

"Yeah, I heard the same thing." Max leaned her elbows against the metal screen. "You guys seen anything of him yet?"

The partners exchanged looks again, this one just as loaded as the last. With mutual grunts, they abandoned the subject. Max watched the pair for a moment longer then settled back, content to look out the window at the passing morning traffic. There wasn't a reason in the world for not telling these two who she was, but there was something about answering questions from the rear of a police car that had always brought out a certain reticence.

The house was hidden from the road by a high brick wall. An ornamental black iron gate stood open at the entrance to the drive, displaying a paved court filled with half a dozen cars, a van from the coroners office and two bright blue compacts with the crest of the Palos Verdes Police emblazoned on the side. The roadway, twisting up the side of the hill, held another dozen or so black and whites, two news vans from the local stations and assorted cars belonging to press, puzzled neighbors and general busybodies.

Max slid down in the seat, pulling the collar of her jacket across her face as the black and white threaded its way through the reporters and camera crews clustered around the front gate. A camera man turned the lens of a mini-cam toward the rear window of the car as they passed. Max held up a stiffened middle finger making certain that even if he did have a good shot of her it would never make it past editing. Censorship allowed any number of dismembered body parts during the six o'clock news, but a blatantly sexual reference was still taboo.

Once inside the courtyard Max jumped out of the car as soon as the door opened. Ducking her head, she made a dash for the front door, ignoring the shouts of reporters from the gate trying to pin down her relationship to the deceased. Inside the door two policemen blocked the way.

"I'm sorry, ma'am, but . . ."

"Morgan. I'm with the Task Force."

Before things could get tedious Chang elbowed his way through the boys in bright blue. "Max? I thought I heard the hyenas barking." Hy smiled crookedly, ushering her toward the rear of the house. "I hope you had your breakfast 'cause a look at this one is gonna put your stomach outa the mood."

Max glanced into the living room where most of the members of the Task Force were gathered around a particularly attractive redhead. Duncan, taking up a proprietary lean against the mantle, was one degree away from a lecherous leer. "Fan club?" Max smirked back at Chang.

Leaning close he said quietly, "Wife of the victim. Mrs. Claire Caldicott."

"And the hulk?"

Hy frowned, turning around to locate the source of Max's reference. When he turned back his smile got a lot tighter. "Ah, that's Mr. Victor, her aerobics instructor."

"Ah," Max nodded knowingly. "And I've been wasting all this time with Jane Fonda," she muttered, falling in behind Chang.

The traffic swelled proportionately as they neared the crime scene. Max noticed, managing not to stare, a young woman in a lab coat doubled over trying to put her head between her knees and drink a glass of water all at the same time, thanks to the genuine but conflicting concern of two helpful uniform cops. Another casualty, an older detective who looked more like a senator than a cop, leaned against the wall nursing a cup of something Max doubted seriously was water. Feeling her gaze, he flashed her a watery smile and quickly downed the last of the cup's contents before retreating from the scene.

"Here we are," Hy said, stepping aside allowing her to pass through the doorway ahead of him.

Max viewed the activity inside. A short, stocky man with several camera's slung around his neck was busily recording the debris for posterity. Three other men dusted for prints, each busily avoiding the desk area. As Max turned in that direction a tall, thin figure rose up from behind the desk, stroking his chin and studying something on the floor.

"Hey, Jasper," Chang called out.

Heep looked up, squinting toward the doorway like a gopher in bright sunlight. With a nod he motioned the pair over. Max rounded the desk, leaving Hy firmly planted in front of it, Jasper cautioned, "This one's a little on the ripe side. I'd breathe through my nose if I were you."

"It doesn't help." Max grimaced. "You can smell it from the driveway." Max looked down at the chair.

The lower portion of a heavyset man clung tenaciously to the seat of the chair. On the floor beside the chair lay the other half. Max, breathing through her mouth, bent forward, leaning closer to the upper half. She studied it for several moments then straightened. Jasper watched her quietly.

Max looked at him and sighed softly. "Feet and hands missing like the others."

"Right."

"Separation starting from a central core rupture?"

"Right again."

She turned her attention to the lower extremity, giving it the same kind of scrutiny as the other. With a small frown she looked to Jasper. "Does that rupture look different to you?"

"You think so?" He leaned forward, focusing on the area in question.

"I'm not sure. This is the freshest one I've seen. It looks slightly different from the others."

"There is a new twist, you should excuse the pun. I can't be sure yet, but I've got a hunch that when our nasty friend left the deceased was still in one piece."

"Really? What makes you think that?"

Jasper squatted down beside the chair. "Notice the area here." He pointed to the flesh at the rear of the rupture nearest to the spine. "Can you see the difference in the coloration of the ligatures as opposed to those in this area." He pointed to the front of the corpse nearest the abdomen, the initial point of rupture.

"Possibly a bit lighter in color at the rear?" Max answered hesitantly like a pupil at examinations.

"Good eyes."

Max smiled. "Thank you, sir."

"You have any idea what that indicates?"

Max's eyes narrowed. You could see the wheels turning. "That the rupture at the rear of the body occurred later than that in the front?"

Jasper stood up. "You're no fun."

"Sorry."

"I'll know for certain once I get him downtown, but I'm betting there'll be a difference."

"I wonder what that means," Max thought aloud.

"Maybe nothing." Jasper shrugged. "Then again it could mean our friend is getting tired of his work."

"Don't get your hopes up. It could also mean Mr . . ."

"Caldicott."

"Mr. Caldicott here is a much larger individual then any of the other victims. When the top half slumped forward the strain was just too much. Snap—two pieces."

Jasper considered that for a moment. "Yeah, I suppose that could account for it," he said, not sounding overly confident. While Jasper toyed with that idea, Max turned her gaze to the desk. Clasping her hands behind her back she bent over the desk, peering at the papers and files covering its surface.

"I got something else you might be interested in."

Max's head snapped up, a look of almost childish eagerness on her face. "What?"

Jasper glanced at the others in the room, a gesture Max copied automatically, then he inched closer pulling a small polyethylene bag from his pocket. He waggled it between his thumb and forefinger.

Max stared at the bag and squinted at the contents. "Dust?"

"You've played this game before."

Max's face lit up as she realized what Jasper was trying cryptically to tell her. "Where is it?"

Jasper pointed to the shelves on the wall behind the desk. Max slipped between the desk and the chair beside Heep. The sculpture sat on the second shelf, the lip of that shelf at the height of Max's nose.

"Need a little help?"

Jasper and Max both jumped like childish conspirators at the sound of Chang's deep voice.

"I'm about three inches shy." Max grinned sheepishly.

"What do you want?" Hy asked, gazing at the shelf.

"I'd like to take a look at that sculpture."

Chang nodded and started to reach for the piece then stopped. Looking back over his shoulder he shouted, "Hey, Fred, is this area still hot?"

A man in a shiny gray suit pushed thick glasses back against the bridge of his nose and looked up from his work. "Naw, we finished that end of the room. You got something you want printed?"

Chang looked down at Max. "Do I?"

She shook her head.

"Naw, so it's all right to . . ."

"Yeah, yeah. Knock yourself out." Fred grumbled and turned back to his current project. "Place's as clean as your granny's skivies. Same fuckin' shit. I don't know why they even bother havin' us go over this crap. They know we ain't gonna find nothing like a print in this kinda . . ." His monologue gradually decreased in volume until the words took on the sound of grinding teeth.

Chang reached up and took the statue down from the shelf. He looked for a likely spot to set it down, but when none presented itself he simply stood there holding it.

Max leaned close to the piece. Running a finger over the sculpture's crown, she pulled it back and studied the residue collected on her fingertip. Rubbing the gray substance between her fingers she nodded. "Feels the same as the others."

"The results on the other samples should be done by the time I get back to the office. I'll add this one to the lot," Jasper said, tucking the bag back into his pocket.

"Great. I'm curious about the content of this stuff."

"What stuff?" Hy asked.

Jasper and Max exchanged a quick glance. As Max began to explain Jasper edged away a bit. "Dust particles found on these sculptures at four of the other five sites."

"What not all five?" Hy frowned.

"I overlooked Mrs. Worthington's statue."

Chang nodded. "Is it important, this dust thing?"

"Who knows? Maybe, maybe not. Anyway it's certainly more than a coincidence, so I figured we'd take a look at it."

"You tell anybody else about this stuff?"

"Yeah, it's in my report."

"The one nobody but the brass got a look at, right?"

"Bingo." Max studied the expression on Chang's face. "You got some problem with that?"

He sighed and twisted up his mouth, chewing on the inside of his lip. After a brief pause to consider his position, he shrugged. "No, I guess not. Not your fault if they don't want to hear what you got to say. Only, if it wouldn't be outa line, you find anything else like this, let me and Dunc in on it, O.K.?"

"O.K.," Max said quietly, a small smile turning up one side of her mouth.

"In the meantime, what do you want me to do with this ugly little bastard?"

"Put it back?" Max shrugged. "I know this may not be a good time to bring this up, but what are the chances of me getting some time in here alone?"

"For your stuff, right?" Chang asked, replacing the statue.

"Right. How's my chances?"

Chang looked around the room. Two of the three forensic men had disappeared, and Fred was busily packing up his gear. Hy turned to Jasper. "You about ready to remove the deceased?"

"I don't suppose Janet has recovered yet?" Heep asked not unkindly.

"Why did you bring her in the first place? She's a long way from being ready for this kind of thing," Hy grumbled irritably.

"It's been a busy night and now it's a busy day, and if you'll notice the sun is out and I'm still on duty. Don't blame me, blame the mayor. He's the whiz kid cut our budget. Besides Janet signed on for the training program. She wants to be an investigator."

"Yeah, yeah, I know all that, still . . ." The rest of Chang's sentence trailed off, leaving his frustration clearly etched on his face.

"I'll give you a hand."

Both men looked at Max.

"You don't have to do that," Chang announced firmly.

"I know," she said, calmly lowering the tote to the floor. "What do you need?"

Chang and Heep exchanged glances.

"I need to tape . . ."

"Where's the roll?"

Jasper stared at her uncertainly.

Max sighed. "Trust me. I've seen it done a few times."

Jasper looked at Chang a last time and shrugged. "It's alright with me. What do you think?"

Chang shook his head as much in disbelief as an indication of denial. "Don't ask me. It's your department."

"Well, sure . . . yeah, okay." Jasper pulled a roll of thick white tape from an inside pocket and handed it to Max. "You want gloves?"

"That would be nice."

"I think I'll see if Janet's up to showing me where you guys stashed the stretcher," Chang announced, heading for the door.

"Get the bags, too," Jasper ordered quickly.

"Right," Chang called, disappearing out the door.

The pair moved through their routine like they'd worked together before.

Later, when Mr. Calidcott had been sent on his way and the others had all eagerly departed, Max turned to the business at hand. Squatting down beside the tote, she considered the equipment inside. Taking a deep breath she looked up at the ceiling, a sense of deep weariness gnawing at her. There appeared at the core of this weariness a nagging suspicion that this part of her investigation had yielded all of the useful evidence it was ever likely to. The process of video taping the scene and recording her impressions no longer served a useful purpose to the solution. The solution now revolved around other methods, methods of a more personal nature, methods more lethal.

Refusing to face the inevitable, Max pulled out the recorder and the camera, promising herself to give this element a smaller portion of her time. Settling the recorder and mike in their respective places, she lifted the small camcorder to her eye and began moving slowly around the room. She dutifully recorded the area even to the view out the north window. She worked steadily but with a noticeable hesitancy the nearer she came to the desk.

Unable to postpone the inevitable any longer Max shut off the camcorder and stood silently staring down at the bloodstained carpet. Slowly she pulled her gaze upward, fixing on the sodden desk chair. It was old and well-worn. The impression of its former owner was deeply carved in its faded and battered surface. A grease-stained impression on the high back marked the spot where Caldicott's head had rested—how many nights? How many hours had he filled this chair, laboring over his facts and figures in the pursuit of what? Of wealth?

Max studied the room and the cluttered desk. No, this wasn't the abode of a man who chased after wealth for the sheer desire of possession. This was a man who labored at something he loved, perhaps the only thing in his long life that had ever loved him in return. Sharp pinpricks of anger nipped at Max's conscience as stronger and stronger impressions of the deceased imposed themselves on her senses. Carefully she placed the camcorder on a shelf out of the way. Looking around for something with which to cover the sticky surface of the chair she found a stack of *Wall Street Journals* and carefully pasted a thick layering of newsprint over the back and seat of the chair. When this had been completed to her satisfaction Max sat down.

Even as she attempted to clear her mind in preparation, impressions of the deceased and that night clamored for access. Max's head snapped up, turning sharply toward the windows. Before her eyes the windows grew dark, any view blocked by a bright circle of light issuing from the desk lamp. Without moving from the chair she watched, an imprisoned spectator, seeing the world and that night through the eyes of a dead man as he crossed to the windows and peered out into the night beyond. She saw the bush brushing the window, his retreat back to the desk, sitting down, picking up the small recorder, returning to his work, all of his movements.

The thought slammed into her with such impact that she sat up abruptly in the chair.

Her fingers grazed the cool metal surface of the recorder buried under the scattered papers. Slowly she closed her hand around it and pulled it from under the debris. For a moment she hesitated, staring at the small machine then, almost as if exerting a great force of will, she depressed the play button. No sooner had she depressed it than the machine made a faint groan of compliance and the button popped up, shutting the recorder off. Looking more closely Max could see the small tape cassette had been wound to the limit. Depressing the rewind she waited for a moment or two then stopped the machine. Depressing the play button a second time she waited.

Straining, she listened. Nothing.

Frowning, she quickly rewound the tape a little further. Depressing the play button a third time she was rewarded for her persistence.

A tight knot of uniforms and rumpled suits collected near the front door. Commander Liebschuetz orbited around the perimeter of the group like an uncertain moon. He listened to the other men talk, nodding and laughing when they did, shaking his head and grumbling when they did, all of his efforts going unnoticed by the group. Forbes and Chang entered from the vicinity of the living room. Forbes muttered something under his breath, causing Chang to grin as they joined the gathering.

"Me and Hy will stick around to seal the place up and then give Morgan a ride home," Forbes said to Liebschuetz.

"My thoughts exactly. Tell Ms. Morgan I'll be expecting her . . ."

"Hey, Forbes, see what your physic likes in the fifth race, will ya?" A big, beefy policeman called out.

Duncan grinned tightly. "What'da'ya care for? You ain't had two fuckin' nickels to rub together since your first old lady dumped ya."

The men grinned, some more than others, and one who had yet to marry thus been spared the financial indignity of divorce even laughed.

"Yeah, well maybe if you can get the witch to stir something up for me I could get a couple of nickels."

"You couldn't win a fu . . ."

"Gentlemen, I think you better come back into the office."

Forbes swung around like he'd just heard the chamber click on an empty cylinder. Max stood in the hallway, her face an unreadable mask save for the glassy condition of her red-rimmed eyes. Duncan started toward her as did Chang, when another voice stopped them.

"Now see here, Ms. Morgan," Liebschuetz squeaked loudly. "if you've found something why don't you just tell us what it is and drop the histri . . ."

Duncan opened his mouth to tell the commander politely to shut the fuck up when Max settled the issue.

"Now," she said in the same even, steely voice she'd made the first announcement with. Then not bothering to wait for any reply, she turned abruptly and headed back toward the rear of the house.

The detectives crowded into the small office, leaving Commander Liebschuetz lingering on the fringe once more. Stepping behind the desk Max turned and faced the group. "We have a witness to the Caldicott murder."

Everything after the word witness was lost as the men voiced their mutual surprise and disbelief.

Nonplussed by their response she lifted the small recorder from the desk and held it up in front of the group. "The death of Mr. Caldicott was recorded on this machine."

"By who?"

"The murderer?"

"How?"

Overriding the questions she continued calmly. "Caldicott was dictating a letter on the recorder. The play record mechanism was depressed, and the machine continued to record until the tape ran out and it shut itself off." She held up the small machine. "This is our witness."

There was a long leaden silence in the room as the detectives glanced at one another and at the small recorder.

"Perhaps you'd care to tell us just how you can be so very certain as to the sequence of events," Liebschuetz asked nervously.

Max turned her head slowly in his direction, fixed him in a hard gaze then looked back to the machine. Depressing the play button she boosted the volume then sat down in the red-stained, newsprint-covered chair.

A low groan slipped over more than one pair of lips in that room as she sat in the dead man's chair, but those groans were soon replaced by the strong resonance of the deceased's voice.

As the tape played, Max's gaze drifted over the men gathered around the desk. "He pauses here, thinking he's heard something in the hallway." Caldicott's voice took over the narration again. "And here he rises crossing to the window." In the flat, emotionless monotone of an instructor Max narrated the nonvocal sounds captured on the tape, using her own visions of the events as a scenario. Fourteen minutes later she shut the recorder off.

The men in the room glanced at one another furtively, some cleared suddenly clogged throats, others fidgeted nervously, while others blotted damp foreheads and palms—but none spoke. Eyes directed at the surface of the desk, Max vocalized what none of them wanted to hear.

"In less time that it takes to brew a pot of coffee the deceased was reduced to the consistency of a side of beef all without the benefit of equipment of any kind, without physical assistance from additional sources and without disturbing another member of the family a few rooms away in the dead of night. And once having completed this heinous crime the perpetrator vanishes without leaving a trace of either entry, departure or presence. What, gentlemen, does that do to your theory of a *human* perpetrator?"

"If the perpetrator isn't human, what do you think it is?"

Max lifted her gaze, locating the speaker in the form of a dark, intense-looking man who would more easily have passed for an aging golf pro than a detective. "What I believe is," she began slowly, "we are dealing with forces brought into being, the nature of which is as yet unknown, by person or persons unknown."

This response was greeted with groans, mumbled epithets and much coughing and throat clearing.

"What does that mean in English?"

"Are you talking about ghosts and poltergeists?"

"Ghosts? Shit!"

"Now hold on here," Liebschuetz squeaked over the growing tumult. "I'm sure Ms. Morgan doesn't mean to imply . . ."

"Let her tell us just what she does mean, in English."

"Santee, shut up!" Chang snapped.

"Fuck you," Santee grumbled, refusing to meet Hy's stern gaze.

"We've got a lot of conjecture going arou . . ."

"Conjecture?" Max snapped, cutting Liebschuetz off in midsentence. She shook her head and studied the ceiling for several moments.

"What we need to do is get some perspective on what is turning into a very emotional situation."

"You want perspective? How about this?" Max snatched up the recorder and marched across the room to Liebschuetz. Taking hold of his hand she slapped the recorder into his palm. "Right now in one of those shiny white laboratories over at U.C.L.A., they've got a collection of very bright young people who spend their entire day doing nothing but identifying and charting sounds. You might be amazed at just what some of those folks can tell you about yourself after putting your voice through some of their machines. Now you take this tape over to them and see what they have to say about it. Tell them nothing about what I've told you here, nothing concerning the victim, not even his name. Now it may take them a little while 'cause I don't think they've ever run across a tape recording of a human being torn apart before, but don't be too surprised when they come back and tell you this is the recording of an elderly, white male, who while dictating a letter was turned into stew meat by means and persons unknown. And if that isn't enough perspective for you, how's this? If their report deviates in any way from what I've told you here today I'm gone. How's that for perspective?" Before Liebschuetz could close his mouth Max turned on the other men in the room. "Is that clear enough English for you?"

Recrossing the room she picked up her jacket and tote and turned back to them. "If a doctor tells you a disease can come into your house on a draft of wind and kill you and your entire family in a single night you believe him without question. I'd be surprised to find a single man amongst you who does not believe in some form of a god, a great invisible force for which there never has nor will be one ounce of tangible proof as to its existence. You've seen five victims of this thing you call the Butcher. Can any of you demonstrate one shred of evidence that leads you to believe these crimes were committed by another human being?"

"Well . . . ah . . . there is a great deal of information to collate . . ." Liebschuetz stammered.

"And when you've done all the collating of all the information from all the murders and the bodies are stacked up in the morgue like cordwood, maybe then you'll be willing to admit what you suspect even now is true. The fact is, no human being did this, and you'll never convince either yourself or me that one did."

There was a momentary pause before an all too familiar voice took the floor.

"You're right. We believe in a lot of things that we should probably look a lot closer at, but we don't,"

Duncan said calmly. "There are a lot of us in this room who've believed a scared fourteen-year-old shoplifter and given the little bastard a break only to have our wallets snatched. Believed a mother couldn't hurt her own kid only to find the poor little bastard drowned in his own tub or hookin' on Hollywood Boulevard to cover her old lady's habit. Yeah, most of us still believe in a lot of impossible things, but I'll tell you what none of us believe. We don't believe in the Tooth Fairy, the Easter Bunny, Father Christmas or things that go bump in the night. We don't believe in spooks or evil spirits or devils with pitchforks and tails wandering around at night jumping wealthy patrons of museums. We know—not believe, lady—we know there are too many two-legged things out there practicing the trade for spooks to even get a hoof in the door. You talk about proof? Where's yours?"

"All around you," Max said quietly.

The men had found their spokesman, and they greeted his declaration with approval. Max hitched the strap of the tote up onto her shoulder, and moving outside into the hallway, she paused looking back into the room. Forbes was surrounded by his fans. She watched the show for several seconds before, with a tight shaking of her head, she continued down the hall and out of the house.

"You gonna walk back to the Marina or you want a lift," Duncan growled, stepping out onto the walk.

Max sat on a small, white, wrought-iron bench hidden amongst the ivy covering the front portico. Slinging the tote over her shoulder she followed after him.

Duncan unlocked the car, opened the rear door for her then moved on around to the driver's side. He looked over the roof as she started to get in. "You gave up awfully easy in there just now."

"What makes you say that?"

He shrugged then climbed into the driver's seat. "I didn't figure on you letting me have the last word is all."

Closing the door behind her she pulled out a cigarette

and lit it. Exhaling, she said evenly, "Unfortunately the last word on this subject is a long way off."

Duncan adjusted the mirror to look at her. Max did not bother to return his gaze.

"Come on, will ya?" Forbes called to Chang, pounding the horn impatiently.

Huddled on the brick courtyard Chang scrambled to reclaim some papers he had dropped. His back to the car, he stood slowly.

Max watched as Chang's dark suit took on the coloration of an apparition in a dream she had the night before. Before her eyes, the scene shifted taking on the elements of the dream. A fog curled around his feet, and she could feel the dampness of the ocean's breath against her cheek. He turned slowly toward her. Overhead the cry of a lone gull pierced the atmosphere with such shrill intensity it drove all other sounds from her mind. At that instant, as his face swung into view, a shadow glided over it as the gull passed overhead, and a chill clamped itself around Max's intestines.

It was definitely the damn dream.

As Chang approached the car Max looked away abruptly. Hy climbed into the front seat, the ignition ground then caught, and the car lurched out of the courtyard.

While the men spared verbally Max shuffled the collection of random thoughts littering her thinking processes. In one relatively neat corner of her mind she began assembling the elements of the strange impressions she had been registering in reference to Hyiam Chang since their first meeting. At the bottom of that column she included the imagery of the dream. Quickly adding the column she discovered that through either fatigue or stupidity two and two suddenly added up to seven.

With a mental groan she pushed away from the equation, trying to erase all thought of it and the dream from her mind. Looking out the window she watched the cluttered, pleasant scenery of Redondo, Hermosa and then Manhattan Beach slip by, but always the images of the dream were brooding in her mind.

Arriving at the Marina, Max beat a hasty retreat to the sanctity of the apartment, unsettled by the revelations of the tape recorder, angered by the reactions of the Task Force, and irritated by her inability to solve the riddle of the dream.

She bolted and chained the door as if preparing for an assault, unable to break a habit formed out of years spent living alone in hostile territory. With a bone-grinding weariness, she crossed to the edge of the living room and dropped down on the uppermost of the three steps leading down into it. Resting her elbows on her knees she propped her chin up with her hands and sat staring out the glass wall.

Later that night, watching the first stars of evening appear, she centered her concentration on the facts she'd spent the afternoon trying to unscramble. In the quiet solitude of the apartment any of the lingering confusion as to the meaning of the dream was driven away as she focused on the vision of Hyiam Chang's face, shadowed by the soaring gull. Suddenly it was all painfully clear. Through his work on this case and more distressingly by his close association with her, Chang would die. What should she do with this information?

Logic dictated she take steps to avoid the predicted disaster. However, logic took a back seat to other concerns. The doctrines that controlled her world were most precise and the tenets surrounding precognitive dreams were equally specific. To act in an aggressive nature on the information revealed in a dream of this type was to bring down the most dire of consequences upon all parties concerned. In this case, if she were to take the direct method and simply warn Chang, by virtue of her warning she would bring him to harm.

No, that path was closed to her.

She had a brief, uncomfortable, mental image of herself confronting Commander Deihl with her concerns over a dream. No, that avenue was definitely closed. If she were to abide by the aged doctrines, she must do so with passive activity. A frown of consternation twisted up the space between her pale brows. How was it possible to act on the prediction of the dream passively?

"Lie." The word tiptoed through her mind like a cat burglar.

She considered this advice a moment then began to smile. She would have to convince Chief Merchinson that Hyiam Chang constituted a hindrance to her further investigation, taking the form of the so-called personality conflict. It was a long shot. Anyone who knew Chang, even slightly, would find it difficult to believe the picture she planned on painting, therefore the burden of believability rested firmly in her court. To this end she decided on an altering of her own persona. This performance called for a serious dose of the old I.D.B. mode, commonly known and widely accepted by male audiences as the irrational dyke bitch.

Shortly after 8:15 Max was on the phone. She had a firm grasp on her new persona, the scenario was as good as it was ever going to get, and if all else failed she had a back-up story that came as close to the truth as she could get and still remain in what she fervently hoped would be seen as a passive mode by higher sources.

"Good evening, Ms. Morgan. I'm sorry for the delay, but its our daughter's engagement party. What can I do for you?"

Max cringed mentally at the happy ring in Chief Merchinson's voice. Slamming the door on feelings to the contrary, she launched the performance. For 22 minutes, with barely space enough for him to get in more than a syllable or two, she ranted, raged, protested, argued, whined, threatened and cajoled until in the end Merchinson surrendered, throwing down his standard and running away to the sanctuary of his family.

As she hung up the phone Max was at once elated and contrite. A born fighter she relished the victory even as the knowledge of the price payable for it chipped away at her elation. The ploy was not without its drawbacks. It could and did, in most situations, drain one's credibility seriously in the eyes of those she was forced to work with.

This little act would undoubtedly come back to haunt her when and if it became necessary for her to seek assistance from the chief at some future date. She winced at the images that thought conjured.

January 28th—10:00 a.m.

FRANKLIN OSGOOD MARSHALL WAS A TIDY MAN. IN ANOTHER time he would have been called dapper, but that word like the suits he wore belonged to another era and the refuse bin of the late show.

Franklin parked his immaculate brown, 1963 Fairlane convertible precisely in the center of the last space of the last row in the parking lot of the Pasadena Amtrak Station as he had everyday for the past 31 years. After locking the vehicle, he pulled from the trunk a cloth car cover and settled it over the car. Satisfied that his last fling at youthful extravagance was protected from the indignities of Pasadena's brutal sunlight and polluted air he crossed the lot to the crumpling, defiant grandeur of what was to his mind, the grande dame of southern California railway stations.

Inside the station, his slightly elongated nose twitched at the particularly stale quality of the air, even at this early time of day.

As Franklin crossed the concrete expanse of what he referred to as the main concourse, he smiled slyly at the flurry of activity in his otherwise turgid employees. The station's lone security guard, a man of rapidly encroaching middle age and spreading midsection, abandoned his perch at the snack bar and headed for the rest rooms and any unsuspecting transient foolish enough to have overstayed his welcome. Mable, 11 months shy of mandatory retirement, shifted her ample bosom to a better elevation and smiled with faintly yellowish dentures in his direction as he passed, all the while neatly avoiding eye contact with the ratty pair of aging hippies at her window trying to purchase one way tickets to Butte, Montana.

Tyrell Watson, 43-years-old but with a body any 20-year-old would and did on numerous occasions lust after, split his broad black face with a smile at once frightening and friendly. "Morning, Mr. Marshall."

Franklin nodded. "Tyrell." He made to step around the towering black man, who always made Franklin nervous, but found his forward progress hindered.

"Seems we got something of a problem this morning, sir."

A shadow drifted over Franklin's cloudy blue eyes. He hated problems. Problems called for solutions and solutions meant taking initiative, and if there was one thing AmTrak discouraged in it's assistant station managers it was initiative. "Well, I'm certain that you can handle whatever seems to be amiss. What seems to be the problem?" Franklin asked, not really caring but only stalling in hope of discovering a technical loophole.

"Have you noticed that interesting aroma in the air this morning? Well, it sure ain't Mable's new perfume."

Franklin frowned.

"48 E, last one in the row back there. It's stinking up that whole end of the station."

A wave of relief spilled over Franklin's pale face, and his blood pressure began edging back towards sea level. Somebody's forgotten lunch was a situation that called for an acceptable amount of initiative. "I'll get the keys." he said.

To describe the smell as overpowering was the same as saying a dragon was an oversized lizard—accurate, perhaps, but suffering in the translation. Franklin, his pale blue handkerchief pressed tightly over his nose, could still smell the stench even standing several feet from the offending locker. Rick and Manuel, the station's two resident janitors, stood by armed with rubber gloves, trash bag and mop and pail ready to scrub the stink out of the bin. The locker door popped open at a touch of the key, seemingly eager to put as much distance between itself and the smell as it's hinges would allow.

"Sweet Jesus fuckin' Christ." Tyrell winced, turning away at the blast of polluted air.

The Hispanic janitors giggled, wriggling their blunt brown noses, a reaction for most anything from a train wreck to a wedding.

Franklin retreated several steps but felt certain across the street would not be far enough to escape the blistering odor.

The quartet stood there in silence for several seconds, all four sets of eyes in various stages of watering, all glaring in at the dingy, yellow, vinyl suitcase jammed into the tall, narrow confines of the locker.

"That's where the stink's comin' from," Tyrell informed the group unnecessarily.

"Well? Get it out of there and throw it in the trash," Franklin ordered behind his wilting handkerchief.

"I'll pull it out allright, but rules says we got to look for identification and notify the owners. Can't just throw it away."

"I'm not touching that thing," Franklin announced firmly.

"Suit yourself. You're the one's got to fill out the paperwork, not me." Tyrell shrugged, reaching for the case's worn handles. He gave an experimental tug without any luck. Grumbling behind his big white teeth he wrapped a ham-sized hand around the handles and pulled. The suitcase slid forward a quarter of an inch then stood it's ground.

"Bitch don't want to come out," he mumbled to no one in particular.

Abandoning any previous delicacy, Tyrell took a firm grip on the handles with both hands, and applying the not inconsiderable power of his broad back and arms he gave a might tug. One of the rivets holding the handles in place snapped off, shooting across the floor.

"Careful. Don't damage it," Franklin warned, suddenly concerned over the thing's condition and the complaints of its errant owner.

Tyrell gritted his teeth and set his legs into a wider stance. Taking a firm hold on the handles, he gave an awesome tug, and with that single movement not only tore the handles off but relocated the row of lockers five inches out from the wall as well.

"Fuckin' thing's jammed in there tighter than a hooker's cunt at a Shriner's convention." A fine beading of sweat glistened on Tyrell's broad forehead. Looking around he snatched the mop out of Rick's hands so abruptly the small Hispanic, who had been using the tool as a crutch, nearly fell on his face. Jamming the mop handle between the back of the case and the rear wall of the locker he looked over his shoulder at the janitors. "Get in here and get a hold of this bitch. When I shove, you pull."

With considerable giggling and muttered complaints the two boys took up positions that met with Tyrell's approval. "On the count of three, ready?" Without waiting for a response he flexed his big shoulders and focused on the obstinate suitcase. "One . . . two . . . three!" Tyrell grunted, pressing down on the mop handle with ever increasing pressure until the whites of his eyes turned faintly pink with the effort. "Pull, damn it," he groaned between clenched teeth.

The suitcase extracted itself from the locker with all the surly grace of a fat lady's shoe, an inch at a time. When nearly half of the case leaned out of the locker Tyrell pulled out the mop, pushed the boys aside and took a firm grip on the thing and managed to wrestle it a little further out. As the last quarter of the large case slid grudgingly forward an area covered by a thick brownish stain appeared.

Franklin was about to remark on the stain when Tyrell gave one final jerk. The case, no longer able to repel his advances, split open along the area of that stain, disgorging it's contents onto the floor. Thus unburdened, the ruined suitcase easily sprung free of the locker.

Tyrell lurched backwards. Rick and Manuel retreated behind a row of wooden seats, leaving Franklin to face the brownish, green glob lying at the foot of the locker.

For several moments none of the men moved, each silently observing the thing. Tyrell swallowed back the bitter taste scratching at his throat. He considered the thing, trying to correlate it's current state with something familiar but could not. Glancing in the direction of the two janitors he grumbled, "Get a shovel, you guys, and get that thing outa here."

The guys response was quick and predictable.

"Then get the damn shovel, and I'll do it," Tyrell growled. He tiptoed his way around the mess, approaching it from the rear. Using the mop handle he pushed the torn suitcase away from the slowly spreading area of ooze. "Give me a couple of them bags," he snapped to Rick. Using the mop handle again, he pushed at the thing moving it further out from the locker so he could get the shovel, when and if it arrived, under it. The ring of liquid surrounding it began to spread, moving slowly but surely in the direction of Franklin's neat gray lace-ups. Tyrell looked at Franklin, standing there with the handkerchief pressed tightly over his nose and mouth. "You better be movin' back, Mr. Marshall. You don't want any of this stuff to get on your shoes."

Franklin's brain was dispatching orders to his feet when all lines of communications went dead. The brownish, green lump, now free of it's prison, chose that particular moment in time to make a break for it. In front of Franklin's bulging eyes the thing began falling apart. Great, greasy brown globs of it began dropping away from a central core. As he watched, unable to turn away, the core slowly exposed itself.

Franklin's eyes rolled up in his skull and his knees buckled, dropping him to the concrete floor, his own face inches from the one staring blankly out at him from the center of the goo.

Their discussion could be heard two floors below in the drunk tank.

Commander Diehl squinted up at Forbes from behind the smoky blue haze of his cigar. In a voice, the volume of which could peel paint, he roared. "One more fucking word outa you and you can join him. Come to think of it, we got too many flies on this pile of shit as is. Might not be so bad an idea you cool your heels in the office with your partner for a while, 'cepting I don't want to look at that nasty ass face of yours over my coffee every morning. So before I change my mind, why don't you go out and do something constructive, like hose down a witness or two? Go find your little queer friend. That oughta keep you outa my hair for the next year or so."

Duncan's face was the color of fresh pasta sauce. "You want constructive? How's this? I'm gonna construct a sling for the ass of the cocksucker what came up with this brilliant idea and shove him in it head first. How's that for constructive? You ain't heard the fuckin' last of this."

"I fucking well better have," Diehl screamed, his own face matching Forbes in hue.

Duncan exited, slamming the door on Diehl's threat. The glass rattled but did not break, saved no doubt by the accumulation of grime on its surface. During the confrontation all eyes in the squad room had been locked on the cubicle, but at Duncan's heated exit all those eyes suddenly found the material on their own desks of much more pressing interest—all save one pair which had never looked up in the first place.

Hyiam Chang sat at his desk, his gaze directed at a half-eaten jelly donut quietly going stale where he had abandoned it over an hour ago. Anyone who knew Chang understood that anything left around him half-eaten was an indication of trouble, but a jelly donut in particular was cause for general alarm.

Forbes rumbled up to Chang's desk like an overworked freight train, a string of muttered curses trailing behind him like steam. "Don't make no sense. No fucking sense at all. Some silly son-of-a-bitch is playin' around, you ask me. Why you? Why now? It don't make no sense. No fucking . . ."

Chang cleared his throat. When he spoke his voice came out all smoky and quiet. "I've never been pulled off an investigation in my whole life."

The ice water of that simple statement cooled a big piece of Duncan's anger. "And you ain't been this time."

"What do you call it? Stuck behind this desk, answerin' phones, runnin' down paper leads. Next thing you know I'll be makin' coffee and goin' for donuts." Chang looked up at his partner, his great brown eyes shining glassily. "I ain't no desk cop."

"Nobody in his right fucking mind ever said you were."

"Well, somebody somewhere thinks I am. Why else would I be pulled off this case and dumped in here?"

"Will you stop sayin that? You ain't been pulled off the case."

"What do you call it?"

The two men glared at one another, then in one voice they both grumbled, "Temporary support detail reassignment."

"Shit," Forbes snarled.

Chang sighed loudly then crumpled his half-eaten jelly donut in the report form it had been resting on and dropped both into the wastebasket. Pushing around the files on his desk he muttered, "Well, I guess I better go see what Ramey wants me to do." Lingering, he looked sideways at his partner. "What are you gonna be up . . ."

Forbes screwed up his face in an expression that on anyone else would have indicated severe pain or constipation but on him only indicated deep thinking in progress.

Chang frowned, recognizing the grimace. "What's going on in that feeble brain of yours now?"

"Diehl won't say exactly where the order came from, right?"

"Yeah."

"Well, I got a hunch if there's one person who knows everything that's goin' on around here it's Marks, right?"

"Yeah, right, and you and the chief's fair-haired boy get along so well he's just gonna tell you what you want to know. That your plan?"

"We'll discuss it." Duncan grinned innocently.

Chang sighed loudly. "Brother. You discuss it with

Marks like you did Diehl and we'll both wind up walking a beat in Watts, which might be your idea of a picnic but ain't mine. Look, you know how things go around here. Give it a day or two, a week at most, and Diehl will forget where I'm supposed to be. I'll be out on the street before you get a chance to miss me."

Forbes ground his teeth. Rolling his eyes he added a groan to the routine. "Forget, my ass, and you know . . ."

The rest of Duncan's sentence got lost in a traffic jam behind his teeth. Eyes narrowing, he gazed across the room. Chang followed the direction of that gaze.

"Oh, good morning, Ms. Morgan." A young female officer who looked more like a cheerleader than a cop smiled up at Max.

"Hi." Max smiled back quietly. "Listen, I need a copy of the reports from last night. Would you have those in yet?"

"Support's running copies right now. They should be up here in a few minutes. In the meantime you have a message."

Max frowned, taking the pink slip. "When did this come in?"

"Must have been sometime last night. I didn't take it. I was off duty. I always put down the time. Must have been the second shift."

Max smiled and nodded. "I'll stick around until those copies come in. Is there a phone I can use?"

"Just find an empty desk. Would you like some coffee?"

"No thanks, cutting back."

Max looked quickly around the squad room, located an empty desk and crossed to it, all the while avoiding the heated gazes Duncan Forbes was aiming in her direction. Max settled in at the desk and began dialing.

"Coroner's office."

"Jasper Heep, please."

"Just a minute."

Forbes sat down in the chair beside her desk and bared his teeth in a fashion that faintly resembled a smile. Max returned the grimace. Neither spoke. She could have easily told him she was holding, but knowing full well the inevitability of the pending conversation she decided to allow him the opening gambit. No sense in using up a good alibi if it wasn't necessary yet.

"Hello."

"Jasper Heep, please."

"Mr. Heep will be on duty at four."

"Oh. Could I leave a message?"

"Sure," the voice on the other end said with obvious discomfort. "Shoot."

"This is Max Morgan returning his call. I'll call back after four. Got that?"

"Sure, Morgan call back after four. Anything else?"

"No, that should—"

The boredom of finishing that sentence became unnecessary as the other end of the line went dead with a click. Max pursed her lips and for the briefest of moments considered redialing the number in order to give the cranky civil servant a refresher course in common courtesies, but she abandoned the urge, realizing it was just an effort to postpone the inevitable. She turned her attention to Forbes. As she looked at him he reaffirmed the slightly demented grin he had earlier displayed, and for the second time Max matched it.

For several seconds the pair sat there grimacing at one another. Just as Max had decided to concede the first fall to Forbes, he spared her the effort.

"What do you know about Chang being taken off the Butcher case?"

"Fine thank you, and yourself?"

"Don't be cute."

"Do be polite."

"I asked you a question."

"Oh, did you? I'm sorry. What did you ask?"

"Why did you get Chang pulled off the Butcher case?"

"That is not what you asked."

"If you knew why'd you have me repeat it?"

"And where the bloody hell do you get off jumping on my case with a ridiculous accusation?"

Duncan's grimace tightened as he caught the whiff of victory. "A simple 'no, I didn't' would have sufficed."

The pair glared at one another. Max's eyes narrowed. She grumbled something under her breath, then pushed back from the desk and stood.

"Beg pardon, I didn't catch that," Duncan said.

Max looked down at him and purred, "Piss off."

Like the hare and the hound the pair began to weave a trail around the squad room with Max in the lead and Duncan fast on her heels. From the coffee urn to the message center to the reception desk and back to their original starting position the pair continued their heated exchange, all the while managing to complete certain items of necessary business at each of these stops without losing a beat in their conversation.

"How would you like it if I was to go in there and tell Diehl about your little expedition?" Duncan asked slyly.

Max lowered the sheaf of report copies she had been attempting to scan and fixed Forbes with a blistering glare, then slammed the copies down. "Fine. Why don't we do it now?"

"What?" Forbes frowned.

Rounding the desk she tried to take hold of his arm, but he pulled free. "What's the matter, cat got your feet? Diehl's office is that way. If you're in such a hurry to talk to him all you have to do is put one foot in front of the other."

"You don't think I'll do it, do you?" Forbes grumbled, taking several steps in that direction.

"Frankly, Scarlett, I don't give a flying rat's ass what you do. Only do it without me!"

"That's just fine by me, lady. From now on you need somebody to haul your ass around town or blow your nose for you you can find somebody else, 'cause as far as I'm concerned you and me are quits."

"Oh, don't make it sound like such a threat," Max snapped, snatching up the reports and stuffing them into her tote. "Seeing the back end of you would be a pleasure."

"Likewise. Only don't think you've heard the last of

this. I'll bet my pension you're the one dumped on Chang, and I'm gonna prove it if it's the last thing I do."

Forbes snarled at her under his breath one last time then turned on his heel and stormed off. Max glared at his retreating back, then chewing on her anger she turned and froze.

There were no words eloquent enough to say what the simple, sad expression on Hyiam Chang's face did. In that expression was captured all the faces of every injured kitten, abandoned puppy, starving child and aged parent the world had ever produced. All traces of Max's former anger were driven from her mind by the look on his face.

Max swallowed. One part of her mind shouted out in anger, demanding she explain, demanding she ease Chang's pain, while another voice from a deeper, darker part of her mind calmly reminded her of the tenet she must not disobey. Max looked away for an instant's reprieve, but when she looked back Chang had turned away from her. She watched him move quietly back to his desk.

"Fuck," Max snarled through clenched teeth.

In the parking lot, locked within the snug security of the Packard, Max leaned her forehead against the cool surface of the steering wheel. Within a few minutes she felt much calmer, more focused, more in control, but for all of her returning confidence there still remained a bitter aftertaste.

Starting the car she accepted that bitterness, adding it to others she'd acquired over the years and taking small comfort in the knowledge that even as she strove to protect, she caused pain.

Tiffany Childress was a 109 pound, blonde, green-eyed, tanned piece of the American dream that cured adolescent acne and geriatric impotence and gave a whole new perspective to the prospect of dying in bed. With a bust measurement slightly smaller than her I.Q., she was, to Riley's mind, a goddess.

The last dregs of the lunch hour rush had been swept

away when Max walked into the bar. She paused just inside the doorway to allow her eyes to adjust after the heady glare of a Southern California winter sun working overtime. Sean, sitting at the end of the bar, waved her over.

"Can I get you something?" Sean smiled shyly.

"Orange juice would be nice. Where is everybody?"

"The lunch crowd is gone, and the regulars won't be in for a little while yet."

Max looked over her shoulder, a small smile turning up one corner of her mouth at the sight of Riley and his buxom captive. Sean put her drink on the bar and, following the line of her gaze, frowned. "Did you want to see Da?"

"He seems a bit tied up, doesn't he?"

Sean shrugged "Nothing he can't get out of. I'll get him for you."

Max turned to her drink and had nearly finished it by the time Sean returned, trailing an agitated Riley behind him.

Half-straddling the barstool beside her Riley leaned close. "Listen, darlin', I got that information you wanted, but something important has come up so if we could—"

Max bit back a smile. "Why don't you just give me what you've got?"

"I could do that right enough only it's a bit complicated. Would it be such a disaster if this was to wait for a day or two?"

"I hate to be difficult about this, but yes, it would."

"Max, now surin' you're not gonna be makin' things hard for ole Da, are ya?" Under pressure Riley's accent thickened.

Max studied his artfully crafted pose and bit back a giggle. "You old grafter, what are you on to?"

"Sometime tomorrow I'll bring the material over to your place, and we can have a nice sit down and . . ."

Riley swallowed the rest of his sentence as his gaze swept the back booths. His usually ruddy complexion took on an unhealthy pallor, his eyes widening to twice their normal size. The booth where he had left his goddess had been defiled; she was gone. He swung around and scanned the deserted bar. When no sign of her was to be found he turned toward his office muttering, "Come on."

Max looked over the simple one page bio with undisguised disappointment. Tossing the sheet onto the desk she pouted. "Malcom Westeridge, son of wealthy parents, educated in Europe, returns home to take a position at the White. Inherits family fortune after a hunting accident and still lives in the family mansion. Wonderful. I could have gotten that much out of the library myself. What I had in mind was something a bit more colorful, and this, my friend, is definitely not it."

Riley smiled behind his coffee mug.

Max leaned back and studied Riley's relaxed posture. With a tight grin she looked away briefly then back to him. "Can I assume by that grin, you've suckered me into the trap and are now ready to light the fire?"

Riley smiled slyly, took a gulp of his coffee then launched into the Westeridge saga. "To get a complete picture on the junior Westeridge we need to go back a bit," he said, preparing the stage.

"Jonathan Westeridge, Malcom's sire, was no stranger to the White Museum. Jonathan was something of an archaeologist. In fact, you could say he was something of a legend. The term most often linked to his name in reference to the field would be infamous. Seems Jonathan had something of a reputation for the liberties he took with other people's work—up to and not excluding putting his name on it. It was broadly hinted that several rather spectacular discoveries he made were in fact discovered in the back rooms of certain professional tomb robbers." Riley suppressed a smile at Max's raised eyebrows.

"And it seems that this wasn't all to the senior Westeridge's reputation. Old Jonathan was something of a rake. On one particular dig his behavior became so scandalous that his superiors demanded he leave Mexico or forfeit the patronage of the White Museum. This had little bearing on the feelings of a certain Miss Margaret White, only child of the White family and heir to the estate, because shortly after Jonathan's return from the Mexican dig they were married."

With studied casualness Max poured herself a coffee and settled back contentedly, studying the storyteller over the rim of the mug. "Don't stop now. You've got my attention."

"Malcom Jonathan Westeridge was born September 10th, 1946. According to birth records Malcom was male caucasian, blond hair, blue eyes, weight six pounds eleven ounces. The records go on to describe an extremely lengthy and difficult birth which took place in the Westeridge home due to the advanced stage of delivery at the time of the doctor's arrival. There is a very interesting and detailed account of that delivery, which I will skip in lieu of this rather interesting material relating to young Malcom. The child's body was disproportionately small. The head was somewhat enlarged with small, almost nonexistent ear channels, faintly oriental features concentrated in the elongation of the eyes, flattish nose and a forehead with a pronounced forward slope."

"Wait a minute." Max frowned. "Am I crazy, or did you just describe a Down's Syndrome child?"

"In those days it was called Mongoloidism."

"Same thing."

"I know. What I was about to say . . ."

"That can't be," Max said firmly.

"Would you quit interrupting?"

"You've made some kind of a mistake on this one. I've seen Malcolm Westeridge. He doesn't have blond hair nor blue eyes."

"The color of a baby's hair and eyes have been known to change as they've grown up, a fact you'd be knowin' if you stayed at home and had a few."

"Be that as it may, children do not grow out of Down's Syndrome. Malcom Westeridge, the one I'm interested in, looks like he never had anything more serious than a head cold in his entire life. Nope, this time you've gotten the wrong apple out of the barrel."

Riley sat there chewing on his irritation and waiting. "Under the assumption I know a bit more on what I'm about, would ya be the least bit interested in hearing the rest of ma story, or do you want to hire yourself another bloke for the job?"

Max sighed. "I really hate it when you get all shirty."

"And I'm not exactly pleased about bein' told I don't know my ass from my elbow. Now, are you gonna listen or do I scrap this lot?"

"Go on, but I'm telling you you're on the wrong trail."

Riley growled behind his teeth, paused to regain his train of thought, then dove into his tale once more. "Now it was a well-known fact at the time that just because Jonathan had adopted the outward appearance of faithful husband and father he hadn't given up his old ways. It seems old Jonathan had something of a yen for the dark-eyed señoritas. He made a practice of hiring a number of them in his household staff, including a particular young Mexican woman who had with her a young son who some said bore more than a passing resemblance to Westeridge senior. According to my sources, in 1949 a young Mexican lad died of diphtheria on the estate. The mother remained in the Westeridge employ and remains so to this day. In that same year young Malcom was shipped off to Europe to begin his education, where he was to remain for the next eighteen years, and to make things really interesting it was in that same year that Margaret Westeridge, almost completely bedridden since the birth of her son, passed away."

Max made to interrupt, but Riley repelled the attempt. "I'm almost finished. Let me get the rest of this out before senility sets in."

Max rolled her eyes but waved him on.

"Now, in 1957 Malcom returns home just in time to witness his father, now near sixty, marry his second wife, a lady three years Malcom's junior. Once established as the lady of the manor she didn't waste anytime getting rid of any prospective rivals to her new throne, firing all of the señoritas with the exception of one middle-aged Mexican woman. Six months later, a fire of curious origins burned the Westeridge hunting lodge near Big Bear to the ground, killing both Mr. and Mrs. Westeridge as they slept in their beds.

"There was a considerable investigation by local authorities at the time, but when nothing of a suspicious nature could be discovered to explain the fire their demise was ruled death by misadventure and the entire Westeridge estate was turned over to it's sole heir, Malcom Jonathan Westeridge."

Riley paused and refreshed his coffee, indicating his tale was completed. Max put her cup on the desk and asked sarcastically, "Are you through, or am I still on hold?"

"It'd be easier to roll back Belfast Lough. Go ahead and blather your head off," Riley grumbled into his cup.

"Look, I can buy a lot, but the part about Malcom's birth records is a sour note. I'll grant you that medical science has come a long way in the past fifty years, but even at our current elevated state I can assure you that Downs Syndrome is not now, nor ever will be, considered a childhood illness that one simply grows out of."

"Max, open your earholes. Nobody's said anything about growing out of it. I may not have your education, but don't you think I'd know something about retarded children after what I've been through?" Riley snapped irritably.

Max's face flushed a bright crimson as a picture of Conna McCall flashed into mind. "Oh Christ," she moaned. "Da, I didn't mean . . ." She stumbled, searching for the right words. "I'm sorry . . . I . . ."

Riley waved her off. "I know you didn't," he said. "I'm an old man who's had a full day takin' out his disappointments on the first available target." He set his cup down and pushed it away from him. Leaning his elbows on the table he looked at Max, and when he spoke his voice was soft. "When you asked me to look into Mr. Westeridge I covered the usual channels and discovered the gentleman, according to those sources, was a likely candidate for canonization, but something about all that got my itch started up."

Max smiled. Riley's itch was legendary. "And your itch made you look further."

"That it did, and you have no idea the trouble it caused me. Poking around in business fifty years come and gone led me some merry chase, I'll say. Couple of times I'm pretty sure I came damn close to solving the Black Delilah murder."

Max laughed abruptly, but at Riley's bayful gaze she covered the laugh with a cough and the back of her hand.

"All smart remarks aside, think about what I've told you."

"I have, and I'm telling you there's been some kind of . . ."

"No! You're not listening—and stop thinking about today. Think about the time we're talking about. Think about the kind of man Jonathan Westeridge was."

Max slowly began to relax, her full attention focused on Riley's voice and the information he pressed her to consider. As she pushed the obvious conclusions earlier arrived at aside, a picture began to form.

"Forced to marry in order to assure his career with the museum to a woman who I gather was not to his particular taste in feminine companionship. A severely deformed child . . ." Max paused and shook her head. "But you see, that's where it goes bad. Malcom Westeridge could not have been born with Downs Syndrome."

"Ah, perhaps not the Malcom Westeridge you know."

Max frowned. "How many Malcom Jonathan Westeridges born to Jonathan and Margaret Westeridge do you know of?"

"You're bein' daft. Think about it. Westeridge's first-born a hopeless retard. Think what something like that must have meant to a man like himself."

"As it would to anyone, a tragedy."

"You're not getting the picture, girl. What was the man like? What kind of human being was Jonathan Westeridge? And while you're workin on that one, consider the Mexican woman and her young son Westeridge hired on. Does he strike you as the kind of man to make such a magnanimous gesture out of the goodness of his heart?"

Riley's eyes narrowed as he studied Max eagerly. At the first signs of her understanding he smiled gleefully. "Fog lifting, is it?"

Max slid onto the front of her seat. She rubbed her eyes then ran her fingers back through her hair. "Now hold on a minute. Let me get a fix on this. Are you insinuating Jonathan Westeridge did away with his own son and put the illegitimate child of some Hispanic housekeeper in his place? That's crazy, isn't it?"

"The scandal what got ole Johnny boy sent packing outa Mexico in the first place had something to do with him getting a young girl what worked in the cook tent in a family way, at least that's what the rumor was at the time. But when Jonathan married little Margaret, her daddy's money went a long way in providin' for some very convenient lapses of memory."

"And you think the woman he hired at the house was that same girl?" Max asked, each word said with a shadow of hesitancy.

"What I think is that this little Mex lass tracked him down and put the screws to him. What with him bein' married to the boss' daughter and all, what was himself to do about it?"

"And then the two of them blithely plot to murder his real son and replace him with the girl's son? That's a reach even *All My Children* wouldn't go for. What about little Malcom's mother? Might it not occur to her that her son had undergone some pretty radical physiological changes?"

"Might well have—which is why she had to die as well."

"Hold the phone, Da. Christ, are you saying they died together?"

"You're thinkin' current day again."

"That's not exactly what I'm thinking."

"Well, scrub around that and try this on for size. It's a big house, lots of servants, Mama's confined to her bed. How often does she get to see little Malcom? My bet is damn little. I haven't got all the dates sorted out yet, but I'd be willing to bet the Mexican boy's death and Mrs.

Westeridge's were not far apart."

"I'm beginning to get a touch dizzy. Why don't you just lay this all out for me one time from the top." Max eased back in her chair, her attention focused on Riley.

"It's like this. The little Mexican lass shows up at his doorstep with his kid in tow. Jonathan maybe tries to buy her off, but she wants no part of his money. She's lookin for a future for herself and her son. Westeridge is between the rock and a hard place, so he takes them on. It's a pretty safe bet that the lass manages to reestablish herself with Jonathan. Who knows? It might even have been her idea. Maybe she even thought with the son out of the way and the wife next in line she and her boy could step right in."

Max swirled this scenario around in her mind behind narrowed eyes and pursed lips. After several minutes she spoke slowly, as if to herself. "Extrapolating from that assumption, Westeridge ships his illegitimate son to Europe on the pretense of education when in reality the primary goal is to keep him away from prying eyes until he's grown. During this time Miss Mexico works her wiles on Jonathan. Maybe for awhile she manages to keep other rivals at bay, but in the end she loses out to Mrs. Westeridge number two."

"Now you're workin', lass. Play it out."

"Malcom junior returns home to find his mother's plans ruined. Mom could not have been a happy camper at this turn of events. Maybe there was even a fight. What if she tried to blackmail Jonathan, and he threatened to cut her and junior off without a cent?"

"A master at work. I love it," Riley chirped happily.

"Mommy can't take the chance of junior being disinherited so she sabotages the hunting lodge—maybe junior even helps or did the dirty deed himself. Wouldn't be the first time a son's love for his mum caused murder. They off Daddy Westeridge and his floozy wife, and junior and his mommie are now set for life. Is that the kind of picture you had in mind?"

"Rembrandt would be proud." Riley smiled contentedly.

"Balderdash."

"It's all there plain as day."

"Yeah, about as clear as a summer day in L.A."

Riley groaned and slumped back in his chair.

"Don't you see, Riley? It's a snap conclusion based on inconclusive evidence."

"Snap conclusion, is it? And brown shoes wasn't?" Riley grumbled.

"The final piece of a much larger puzzle. Do you have anything other than that infamous itch of yours to back any of this up?"

"Not yet," Riley admitted.

"Not yet . . . wonderful!"

"But I'm working on it."

"Grand—and when you get something I'd be more than interested in having a look see, but if it's all the same to you until that proof arrives we'll just table this little flight of fantasy, allright?"

Riley folded his arms across his chest and studied the ceiling.

"Allright?" Max pressed.

Lowering his gaze, Riley watched her for a minute then unfolded his arms and slid to the edge of his chair. "You think I made all of this up?"

"You know better than that. What I think is that you've found a discrepancy that at the moment you're unable to account for, and you began extrapolating on a faulty information base."

Riley frowned. "Extrapolating on a faulty information base? My, ain't we grand? I'm right, your ladyship, and I'll flamin' well prove it."

Max smiled. "If there's anyone on the face of this earth who could, my money would be on you."

Riley fought it for a moment longer then returned that smile. "A sucker bet."

Max laughed and stood up. Stretching, she groaned at the sound of popping joints. "This has been one pisser of a day."

"That it has."

"What are the chances of me taking a certain randy

old Irishman to an early dinner?"

"Bess should be back in the kitchen by now."

"I was thinking of something on the coast."

"What's wrong with my food?"

"How long have you got? Besides it'll do that nasty disposition of yours a world of good to get out of this den of iniquity. How about it? My treat."

"On the grounds of you bein' the cause of my disappointment—"

"Me?"

"And seeing how you haven't got the good manners to say thank you for all the work—"

"Manners?"

"Not to mention the disparaging remarks you made against my food and my establishment."

"Oh, spare me this grief."

"I'll go."

Max shook her head and giggled. "You are some piece of work, Riley McCall."

"Fine Irish linen," he purred smuggly.

Jasper Heep extracted himself from behind the steering wheel of his 13-year-old Volkswagen bug and made a half-hearted attempt to stretch the kinks out of his spine. It wasn't that he couldn't afford a bigger car or that he didn't want one desperately, and it definitely wasn't a case of the aged bug being in good shape. The problem was Jasper was emotionally attached to the battered blue bug. Each one of its complaints had become personal to him. Every clunk, clatter and weeze of the vehicle formed a kind of alien conversation of which Jasper was the sole linguist, and all the abuses, cruel jokes and scathing japes made by his coworkers brought him to the defense of his rusting friend. In a world lusting after personal relationships, Jasper had learned at an early age to seek the comforting solace of the companionship of inanimate objects. To Jasper the bug was an old friend, and he was truer to his friend than most married couples were to their spouses.

Clutching the brown paper bag containing his lunch,

Jasper ambled across the parking lot and into the coroner's building with only a single backward glance at the sun reflecting off his friend's smudged windshield.

Jasper quietly greeted the duty guard, neither receiving nor expecting a response. Picking up his messages and scanning the duty roster he picked his way through the debris of the cluttered cubicle that served as his office.

So far the day was starting as usual, then, unbeknownst to Jasper, the needle on the gauge of normalcy began to edge into the red.

"I don't give a flying fuck what he wants. It's ten minutes to four, and I'm not getting stuck with the paperwork on that pile of shit," Frank Morilla, day shift supervisor, snarled, glaring first at the bored attendant lounging in the hall and then at the lumpy gray bag and dingy yellow suitcase resting on the gurney in examining room two.

Glancing at the wall clock Frank gnawed the edges of his thick moustache and grumbled, "Just like that creep Heep to be late today of all days."

"Give the poor bastard a break, Frank. He's not on the clock till four," Mike Schuster, lab assistant, said.

"Jasper, my man, we were just talking about you," Frank smiled, showing too many even white teeth.

Jasper grinned weakly, certain Frank had been talking about him. "What's up?" he asked gamely, shoving his hands into the pockets of his lab coat.

"We got a small problem here."

"What?" Heep asked, certain the problem involved himself and additional work.

Frank glanced in Mike's direction, flagging off any potential assistance, then began oozing oily charm. "Well, it's this way. See, there's this little stewardess I been seein' for the past few weeks, and it's her birthday. Her schedule is pretty tight, but I managed to put together this little surprise party for her tonight, and if I don't get out of here right now I'm gonna miss her at the airport."

Jasper shrugged. "No problem. I'm here, so take off."

"Yeah, I would, only we had a late pickup from Pasadena P.D. and if I log it in on my shift I'll have to stay and . . ."

"No problem. I'll handle it." Jasper agreed quickly, unwilling to suffer further exposure to Frank's glowing charm.

Ignoring the disgusted head-shaking of the robust Schuster, Frank forgot himself for a moment and almost clapped an arm around Jaspers thin shoulders. Regaining his composure in time he slapped him quickly on the back and sailed out the door with a brisk, "I'll return the favor sometime," tossed over his shoulder.

"You got three chances of living long enough to see that day," Mike groused.

"What?" Jasper frowned.

"Three chances. You know—slim, fat and none. The big three."

"Oh, yeah." Jasper nodding, not really understanding but getting the drift all same.

"Look, I got nothing planned for tonight. If you want me to . . ."

"Thanks, but it's allright."

"You sure?"

"Yeah, go ahead. Enjoy yourself."

Mike crossed to the door then stood looking back at Heep.

"Something wrong?"

"You think I'll live long enough to see the day you tell that bastard to go fuck himself?"

Jaspers pale face flushed as a confusion of answers tumbled through his mind.

"Forget I asked. When that day comes I want to wallow in it, and the element of surprise will only make it that much better. See ya tomorrow."

"Good night," Jasper mumbled.

Long after the last dregs of the afternoon shift had clocked in Jasper sat at his desk and stared at the log entry. The words on the paper had long since blurred as he searched the nooks and crannies of his memory for an illusive something those now blurred words had awakened there.

He attached the report to his worn clipboard and walked down the short hall to Examining Room 2. Outside the room he paused, clipboard under his arm, and looked through the viewing windows at the plastic-cloaked remains waiting peacefully on the table. His eyes drifted to the worn yellow suitcase glistening under the bright lights in a clear plastic coat of its own, all the while feverishly trying to locate a footprint of the thing he was now certain it was imperative he remember.

Entering the room his nose wrinkled as the scent of death accosted his senses. Turning his back on the table, he pulled a pair of thin rubber gloves from a bin, put aside the clipboard and arranged the proper forms.

Arranging a tray of implements beside the table, he pulled the overhead mike into position, set aside the plastic sheathed suitcase, took a deep breath and drew down the grey bag's long plastic zipper. Turning his face aside he silently counted to 20 allowing the first wave of odor to dissipate.

Carefully he removed the contents of the bag and placed the six grayish-green pieces onto the center of the gleaming chrome table. For several long minutes he looked over the collection, then began moving them into a more orderly pattern. Even when reassembled in this crude manner, the results held only vague similarity to the human form.

Drawn to the open rupture in the chest cavity he clicked on the microphone and began the oral portion of his report. After thousands of these recitations he could move through the preliminary steps without bothering to think, thereby freeing his mind to continue the search begun earlier.

". . . huh?" Jasper started. Squinting toward the door, he blinked trying to focus his eyes.

"Jeez, Jasper, what's the matter with you?"

Jasper grinned sheepishly, his cheeks flushing slightly.

"I'm sorry, Mindy. I was concentrating. Did you want something?"

"I found a message for you in Mr. Morilla's box. I can't make head or tail of it."

"What does it say, Mindy?" Jasper asked patiently.

"Oh, yeah. Sez Morgan to call back p.m. That make sense to you?"

Heep nodded. "Yeah. She hasn't yet, has she?"

Mindy wrinkled up her tiny nose and frowned. "Hasn't what?"

"Ms. Morgan hasn't called back, has she?"

"Jeez, Jasper, how would I know?"

Jasper considered reminding Mindy that as afternoon shift switchboard operator his asking her such a question was not out of line, but his ingrained sense of polite behavior to females would never have allowed it. Instead he simply smiled quietly and said, "If she does you will be sure and put her through to me, won't you?"

"For sure. Boy, it sure smells funny in here. What'cha got?"

She started to come further into the room, but Jasper stepped quickly around the table, putting himself between her and it. "Nothing for you to see. Why don't you go down to the lounge and have a coke or something?"

She shrugged. "Yeah, I could do that. Almost my break time anyway." She turned back toward the door and said, "You know, you work harder than anybody I ever seen. You sure could use an extra pair of hands."

Jasper grinned and tried not to blush. "Thank you, Mindy, that's very nice of you to say . . ." He stopped, his mouth hanging open. Behind his eyes a movie screen had dropped down and something was beginning to appear on its surface, but the pictures were blurred and out of focus.

"What did you say?"

"Huh?"

"Just now, what did you say?"

Mindy thought. "About what?"

Jasper crossed the distance between them with frightening speed. "About me needing help."

Mindy blinked up at him, her bright blue eyes registering alarm. "I . . . I didn't say nothing."

"Hands. You said I needed an extra pair of hands, didn't you?" Jasper reached out and took hold of Mindy's shoulders. "You said hands, didn't you?"

Mindy's alarm was rapidly turning into panic, a transformation that instantly saw full bloom when simultaneously she noticed the dark green stain spreading out from the area on her white blouse where his soiled gloves now held her. It was unfortunate for all concerned that Jasper, overjoyed at Mindy's casual remark having reawakened his recalcitrant memory, smiled.

With a squeak Mindy lurched out of the office and raced down the hall.

Jasper, still overjoyed at his resurrected memory but considerably less demonstrative, stood in the empty corridor and called woefully, "Sorry about the blouse."

January 29th—12:15 a.m

THE SECOND FLOOR OF THE CORONER'S BUILDING WAS NOT AN area accustomed to large crowds. Even at peak hours, the corridor outside the examining rooms was rarely witness to more than groups of two or three individuals, but with the arrival of the early hours of January 29th all previous records were broken.

Commander Diehl scratched at the stubble shadowing his chin. Gnawing on an unlit cigar, Diehl studied the tips of his shoes for a moment longer then grumbled, "What made you put the two of 'em together?"

"Approximately twenty-one days ago the body of a male Hispanic child between the ages of four and seven was discovered by the security police at L.A.X. in an investigation of a stolen luggage report." Jasper kept his eyes riveted to the clipboard in his hand. Jasper hated recitations even to an audience of one. Tonight he was playing to an SRO audience.

"I didn't see the body myself, but when I heard some of the comments about its condition I made a point of looking up the report."

"Too bad you didn't see fit to pass that information on to somebody else," Diehl muttered ruefully.

Jasper looked up. "Actually I did, sir."

"Uh? When?"

Jasper, seeing the gleam in Diehl's cloudy blue eyes, dived back into his clipboard. "In a memo to the Task Force office dated January 1st."

Diehl grumbled like a plugged drain.

"Beg pardon?"

"Indigestion," Diehl snapped. "Get on with it. Then what?"

"When the Pasadena victim, a female Hispanic of the same physical condition came in this afternoon I made a point of looking up that report. Interestingly enough, a notation on the status report indicated a next of kin had never been located on the first victim so the body was still being held." Jasper glanced in Diehl's direction in time to see him making a speed-up motion with his hand.

Mentally sorting through the rest of his story Jasper cut to the chase. "I had the first victim brought up while I did a preliminary on the second."

"And you discovered what?"

"That these children and the Butcher victims have a number of similarities in manner of death including removal of hands and feet, a fact not mentioned on the first victim's report."

"Wonderful," Diehl muttered under his breath. Looking toward the examining room, he shouldered his way through the collection of Task Force personnel clustered there and stared inside. "And exactly what is she doing in there?" he barked over his shoulder.

Everyone within range of Diehl's bellow turned to the

room and to Max, busily poking a dismembered limb with a long probe.

"Ms. Morgan has been quite helpful in certain areas of my work, and I was, of course, following procedure as per departmental memo."

Diehl squinted at Heep for a moment then stepped away from the window. "That's very nice, Mr. Heep. Only if it's all the same to you, from now on notify our office first."

Heep's face flushed. Diehl hooked his thumbs in his belt and grinned ominously.

Max beckoned to Jasper. She watched him until he started toward the door then looked briefly at the other faces staring in at her, avoiding the glaring gaze of Diehl and sweeping past Forbes with his back against the glass.

"What do you need?" Jasper asked, closing the door behind him.

Leading the way back to the table bearing the Pasadena victim, she took the probe and indicated an area on the inside of one tiny, withered thigh. "Take a look at this crusted substance there and tell me what it looks like to you."

Jasper pulled on a clean pair of gloves, picked up an instrument similar to Max's and leaned over the table. "How did you see this?"

"What's it look like?"

"Get me a slide. Over there on the counter."

Max retrieved the slide and gave it to him.

Scratching a bit of the substance onto its surface he stood up. "It's blue," he said.

"So far we agree. What else?"

Jasper glanced at Max then took the slide to the far end of the counter and a large microscope. Max hovered nearby as Jasper adjusted the instrument, added chemicals to the substance and made notes, all the while muttering to himself.

Max fidgeted as the minutes dragged on. Leaning over his shoulder she said, "A dissertation I don't need. A guess will do." She moved around to his side, a hopeful expression on her face, but when after several moments he did not respond she pressed. "Jasper, don't leave me now. A guess. A hint. A clue." Again her requests were met with silence. "Earth to Heep. Jasper, you're making a crazy person here."

Jasper looked up from the microscope, frowned at the wall tile for a moment then looked to Max. "It looks like some kind of paint."

Max looked to the ceiling. "Thank you, whoever."

"Blue paint."

"Bingo!" Max grinned.

"Bingo? Is there some significance to blue paint I'm not grasping?"

"If you look at the base of the skull, on the underside of the hair at what's left of the nape on the first victim, you'll find additional traces of a similar material."

When Jasper placed the second specimen under the microscope, his conclusion was arrived at much more quickly this time.

"A match," he said softly, slowly turning his gaze on her.

"I have a very strong feeling that when you have those samples analyzed you'll discover they are not a standard commercial product. It's just a guess at this stage, but don't be surprised if you find a compound mixture of chalk dust, water and a form of natural vegetable dye."

"I'll get these over to the lab myself tonight, but I don't understand. Does this paint have something to do with why these children were murdered?"

"Not only why, but I should very much suspect how." A small frown began to form between Heep's eyebrows. Unable or unwilling to add his questions to those already on her list, Max continued. "I don't want to say a lot more right now. There are several aspects to this I want to make certain of before I start shooting my mouth off. Unfortunately there are at least three aspects of this situation that I'm very certain about."

"And those are?"

"The murders of these children and the Golden Circle victims are definitely linked. Secondly, there are at least two more little victims like this waiting for us out there somewhere right now." Max paused as she saw the pain register in Heep's great dark eyes.

After a moment he asked quietly, "And the third?"

Max drew in a deep breath and then exhaled. "Until we stop this havoc, for every Golden Circle victim there will be another child victim."

"Oh God," Jasper groaned softly, turning his gaze away.

Max felt the tall man's pain like a cold draft in the warm room. For a moment she stood there beside him, conscious of the eyes watching their every move from beyond the glass but unwilling to allow them to interfere. Reaching out she lay her hand over the top of his.

Jasper sat there, perfectly still, almost holding his breath for fear of breaking the spell. A confusing mixture of emotions were flooding his body. He felt deep sadness for the tiny victims as well as those who might soon join these first two, but at the same time a warm sweet happiness hummed along his veins. Jasper had rarely experienced such kindness from those he knew well and never from strangers.

With a squeeze Max lifted her hand. Jasper looked at her, and she smiled quickly with a little wink. "You can, of course, tell Diehl the basics on this pair, but I think it would be best if you let me drop the bomb on the paint." She said. "He already hates my guts. No sense overburdening his shit list."

One side of Jasper's thin lips curled upward as a small giggle caught in his throat. "Sure, if that's what you want."

"You know what I want?"

"What?"

"For you to give me the dope on those other samples you ran."

"I've got the reports in my office."

"Just the highlights for now."

"Each sample contained simple charcoal, two different commercial varieties."

"The kind of stuff you barbecue with?"

"Yeah, pretty common stuff. All samples contained trace elements of human blood, a substance that tests very much like semen residue, and then each sample had different elements after that. There was animal leather, silk fibers and one hemp and cotton combination—and, oh yeah, human hair."

Max's eyes got all squinty as she considered this new information.

"What does all of this . . . ?" Jasper gestured toward the children wanly then let his slender hand drop onto his knee as if fatigued by the action. "The paint, the ashes . . . I don't understand how . . ."

"Give me tonight, or at least what's left of it. I just want to be very sure in my own mind of the pieces and the way I've put them together. In my business, probably more so than most any other you can name, credibility is a very precious commodity. Most of the folks in this game have about as much of the stuff as your average mail order proctologist. The last thing I want to do is tie certain evidence to a particular cause and then have to change my mind later because I did so too quickly. Can you understand that?"

Jasper nodded. "It's not all that difficult."

"No, you wouldn't think so. Look, tomorrow I'll drop by and lay it all out for you. You'll need to know, under the assumption this isn't the last time we'll be seeing other victims like these."

"And there will be others, won't there?" Jasper said quietly, making the question into a statement of disturbing fact.

Max grimaced. "Yes, I'm very much afraid there will be." Cocking her head at an angle, she squinted at the examining tables. "Curious thing, that."

"What is?"

"You said the first body, the boy, had been here unclaimed for some time."

"That's right."

"And the girl, has anyone . . . ?"

"Too soon to know yet. Pasadena will check with

Missing Persons if a report's even been filed."

"Why wouldn't someone file a report if their child was missing?"

"Illegal aliens or runaways. Sometimes the report is filed in another area and doesn't get on the system right away. There are half a dozen reasons why we can't find—"

"If you two are done with the social part of the evening . . ."

Max groaned behind her teeth, recognizing the speaker without looking up. Jasper turned around on the stool and stood up. "Just coming, Duncan."

"Well, put a little heat under it, will ya? Diehl's gettin awful itchy out here."

Max watched the tall Heep usher Forbes out ahead of him but turned away before she saw the small, reassuring smile Jasper almost gave her over his shoulder as he stepped out into the hallway and closed the door.

Even through the thick glass she could hear the muted rumble as the detectives began pummeling Jasper with their questions. After a few minutes those voices began to fade away. Looking over her shoulder a small smile turned up one side of her mouth. He had lead the pack away from the door, leaving her exit unblocked.

Pulling off the smock she gathered up her coat and the omnipresent tote and crossed out into the corridor. She glanced down the hallway to the lab area and saw the men of the Task Force clustered around Jasper. In the opposite direction the coast was clear all the way to the elevators.

Unwilling to risk a meeting with Diehl and the possibility of being forced to reveal her discoveries prematurely, Max wasted little time in covering the distance to the elevators. But for all her haste sound travels even faster.

"Hold on there, Miss Morgan."

Unwilling to surrender that easily, she pressed on only to find, upon reaching her goal that elevators are only where you want them to be in the movies. Punching the call button with more than the required force she turned slowly, fixing a calm smile on her face. Diehl, a cigar protruding from his face like a flagpole, came trundling toward her.

"What's your hurry? You got another job?"

Several answers with varying degrees of venomous content came easily to mind, but for the sake of a speedy exit she selected the least offensive. "As a matter of fact I moonlight as a mattress tester, and I'm sorely behind in my work."

Diehl rumbled to a stop, blocking her escape route. With a grin that had nothing to do with amusement, he nodded. "Nice to see you can keep a sense of humor after poking over the remains of a couple of dead kids."

Max let her calm smile wither on the vine. "Was there something you wanted?"

"I'm real interested in what you and Heep were so thick about back there. I got the definite feeling you were bendin' his arm more than a bit." Diehl's hooded blue eyes had gone all flinty.

"Had I wanted you in on the conversation I would have—"

"Don't get cute with me, sister. As long as this department is paying your salary you're a member of this Task Force, and if I want to know what you had for breakfast, you goddamn well better be making out a menu. Now, I'm not goin' to repeat myself."

"You can repeat yourself from now until hell freezes over for all I care. I don't have to tell you anything I do not consider relevant to this case, and a personal discussion between myself and a friend—"

"Friend? You never laid eyes on Heep before."

"Be that as it may. Tomorrow morning I will be in your office with a written report in regards to tonight's investigation, which is precisely what my contract requires me to do at this point. However, if that doesn't meet with your requirements, I suggest you take that up with Chief Merchinson. Now if you don't mind I have an elevator to catch!"

The two glared at one another for a moment longer before Diehl stepped aside. Max entered the elevator and pressed the button, but before the machine could move Diehl shoved a meaty arm between the doors.

"You're cutting it mighty thin, lady. There's gonna come a time when you want a favor from this department."

Knowing only too well the unfortunate truth in that statement, Max suppressed an urge to exercise her knowledge of expletives. Instead, using two fingers like tweezers, she took hold of Diehl's cuff and lifted his hand out of the way. As the doors closed she flashed him a dour smile. "Nighty night," she purred, the sound of the doors closing drowning out, "fathead."

All eyes were focused on Max.

Every desk, folding chair and leaning space was filled. The officers of the Task Force, deprived of an earlier performance, weren't going to miss this one. A blackboard had been placed at the front of the squad room in case she felt the need of one, a series of hastily prepared black and white photographs taken of the two small victims were thumbtacked to the board's wooden border, and each officer held a written copy of her report. There was nothing left to do but get on with it.

Max was about to speak when the door opened and Chief Merchinson, closely followed by Marks and Commanders Diehl, Liebschuetz and Helmer, entered. There was muffled throat clearing, chair scraping and significant glances among the detectives. These actions, like native drums in a jungle, was their way of communicating the obvious seriousness of the event they were about to witness. Like sharks they caught the scent of blood in the water, a number of their smiles revealing gleaming incisors.

Max could feel the current of excitement skimming over the small hairs on the backs of her arms like an exhilarating electric charge. Any nervousness she might have felt vanished as her ego, interpreting the sensations as a challenge, answered the call.

"Two victims," she began, her voice controlled, well-modulated and firm. "Both between the ages of four and seven. One male, one female. Both bodies dismembered in identical pattern. Head, arms and legs cut from the torso. Hands, feet and heart missing on both victims.

"The nature of the wounds indicates that these cuts were produced by a small but extremely sharp knife. Pressure indentations in the area of these cuts indicate the size of the weapon and that due to its small size the murderer was an extremely strong individual exerting pressure on the weapon and relying on his own strength as much as the sharpness of the blade. Particles of obsidian found in the wounds indicates the murder weapon was made of stone."

She paused for a moment, looking slowly over the faces of her audience. One officer near the rear of the room hesitantly lifted his hand. "Please hold any questions until I have completed my report." As the man quickly lowered his hand, more at the looks from his fellow officers than from Max's request, she said, "Thank you."

"Contrary to popular belief, these children and the Golden Circle victims are not an indication of a new wave of sadistic criminal behavior. Nor are they an aberration new to society. What they are, in fact, are examples of a very old and well-documented practice. Each of these victims were a sacrifice dispatched by prescribed ritual—in practice even today some place on the face of this earth and dating back since before the birth of Christ."

A low muttering vibrated up from the audience, threatening to increase in volume until Max resumed her monologue in a firmer tone.

"In the case of the Golden Circle victims, we see in each situation a perfect reproduction of the previous victim in everything from the manner of the dismemberment to the removal of the same amount of external skin.

"Each of these repetitions strongly indicates some form of ritual, but nowhere can this be more strongly evident than in the bodies of the two children. The evidence that finally eliminated all other possibilities was found last night in the form of pigments of blue paint found on each child's body.

"The color blue has a long and well-established record of veneration throughout civilization, dating from the times of the ancient Celts up to modern times and the religious ceremonies of the Hopi and Navaho's of the American Southwest. Combining this fact with the repetitive ritualistic nature of the previous victims it is an undeniable conclusion that what we are seeing here is the resurrection of the custom of sacrificial offerings. With the acceptance of this fact, all that remained was to deduce the origins of the practice using the specifics gathered from the remains."

After a quick glance around the room and a swallow of coffee Max pressed on. "The removal of a victim's heart is not an uncommon practice among a number of ancient cultures as well as several existing ones today. Dismemberment, again, is not an uncommon practice in acts of religious sacrifice, however skinning of the victims is an act limited to ritual practices recorded by considerably few cultures. Tribes in Africa have for centuries skinned animal victims and worn the skins in the hopes of taking on the attributes of those animals, but they refrained from doing so to human enemies, preferring to eat certain organs of the victim for that same purpose.

"However, the records of ritual skinning of victims and use of that skin as part of religious ceremonies is curiously limited to natives of the Americas. Several tribes of North American Indians not only scalped their victims but in religious ceremonies used pieces of skin from their victims, at times even the whole face as well as the scalp. But given the amount of skinning on our victims there is only one collection of cultures whose practices were identical. These cultures are those of the Indians of the Meso-Americas.

"In a number of ceremonies endemic to each of these cultures, practitioners ritually removed the heart of their victims, offering it to their gods. They removed the skin to be worn in other ceremonies and removed the hands and feet. These parts of the body were considered of nearly as great a significance as the heart and were given to priests, nobles or warriors as rewards. They then dismembered the remaining parts of the body, using them as food either for participants in other ceremonies, prisoners of war or even zoo animals. The cultures who exercised these practices were the Aztecs, Toltecs and the Maya."

For several minutes after that statement the room was quite still. All fidgeting had ceased, and all eyes were trained on her. Max returned their gazes, knowing only too well the shock would soon wear off.

"Excuse me," came the well-modulated voice of Daniel Marks. "Ms. Morgan, are you suggesting that these murders were committed by Aztecs?" Daniel's expression was beautifully neutral.

Suppressing a smile she replied calmly. "Absolutely not. In fact I am not suggesting anything of the kind. What I am telling you is that out there somewhere, at this very moment, there is a group of individuals who are resurrecting the religious practices of these cultures for reasons, as yet, unknown."

Chief Merchinson had heard enough. With a stern glance in Diehl's direction he looked quickly to Max. "You've done your homework, Ms. Morgan. You will see that I get a copy of all your reports from now on."

"Certainly."

"Fine. Gentlemen please remain seated." Merchinson turned toward the door, but as he passed Diehl, he said something which caused the heavyset commander to respond nervously as the chief disappeared out the door, trailing Marks behind him.

Almost at the same instant the door closed behind them the questions began.

"I'm confused," a voice called.

Several other voices made disparaging remarks about that being the usual status of the speaker. Max looked around until she located him in the figure of a young detective with a sparse moustache and dishwater hair.

"Seaver," he said identifying himself. "I thought you

said the killer was some kind of spook or something."

"Your words, not mine, but in essence you're correct."

The muttering sprang up once more, this time rapidly escalating to vocal protest.

"Wait a minute, lady. You can't have it both ways."

"Of course I can," Max responded easily.

The verbal volume increased, punctuated by several groans.

"What kind of bullshit is this?" a voice, sounding suspiciously like Duncan Forbes, rumbled.

"I think you better explain yourself, Morgan," Diehl bellowed, quelling the disturbance.

"Although the victims bear strong similarities in the manner of their deaths it is an undeniable fact that the Golden Circle victims were committed by a considerably different force then the children. It is my belief, one which I trust the Coroner's department shares, that the children were murdered by very human subjects, possibly the same individual in each case." Before further questions could be posed on that conclusion Max hurried on to deliver the rest of the bad news. "There is considerable reason to believe these two children are but the first of at least three more which may or may not be discovered. Further, for every additional Golden Circle victim there will be another child murdered, just as these two and the remaining three we have yet to discover have been."

This time when she finished the silence in the room was a thick tangible entity.

"Why are they killing children?"

Max turned slowly to face the speaker. She met Hyiam Chang's even, hard gaze, but after only a few seconds he broke off, looking away.

Pushing aside the sharp stab of despair his brief gaze brought to her, Max spoke in a calm, even tone. "Sacrifices of this kind are often of a multi-victim nature. Simply put, a priest or practitioner must make a sacrifice of sufficient weight or importance in order to gain the attention of the god or spirit they are trying to attract. Young children, particularly those under the age of five, are considered excellent subjects. They are virgins, although some rituals do not require this and in fact dictate that the child must be violated before it can be sacrificed."

Groans and angry muttering greeted this information.

"Are you saying those little kids were raped before they were murdered?" Commander Diehl challenged hotly.

"We have no reason to believe that at this juncture."

A silent, group sigh could be felt moving across the room like a wave.

"Once the child is offered up, the spirit or god the practitioner is seeking to arouse will seek out its victim in order to appease its master. Usually in this kind of ritual the practitioner is asking the aid of this spirit or minor god in reaching a higher source. This part of the ritual is used to gain the attention of the higher god who may or may not, depending on the accuracy of the sacrifices and rituals, aid the priest or practitioner."

Max recognized the scattering of fuzzy looks and began searching around for an analogy. "It's rather like the actor who wants a part. He can't go to the director and get an audition. He must first have an agent speak for him."

A couple of heads nodded.

"So what is this guy trying to get the big boss to do?" Forbes asked with more than a trace of sarcasm.

"If we knew that we'd have the party responsible for the children's murder," Max lied artfully. It was possible this might be the case, but there was no precedent for such speculation. There was no use telling them the truth at this juncture. After hearing the kind of news she'd delivered thus far a cause for some hope, no matter how small, was a necessary escape valve.

"Would the locations where the children's bodies were found help us to form some kind of pattern that might enable us to predict future victims?" A new county was heard from.

"It's possible. I think you'll find when the three victims which we have yet to discover are located we'll see they are in close proximity to the Golden Circle victims. For example, we had one in Pasadena and one child was discovered there. The boy found at L.A.X. could easily be grouped with either the Brentwood or Pacific Palisades victims."

"Is that common? I mean, could they have been committed at the same place?"

Max frowned. "If you mean could the child found in Pasadena have been murdered at . . ."

"Dr. Paxon's," a helpful voice offered.

"Yes, Dr. Paxon's residence. No, we have no evidence of such a multiple murder, but I believe that it would be safe to say the child was dispatched somewhere nearby."

"Why?"

"As I have said there are very strict rules of procedure in rituals of this kind. There are, in a number of rituals of this type, a need for fairly close supervision of the lesser spirit. It was generally believed that the lesser spirits weren't terribly bright entities, and allowing too great a distance to separate them and their victims was not a wise course to follow." Max paused as another part of the puzzle dropped into place for her. "In fact it was not an uncommon practice for the priest or one of his acolytes to place an object or talisman with the prospective victim that the spirit could use as a kind of directional beacon to aid in locating the subject."

There was a buzz of a different kind with this news. At last she was beginning to give them something of a more tangible nature. Several voices at once clamored for further information.

"A talisman is an object used by a believer."

"That's all well and good, but you say the bastards that killed these kids are human. What can you tell us about them?" Diehl was steering his bulk through the maze of seated bodies toward the front of the room. Coming to a stop across from her, he growled, "Huh? What about them?"

"What would you like to know?"

The question ignited a small spark of surprise in Diehl's glassy blue eyes, but he kept any sign of it from showing in his face. "I don't suppose you have anything in the way of a description on these human perpetrators, do you?"

Max waited patiently, recognizing the routine all too well. Diehl's ego was smarting. He'd gone to Merchinson last night with complaints undoubtedly in reference to her belligerent attitude, uncooperativeness and lack of useful information on the case. She knew the litany by heart. He brought Merchinson in to hear her report, believing that her own words would do her in. The plan hadn't worked. He knew it, the men knew it, the chief most certainly knew it, and worst of all Diehl knew that she knew.

"No visions of the killers gathered by rubbing the paint chips?" A smile was oozing its way across Diehl's face that was decidedly insulting. "No voices of the deceased giving you clues from beyond?"

Max swallowed a sigh. Shuffling the pages of her report into a rough order she began gathering her possessions.

"Well, I guess not. Looks like we've heard the end of your report. Now unless you've got any suggestions of a useful . . ."

Max gave a deep, throaty laugh, slung the tote over her shoulder, rounded the desk under a full head of steam and exited.

By the time Max reached the parking lot and climbed behind the wheel of the Packard, there was a spring in her step. Her dramatic exit had dispelled all the hostilities Diehl's performance had inspired.

High above the San Gabriel's thunderheads were boiling over out of the high desert, bringing another in a series of storms pushed in by a low pressure area near Lake Tahoe.

Swinging up onto the Golden State Freeway from the narrow confines of the decaying Pasadena Freeway the Packard cut through throngs of tiny imports and brooding, diesel-belching trucks.

Before leaving the apartment that morning Max had contacted an acquaintance of hers, Dr. Martin Merriam, at the Los Angeles County Museum of Natural History where he served as assistant curator specializing in Meso-American antiquities. She was seeking additional information on the Peten Chac Mool. Dr. Merriam offered what he knew on the subject eagerly but suggested that for a fuller accounting on that particular item she should look up a certain Dr. Linda Osprey at Occidental College. After a brief phone conversation Dr. Osprey made an appointment for Max to visit her.

Suddenly, racing past her car was an impossibly large, white-walled tire—just a single tire independent of either a car or any of its fellow tires.

The steering wheel of the Packard abruptly whipped to the left with the force of a thing gone mad, the cross member of the huge wheel striking the first two fingers and thumb of Max's left hand with sufficient force to banish all feeling. The left front tire rim slammed down against the pavement, sending up a shower of sparks as the weight of the heavy vehicle ground steel splinters into the center lane of the freeway. Its forward momentum stunted, the car swung around wildly until the Packard faced the oncoming flow of traffic.

A small van in the fast lane clipped the rear end of the Packard as it swung into his lane then ricocheted off the center divider where it stalled and rolled to a stop. The collision did little to slow the madly careening Packard.

Max hung onto the huge steering wheel, doing what she could to guide the listing vehicle when possible while working the gas pedal, brake and clutch almost simultaneously. She wanted desperately to stop the Packard's erratic movements but not across three lanes of the Golden State Freeway with oncoming traffic. The driver of a moving van created a miracle in her favor by manhandling his huge rig around the limping, lurching Packard, a feat a nasty-looking Buick did not copy. All things considered the rude push the Buick gave the Packard was just the incentive the battered old queen needed to launch herself up out of the concrete ditch of the freeway and onto the comparative safety of the grassy shoulder strip separating the freeway from the swollen wash of the L.A. river. Unfortunately for Max the Packard took too much of a good thing, and instead of having the common sense to crash into the fence and hang there, she lurched through it and down the concrete embankment toward the swirling waters below. Just exactly how Max managed to stop the lumbering leviathan with no more than a portion of the front bumper awash wasn't completely clear, although upon later reflection she would credit the creatively rich flow of curses that had spewed from her mouth as much as her manipulations of gearshift and parking brake.

Forbes sauntered into the emergency entrance of the Glendale Adventist Hospital, paused long enough to light a cigarette directly under the "Thank you for not Smoking" sign, then puffed his way through the swinging doors leading to the interior of the emergency room. Several moderately busy nurses looked up from the front desk as his smoke wafted in their direction, but none seemed concerned enough with the offense to give chase. A short, rotund orderly waddled purposefully across Duncan's path and got buttonholed for his trouble.

"Detective Forbes, Homicide. I'm lookin' for a . . ."

Before he could finish the statement he caught sight of a small covey of Glendale's finest and two chippies from the California Highway Patrol. Releasing the startled orderly, he moved in their direction.

"You can't smoke in here," the orderly grunted by way of a parting shot.

As Duncan approached, he could see the gathering was listening intently to something he could not quite make out. Stepping into their midst he announced abruptly, "I'm Forbes, Homicide. Which one of you lot is Ferguson?"

"Me. I'm Ferguson," a tall, blonde-haired young officer in the uniform of the CHP said evenly, looking every bit a model for Hitler's ideal of the Aryan youth.

Forbes looked the lad up and down. "I understand you got something belongs to us?"

"If you mean Miss Morgan, then I guess we do."

"What's the story?"

Ferguson reached for his notebook, but Duncan waved him off. "Spare me the details. Just give me the punch line."

"Well, she lost the left front wheel off that—what was that thing, Charlie?"

"Packard," Forbes interceded. "How the hell did she lose the left front wheel?"

"Lose ain't exactly the right word."

Duncan swung around to the new speaker, a stocky, red-haired veteran of the road closer to his own age. "What exactly would the right one be?" Duncan squinted at the man's name tag—Lasky.

"Looked like to me somebody wanted that wheel to come off in a bad way."

"What exactly leads you to that conclusion?"

"The way the wheel was all scarred up and not from the accident. Looked like somebody beat the shit out of the thing and loosened the lugnuts."

Duncan ground out his cigarette on the tile. "You got anything on that more than your hunch?"

Lasky said, "When we found out she was with the Task Force we figured you boys might want to take a look at the wheel, so its wrapped up in the trunk of my unit. Would have hauled it over to our lab, but we figured why take the chance on botching anything with the primitive stuff our boys got to work with. Figured we'd save it for the bright boys downtown."

Duncan stuck another cigarette in his mouth. "You done good, Lasky." With one last glare in Lasky's direction he turned his attention back to Ferguson. "What's the damage on her ladyship?"

"Shit, damn, piss!"

Everything stopped as the curses drifted out of the examining room.

Forbes cleared his throat. "Well, there's no damage to her lungs."

"You shoulda been here earlier."

"Yeah, Ferguson was takin' notes. Said he never heard language like that before."

"Wonderful," Duncan muttered under his breath. Pushing through the men, he reached for the door to the examining room, then paused. Looking back over his shoulder he said to no one in particular, "Make sure you send copies of the traffic report to the office." Then looking at Ferguson he asked, "How'd you know she was workin' with us? She tell ya?"

"No, and she wasn't thrilled when I told her we called you guys."

"Then how?"

"She had that I.D. badge pinned to her coat so I just figured."

Forbes grimaced. "Thanks—for nothin."

Pushing through the door to the examining room Forbes was already preparing the razzing he intended on delivering to Ms. Morgan for ruining the Packard, but the scene that greeted him inside brought him up short.

Max sat perched on the edge of the examining table. Her left hand, two-thirds of which was turning a lovely shade of greenish purple, rested on her knee, while clenched in her right hand was a metal bowl not unlike those dentist's are so fond of demanding you spit in. Brandishing this unlikely weapon she was managing neatly to keep a tall, black intern at bay.

"And I say I can still feel the damn thing," she grunted through clenched teeth.

"And I'm telling you you can't," the intern insisted. "I gave you that shot almost ten minutes ago, and by now it would be impossible for you to feel anything in that hand."

"Fine. You come back over here and put my thumb where nature meant it to be, and if I don't feel anything I won't split your skull open with this thing, but if I do . . ." She let the last words trail off with a shrug.

The two opponents eyed one another for a moment longer before the intern straightened and turned toward the door. Pausing there, he looked back at Max. "I'm gonna give you a second shot, but it's totally unnecessary." He looked briefly at Forbes before exiting the room, muttering something odious under his breath.

Max looked at Forbes and groaned. It was difficult to tell whether it was from the pain of her injuries or in response to his presence. Tossing her weapon onto the table beside her she gently tested the injured hand. "It's not like I don't have enough pains. They have to send me another one," she muttered under her breath. After further examination of the injured digit she said more loudly, "What are you doing here?"

"Garbage detail," Forbes purred, enjoying Max's discomfort immensely. "Seems somebody downtown was concerned about your remains cloggin' up rush hour traffic."

Max looked up at him with a weary smile. "And I can just guess whose bright idea it was to send you. Well, you can save us both the grief and push off. I'm perfectly capable of finding my way home."

Under the best of circumstances Forbes barely tolerated orders from his superiors, and he wasn't about to extend his patience to include this pushy outsider. "Well, I guess you should have thought about that before you decided to redesign the Golden State with the front end of the Packard. My orders are to see you make it home in one piece, and that's what I mean to do."

Max glared up at him. "And if I don't see it that way, what are you going to do about it?"

A little bell went off inside Duncan's head. The movie was all but forgotten by the general public but Duncan remembered it, and when an opportunity arose he jumped on it with both feet. "Go ahead, make my day!" he purred.

Max's mouth dropped open, and her eyes bulged. It wasn't exactly the reaction he'd hoped for, but it was better than nothing, at least that's what he thought.

A giggle bubbled in Max's throat. Before she could stop them several more giggles escaped as well. She clamped her good hand over her mouth, but her eyes told the story.

The effects of the accident were being to tell on her, and she teetered on the edge of an hysterical giggling spell. Duncan frowned, and even this set up a whole new barrage of giggles. Max wobbled on the edge of the table and was forced to steady herself with her right hand. "Make my day?" She chortled. "Dirty Duncan Forbes?" Her eyes were beginning to water.

Forbes stood there weathering the barrage of remarks that poured out of Max's mouth, both confused by her reaction and more than a little embarrassed by it. When he felt the color in his face begin to blossom, he turned hurriedly, exiting and muttering a string of curses that only added to Morgan's merriment.

"Look out, will ya?" The black intern snarled jumping back. With the kind of quick hand action any surgeon would be proud of, he snatched a hypodermic needle off the edge of the small tray he carried before it could escape, all the while giving Forbes a look that would chill meat.

Forbes eyed the needle. "That for the U-Boat commander?"

The intern frowned for a second then nodded. "Yeah. Don't tell me you're a specialist, too? If you're thinkin' about tellin' me how to practice medicine like your friend—"

"That ain't no friend of mine, and if that's for her, that needle ain't near big enough."

The two men eyed one another for a moment before the intern smiled. "Maybe, but she's gonna feel it all the same."

Forbes nodded, a small smile playing across his lips. "Good . . . good."

Three hours later Max stepped out of the emergency room doors, paused long enough to pull the sling from her left arm, dropped it into her tote and lit a cigarette. Out of the corner of her eye she could see the battered gray car with Forbes behind the wheel. Inhaling deeply, she considered walking down the long drive to the street and once there trying to find an alternate route home. Her mind may have considered that option, but her feet were already guiding her weary body in the direction of Forbes.

Forbes could see her coming even though his nose was buried in a newspaper. He continued his sham interest in the paper as she rounded the front of the car, opened the door and climbed in.

The pair rode in a thick, palatable silence broken only by the static-ridden reports of the police radio. Dropping down out of the foothills of Glendale, Forbes made his way out onto the Glendale Freeway and headed toward the waiting gridlock known euphemistically as rush hour on Los Angeles Freeways.

Duncan reached for a cigarette but found himself interrupted as the radio belched out his call number, W481.

Snatching up the mike he barked, "W481, Forbes."

"Detective Forbes, please call your office immediately."

Forbes considered the request for a moment, his eyes narrowing as he studied their position in traffic.

"Detective Forbes, do you . . ."

"Yeah, I got ya." He slammed the mike back onto it's cradle with sufficient force to cause Max to wince, an action that was not without certain painful repercussions.

"What's up?" she asked cautiously.

Forbes was craning his neck and looking out the rear window, his left hand already turning the wheel in the direction of the next lane. Max glanced toward the lane next to them and, seeing it was already occupied, snapped, "Look out!"

"I'll do the drivin'. You want to be useful? Pull that light out from underneath the seat and put it on the dash."

Forgetting her ailments Max moved quickly, easily locating the light and setting it into operation, but she had forgotten about the siren that went along with the light. "Fuck," she snarled, clapping her hands over her ears.

"You got some nice mouth on you, lady," Duncan grunted, nosing his way into yet another lane over the protests of several motorists.

From the moment the call was received until the time they careened to a halt in front of a phone booth outside a 7-11, it had taken Duncan a little over eight minutes to cross six lanes of bumper-to-bumper traffic, race down the shoulder to the nearest off-ramp, reach surface streets and locate a phone.

While he busied himself on the phone Max ran into the store and returned bearing cigarettes, Pepsi and a large bottle of Medipren. She had a very nasty feeling it was going to be a very long time before she saw home again, and one look at Forbes' face told her she was right.

Pulling out onto the street Duncan said gruffly, "They've found another one of those kids."

Max nodded, not surprised by the news. "Where?"

"Hermosa Beach."

Forgetting the contents of the bag on her lap, she turned her gaze out the window without seeing the scenery blurring past. It has to be another little girl, she thought. As she thought those grim words equally grim pictures began forming in her mind.

As Chang rolled up the ramp from the station garage to the street a fine mist was turning the city asphalt to glass. He should have been in the station, sitting at his desk and staring at the four walls, but he couldn't help himself. For the first time in his life he wanted desperately to be in that lousy car with Forbes, cursing him at the top of his lungs. Hermosa Beach was probably the tiniest of the Southern California beach communities, slightly less than one square mile on the map, and since there was no direct route there, a speedy approach was out of the question.

Working his way through traffic his spirits began to lift. He realized, of course, that once he arrived he couldn't just stroll onto the scene like he belonged there, at least not as long as Diehl was around. But Diehl wasn't noted for spending time at crime scenes anyway. With any kind of luck Diehl would be gone before the coroner's boys, and then he could just casually join the others. Maybe he and Forbes could stop for a drink afterwards and talk things over, like old times.

"Old times?" he chided himself aloud. Jesus Christ, he was being to sound like some dottering retiree. What was the matter with him? He knew what the matter was. It was a feeling that every cop the world over had about his partner at some time or other.

Tonight, somehow or someway, Duncan Forbes' life was going to be in jeopardy. Hy didn't know how he knew, but the important thing was that he did know. With almost equal certainty he realized he was the only one who did, and it was up to him to make damn sure whatever was going to happen didn't.

Ten blocks north of Hermosa Beach pier at the dead end of 34th street, a small, sad circus of blue and red flashing lights, dripping-slicker-clad clowns, and gun-toting lions were moving through their age-old routine under the watchful eyes of a bedraggled audience. The rain had quickened to a steady drizzle, and a fog suitable for any Hitchcock film was slithering around the partici-pants in this little drama. Only this wasn't a Hitchcock film. There were no neat, tidy corpses or slick, polished professionals going about their duty with cool efficiency, and no guaranteed solution was visible just over the horizon in the final reel.

The actors in this drama were all too real. The rain soaked their clothing, the sand clung to their shoes, and the only eye witnesses were six crusted urinals, and according to the report a 16-year-old junkie. Several of the detectives, who'd been around long enough to have a fair working knowledge of what street life could do to the young, doubted that she was even that old.

"Here," Max said, indicating the blue coloration on the child's neck.

"Right," Jasper whispered.

They worked over the pitifully small collection of body parts for several minutes longer before Jasper rose, pulling off his gloves. "You want to tell Diehl, or should I?"

Max pulled herself up with the aid of a grimy sink and

peeled off the glove covering her uninjured hand. "I'm a bit thin tonight. Why don't you tell him?"

Jasper watched her for a moment longer. "You gonna be all right? You don't look so good, you know."

"I need some air. Let's get out of here."

A small crowd of suits and uniforms waited just outside the door. As they clustered around Heep, Max made her way around to the far side of the small, cement-block building. She sat down in the wet sand and lit a cigarette.

"All right," Diehl bellowed, trying unsuccessfully to drown out the groans. "Suit yourselves. You can stand around here and drown or fan out and cover this side of the Strand and the block leading up to it. I don't care which, only don't show your face at Headquarters until you've talked to everybody in the area." The groans flared up again. "Tomorrow you can go over the rest of the area." More groans. "Or do you want to do that tonight as well?" The groans dropped to an acceptable level. "Well? Get moving!"

The detectives picked their way off the beach, pairing up silently on the firmness of the Strand, and moved off into the fog to disturb the snug comfort of the locals with their questions. Diehl, certain his presence was needed elsewhere, vanished along with several patrolmen no longer needed for crowd control now that the minicam crews were gone. Jasper, enjoying the rare experience of having a full crew, watched from inside the van as the remains were loaded, then settled back for the long, slow ride back to the plant.

Max reached for another cigarette then stopped, realizing she had smoked nearly half a pack since arriving. The fog was thinning out under a freshening wind out of the west, and the drizzle had become a fine, intermittent mist. Pushing herself up, she brushed the clinging sand from her bottom and zipped her jacket, pulling the collar up around her face. Easing her injured hand into her pocket as best she could, she trudged through the sand toward the Strand.

"Where is everybody?" she asked the boys in the single

remaining black and white, surprised by the lack of bodies as much as the realization of the amount of time that had passed.

The driver turned his spotlight in her face.

"Easy," she snapped, shielding her eyes from the light.

"It's all right, Jim. She's with the Task Force," a disembodied voice within the car assured the driver.

"Sorry, miss," Jim offered earnestly. "Most of 'em are gone, and the rest are canvassing the neighborhood. You want to wait inside until they get back?"

Max looked over the roof of the black and white until she located Forbes' car. "You see that car over there?" Two voices quickly confirmed that they did. "When the driver gets back tell him to wait. I'm going to stretch my legs. I won't be long."

Chang had perked up considerably at Max's appearance, but when she turned and walked away he slumped back into the seat, filling out the warm contours he'd been pressing into it for the past two hours. From his vantage point, on the north side of the street just across from the crime scene, he'd had a good view of the action. Cars had come and gone without so much as a sidelong glance in his direction. Diehl had passed by so close Hy could see the blue veins in his nose without Diehl noticing his presence. When he'd seen Duncan and the others fan out through the beachfront homes he had considered joining him, but for some reason he felt it important that he hold his ground. With a grunt, he snuggled deeper into his coat and waited.

Walking along the Strand and listening to the sounds of her boots on the pavement as well as the shrouded tide beyond the sand, Max could easily believe herself stepping back in time. With the exception of several new homes along the route the scenery had changed little in the last ten years. Ten years—had it really been that long? She tried to settle into a little comfortable nostalgia, but the events leading up to this return visit to her old neighborhood refused to be pushed aside by anything so fragile as pleasant memories.

Reaching the pier she paused under a streetlight to pull

a cigarette from the pack. Fishing in her pockets, her gaze drifted up the narrow main street of the downtown business area, Pier Avenue, and she forgot both the cigarette and the search for a light.

Banners fluttered listlessly across the street, their bold lettering announcing an Artist Street Fair on the coming weekend. Filling the center of the street were several small metal booths, trailers and a partially erected Ferris wheel. The ribs of the conveyance stood out in skeletal relief against the fog. Max stared at the thing and realized the Ferris wheel had been in her dream. Turning away from it, she moved quickly back in the direction she had come.

The darkness and the fog that swirled around her now appeared suddenly more sinister. "This is only a coincidence," she thought. "Even if it's not, Chang isn't here. You saw to that. This is not a dream. This is reality." She said the words aloud trying to reassure herself. "There are no dark forms or chessboard patterns where sand should be, like there were in the dream, and sea gulls do not fly at night."

Almost before the words faded from her mind, from a side street a determined jogger lurched out into her path. Max started as the man's dark shape lumbered past and watched as he vanished into the fog. Turning away she lengthened her stride. "No, this is not happening," she shouted, increasing her pace to a lope.

Ahead she could make out the dim glow of the streetlight at 34th. She fixed her concentration on that spot and was about to pick up her pace again when her boot slipped over something uneven, and her ankle twisted painfully. Stumbling, she fell against the retaining wall separating the sand from the concrete. Hanging on to keep from falling she looked down instinctively and immediately regretted it.

There on the pavement, in a childish scrawl, was a hopscotch pattern drawn on a smooth section of blacktop. Several squares had been colored in with white chalk, forming a kind of crude checkerboard pattern.

Max swallowed. Her breathing suddenly labored, she

wheeled around, her gaze directed at the sky. There had been a sea gull in her dream, but sea gulls do not fly at night. Searching the gray fog ceiling, she swung around and around until her balance became faulty and she was forced to lean back against the wall to keep from falling. It was then that she saw it.

Not 20 feet away sat a darkened duplex. On the second floor balcony, moving sporadically in the breeze was a tattered windsock, abandoned by some summer residence. Max staggered across the Strand, coming to a stop directly below the balcony. Staring upward, she could clearly make out the black and white stenciled image that flew silently from the center of the windsock—a sea gull.

Hy sat patiently watching as each of the familiar cars of the Task Force had pulled away from the beach and began the drive back to headquarters until only Duncan's car and the lone black and white remained. When the black and white drove off as well, he felt the need to wait no longer. He could clearly see Forbes pacing beneath the street light. Leaving the car, he walked down the steep, sloping sidewalk toward the beach. Crossing Hermosa Avenue, he frowned as he watched Duncan suddenly wheel around and stare off down the Strand in the direction of the pier. Without conscious thought Chang quickened his pace, reaching for the gun strapped under his arm.

Max ran harder than she could remember having run in a very long time. She could see a figure standing dimly under the streetlight. Straining, she realized it was Forbes. "Duncan, get out of the light! Get out of the light," she screamed waving her arms wildly.

His gaze fixed on Duncan, Chang increased his pace as Forbes began to move out from under the light. Faintly the sound of a woman's voice came to him out of the fog, but it was another sound that pulled his attention away abruptly.

Ahead of him, a dark form moved out of the shadows. Seconds before his eyes could make out the shape he heard a hard metallic click that sounded like a bone breaking in the stillness. His breath caught in his chest as the dark shape moved again, this time into the light. An all too familiar object glinted dully in the shape's outstretched hand.

In the blinking of an eye Chang raised his weapon and screamed, "Forbes! Down!"

The first shot whined off the pavement not six inches to the left of where Max stood. Without a second's thought, she threw herself over the waist-high retaining wall, landing hard in the wet sand.

A series of shots tore through the darkness and then, in less than a few heartbeats, silence held sway once more.

Then the screaming started.

January 31st—12:55 p.m.

THE AIR IN THE TERMINAL WAS COLD.

Max suppressed a shiver, shouldered her bag and moved listlessly toward boarding area 28C. Others moved through the long concourse of Los Angeles International airport but, she neither saw nor heard them. Behind the dark glasses and broad, brimmed hat she managed to cocoon herself from the outside world, but this gave her little protection from the sights and sounds of the past 36 hours repeatedly on view in her mind.

There had been a hushed stillness in the first few seconds after the sounds of gunfire had reverberated away, a stillness when even the tide had held its breath. Soon that stillness was replaced by a shrill high-pitched keening that is like no other sound. Events occurred in kaleidoscope fashion. One minute Max was laying face down in the sand, and the next minute she was cradling the faceless head of Hyiam Chang in her arms, a voice sounding vaguely like her own shrilly calling for a medic. A screaming, crying Duncan Forbes in one breath was cursing the dying Hispanic for killing Chang while damning the man to eternal hell if he dare die himself.

Then others joined her nightmare, jostling her aside, separating her from Forbes and Chang and the dying Hispanic with a wall of flesh and bone, and then they were all gone leaving her alone on the Strand.

Memories of her return to the apartment were dim, but she remembered all too clearly the faces of Diehl, Liebschultz and Helmer as they accepted her resignation.

The waiting area at boarding gate 28C was rapidly filling up. As she stood there surveying the area, a young couple, overburdened with luggage and two small children, surged around her to find seats. Unwilling to join the swell, Max took refuge in the deserted confines of 29C, soothed to have the entire row of seats looking out onto the windswept tarmac to herself.

Gazing out at the runway she centered her attention on a small white sheet of paper that fluttered about the tarmac, hostage to the winds. Concentrating on it, her spine registered a subtle shifting of the seat beneath her.

There was no surprise—only a small whimpering in her soul—as she turned to find the red-rimmed eyes of Duncan Forbes staring into hers. A thick stubble wreathed his chin. His jacket was wrinkled, his tie had vanished and his white shirt bore reddish brown flecks which might have been gravy stains but weren't. They sat there, staring at one another for some time before Duncan broke the silence.

"They're cremating Chang today." His voice had the sound of shallow water running over stones, and she could see traces of tears welling up in the corners of his eyes. "He always wanted it that way. Used to say he couldn't stand the thought of layin' in the ground and gettin' pissed on by squirrels."

Duncan looked away, turning his gaze out to the runway. "You told Merchinson it was going to happen. You made him take Hy off the case. You knew it was going to happen." When he looked back at her, all traces of tears were gone from his eyes. "How did you know?"

Max swallowed hard, willing the lump from her throat.

"Will all passengers with small children or those who need assistance boarding come to the front of the boarding ramp, please?"

Reaching out blindly, Max pulled her luggage into her lap and unsteadily began to stand.

"How did you know?" Duncan demanded a second time.

"I'm so very sorry," she mumbled. Turning away to make good her escape, she found herself brought up short by Duncan's powerful grip locked around her wrist.

"How? How in God's name did you know Chang was gonna' die?"

Max looked at him unable to respond.

"Why didn't you tell Chang or me, huh? Why couldn't you do that much?" Duncan stood, slowly pulling her closer to him until he towered over her. "Tell me that much. Why didn't you tell us?"

Duncan's eyes were bright and hard, and Max could feel the anger building in him like heat in a stoked furnace. "Let go of my arm," she said as calmly as possible.

"No," Duncan growled.

Max tried not to show any of the surprise she felt at his adamant response. "Duncan, don't do this. Let go of my arm. I have a plane to catch."

"No!" Duncan shouted. "No plane! What? You think it's over? Chang's dead and it's over? Well, think again."

Max could feel the eyes of the other passengers drawn to them by Duncan's heated words.

"That dirty little wetback bastard died. He never told us who sent him. He died, and I'm glad he died. I hope he's roasting in hell right now."

"Stop this, Duncan," Max snapped between clenched teeth. With a sharp twist she wrenched free of his hold but succeeded only in gaining a few steps before he was on her again.

"You're not leaving. You're going to find the son-of-a-bitch that sent that little cocksucker . . ."

The rest of his words were blurred as her ears caught the sound of the boarding call.

"All passengers holding first class tickets are asked to board at this time."

A panicky tremor began in the pit of her stomach. Struggling vainly, Max managed to drag Duncan a few steps closer to the boarding area before he brought her up short.

Clamping a firm hold on her upper arm he began steering her out into the concourse. "Let go of me! Damnit, Forbes, I'm sorry about Chang, but I can't help."

Forbes shook her, roughly pulling her along beside him. "Think again, lady. I don't know how you knew they were going to kill Chang, but you're sure as hell gonna' help me get the bastards."

Max was about to speak when she saw the rapid approach of two airport cops. Before Forbes could stop her, she called out to them to help. Everyone tried to talk at once, but with the aid of one of the officers Max managed to free herself of Duncan's grip. Shutting her mind to everything else she spun around and sprinted into the boarding area. Through the windows she could see the nose of the plane easing back from the ramp. A boarding agent tried to block her path, but Max pushed past her.

When the two officers took hold of her arms she was almost unaware of them having done so until they steered her back into the terminal. Looking over her shoulder she saw a look of victory on Duncan's stern face. That look brought her back to life. Max knew she would be hard-pressed to break free of the pair, so anything she did was more of a spiteful nature than a constructive one. By the time their strange quartet reached Forbes' car parked at the curb she took a certain perverse pleasure out of knowing both of the young patrolmen would be nursing bruised shins, swollen toes and numerous contusions thanks to their encounter.

When Forbes, helping them, handcuffed her to the back seat she made up her mind he would not get off so lightly, grief-stricken or not.

The car lurched out into traffic, throwing her against the front seat. "You crazy bastard," Max snarled under her breath while pulling herself back into the seat. Straining to regain some morsel of composure, she urged calmly, "This is no solution. You don't understand. I can't help you. If I could, I would. I hurt, too, but you don't understand. I can't help you. I'm not sure I can even help . . ."

"Shut up!" Duncan growled.

"Fuck you!" Max snarled with equal venom, her anger taking the fore.

Duncan took the curve leaving the airport 20 miles an hour faster than any sane man would have. A small glimmer of amusement flickered in his eyes as Max slid off the seat and onto the floor again.

Forbes raced away from the airport, touching the brake only when the possibility of killing some innocent bystander seemed inevitable. Careening along the roadways bounding the south end of L.A.X., he drove into the beach parking lot entrance, slid past the wildly gesturing attendant and roared down into the lot, finally coming to a stop at the far end in an area normally reserved for the summertime crush of campers.

Jamming the gear shift level into neutral he ripped the keys from the ignition, slid out from under the steering wheel and climbed out of the car. Max watched him like a caged animal, suspicious of his every move, but when she saw him lock the car door, turn and walk away toward the beach she began to shout.

Max searched the surrounding area for a possible rescuer and, finding none, set about rescuing herself. She pulled at the handcuffs, used the heels of her boots on the restraining bolt that held her chained to the seat, cursed, strained, screamed and in the end was forced to face defeat. Silently she cursed Forbes, his parents and all of his ancestors. Laying her cheek against the cool vinyl of the seat, she began to feel the throbbing of her injured thumb.

Some time later Max heard the key in the door and sat up, ready, wary, certain she would again face the wild-. eyed madman who had kidnapped and imprisoned her—but she was mistaken.

Without a word and almost without looking at her he got into the car and unlocked the handcuffs. She watched him closely as he did so. All color seemed drained from his face, an ashen grayness enhancing the dark shadows under his eyes. Letting the handcuffs drop to the floor, he turned slowly toward the windshield.

Max slumped back into the seat, content to simply sit and rub at her swollen wrists for the moment. The spell was broken. Duncan's fury appeared spent, and the relief she experienced at this realization quickly vanished as the pain in her thumb found a twin in a headache building between her eyes.

Without so much as a glance in Duncan's direction she climbed out of the car. Lighting a cigarette she stood there, like Forbes, looking out at the water. As she watched the gray swells, pressures and tensions of the past days seemed to fade into the background. She found herself standing outside it all, looking at the situation as an objective third party rather than one of the injured. She felt a gnawing twinge of guilt as she placed herself in Duncan's position, realizing what she would be capable of in such a situation, and despite his treatment of her she wanted very deeply to ease his pain. But with this desire came the real and certain knowledge of her own part in Chang's death. She had broken the rules, and an innocent had paid the price, a fact that would haunt her for a very long time to come.

Rounding the car she looked down at Forbes then opened the door. Squatting down on her heels, she watched him for a moment longer then reached out, laying her hand on his.

"Duncan," she said quietly, feeling the lump forming in her throat again, "believe me when I tell you that I really cared about Hy. I tried to alter fate to protect . . ." Her words broke off as Forbes turned his face to hers.

His eyes glistening, he opened his mouth as if to speak but a broken sob was the only sound he made. Then, in that strange, tearless despair that only men seem capable of, he began to cry. His shoulders shook and great wracking sobs escaped his throat. Max whimpered and tried not to cry but failed. Pushing her way onto the seat beside him she put her arms around his shoulders. At first he sat ramrod straight unable to relinquish his stubborn hold on masculine mores, but slowly his posture softened as Max pulled him to her.

Several fashionable joggers pranced past on the bike path which ran along the front of the parking lot. A shiny new Winnebago from Illinois parked less than 200 feet away from their car, and three loud surfers raced toward the fitful waves less than a foot from their open door without so much as a curious glance inside. In paradise, pain is a spectator sport only to be witnessed from the safety of the six o'clock news.

February 1st—2:30 p.m.

THE DOORBELL RANG.

"Can you hold that thought for a minute? There's somebody at the door."

"No, I can't. I've been holding it since last night, and I'm bored with it," Riley McCall said.

"Think how I feel about it," Max muttered, crossing up out of the living room and into the foyer.

After a quick check through the security peephole, Max announced, "It's Forbes."

"The copper? How bleedin' grand," Riley muttered.

"How'd it go?" Max smiled while opening the door, but one look at Duncan's face gave her more than a sufficient answer.

Stepping inside he shrugged. "I got some good news and some bad."

"How wonderfully original," Riley grumbled.

"Will you shut up a minute?" Max snapped, cradling the phone against her shoulder. Following Duncan into the living room she waited until he flopped onto the couch then said, "Let me guess. The bad news is Diehl doesn't want me back on the case. I told you I should have gone direct to Merchinson. Maybe it's not too—"

"Will you put away the crystal ball and let me tell it?" Duncan said flatly.

"Well, get on with it you great silly . . ."

"Da!" Max barked into the phone. "If you don't be still, I'm going to hang up."

"You hang up, and I'll come over there and put you on the next plane outa here myself."

"Please," she whined. Looking sharply to Duncan she gestured for him to continue.

"Well, you're right about Diehl not wanting you back. And you can forget about Merchinson. He's in the hospital on sick leave."

"What happened to him?"

"Gall bladder."

"Wonderful. Who took his place?"

"For the time being D.A. Jacobson is stepping in."

"Jacobson? I don't think I met him."

"Don't bother. You think you had problems with Diehl? Compared to Blackjack Jacobson, Diehl is a stroll in the park. Besides that's not the bad news."

Max sighed and ran her free hand back over her hair. "If that's your idea of the good news, should I be seated for the rest?"

"Suit yourself." Duncan shrugged sullenly.

"Don't sit, pack!" Riley shouted in her ear.

"One more word and I hang up. Let me have it, Forbes."

Duncan sighed loudly, burrowing deeper into the couch. "Seems Diehl took offense at my position on the issue."

"You called him an asshole."

"Not in so many words. Anyway he's decided he can do without my services as well for awhile."

"You're off the case, too?" Max frowned.

"Sort of a three week vacation—without pay."

"So where does that leave us?"

"On a plane home?" Riley ventured.

Before Duncan could offer any opinion on that score Max waved him off, crossed into the kitchen and disappeared. Several minutes later she returned, placing the receiver of the portable phone back on its base. She smiled quickly at Forbes then sat down across from him.

"All right, now where exactly—"

"Who was that on the phone?" Forbes asked quietly, changing the subject, not quite ready to take it up again.

Max studied him for a moment. She wanted to further scrutinize their standing with the department, but it was obvious Duncan did not. Perhaps for now, that was for the best.

"My maiden aunt—an obsessive worrier."

"Your line of work must give her a lot of practice," Duncan said listlessly.

A tender silence stretched between the pair as Duncan worried the crease in his slacks with a broken fingernail while Max watched.

"Look, you feel like some coffee? I just put on a fresh pot."

"Yeah, that would be nice."

Max moved to get the coffee only to find Duncan suddenly on her heels.

"That's O.K. I'll bring it into the living room."

"If it's all the same to you, could we have it in the kitchen?" he asked, tagging along behind her.

"Yeah, I guess so. Why?"

"That living room reminds me of Terminal Annex. High ceilings do that to me."

"Oh. How do you feel about space travel?"

"Huh?"

"Never mind."

An hour later, after tap dancing around the subject as long as humanly possible, snugly ensconced in the most conservative room in the apartment, the den, the pair were beginning to lay out the parameters of their task.

". . . no problem. Heep'll make sure I get reports from his section. He keeps me up on anything he hears, and what I miss I tag down from Laurie at records. Course we can forget about being on the crime scene."

"I think my dance card is full on that score, thank you very much," Max replied drily.

"So much for my end. What about you?"

"This morning, in between rounds two and three with Auntie, I managed to get a hold of Dr. Osprey at Oxy. We had a rather productive talk. She wasn't much help on Westeridge since she's strictly a part of the scholastic community. Seems the politics of the field were too fast a track for her tastes, but she's aces when it comes to the study of Meso-American cultures. The Mayans are of particular interest to her."

Duncan gave a squinty smile, his equivalent of a wind-up gesture.

"It appears the study of those cultures is far from a defined science. Thinking on the subject changes almost every day. Written records from that period are almost nonexistent, thanks to the efforts of certain Spanish priests around the time of the Conquistadors, but there are a few constants. One of those is the Chac Mool. Duncan, they don't even know what the damn things are. They don't know for sure who created them. They think the Toltecs did and then the later races just copied the art form, but they're not really sure. Everybody's got a different idea on the subject but nothing to back up their theories. I asked her about the Peten Chac Mool, and you know what she said? Until the big ugly bastard turned up everybody was convinced it was nothing more than a myth. There's about forty stories concerning its origin. She's gonna run down some sources for me. One of us will have to go out there and pick the material up when she calls."

"Fine. I'll be more than happy to do that, but what has the big one to do with us?"

"It's a crucial ingredient in these murders. Exactly what part of the final quotient it plays I'm not quite certain of—yet. One thing I'm bloody well certain about though is those little copies we found at each of the murder sites were used by the murderer as some kind of homing beacon."

"Can you prove that?"

"Somehow, if I have to. In the meantime I want to get a list of the Golden Circle members."

"I don't know how you're going to manage that one. When the Task Force asked for one Westeridge put up a real fuss. Said there were too many very important people on that list to allow it to lay around so that just anyone could get hold of it. We wound up interviewing them in a group at the museum."

"Isn't that rather unusual?"

"There are a lot of things unusual about this lot but with the kind of money and clout we're looking at you can buy a lot of privacy."

Max considered the proposition for a moment, then brightened. "No problem. I think I can find us a copy of the list."

"How?"

"That reminds me," Max said, ignoring the question though she had heard it plainly, "could I borrow your car for a couple of hours?"

"No," Duncan said quickly.

Max seemed stunned by the refusal. "I'm quite a good driver, you know. Those cops in the hospital the other day said . . ."

"Never mind the references. I believe you, but the answer is still no. You want to go somewhere, fine. I'll take you."

"Oh, that's too much trouble. I couldn't ask you to."

"You didn't. I'm offering."

"You're too kind, but I couldn't."

"I'm not, and the answer's still no. The way I figure i
we're a team now, and I'm not going to lose anothe
partner."

Max studied him for a moment then stood up. "Yo
win this time, but I'm telling you right now it won't work
a second time so don't think about an encore." Max
retrieved her jacket from the hall closet then paused
Looking Forbes up and down she shook her head
"When we get where we're going, try not to look like a
cop. Could you do that for me?"

"What's the matter? Your friend doesn't like cops?"

"It's an allergy, and one look at you and he's gonna
break out in a rash."

The door to Riley's private office slammed with sufficient force to loosen several dusty antiques from thei
hooks on the wall and to cause nearly all of the early
diners to stare.

Max looked back at the curious patrons with a sheep-
ish expression. At a corner booth, near the front door,
she could see Forbes still absorbed in alternating angry
glares between Conna and Sean McCall who were keeping him from becoming further involved. Max ground
her teeth. Forbes was going to let her hear about this
later—she could count on it—but first things first.

Facing the office door she tried the doorknob and
found it locked. It figures, she thought, no sense on
things getting easy now. "Da?" she called pleasantly.
"Da? Open the door, Da. I want to explain."

"Piss off!!!"

A small ripple of titters raced around the room and
one exclamation of shock. Max smiled weakly at the
elderly matron with the shocked expression and mumbled, "Sorry."

Max leaned closer to the door this time and said
through clenched teeth, "Open this goddamned door
and stop acting like a child, you old coot!"

"Shit," Max yelped as from the other side something
heavy bounced loudly off the door and clattered to the
floor.

"You rat-brained, pig-eyed Mick," Max shouted, clobbering the door with her fist.

"If you wouldn't mind."

"Huh?" Max started swinging around.

Ruth Elizabeth held out a key. "Before you two run off what's left of the dinner rush."

Max's face colored. "Sorry. It's just he's such a pig-headed . . ."

"That's between him and you. If it's all the same, thank you very much, would you be doing your fightin' on the other side a the door, and quietly, if you please."

Ruth Elizabeth turned and walked off, indicating either the question had been rhetorical or she wasn't interested in any answer Max considered giving. Either way it was additional kindling on the fire. Jamming the key into the lock, Max turned the latch and pushed the door open.

From behind his desk Riley shouted, "Who the bleedin' hell let you in here?"

Max slammed the door behind her. "Sit down and shut up. I want to talk to you."

"Well, I don't want to talk to you. In fact," he growled, standing abruptly and marching around the desk, "I don't even want you in my pub. Get out and take the crusher with ya." He crossed the room toward her under a full head of steam. "Come on, get out." When Max didn't appear to be moving in the direction he indicated, Riley reached out to assist her departure.

At least that was his intention.

Instead of backing away from his approach Max stepped into it, grabbed onto his outstretched arm and twisted his little finger in a direction nature had never intended. The look of utter shock on his face only began to dim when she increased the pressure on it, driving all thoughts, save those of quick and passive obedience, from his mind.

"This week, so far, someone loosened the wheel on my car, hoping to spread my guts all over the Golden State Freeway, and when that didn't work they tried ventilating my brain with a high caliber handgun. I've been kidnapped under the noses of three hundred odd witnesses, manhandled by everything in pants and handcuffed in the back of a car driven by a madman. So right now is not a good time for anybody to think about increasing my score of physical abuse for the week."

"You're breaking my finger," Riley whimpered, genuine tears in his eyes.

"Not yet, but if you're not a very good boy I most certainly will. Do you understand me?"

"Yes," he whined, "I understand, I understand." In a firmer voice he grumbled, "I'm in pain, not deaf, you silly—"

Max pressed a little harder. "Now, now," she cautioned. Steering Riley where she wanted him she cautioned, "I'm going to give your finger back, but if you even look like you're about to start any goofiness I'm going to get irrational."

"All right, all right, only bleedin' well do it."

Max released her grip and stepped to the opposite side of the desk with casual but quick movements. She watched him vainly trying to rub life back into his numb finger. Pulling a chair up to the desk, she sat down.

"The refreshing news in all this mayhem is that nobody new has had a go at me, a trend I doubt we'll see continued for much longer."

Riley gnawed on a ragged thumbnail for a moment then asked, "And there's nothing I can say to change your mind? You're bound to stay and see this thing done?"

"I owe it to Chang."

Riley nodded. "I think you're daft."

"You always did." Max grinned.

"Which means I might as well hang about and see to it you don't get into any trouble."

"You always have, which is why I came here tonight. I want you to see what you can do about getting ahold of the contributions list for the White—"

"Ah ha!" Riley barked, clapping his hands together. "How would you like to have a complete list of all the

White's contributors, including those taffy noses in the Golden Circle Society as well as a list of all the museum's acquisitions purchased with those funds. How would that little item do ya?"

Max smiled, completely puzzled. "I'd love it. Who's the psychie here anyway?"

"Ta, ain't nothing." Digging into his desk he pulled out a large manila envelope and pulled from it a thick pile of computer print-outs. Handing them across to her he grinned. "And that's not all."

Max studied him for a moment then thumbed quickly through the pages. "Addresses, phone numbers, social security numbers, dates and amounts of contribution . . ." Max looked at Riley. "What are you doing with this?"

"Incorrigibly nosey." ·

"How did you manage this bit of sleight of hand when the Task Force boys drew a blank?"

"Slid right under the red tape," he purred. Seeing Max's skeptical expression he added quickly, "Nothing so mysterious about it. If you've got a computer today, a little know-how and a lot of patience, you can get about anything."

"Who's the wiz?" Max asked casually, turning back to the list. Riley ignored the question. Max squinted down at one set of figures then leaned closer as if to confirm what her eyes were seeing. "Bloody 'ell," she muttered. Looking up to Riley she shook her head. "Senior citizens freezing to death on the streets of New York and these folks spending this kind of money on a clay pot. Something's faintly out of kilter in the world."

"Well, adjust your horizontal hold, love, 'cause the best is yet to come."

Closing the file Max turned her attention to him. "What else?"

"You remember our little discussion last time."

"Clearly."

"Well, I've been digging." He smiled, folding his arms across his chest and leaning back in his chair. "Interested in what I've uncovered?"

"Get on with it. You're becoming unbearable." She smiled.

"Right. Now as you recall my little tale ended with young Malcom inheriting the whole kit and caboodle, right?"

"Right."

"Not right."

"What?"

"Seems that since old man White outlived his daughter, he decided to hang on to the museum for as long as possible. In fact when he knew he was dying he decided to stretch the point and added a codicil to his will, making certain the White would be controlled by a board of directors elected on a yearly basis by the members."

"But Malcom still had the Westeridge money, right?"

"Right. Which he tried to use to buy his way onto the board and failed. Seemed too many people remembered Senior Westeridge and didn't care to have Junior around taking over where Dad left off. So Malcom decided on another route. He announced a dig, to be headed up by himself, in the jungles of Central Mexico. The basis of this expedition was an extremely questionable paper published in the mid-thirties by Poppa Westeridge which most scholars of the time claim was not only ludicrous but stolen from a much earlier work. This put a cloud over the dig along with the inexperience of its young director, and because of this no accredited archaeologist applied for membership. There was even some difficulty getting the proper permits from the local government. Yet despite all this Malcom pressed on. Within a short time the dig disintegrated. When Malcom finally returned home he brought with him a considerable number of artifacts, presenting them as the results of his expedition.

"When he attempted to gain recognition for his alleged discoveries it was learned that not only were several of the smaller pieces known to have been stolen from the National Museum of Mexico, but the rest were nothing more than extremely well-made forgeries. Westeridge was ruined in the eyes of the archaeological community and the museum as well.

"After several months of seclusion Malcom returned to the White and persuaded them to allow him to resume his old job. Two years later, with the death of the museum's director the board of directors had every intention of closing the facility due to low revenues and lack of public interest, but thanks to a healthy grant from the Westeridge Foundation the museum was not closed. Within the next two years, with the continuing financial support of the foundation, guess who became director?"

"Malcom Westeridge. But how?"

Riley held up his hand. "Listen and learn. In 1968 Malcom, under the guiding wing of Mr. and Mrs. Michael Charles Worthington, formed the Golden Circle Society. With the Worthington name and the Westeridge financial resources the museum began slowly and with great care to acquire stunning pieces to bolster their sagging Meso-American collections. Soon the museum had abandoned all of its other collections to concentrate solely on pre-Columbian artifacts. Today they are generally considered to be the third largest holder of pre-Columbian artifacts in the world."

"But why would the board of directors accept Malcom when White himself went to such lengths to keep the Westeridge name out?"

"New money, new members. Time and cash heals all wounds."

"Wonderful. I see what Dr. Osprey meant by fast tide."

"There is one other thing you might find amusing."

Max frowned. "Like?"

"Remember my preposterous scenario?"

"About the two Malcoms?" Riley nodded, smiling. "I never said it was preposterous," Max said, "just lacking proof."

Slowly and with great showmanship Riley reached

into his desk once more. This time he pulled out a single sheet of paper. Pushing it across the desk to her he sat back and waited.

It was a photocopy of an old and faded academic record from a South Pasadena elementary school. The name referred to a nine-year-old boy born in Mexico in 1940. His name was Manuel Renaldo Ortega. At the bottom of the file was attached a class picture of the youth.

Max looked up slowly.

"See anything familiar?"

Max looked back to the photograph. Even considering the age of the print, the quality of the photocopy and the boy's age, there could be little doubt. It was Malcom Westeridge.

"That's your boy, isn't it?" Riley asked, already knowing the answer. "And unless you've gone completely daft you've got to have at least a very nasty suspicion that our little friend there is at the bottom of your recent spate of accidents, right?"

"Another gift of the computer?"

"Actually I did the legwork," Riley chirped. "Thirty years ago the city transferred all paper records to microfilm—tax records, birth and death certificates, trial records. The Board of Education got into the act a few years later. When everybody went to computers, most records just got automatically copied and stored. It's all there. All you gotta know is where and what to look for."

"But there must be thousands of Ortegas in Pasadena."

"Attending school in Pasadena in the 1940's? Think again."

Max looked down at the photocopy. "Looks like we may be dealing with a very nasty piece of work here."

"Exactly." Riley reached into his desk one last time and pulled out a large, flat, black 9mm automatic. Sliding it across the desk, he smiled. "May I suggest you take up with this little fellow."

Max looked from the photocopy to Riley and then

down at the gun. Picking it up she checked the load, slipped it into the waistband of her Levi's at the small of her spine and settled back once more.

"All right, let's run this over from the top one more time just to polish off the rough edges."

February 2nd—4:15 p.m.

A PALE, BLUISH GRAY PALL, NOT UNLIKE THE ONE FOUND filling the San Gabriel Valley on a hot August day, drifted on the air currents over the computer. Adding to that pall, Max lit another cigarette, oblivious to the one burning away in the ashtray. With a wavering concentration, she stared at the small green-lit screen still suffering the aftereffects of a late night.

After soothing Duncan's ruffled feathers the pair had spent several hours discussing, dissecting and reassembling the information Riley's covert investigation had uncovered. Following Duncan's reluctant exit came a frantic call from Michael Bloom who had just that moment returned from a remote jungle location and gotten the message about the accident. All of this had left Max exhausted, hoarse and bored with the sound of her own voice.

Unable to focus Max pushed back from the computer, rubbing at her tired eyes. Moving aimlessly around the large living room she stretched then dropped into an overstuffed easy chair. Stretching her legs out in front of her she stared at the ceiling, trying desperately to focus her thoughts.

Before she could even get a toehold on a single line of coherent thought a whole basketful of question began emptying itself into the flow. As if that weren't enough, the doorbell rang. Even money said it was Forbes.

"Sanctuary!" Max cried.

If she had any witty remark to greet his arrival it ran away in the face of the vision standing on her doorstep.

"Don't just stand there with your mouth open, grab something," he said, then shoved a heavy plastic shopping bag into her hands. "Put that in the fridge."

Marching past her, his arms still ladened with several newspapers, two large manila envelopes, a large pizza carton and a Dunkin' Donuts box, he headed straight for the living room. Emptying the paper contents of his swag onto the couch, he carefully placed his two cartons onto the coffee table directly on top of Max's papers.

Standing at the top of the stairs, Max continued to stare. At slightly over six foot three and just under 210 pounds, Forbes could easily stand out in a crowd of lesser men, but in his present guise he was almost breathtaking. He was wearing a Vandergellen warm-up suit that was so new the jacket still had creases along the arms and $100 Georgian running shoes that were even newer, judging from the squeaking noises they made when he walked. As if that weren't enough to dazzle the eyes, he was clean-shaven and his hair was neatly combed.

"Don't just stand there. Put the beer in the fridge. I hate warm beer." He frowned with just the smallest hint of embarrassment at her brazen stare.

Shaking off her amazement, Max turned toward the kitchen, muttering under her breath as she went. By the time she returned all the smart remarks were out of her system, and she promised herself she wouldn't think up any new ones.

"What is all this?" she asked, picking up the newspapers.

"Copies of yesterday's newspapers. They're both running stories on the murders to date. I thought maybe you might want to see 'em. In that envelope marked *Times* I've got some clippings on the museum, Westeridge and any on the Golden Circle Society I could find. That other one is copies of Heep's report on that last kid." Pulling down the zipper of his jacket he pulled out several wrinkled photocopies. "And these are copies of some of the on-scene reports from that night. I also got a copy of the file on the shooter."

"And this?" Max said, lifting the lid of the pizza box. "Forget I asked." She quickly lowered it, overwhelmed by the sight of so many cold anchovies. Finding something more to her liking with the donuts she perused the selection. "You have been busy, haven't you?"

"I could have gotten all the reports, but Diehl showed up early today and I had to scoot out the back door."

Max smiled.

"What about you? Any luck on making any sense of all this?"

"Not much, I'm afraid. The closest I've come to working up anything constructive is a headache."

"I was thinking that maybe I could work a trace back on the shooter. You know, check with his landlord or family for known associates, that kind of thing, but according to Helmer the boys have pretty much drawn a blank in that area."

"How so?"

"A drifter nine days out of Chino on a seven year arson rap. No family—in this country anyway. Spent three days at a flop house on Wall Street courtesy of the city, then disappeared. Missed his weekly appointment with his parole officer, but that joker forgot to put him on the skip list so nobody went looking for the sucker. It's a dead end," Forbes said, valiantly trying not to show the depths of his dejection.

"Maybe, maybe not. Somebody knew him. Knew he was out. Knew he'd take on a job like this. He wasn't a zero. Somebody somewhere knew him pretty well."

"But how do we find this somebody?"

"Ah, take a number and get in line. I've got a list with at least forty other question ahead of yours. We'll just add that one to the bottom and work our way down to it."

"All right, where do we start?"

"For starters we need a list of similarities among the Golden Circle members—anything from where they live, other clubs, physical attributes whatever."

"I could go through your friend's print-outs and see if I can find anything there," Duncan said with almost schoolboy zeal.

"You got it. I hate reading those damn print-outs. They make my eyes water. And while you're at that I'll sort through these clippings and see if I turn anything there."

"Let's get to it then."

While Max dumped the clippings out onto her lap Duncan settled onto the floor using the coffee table as a desk. They had both begun their individual tasks when Max said quietly, "Nice outfit."

Duncan looked up, slightly startled by the remark. Turning back to his print-outs, he responded softly, "Thanks."

Afternoon turned into evening and evening into night. They changed positions, argued potential clues, took breaks to stretch, raided the refrigerator and cleaned away the debris before starting anew. Along about ten Max found herself laying on the couch amidst the clutter, staring up at the ceiling and thinking illegal thoughts about Malcom Westeridge. As an enticing idea took form she quickly sat up, eager to share it with Forbes only to find she had no audience.

Duncan had stretched out on the carpet. Head down, his face smashed into the pillow like a Persian cat with a cold nose, he snored softly, sound asleep. Max watched him sleep, a tight smile playing across her lips, then suddenly her eyes narrowed. She had planned on tempting him with the possibility of the two of them paying an unscheduled visit to the Westeridge home. She hadn't quite worked out the details of this proposed visit, but as she watched him sleep a better option came to mind. Why not go on her own?

That would make matters much simpler. She could go out there, look the place over, and if all was quiet perhaps pay Westeridge a more personal visit, hopefully without his knowledge. Failing that, Forbes would be here and she could use her one call for him. Yeah, she thought, that's much ·better.

Questions as to the rhyme or reason for her visit hammered at her enthusiasm, but she pushed them aside.

Crossing quietly to the hall closet she was pulling her coat off the hanger when a more pressing problem presented itself. No transport. The Packard was out of commission for the duration, and she hadn't taken the time to find a rental car. But with her native deviousness she quickly solved that small hang-up.

Picking through the debris of their work area she could find no trace of Duncan's car keys. She turned to his warm-up jacket laying across the back of the sofa. It only took a moment to know that source was barren, leaving only one possibility. Briefly studying her approach, she knelt down beside him and tried easing her hand into the pants pocket closest to her. Thanks to his position whatever was inside the pocket was buried beneath him. Gingerly she tried encouraging him to shift his position but nothing, not even cautious tickling, worked. That left only one alternative.

Carefully she wedged her fingers between his hip and the floor. Slowly she began to lift. Suddenly he shifted, but instead of raising up on that side he rolled over and trapped her hands beneath him.

"Get off," she yelled.

Duncan looked up groggily. "Uhhh, what?"

"Get off my hands, you great . . ."

Duncan lurched onto all fours. "What the hell were you doing?" he grumbled, sitting down heavily as she pulled away her hands.

Messaging her sore digits she countered quickly. "I lost a clipping. I thought you might be lying on it."

It was difficult to tell if he was frowning or simply still groggy. Slowly gaining his feet, sleep still thick in his eyes, he brushed off his pants. Looking around, he said evenly, "I don't see anything, do you?"

The question was rhetorical. Standing, Max shrugged and turned to the pile of papers on the couch. "It's got to be here somewhere."

"Tell me what it was and maybe I can help you find it."

Max sighed loudly. "Look, you're tired. Why don't we call this off?"

"Nonsense. I'm just getting my second wind."

Wonderful, Max thought.

"Look, why don't you make us a pot of coffee and we'll have another go at this stuff?"

For the briefest of moments she considered arguing the point, but in the end, unwilling to face another defeat, she retreated. "Sure, why not?"

In the kitchen, as the coffeemaker gurgled through the brewing cycle, Max tore a slip of notepaper off the pad and made the simple notation, "Rent Car—Urgent!"

February 3rd—11:35 a.m.

LITTLE RITA RAMOS WAS A HAPPY, OUTGOING CHILD. AT NEAR-ly five she had an admirable grasp of English, knew the alphabet and could count up to 50. She liked orange sherbet, her Robotron dolls and fuzzy cute animals, but she didn't like the zoo. The animals smelled funny and they made strange noises that frightened her and the fences were so high that she couldn't see over most of them and today Linda Sherman, her favorite adult from the agency, was spending all her time with dumb old Richard Mathews who was only good for wetting his pants and crying all the time. All things considered, this was not one of Rita's better days.

The other 11 children from St. Teresa's Home for Orphaned and Abused Children didn't appear to be suffering from the same afflictions as Rita. They chattered and ran from exhibit to exhibit despite the protests of their guides and stuffed their little bellies with as many hot dogs and cokes as they could hold while carefully saving just enough room for the promised ice cream on the ride home.

Arriving at the elephant habitat, the other children squirmed their way to the front of the other viewers there while Rita, like that old camel, suffered her last straw. She watched with pouting belligerence as Linda, with Richard Mathews in tow, split off from the group and headed back down the path toward the rest rooms. Watching the pair until they were out of sight she kicked at an invisible target and scuffed her way to the outskirts of the group. There, clearly showing her boredom and indifference to the dumb old elephants, she hung on the bars, stared into the shrubbery and sighed a lot.

She was pressing her face between the bars when something dark flickered at the corner of her vision. Turning her head, ever so slightly, she could see the movement of a long dark skirt. She watched the material move in the breeze for several minutes until her curiosity made her look up. Squinting against the sunlight she could just make out an adult shape. Shading her eyes she saw the face of an old woman, brown, wrinkled and round.

"Hi," Rita said smiling shyly.

The woman smiled and brushed Rita's long dark hair with a pudgy brown hand. Rita smiled back.

When Linda Sherman returned and looked over her brood she did a quick nose count. "Where's Rita?" she asked aloud. "Rita? . . . Rita?" she called, searching the immediate area. When she got no response to her calls, she left the children in the care of Steven, her teenage aide, and rushed back down the path toward the elephant pens.

Rita crouched down and dragged her feet trying to slow the woman's progress but she lacked the weight to make the action work. She tried prying the woman's fingers loose of their hold on her wrist but the grip was too tight. Tears welled up in Rita's dark eyes as she looked frantically at the faces of the people they passed, but if any of them noticed her predicament they made no visible move to come to her assistance.

The heavyset woman, with short purposeful strides, was making good speed despite her reluctant burden. Near the entrance to the zoo, she swung the now crying Rita up onto her hip and increased her speed into a wobbly kind of lope.

As she approached the car the driver, a thin dark man with nervous mannerisms and angry black eyes, pushed open the front door, racing the small engine and called to the woman in Spanish.

Linda, now trailing two security guards and a nurse, ran out onto the steps leading down to the parking lot just in time to see a small smoke-belching, orange Toyota roar out of the parking lot. Though she noticed the car at the time it would be another hour before she would learn it was into this vehicle that little Rita had disappeared.

Max stepped into the apartment and bumped the door closed with her hip. Moving quickly into the kitchen, she dropped her packages onto the island counter and plopped down onto one of the tall stools drawn up in front of it. After a minute or two spent in heavy breathing she pulled off her jacket, after unloading the pockets, and dropped it onto the stool as she stood up.

It had been a very busy morning. Up before eight, she'd secured a rental car by nine. Before noon she'd done sufficient grocery shopping to tide herself and the rapacious Forbes over for the remainder of the week, stopped at the Banana Republic to pick up a few items of specialized clothing not generally carried by the average department store, then roused a belligerent Riley McCall out of bed to garner his particular expertise on a matter of some importance.

With the groceries put away, a fresh pot of coffee brewing and Riley's secret weapon stored safely in a handy spot in case of emergency, Max settled down on the sofa to relax, but before she could even swing her feet up onto the coffee table the doorbell rang.

"Where were you this morning? I tried to call you twice."

Max flickered a glance in the direction of the answering machine and noticed the flashing red light for the first time. "I went over to the mall to do some shopping. Just got back a few minutes ago. Something important?" Max asked.

"No, I just wanted to pass the time of day. Of course it was important."

"Well? I'm here now, so let's hear it."

Duncan perched on the arm of the couch, his gaze trained on her as he spoke. "Remember last night we talked about those statue things?"

Max frowned. "What statue things?"

"Those little ones like that big thing at the White. The ones you thought might be some kind of . . ."

"Yeah, what about them?"

"Well, I got to thinking about 'em. So I paid a little visit to Victor Stein, Dawson Gillis' houseguest."

"And?"

"According to the sticker on the bottom it was made by Skylark Studios in San Jose, California."

"Very nice."

"I figure we give them a call and maybe find out how many of the little suckers they made."

"To what end?"

"What do ya mean?"

"All right, we call and find out that, let's say, there were twelve of them made. And then suppose we sit down and start phoning each of the Golden Circle members. 'Excuse me, sir or madame, but we're taking a survey. Would you by any chance have a replica of the Peten Chac Mool in your home at this time?' Assuming anyone will tell us anything other than piss off, then what?"

Duncan snapped, "Well, I don't see you coming up with anything."

Max bit back a smile. "Now you know how I've felt for the past ten days."

"You rotten little . . ."

Turning toward the kitchen Max asked, "You want some coffee?"

"No," Duncan snapped petulantly then quickly reversed himself. "Yeah."

Setting out two cups and saucers she continued, "Actually your discovery isn't a total loss."

"Oh yeah?"

"What I'd really be interested in knowing is how the replicas were made."

"What's that got to do with anything?"

"Could be a lot. If we assume someone within the museum is using the replicas as a kind of homing device then we have to agree that he or she is too smart to just give them to the intended victims."

"Why?"

"Remember the samples I took from the replicas? Well, each one of them showed traces of at least two common elements, then the remainders varied with each site. One had silk fibers, another wool and leather."

"O.K, so what does that mean?"

"Simply put, he's using the replica as a beacon, but in order to draw the spirit to the right victim he has to give it the scent of that person, in a manner of speaking."

"Kind of like a bloodhound."

"Exactly."

"So how does what the statues are made out of fit in?"

"It's a lot like doing a problem in chemistry."

"I was rotten at chemistry," Duncan remarked casually, taking a sip of his coffee.

"Weren't we all? And one of the biggest problems was we didn't follow directions. We'd leave something out or put too much of something else in. Well, in ritual magic, which is what we're discussing here, it's exactly the same. There are instructions that must be followed to the letter. Screw up just one small part of any equation and blowing up the schoolhouse is the least you can expect. So far he's doing everything by the numbers, and unless I miss my guess that will include something unusual involved in the construction of the replicas."

"Wouldn't that indicate that these guys at Skylark are in on it, too?" Duncan asked following Max back into the living room.

"Not necessarily. I have a sneaking hunch the clay

these replicas are made of is our key. I'd be willing to bet it didn't come from Skylark's usual supplier."

"And if it didn't, we find out where they got it and we're onto their trail."

"Precisely." Max smiled.

"You want to call or shall I?"

"It's your lead, be my guest."

Max watched Duncan over the rim of her coffee cup as he pounced on the phone. She wasn't fooled for a minute by his seemingly easy acceptance of her occult theories. He was doing a credible job of hiding it, but Max could read the signals as clearly as if they were stenciled in red across his forehead. But she wouldn't call him on it because along with that knowledge came the clear and certain understanding of Duncan Forbes' not so ulterior motive. Frustrated by the loss of his partner and inability to apprehend his killers, some part of him believed, like a drowning man clinging to a life raft, she would lead him to the man behind the killer. He didn't know how this would happen, but in the meantime he accepted any quest that would fill the waiting hours and keep him close to her. It wasn't the best of working relationships, but it was better than most.

"You are some piece of work, Duncan Forbes. You sure there's not a little con man in you somewhere?" Max purred as he hung up the receiver.

Forbes smiled crookedly, despite an effort not to. "You want to hear this?" She gestured for him to continue. "It was a small order, but they specialize in that sort of thing. A total of sixty-five pieces were contracted on the eleventh of November by Westeridge himself."

Max nodded. "And the clay?"

"A special order shipped in from Los Angeles."

"Rats," Max grumbled. "That shoots that theory all to hell."

"Not really."

"Oh?"

"Seems there wasn't quite enough to finish the job."

"Oh, really."

"Really." He smiled, enjoying this immensely. "Seems

they had to get an additional shipment from the original source, someplace in San Andres, Belize. That ring any bells?"

Max frowned. "Well, Belize certainly does. And I'd be willing to bet that this San Andres is within spitting distance of the Peten site."

"Hey, would any of that stuff Dr. Osprey sent over for you have a map in it?"

"It might, if it were here, which it isn't."

"But it is. I picked it up this morning."

"Well, where is it?"

"In the car."

"Well, do you want to bring it up or should I go down there and read it?"

"You got a smart mouth, you know that? I hate smart-mouthed broads," he muttered, adding other less flattering opinions regarding women in general and Max in particular as he went to retrieve the materials in question. He was still grumbling when he returned. "You know I didn't have to drive all the way over to Eagle Rock to pick this crap up. I had better things I could have done."

"Did I mention how nice it was of you to pick these up for me?" Max smiled broadly.

"No, you didn't," he announced flatly.

"All right. That was very nice of you to pick up my books for me. Now can I have the goddamned things?"

"Sure." He grinned, dropping the lot into her lap.

Max muttered something under her breath, but Duncan chose to ignore it. For awhile he watched over her shoulder but soon grew bored with that. "I'm hungry. Got anything in the fridge?"

"Yeah, sure. Help yourself," Max said distractedly.

When he returned to the living room, balancing a plate with two ungainly ham sandwiches in one hand and a second cup of coffee in the other, he took up his usual place across the coffee table from her. He watched her for awhile longer as he ate, then pulling one of the abandoned books to him began to browse through its contents concentrating chiefly on the pictures.

Nearly an hour later Max pushed aside the books she had been searching and rubbed her eyes, weary from the small print. Duncan looked up expectantly.

"Find something?"

"Found nothing. If there is a San Andres in Belize it is so small it's not on any of the maps we've got."

"Is it important?"

"It could be. I'm just not sure right now, and there are too many other questions ahead of that one for me to be able to tell."

"Will any of these books help with those questions?"

"Maybe, maybe not. Won't know till I look, will I?"

"Can I help?"

"Yeah, maybe you can." Carefully selecting the tome with the dullest potential she handed it across to him with a yellow legal pad and pen, hoping to bore him enough so he'd leave. "Scan through and make notations on any reference to the Chac Mools and any religious ceremony having to do with human sacrifice." Max rattled off a list of items for his search, so many that Duncan began making notes about the things he was suppose to be making notes on.

When she was certain he was fully involved she picked up Dr. Osprey's paper and settled back, convinced that within a short period of time Forbes would be begging for release.

But like all best laid plans, Max shortly found hers sliding neatly down the drain. Not only did Forbes not complain about the dullness of his pursuit, but he actually seemed to be enjoying himself. He finished off the first book in surprisingly quick time and had started on a second. Around four o'clock, Max thought her perseverance had finally paid off when Duncan opted for a break. Moving around the living room, he rubbed at his back, sore from leaning over his studies. She was about to suggest they call it a day and start fresh tomorrow when he switched on the TV to catch the early news.

It wasn't the lead, but sandwiched in between the sports and weather came a report of a child missing from an outing at the zoo. There was a brief interview with a harried-looking young woman who had been charged with the care of the children and then a description of the child.

". . . she is four and a half years-old, approximately three feet tall, weighs about forty-eight pounds with long black hair and dark eyes. When last seen she was wearing a light green T-shirt and dark green skirt . . ."

"You listening to this?"

"Little girl missing from the zoo," Max said casually without even looking up from her work.

"Yeah, but doesn't that description sound like the two little girls we found?"

Max sighed and looked up. "I suppose."

"Well?"

"Well what?" she snapped irritably.

"You think this could have something to do with the Butcher crimes?"

"It's possible. Now what are you doing?"

"I'm gonna see what the boys downtown have to say about this," he responded, already dialing the phone.

"Wonderful," Max grumbled. It wasn't that she didn't see the possibility of a connection. She was as suspicious as the next guy, but she had other fish to fry and Duncan was getting in the way.

When Duncan got off the phone he had one of those I-told-you-so grins. "They're pretty certain it was a snatch. That report was an early one. Since then they've got witnesses who claim to have seen a little girl fitting this description being carried away by a fat Mexican broad. With luck they should have a composite by sometime tomorrow."

"Isn't that a little longer than that sort of thing usually takes?"

"Yeah, well, seems most of the eyewitnesses are about two days shy of a one way visit to Forest Lawn and they're havin' trouble keepin 'em awake long enough to get everybody to agree on the description."

"Wonderful," Max muttered, stifling a giggle. Returning to the Osprey paper, having found a passage that interested her, Max believed their discussion had ended but Duncan didn't quite see things that way.

"If it is some of the Butcher's thugs who got that kid, according to your theory wouldn't that mean he's getting ready to strike again?"

"Possibly," Max muttered.

"And if that's what's happening, wouldn't it also mean that their next victim would be somebody in that area? Close to the zoo, I mean."

Finding herself reading the same sentence for the third time Max looked up and frowned. "What did you say?"

Duncan dutifully repeated himself.

"No, it wouldn't."

"But you said . . ."

"What I said was the sacrifice must take place within a prescribed distance of the intended victim. The reason we found the children's bodies in the same general area as the Golden Circle victims I believe is simply a matter of laziness on the part of the killers."

"Give me a break," he moaned. "Laziness?"

Max ground her teeth. Explaining matters of this nature to the average person was, to say the least, difficult. With Forbes you suddenly knew what the first human being who tries to explain Catholicism to a Martian was going to feel like. But in all honesty that wasn't the whole problem. She had a nasty feeling Duncan's thoughts on the child's kidnapping might be on the money, and that only made the urgency of her visit to the Westeridge compound all the more pressing.

"You want a beer?"

"Sure, but don't think that gets you off the hook."

"Not for a minute," Max called over her shoulder, already heading for the kitchen.

Quickly retrieving the beer, she removed the small bottle Riley had prepared from its hiding place. Forcing herself not to hesitate she uncapped the bottle and emptied a portion of its contents into the beer bottle, quickly wiping away the small amount of foam that slipped over its sides. She didn't like the idea of using Riley's concoction despite his assurances the potion was efficient and reasonably harmless, but that couldn't be helped now.

She started out of the kitchen, then stopped and grabbed a Pepsi from the fridge. Max was taking no chance that any nervousness on her part might tip her hand. With them both drinking things would look more natural.

Casually Max placed Duncan's beer on the coffee table and sat down.

"All right, now explain that last remark," Duncan demanded.

"O.K., but do me a favor and sit down and drink your beer while I collect my thoughts." Duncan muttered something under his breath but did as she requested. Satisfied by the first gulps he took, she began. "Now you already understand some of the rules . . ."

"Yeah, there are rules like chemistry. Jeez, you're not going to go through that again, are ya?" Impatiently he took swigs of the loaded beer.

"You want to do this?"

Duncan gestured his surrender and, sliding off the sofa onto the floor, looked at her expectantly.

"When you make a sacrifice you don't just slip into a darkened room and do the thing. Each ceremony has detailed requirements on everything from color, sex and age of the offering to the time of day, the place—even down to the costume of the adept and his acolytes. Since it's obvious our boy's ceremony calls for an extreme service by the attendant spirit, it's a relatively safe bet that an offering will have to be made either with the onset of night, right at sunset, or certain specific hours of the moon."

"Don't you mean phases?"

"I said hour and I meant hour. In ritual magic there are hours for the sun, the moon and the planets. In specific forms of that magic, say, like the Druids—"

"Druids?"

"Yeah, you know the folks people used to think piled those big rocks up in England at Stonehenge."

"Yeah, so what about'em?"

Was that a slight slurring in his speech, or was she hoping again? "In some forms of Druid magic they named the hours of the day after animals they were familiar with and who had some bearing on the type of ceremony conducted at that hour. For example, the hour of the lamb, dawn, was reserved for ceremonies revolving around easing the labor of pregnant women, caring for infants, protection of virgins, etc. While the hour of the raven, midnight, was used for darker deeds, curses, blood rites, some fertility ceremonies, etc. Get the idea?"

Duncan finished peeling the label off his bottle, then setting in down on the floor beside him he said slowly, "And this guy would have a certain time to do his thing, and if he didn't do it at the right time it could screw up the rest of the rite, right?"

"Yeah, that's pretty much it."

"So what time does he have to do this thing?"

"I wouldn't know that yet, would I?"

"Well, how do we find out?"

Max held up the material she had been studying earlier and waved it at him.

"Then we better get back to it, hadn't we?"

"Yes, I suppose we had," Max said slowly. It wasn't her imagination, but he really was beginning to get a bit sloppy. Thank you, Riley, she thought. Now if he nods off in the next 20 minutes and stays out for at least a couple of hours and I get in and out of brother Malcom's digs without getting arrested or shot in the process, this day will not have been a complete waste. For a moment she considered offering a few quick prayers to smooth the way but quickly decided there were too many possible godheads involved, and she lacked the concentration or the patience necessary to sort them all out.

With a furtive glance in Duncan's direction, she scrunched down in the couch and tried to concentrate on the material in front of her.

Duncan frowned. The words on the page were getting fuzzier by the minute. Rubbing his eyes briskly he smiled as the words cleared slightly. Reaching down he made to retrieve his beer, but his fingers suddenly seemed fatter and less cooperative than usual. In his mind he saw the error and tried to correct it, but somehow the message was taking it's time getting to his fingertips. As he watched, the beer bottle wobbled then fell over on it's side, spilling its contents out onto the pale gray carpeting. Looking up to Max a small voice in his head sighed when he saw she was reading and not watching him. Without looking down he walked his fingers over to the bottom of the bottle then slid them along its middle until he got a good hold on it and picked it up, bringing it to his lips as if nothing had happened. Draining what little liquid remained in the bottle he burped contentedly and set it down on the table beside him.

Max looked up at the sound of the bottle hitting the table. Duncan grinned broadly at her. She returned a small, quizzical smile then went back to her reading. Looking down at the wet spot he frowned, noting that the carpet was turning a funny color. Watching Max closely, he squiggled his bottom across the carpet until he sat atop the wet spot, sighed and then looked back at his book, registering no particular surprise to find the words on the page a jumble of fuzzy black lines again.

Duncan laid his head down on the book without realizing he was doing so, and as his eyes began to close he suddenly remembered Max had not explained about the lazy killers. He wanted to bring this to her attention, but suddenly he couldn't remember what it was he wanted to remind her of.

Slowly closing her book and laying it on the couch she watched him for a moment longer. "Duncan? Oh, Duncan?" she called quietly. "This is stupid. Duncan! Yo, Duncan!" She held her breath, and when he did not respond she literally leapt off the couch. One part of her being urged her to move slowly with caution, while the other shouted for her to get on with it before King Kong came to and ate her spleen. Max opted for the later.

Hanover Drive was one of those streets that clung to the foothills of Pasadena above the Rosebowl. There were only six homes situated on the street, each with some form of concealing wall, fence or shrubbery protecting it from the eyes of its nearest neighbor or casual inspection from the curb. Two of the homes featured lighted gates, each bearing plaques that proudly stated the family name but declined to indicate an address. The remainder lacked even this, but thanks to the efforts of some industrious soul, street addresses had been stenciled in white paint on the curb in front of each house.

The Westeridge estate was the last on the block, filling the small cul-de-sac from the edge of the cliff to the face of the mountains. A black iron gate, set in the center of a six foot high, red brick wall, guarded a long white gravel drive that disappeared back into the dark landscaping of the estate. From the street it was impossible to see lights inside or even the front of the house.

Turning around in the cul-de-sac, Max parked the rental halfway between the Westeridge drive and that of their nearest neighbor. It was important that it appear, on casual inspection at least, as if its occupants might be visiting either home. Leaving the key in the ignition and the driver's door closed but not locked, she made as many concessions as possible to a speedy exit if one became necessary. Luckily it was not a well-traveled street and there were no overhead lights, so leaving a car so available for the first handy thief was not quite as risky as it might appear.

Slipping away from the car, she walked back to the Westeridge property, taking advantage of the overgrown hedge of the neighbor. A quick inspection of the gate, considerably newer in construction than the wall itself, proved to her satisfaction that no electronic security devices barred her further progress.

Now it is undeniable, as any ten-year-old boy will tell you, that the gate was a much easier target for scaling, but if her luck suddenly turned sour and Westeridge pulled up, the last thing she wanted was to be spotlighted there like a spider in a web. Moving back down the wall in the direction of her waiting car, she found a place where a large tree grew up on the other side. Though none of its limbs hung over the outside wall it would make an excellent marker to return by and just might make her descent on the other side an easier one. Pulling on a pair of black leather gloves with open fingertips she began examining the wall.

Within a few minutes she had discovered sufficient potential hand and toe holds to begin her assent. After only one or two near disasters, she mounted the top of the wall and sat there concealed from both sides by the lush foliage of the tree. Hanging over the side of the wall she managed a quick survey of the terrain ahead. In the darkness she could just barely make out the impression of a large, rambling hacienda-style house. If there was anyone at home they weren't adding to the electric bill.

Dropping down onto the lawn on the other side, she froze there, silently cursing herself for not checking for the presence of dogs before doing so, but when after a few moments none arrived, she proceeded on.

Moving as cautiously as the darkness and terrain allowed she approached the house at a diagonal, knowing that most people looking for prowlers did so at 90 degree angles. Even in the darkness there was an air of abandonment to the place. The lawn was sparse, showing large sections bare of foliage. Shrubbery, though not overgrown, showed clearly the lack of more than just the most rudimentary of care. The adobe walls of the house displayed signs of broken plaster visible even in the darkness.

Giving no time to so bold a plan as entry by the front door, she picked her way around the side of the house, just barely avoiding the booby trap of an overgrown rockery. The rear of the house suffered from the same lack of attention as the front, perhaps even more so.

Stretching back from the rear of the house was a patio. At another time, three-quarters of this area had been covered by a network of vines supported by a wooden frame and large masonry pillars. The vines, like pieces of the wooden framework, had long since vanished. At the end of the patio two long low steps lead down to a pool area. The only thing that floated in the pool now was several inches of moldering leaves, soaking up the rain water of the past few days.

Crossing the patio, she approached a series of broad glass doors. Heavy curtains closed off the interior but she could see no telltale glimmer of light under their hems. What she did notice, leaning close to the door furthest from the center of the grouping, was the yellowed circles of water damage on the white lining of the drapes. Looking closely at the doors she could see they were just as lacking in care as everything else she had seen.

Removing a thin metal card from one of her many pockets, she carefully inserted it between the doors, sliding it downward until she could feel the resistance of the latch under the edge of the device. Letting go of the card she shifted her hand position until her thumb and forefinger enclosed the top and bottom then squeezed. On the other side of the door a flat metal hook slid out of the card and dropped down over the latch. Switching hand positions once more she simply lifted up on the card and the door swung outward. Max stepped through the drapes, closing the door quietly behind her.

Standing perfectly still she used the time her eyes took adjusting to the even thicker darkness of the house to allow her other senses to move about the room. Ordinary household smells were masked under several layers of harsh cleaning compounds and the distinct odor of age. Faintly her internal ears heard sharp ceramic sounds, the clink of soft metals and something even fainter and more indistinct. Even before her eyes could take in the dim outline of the long heavy wooden table and high-backed chairs she knew this was a dining area and thought it was cleaned with some regularity though it had been considerable time since its last use.

Removing a small penlight, she used its thin bright beam as a guide across the broad floor to avoid the possibility of any embarrassing collisions. Heavy, darkly stained double doors opened onto a long corridor outside the dining room. Almost directly across from these door stood another pair, slightly ajar. Max listened to the house but could not detect the slightest trace of habitation. She considered the second set of doors for a moment longer then crossed the hall and entered the other room.

Tall bookcases lined the walls, but their shelves were bare. A large, old-fashioned desk sat in front of one wall of vacant shelves. A somewhat newer desk chair sat behind it, dwarfed by the immense piece of furniture. Save for these two mismatched pieces, the room was empty. Crossing to the desk she moved the flashlight over its surface. A large leather-bound blotter filled a good portion of the desk surface, and a cheap, black, plastic, ballpoint pen lay in the center of the blotter like some strange form of decoration.

Pulling out the chair, Max sat down, turning immediately to the desk drawers. The three on the left side were empty, save for a thin layer of dust and one extremely industrious spider in the larger lower drawer. On the right side she fared slightly better. In the lowest she found a small collection of crude drawings done in a childish scrawl with crayons. Max examined them, puzzled by their composition as much by the age of the paper. At first she thought they might be remnants from Malcom's childhood, but the paper was crisp and new, little more than a few months old. Returning them to their place, she moved onto the next drawer. Here the eyes of two very old peacock feathers stared out at her. She was about to close the drawer and move onto the last when her hand, almost as if moving by its own volition, snatched out the two feathered eyes and deposited them in a spare pocket. Rather than spend valuable time puzzling out the theft—Max knew she rarely did such things without reason—she moved along. The top drawer held an old cigar box with Spanish printing on it. Inside lay a jumble of broken and new crayons. Closing the box and drawer, she sat back and considered the room in the face of her meager discoveries. It was then it occurred to her she had overlooked the center drawer. She pulled on the handle and met with immediate resistance. Max frowned. Why lock a desk that was obviously only the plaything of a child? Using a thin metal pick she worked at the lock, surprised by it obstinacy. Just as she was about to try another approach, she heard the telltale metal click. She pulled the drawer open eagerly, expecting to unearth a treasure, and instead got a nose full of dust. Frustrated by the silliness of locking an empty drawer, Max probed its depths, even going so far as to pull it out and search the underside, knowing full well that envelopes filled with secrets taped to the bottom of such drawers were the providence of detective stories and spy movies.

With slightly dampened spirits she returned everything to its proper place and abandoned the room. Whatever secrets it might hold could bloody well wait for another time. Following the corridor outside she came to a broad foyer and stairs leading to the second floor. Facing the foyer, on the same side of the house as the dining room was a long narrow living room visible through a wide archway.

Standing in that archway she moved the beam of her flashlight over the contents of the room and was slightly confused by her findings. She expected to find heavy, massive furniture similar to that in the dining room and den. Instead she was greeted by a confusing assortment of newer furnishings. It was almost as if someone, in a slightly demented state, had run amuck with a Sears catalogue. And if the eccentric decorator's misplaced sense of style wasn't bad enough, the color combinations were enough to make one feel faintly airsick.

On the other side of the living room the corridor began again, only to end abruptly with a small powder room and across the hall another room with closed doors. She almost abandoned this room, wanting to get to the second floor, but one of her small itches urged her to give it a go.

And just by opening these doors she solved one mystery and opened another. The room was the smallest of the three she had seen thus far but with three times the furnishings. Here was the furnishings she had expected to find in the living room. They were jammed against the walls, stacked one piece atop another, covered, uncovered, damaged, whole. Filling one corner behind the doors sat a huge old grand piano. It was here that most of the books from the library had been piled. A river of decaying magazines spilled off its side onto several thick rugs rolled up and tied with rope under the piano. A fringed shade, minus its lamp, was crushed against the wall by a spill of heavy leather-bound books. In the opposite corner stood the stately skeleton of a concert harp, its center strings torn away by a large heavy candelabra thrust through its middle. The obvious wanton destruction of so beautiful a piece set off a jarring cord in her mind, and the vibrating of that cord loosed another mystery. If these pieces brought out such animosity in their owners, why not just get rid of them? By keeping them in this manner it was almost as if they were being punished for the memories they inspired, and if that were so, what kind of mind punished inanimate objects?

Max backed out of the room and moved purposefully to the staircase. This was another piece to add to the growing jigsaw puzzle her impressions of this house and its owners were forming.

The second floor faced off an open balcony overlooking the foyer below. Against the west wall were the doors to four bedrooms and a fairly large bathroom with old fashioned fixtures, no doubt dating from the time of the construction of the house. Each of the bedrooms, likewise, had furnishings that appeared to be somewhat new, and each was freshly cleaned as if waiting for guests, though no signs of recent use could be found.

At the far end of the floor, filling the north wall, were the doors to a master suite complete with dressing room, private bathroom and a small sitting area, but unlike anywhere else in the house, Max could feel the presence of recent life.

The suite had been remodeled sometime within the past few years. Here the kind of money that can buy good taste but does not necessarily possess it was in evidence. Without turning on any lights Max could not get a full picture of her surroundings, but she could sense what it must look like and that picture was not unlike something one might find on the pages of *Architectural Digest*. This was his room. You didn't need to be a psychic to detect the thick residue of his after-shave permeating everything from the linens to the wall paper.

Max cleared all previous knowledge of the man from her mind and began a thorough examination of the room. No closet space, wardrobe, bedside table or sock drawer escaped her perusal. Moving into the bathroom she ran her hands over his toilet articles, pausing long enough to collect a clump of hair from his brush and from the waste bin several scraps of bloodied tissue paper, remnants from his morning shave, and two large white fingernails. These treasures she sealed in an envelope and tucked it away for possible future use.

Out in the bedroom once more she sat down on a padded chest at the foot of the bed. Opening herself to the room she silently recorded the garbled images that pressed themselves upon her. Impressions from the past mixed with those of the present, then faded back into the darkness as those more dominant in nature took center stage. Max tried to bring the conflicting images into clearer focus but each time they somehow evaded her, all but one remaining constantly unfocused and indistinct. Beyond each of the flickering images there moved a clearly defined darkness similar to a man's shadow in a lighted room. Willing aside the others, she concentrated on the moving shadow.

Like a willful cat, its movements teased her, coming close, in one instant almost within reach, then darting away. Minutes stretched out tediously as she strained to pull the dancing phantom closer to her, willing it to respond to her open touch. A fine patina of sweat spread across her forehead as the strain increased. Then, like a moth coming too close to the light, Max flinched as in that instant the shadow rushed forward, moving through her being like a chill wind, then vanishing into the deeper darkness beyond her reach.

The impression stamped itself on her consciousness with an almost frightening clarity and left confusing symbolism implanted there—a long, dark, stone corridor with sand thick upon the floor. Floating in the center of that corridor was a garish mask crudely fashioned in the style of Mexican masks of the dead. As she approached it danced away, the sound of a child's taunting laughter urging her on. Finally she reached out and snatched it away, expecting to see the childish form, but was instead confronted by the wriggling form of a snake. Max drew in a deep breath and forced herself to mentally catalogue the impressions and store them away. Now was not the time for contemplation. Now was the time for escape.

Quickly making certain she had left no evidence of her visit, she stepped out into the hall. Suddenly she felt, more than heard, a strange, far-off kind of scratching noise not unlike the movement of mice. Nearing the stairway, she heard the sound a second time more clearly. Trapped at the head of the stairs by the sound, she paused, listening. When it did not come again she turned toward the stairs only to be frozen a second time as the sound repeated itself.

Max turned the beam of her small flashlight toward the ceiling for it was definitely from that direction the sounds came. Was there a third floor? The outside of the house gave no indication of there being one. Perhaps an attic? Lowering the light, she shone it across the faces of the doors of the other bedrooms. It was then she discovered the small door jammed into the southernmost corner of the hall.

Max stood there, studying the narrow door held in the beam of her flashlight. Her inner voices were beginning to make their presence known again. One shouted for her to push off, while the softer one proclaimed patiently that no rodents were responsible for the sounds.

She crossed the corridor to the narrow door, aware that the sudden focusing of her senses on the singularity of this new target obliterated all other sights and sounds from her mind. The door sprung open at her touch almost eagerly. A few feet inside that door a flight of tight, narrow stairs led up into the eaves of the house. Shining her light upward she could see a small unfinished landing and another door. With one last glance back over her shoulder she stepped inside the first door and closed it softly behind her in such a fashion that would assure quick egress if necessary.

With the door closed, Max quickly became aware of a subtle change in the air. It was predictable that it should be close and slightly stale, but there was something else—something faint, teasing almost, but somehow familiar in a way she could not name.

She put her foot on the first step and stopped. Playing her light over the stairs, she studied their rough, unfinished surface. The center footpath was well-worn, the dirt driven into the once light-colored wood. If someone was here there was no sense in alerting them to her presence before it became necessary.

Holding the flashlight in her right hand, she dropped down onto all fours and began the climb. It was a ridiculous posture looking not unlike an arthritic spider, but centuries of use by Japanese assassins had given more than ample proof that by distributing the body's weight more widely you were less likely to have your arrival announced by a squeaking step.

At the top of the landing, she stood up and brushed the grit from her palms. In front of her now stood a second door. Its wood was worn and scratched. Dark stains orbited the face plate of the doorknob and keyhole. Max considered the large keyhole hoping it was not locked. She listened for a moment. Hearing nothing she turned the knob and pushed gently.

If smells can be said to have weight and substance then this one's weight was considerable for it stung her nostrils. A faint glimpse of rafters confirmed that the area the door opened onto was in fact an attic.

The walls of the entrance were made up of thousands of newspapers, some tied up with string, others simply tossed on the pile to be crushed by the weight of others placed on top. With the newspapers were magazines, all sizes and varieties of books, small household objects and bits of cloth and whole pieces of clothing. Curiosity overriding all other emotions, Max stepped into the tunnel formed by the debris, knowing with a gnawing certainty she could not leave until she had searched its farthest reaches.

Moving forward as quietly as the uncertain footing would allow, she tried not to allow her attention to be drawn to any one object for too long. Like the screen of an infrared scanner, her mind registered the cold blue impressions of the past, but as she progressed deeper into the attic she began registering impressions of a different, brighter hue. Almost like a warm draft in a cold room she could sense the impression of more recent life. It was to these readings that she kept her attention attuned.

At approximately ten feet into the pathway it began to change. It widened in some places while elsewhere arteries ran off from the central core. At the first few of these offshoots she did little more than shine her light into their congested confines, but coming upon one even broader than the main channel she opted for a quick investigation. As she began to follow this wider corridor she realized that the content of the tunnel walls had changed as well.

Here the walls were formed by rolled rugs, loosely stacked piles of clothing, draperies and linens. At one point Max struck her shin on the protruding runners of an old cane rocker buried under a pile of animal skins. One was easily recognizable as a zebra skin; another might have been that of a bear. The rest were tied in a dingy lace curtain with bits of tails and feet dangling through holes in the material. Turning a sharp corner, Max ran into a heavy wooden screen, covered with figures of a medieval design, its painted surface chipped and peeling. But it was not the screen which drew her attention but what lay beyond it.

A nest was the only word to describe it, a nest put together by a sloppy but very human bird. The base of the nest was made up of a layer of rugs, linens and assorted clothing no less than a foot deep. Over this was thrown what must have been at one time a rather handsome silk comforter, though not one of modern design or construction. Several soiled sheets lay on top of this along with a pillow, the case of which bore a greasy black stain made by a head gone too long without washing. In one corner, a tattered yellow blanket lay in a bundle as if kicked aside by a restless sleeper, and over all there lay the undeniable stench of human urine. There were other objects littering this nest—a broken tea cup, pieces of jewelry, stubs of burnt-out candles perched on a cement brick. Max reminded herself to record it but not dwell on it now. Later. Time was too short.

Moving quickly, an uneasy sickness growing in her stomach, she made her way back to the main path. Shining her light on her watch she felt anxiety fueling her steps as she realized she had been inside the house just over an hour. Too long, much to long. A debate was beginning between her voices when her next steps made that debate moot.

Max's flashlight suddenly revealed an opening broad enough and free enough of refuse to swallow up her light's fragile beam. She paused considering this new opening for a moment, listening and reaching out with her senses. Though she could hear nothing she sensed an increase in the sensation of recent life. Mysteriously though, at the same time, she also registered impressions of life much older than anything she had thus far felt within the house. They were conflicting impressions only serving to dull her already overworked receptors. Recognizing this weakening of her vital instincts she transferred the flashlight to her left hand, sliding her right to the comforting reassurance of Riley's 9mm tucked in the waistband of her jeans. Drawing a deep breath, Max stepped through the opening.

After the confining closeness of the pathway the air outside of it seemed chilly in comparison. Max also noted, with no small relief, the smell of mildew, decay and waste were less prevalent here. As best as she could judge, the area she now stood in was almost the exact halfway point of the attic. The uneven footing of the pathway was once again replaced by the firm comfort of a natural floor. It was during a brief survey of the footing ahead that she discovered, just under a mat of gritty black grime a network of crudely drawn figures standing out in stark relief against the darkened wood. Though the artist's work suffered from a number of handicaps, not the least of which was talent, it became quickly evident the figures were similar to those she had seen in Dr. Osprey's books, nearly copies of the kind of friezes found bordering the walls of Mayan ruins.

The beam of the small flashlight was being eaten up by the broad space she now moved through, and Max wished she had opted for a larger model. But time was growing critical and, prowlers can not afford such luxuries as extended curiosity. Moving constantly forward, the darkness drawn tight around her save for the meager light of her flashlight, she found herself strangely unnerved by the openness of this space, more than once almost eagerly wishing for a return to the confines of the tunnel. It was during one of these moments when the beam of her light bumped into a wooden obstruction, halting her forward progress.

At first glimpse she was convinced it was some kind of wooden riser, but on closer scrutiny it became the end of a very long table, the legs hacked off at the base and then set on the floor.

The once smooth, polished surface of the table still retained some of its former glory, but a trail of grimy footprints marked the center. Like a thin, narrow runway, the table led to another raised area only slight higher than the table itself. Its surface was covered by a large hide similar to a buffalo's, but it was not the moth-eaten hide that drew Max's complete attention, but the low seat resting on top of it.

Carved from a single large stone, the thing was crafted in such a fashion as to take on the appearance of a crouching leopard. It was during a kneeling inspection of the wonderful piece that Max's attention was drawn upward to a tall shadow standing out from the other shadows. Shining the light on the subject, Max gasped as the light disclosed a stone carving well over seven feet tall.

In her haste to examine the piece Max climbed up onto the hide-covered riser, stumbling over the low stool and barking her shin in the process. Pressing close to the tall piece, she ran her hand over the carving, her finger tracing the deep impressions cut in the stone. Though no expert on the subject, she was convinced this was no counterfeit. Impressions of great age leapt into her mind with her first tentative touches. Pieces not unlike this one could be found in museums around the world. It was undeniably Meso-American—a single inhabitant of Mayan ancestry seated upon a crouching leopard, the sign of royalty among those ancient people. As her eyes devoured the ancient relic, a small sound scratched at her consciousness.

It wasn't a particularly threatening sound when Max's busy senses first detected it. In fact, upon first hearing, she quickly categorized it as nothing more than the rustling of dry leaves and put it aside. But a few minutes later that sound of rustling leaves began to change in pitch and intensity. Her light still trained on the carving, Max was listening for it now, and the more she heard the less she liked, and with that dislike came a quick altering of her earlier opinion. Rustling leaves had now turned undeniably into the hissing sounds of moving snakes.

Max opened her mouth, drawing in deep breaths to calm herself. "Get a grip on yourself, goddamn it," she shouted mentally. She began sorting through her current knowledge of reptiles, realizing just how little that was. Listening with every pore of her body while trying to come up with some plan of attack was beginning to take its toll on her when suddenly a new element was added to the equation.

Something was moving behind her. It was moving across the open space between the risers and the rat's nest that filled the remainder of the area, and it wasn't small. As it moved closer the hissing sound grew louder. Shifting the flashlight to her left hand she drew the 9mm out of her waistband and clicked off the safety.

Max spun around, shining the small light across the area directly in front of the riser. Finding nothing, she took a step forward, colliding again with the small stool.

"Shit!" she snapped aloud. Lowering the light momentarily to see her way around the stool, she pushed aside an overwhelming urge to kick the silly thing as far across the room as possible. Lifting the light a shudder raced over her body, causing the light to jump as its beam reflected dully off the head of a small dun-colored serpent. In that instant the light illuminated other reptiles, but there was a bizarre, dreamlike quality about them.

Max steadied the light. The snakes in question, though moving slightly, were suspended, hanging by their tails —but from what? Moving the light up their glistening bodies, Max paused as she discovered the answer. The suspended reptiles' tails ended in a wide thick belt formed of an even larger serpents body. A white skull, no bigger than a child's, formed the buckle of that strange belt. Above the buckle sat three sets of dwarfed human forearms and hands, and above this, where one would logically expect to find the figure's head, sat a carving of two large serpents heads, facing one another, their tongues entwined.

Max stared at the bizarre sight, her curiosity pushing aside earlier feelings of fear. It was a costume, her voices shouted in unison, a dry and aged costume. She was about to move closer to the oddity when a stirring at the thing's side startled her.

It moved, separating itself from the scaly confusion of its brothers with a sinewy grace that was at once magnificently alluring and terrifying. Even in the meager light of Max's small flashlight its small black eyes glittered with menacing beauty. The light wavered slightly as the snake's broad, triangular head moved forward, its long neck stretching towards her at nearly eye level. It may not have been the biggest snake Max had ever seen, but it was way ahead of whatever reptile currently held second place—and unlike its brothers it was very much alive.

Sensing her nervousness, the snake hissed loudly, its tongue raking the air in front of it.

With infinite slowness, Max lifted the 9mm, taking a steady aim on the reptile's blunt snout, her finger snuggling up against the trigger. Max didn't like the thought of killing the big reptile, but one more slither and she would.

If one believes in psychic communication between humans, then it's a far less lengthy stride of imagination to recognize the link between humans and animal life. For the next few minutes, Max and the giant reptile exhibited an excellent example of such communication. Neither of them moving, each stared warily at the other when a third party declared the match a draw.

In the bare bones construction of the attic, sounds from outside easily penetrated the structure. The unmistakable crunch of automobile tires on the gravel driveway below echoed through the attic like muffled .22 shots in the night.

Moving more by instinct than conscious thought, Max threw the flashlight to the left directly at the snake's head, then jumped off the riser, rushing around the towering costumed figure on the right. If the being behind the strange costume moved in her direction she was past it before it could prove a threat. But just to be certain no one, the big reptile in particular, gave chase, Max dashed into the tunnel, pulling whatever her hands could close on into the pathway behind her, once almost burying herself in an avalanche of her own making.

Her mad dash through the warren seemed, to her at least, to take hours. Slamming the door behind her, she took the steps to the second level two at a time, and as she stepped out onto the balcony overlooking the foyer, the sound of a heavy car door closing outside reached her ears. For a panicky moment she considered stepping back inside the doorway leading to the attic but quickly abandoned it, opting instead for another hiding place.

Stepping through the nearest portal, she had no sooner closed that door behind her than the front door below opened. Max pressed her back to the wall the 9mm clenched firmly in her hand. She listened as the new arrival moved across the foyer and ascended the stairs. From the volume of the footsteps and the length of the stride it was easily that of a man or even possibly a very heavy woman wearing workman's boots. But Max knew better than to kid herself. Malcom Westeridge had come home. Max closed her eyes, her breath slowing automatically as the heavy footsteps crossed the landing then began moving away toward the north end of the house. Westeridge was heading for his bedroom.

Max lay her head back against the cold tiles. A shiver raced over her body, but embarrassingly the shiver had nothing to do with fear. Her kidney's were shot. Max suddenly had to urinate—badly; fear often did that to her. Max gritted her teeth and tried to think dry thoughts. As she eased the door open a crack she could hear movement from the direction of the bedroom, but it seemed confined there. The empty hallway beckoned seductively; surely escape was just a quick dash away.

Tucking the gun into her waistband, she inched the door open slowly when a heavy thumping drew her attention, but the sound was coming from a new direction—the attic. Max closed the door, quickly resuming her previous position, a string of curses filling her mind. Her friend in the attic was about to spill the beans.

The door to the attic closed loudly, heavy footsteps crossing the balcony and moving toward the master bedroom. Max eased the door open a crack. Past her line of sight moved a dark figure with long, matted hair. Waiting until the footsteps had vanished, she eased open the door. She listened but could hear nothing which as an omen was a lousy one. Taking a deep breath she muttered, "Fuck it," and stepped out into the hall. Keeping her eyes trained on the half-open door of the master suite, she crossed to the landing and was about to descend when the sound of harsh angry voices drew her attention.

Her heartbeat accelerated and her feet struggled toward the first step, but her brain was pulling her closer to the open door. Max strained, trying to hear the actual words, then groaned as she realized the pair were speaking in Spanish. Outside of a few colorful words and phrases, none of which she'd bet would be found in this particular conversation, her Spanish was nil. Still there was something about this heated conversation that drew her away from the stairs.

Less than 15 feet from the partially open door, Max realized that one of the voices was female. She stood there, easily visible had anyone taken the trouble to look out the door, incapable of movement. Luckily this only lasted a few more seconds.

The male voice, deep, barking and extremely irritated, shouted something. Then there was a striking sound, and something heavy and solid hit the floor and rolled into sight in the open doorway. Max had only a split second's view of the large serpent's head, but it was enough to spur her to movement.

Max leapt onto the banister, sliding down its length, the sound of her pounding heart and the wailing from above filling her ears. With as much quiet as her hasty exit would allow, she raced through the corridor, into the dining room and out through the same door by which she had entered. Here she paused just long enough to make certain the door latch closed before rushing out into the dark grounds.

Max located the marker tree but scrambled up and over the brick wall without its aid. Sliding down the other side, her knees let go when her feet touched the ground, and she sat in the damp grass panting like a winded St. Bernard. Sitting there in the darkness, the chill damp wind feeling refreshingly brisk and clean after the cloying atmosphere of the house, she smiled broadly as a wave of relief swept over her. Her smile turned into a soft throaty laugh that stopped abruptly as her kidneys kicked her bladder across the 40 yard line. Scrambling to her feet, she looked around feverishly then plunged into the overgrown hedge next door.

The drive back to the apartment from Pasadena was accomplished by auto-pilot, her mind occupied by the odd collection of material her nocturnal rambling had acquired. Max pulled into the space once reserved for the Packard, took a few minutes to repair her disheveled appearance, relocated the 9mm to the small of her back then got out of the car. As she bent forward to lock the door she sensed movement behind her, but before she could do more than register the fact, two strong hands clamped onto her shoulders and spun her around.

"I ought to rip your fucking head off at the roots," Forbes snarled, his face a nasty shade of red.

Before she could do more than croak out his name, he lifted her literally off her feet, jerking her away from the car, then slamming her back against it. Shoving his face up to hers he growled, "Who the fuck do you think you are, giving me that shit? You could have killed me, you silly bitch." His spittle flecked her cheek, but her only response registered in her eyes as they rolled up in her head. Suddenly she went slack in his hands. The words choked off in his throat as a frown swallowed up his face. He quickly shifted his hands and tried to catch her but failed, watching with stunned confusion as she slumped to the floor. He reached down to pull her up when a circus train full of brightly colored lights went off in his head.

Max swung both fists up between Duncan's spread legs, driving them hard into his crotch. Even before his eyes had a chance to clear from the first blow, Max shifted her position slightly and, digging her fingers in between his now tightly clamped thighs, took a firm, two-handed grip on his aching testicles.

Duncan shook his head and bellowed like a wounded animal. Through watering eyes he focused on Max's face and swung in her general direction with a blow. Max dodged the blow easily and applied a half centimeters worth of additional pressure to his balls.

"Put that fist down. Now!" Max ordered sharply, her voice booming in Duncan's head like a cannon. "Put it down or I'll rip these fuckers out and give 'em back to you mounted and stuffed."

Forbes wanted to reach down her throat, pull out her tongue and strangle her with it, but all he could do was whimper, weakly feeling certain she had already torn one of the little acorns off his tree.

Max watched him warily as he lowered his hands. Standing slowly, careful not to slack off on her hold, she watched him for a moment longer then said in a quiet even voice, "I've been more than a little patient with your ass. I don't have to be here. I'm off this case, remember." When he didn't respond immediately, she twisted one wrist slightly. Forbes nodded enthusiastically. "Now I want to get one thing very clear with you. I am not your punching bag. No matter what you think of me, my occupation or my friends, I am not here for you to abuse everytime you don't like something about me, this case or life in general. You getting all this?" He nodded quickly. "Good, 'cause there's more. I'm staying because I owe it to Chang. Not for you, not even for myself, but for him. I know his getting killed that way tore a big whole in your guts and you're hurting, but you have taken your pain and frustration out on me for the last time. Believe me, by whatever you hold sacred, if you ever touch me like that again I'll give you back in kind if I have to go out of town to buy somebody big enough to do the job and it takes me a year to find him. Is that straight enough for you?

"Let go of me," Duncan managed between clenched teeth.

"Wrong answer," Max snapped, increasing the pressure ever so slightly.

"Yes, yes, goddamn you to fucking hell," he shouted.

"All right. Now I've got a brain full of very interesting information which I'll share with you if you're interested. If not, say so now and I'll shake you loose and handle this one on my own. You in or out?" She eased back on her grip slightly.

Duncan looked at her, a little of the anger fading from his gaze. "In," he said quietly.

"Fine." She turned and started to walk away still holding fast to his crotch.

"Let go," he yelped, quick-stepping beside her.

She studied him a moment longer then released him.

Something like a groan rushed out of his mouth. Max turned away, crossing the garage with long purposeful strides, Duncan bringing up the rear. As they approached the elevator the door opened and a well-dressed elderly couple stepped into the garage. Forbes groaned as the pair stared at him.

Straightening quickly he stepped into the elevator beside Max. "I'm gonna murder you," he growled under his breath.

"In your dreams," Max responded, smiling broadly as the doors slid closed.

February 4th—10:00 a.m.

IF SNORING COULD BE REGISTERED ON THE RICHTER SCALE, Duncan's would have come in at a 6.2.

Max looked down at him spread across the couch, one leg slung over the coffee table, head thrown back, mouth wide open. There was a momentary urge to drop something in, but after last night's confrontation choking the man to death would not be a good way to start a new day. Instead she opted for dropping the heavy morning edition of *The Times* onto his chest.

Duncan sat bolt upright, the newspaper flying into the air. He blinked his eyes rapidly and looked around as if confused by his surroundings.

"The shower's free, if you're still interested," Max said innocently, slipping into the kitchen without waiting for his answer.

A half hour later, when he returned from his shower wrapped in a borrowed robe, his pillow and blanket had vanished from the couch, his jacket was laying neatly folded over the couch, and Max sat comfortably on the couch engrossed in one of her borrowed books. He sat down across from her.

"Have some coffee," she said indicating a tray on the table with ceramic coffee pot, cups and saucers and a covered dish holding lightly buttered toast. As he poured his first cup, Max held out the neatly folded front page of *The Times*. "Does this face look familiar to you?"

Squinting at the artist's sketch of the suspected kidnapper of little Rita Ramos, he put on his glasses. After a few minutes he lay the paper aside and reached for his coffee. "Right off the top of my head I'd say it reminds me of an old bag lady that used to hang around Hollywood Division. I take it that's not the answer you were hoping for."

Max closed the book she was reading and looked up. "I rather thought it looked a bit like Westeridge's secretary, or is that wishful thinking?"

Duncan looked at the sketch a second time, then around a mouthful of toast said, "It could be. I don't remember her that clearly, but it's possible. The trouble is that these things usually look like a lot of people. One of the artists told me they try to get the sketch as close to the witness' description as they can, but they also tend to make the drawing as general as possible. They claim it's better to get a lot of leads and narrow it down than to make the sketch too close and miss the right guy. It didn't make a lot of sense to me at the time, and it still doesn't."

Max picked up a book from the pile beside her and held it out to him, opened at a strange picture of a figure with a skirt of snakes.

"Nope, don't know this one either," he quipped.

"Wish I could say the same."

"What is this?"

"Coatlicue."

"Coat-who?"

"Coatlicue, the Mayan goddess of fertility. Mother Westeridge's favorite at-home attire," Max said drily, reaching for the coffee pot.

"Is this the thing you ran into in the attic last night?"

"Uh huh."

"Can't say I'd like running into this thing in a dark alley."

Max gave a small laugh. "Once I got over the original shock, big brother reared his ugly head and I damn near wet my pants."

"The big snake you think Westeridge killed?"

"Well, I didn't actually see him do it and I didn't stick around for the autopsy, but unless snakes can grow a new head and some strange man is in the habit of using Westeridges bedroom, I'd say that about sums it up."

"I don't think we could even interest the A.S.P.C.A in a snake murder. It's a shame you didn't get a chance to talk to the old lady." Duncan leaned back on the couch, lighting a cigarette.

"Oh, I could have. Don't know how much good it would have done, me not speaking Spanish," Max said with a slight trace of irritation. Lighting a cigarette she exhaled quickly, adding, "It's not like I went there expecting to find the bloodstained weapon."

"I'm still not real clear on why you did go." Max gave him a long look that clearly said she was tired of explaining her reasons to him. "O.K., so maybe I can understand. Cops do research on their suspects as well but not exactly the way you do." Max arched an eyebrow in his direction. "Well, not with any regularity anyway. What did you get for your trouble?"

"Maybe not as much as I would have liked to, I'll grant you," Max admitted. She had left out the part about the specimens she collected in Westeridge's bathroom. As yet she wasn't fully clear on the reason behind that move herself. "The one thing last night's little trek has done is make me give a whole lot more credence to Riley's pet theory."

"Another grand collection of interesting tidbits that doesn't add up to a hill of beans."

"Maybe, maybe not, but when you put together the pieces of the puzzle we've got so far you begin to get a very clear picture of a man who would not be the least bit squeamish about getting his hands dirty with the kind of killings we're talking about."

"Too bad you can't come up with the frame as well—in a manner of speaking," he quickly added.

"Our biggest problem is we've got a lot of circumstantial evidence. If this were a normal murder you might be able to at least get a D.A. to take a look at it, maybe even spring for a search warrant, but the minute you start talking about murderous spirits and ritual magic, nobody wants to talk to you unless you've got video tape of the murderer in the act and a signed confession."

"It'd be rough even then," Duncan said flatly.

"Thank you so very much."

"You're welcome," he said absent-mindedly.

"With this lot I'd be lucky if they'd believe me if I conjured up the devil right in the middle of the squad room. 'Yes, well, that's all very nice, Miz Morgan, but what's your point?'" she said in a reasonable imitation of Commander Diehl's gruff baritone. "I will never understand why people waste money hiring me on cases like this, then spend all their time making me out to be something that hangs around under a rock until the first full moon."

"You know the key to all this, don't you?" Duncan said, suddenly rejoining the conversation.

"Yeah, move and have the phone taken out."

"Mother."

"She's dead," Max said flatly.

"What? Since when? Why didn't you tell me?"

"You never asked."

"I have to ask a thing like that? When? How?"

"Excuse me if this seems rude, but what has my mother's being dead have to do with anything?"

"Who's talking about your mother?"

"Then whose are we talking about?"

"Westeridge's."

"What's wrong with her?"

"You said she was dead."

"I did not."

"Wait a minute, this is getting silly."

"You're telling me," Max said, running a hand over her forehead. "I think I've got a fever. I hope I'm not coming down with a cold."

"Get dressed," Duncan ordered briskly, jumping up off the couch.

"I don't want to go."

"You don't even know where we're going yet."

"That's because I don't want to go."

"Come on. You can't go see Mother Westeridge dressed like that," he called, dashing up the stairs to the bedroom.

"Good," she shouted, folding her arms over her chest defiantly. "'Cause I don't want to go!"

"I do not want to do this," Max said doggedly 40 minutes later as Duncan turned onto Hanover Drive.

"Nice neighborhood. Old but nice," Duncan said. "That it? Down there on the left?"

"Considering there are no houses on the right," Max muttered under her breath, staring glumly out the passenger window.

"What?"

"Yes."

Duncan turned around at the gate then drove slowly back and parked in the general area Max had parked the night before.

"What're you doing? You're not thinking about going over that fence in broad daylight, are you?"

Duncan looked around. "Don't see anybody watching, do you?"

"This is nuts," she yelped, jumping out of the car.

"And everything you do is so rational." He smiled and walked away from the car.

"Come back here," she called, scrambling out of the car after him. "You can't do this."

"Calm yourself. We'll try the gate first."

"Oh, wonderful. What if little Malcom's home?"

"He'll invite me in, and we'll have a little chat. People do that with the police, you know."

"Yeah, sure. We can chat about things like why he

keeps his mother in the attic and how come he killed her pet snake. May I remind you you're a cop without a case right at this moment."

"He doesn't know that," Duncan purred, leaning on the gate buzzer.

"Bloody wonderful," Max groaned, looking around furtively.

Duncan continued to press the buzzer despite Max's nervous fidgeting for another five minutes then abandoned it, opting for a frontal assault.

"Now we go home, right?" Max asked, knowing better.

"Is that the tree you mentioned last night?" he asked, pointing to the very tree in question.

"No!"

"No, that's not it? I don't see any . . ."

"No, you are not going to drag me into this. No, I am not going over that wall again, and neither are you!"

"What's your problem? It's a quiet neighborhood. Nobody's around to see us."

"What about her?" Max asked happily.

"Who?"

"Her," Max said pointing to a short, heavyset black woman carrying a white plastic garbage sack to the trash cans at the curb of the house next door.

Duncan frowned at the woman just about the same time she spotted them. For several moments both camps eyed one another.

"Wonderful. Got any plan to cover this?"

Before Duncan could respond, Max waved to the woman cheerily and started in her direction. "Hello there, could you help us?"

Duncan stood by the wall watching as Max trotted over to the old woman. He watched as the pair talked then realized his position might be less curious if he were to move back to the car. On route, he strained to catch a bit of the conversation but could not. He did however see Max pull something from the pocket of her jeans and press it into the woman's hand before moving away.

"We've made a mistake, hon," Max called cheerfully. "This house isn't for sale."

Duncan frowned. "Why are you shouting, dear?" he called through clenched teeth.

"Get in the damn car and get us out of here, dear," Max snarled through a smile.

They both continued to smile as he started the car and pulled away from the curb. Max waved at the old woman as they passed.

"You want to tell me what that was all about?"

"Domestics, especially the older variety, are convinced all rich people are nuts, and that little lady has just had ample proof of that."

"Oh yeah? How's that?"

"She just earned herself a fast, tax-free fifty telling two yahoos with more bucks than brains they were at the wrong address."

"Ah."

"Now that you've cost me fifty bucks and alerted everybody in the area to our presence, can we go home?"

At the bottom of the hill Duncan turned away from the freeway, heading into the canyon where the Rose Bowl sat. Even seeing that well-known landmark glide past, Max continued to press her case for them to get the hell out of Pasadena. She was still pleading her case as Duncan turned the car away from the canyon floor and began working his way back toward the hillside upon which Hanover Drive sat. Following a worn stretch of blacktop past a small construction site, he found what could only be described as an abandoned fire road. Max's spirits picked up when he turned the car around but sank immediately when he parked it among the trucks and other cars at the construction site.

"Come on, let's go for a little walk," he said cheerfully, climbing out of the car.

Max was determined to stand her ground and told him so in no uncertain terms, but when she saw him disappearing into the underbrush she abandoned her post and rushed after him.

The winter months or rainy season in Southern California is fabled for turning everything green. What they don't tell you about is the mud. The old fire road hadn't seen any use since the last fire season and now could more aptly be called two muddy ruts with a row of high weeds down the middle. They had followed the ruts for about three-quarters of a mile when Duncan paused to study the terrain.

"Now where, Tonto?" Max grimaced, trying to scrape the mud off her expensive boots.

"Up there," Duncan said, heading into the brush.

"Of course, where bleedin' else?"

They worked their way up the side of the hill and reached the crest in a little over half an hour.

Max was the first over the crest. Any caution she might have passed on to Duncan was lost as he pushed his way through the hedge and into the yard. Muttering under her breath and with more than a few nervous glances around, Max followed along behind.

Catching up to him on the patio she made her opinion of his skills known. "If you ever give any thought to leaving the department for another trade I can think of at least two you can scratch off your list right away. You'd make a lousy—"

"This where you got in last night?" Duncan asked, indicating the long row of glass doors.

"Yes," she said with a weary sigh.

"Well?"

Max hesitated for a moment then, grumbling under her breath, pulled out her tools. Crossing to the door she had used before, she paused in front of him for one last plea for sanity. "I guess it's no use trying to talk you out of this?" He just smiled and tilted his head toward the doors.

"Have you considered the possibility Mommy may have told Malcom about my little visit last night, and he may well be waiting in there right now with a very large gun?"

Duncan sighed theatrically. "If you were Malcom Westeridge how seriously would you take the word of a crazy old woman who lives in the attic with her pet snake and likes to play dress-up?" Max started to protest, but he waved her off. "Don't be silly. You wouldn't, and neither would he. So quit stalling and get on with it."

Max ground her teeth. "Fine, but before you take one step in that house get some of that mud off your shoes."

Duncan looked down at his shoes. With a mental shrug he scuffed his shoes against the patio half-heartedly.

Max quietly opened the door, listening for sounds from within and using all the caution she had exhibited on her previous visit.

"Nice dining room," Duncan remarked, crowding in behind her. "Where's this den you mentioned?"

"Would it be all right with you if we kept our voices down?"

Duncan shrugged. "Whatever. Which way?"

Max lips moved but made no sound as she led the way. Crossing the corridor, she stopped in front of the den doors and turned to tell Duncan when she found him moving off on a course of his own.

"Where are you going?" she cried softly, rushing after him.

"What's in there?" he asked pointing to a doorway at the end of the corridor she hadn't noticed on her earlier trip.

"I don't know," she hissed peevishly.

"Some detective you'd make," he said, pushing open the door and stepping inside.

"A kitchen. So much for that mystery. Now can we move on?" Max grumbled nervously.

"Calm down," he said patronizingly. "I don't know what you're so nervous about."

"Oh nothing, really. Breaking into a house in broad daylight. Mucking about when we should get on with what we came for."

"Just get a grip. Jeez, I don't know what you're so hyper about all of a sudden."

"You don't know? What if little Malcom comes home early, or better yet, what if one of the thousands of people who saw us scale Mount Muddy decide to have the coppers in, then what?"

"No problem."

Max gagged unable to speak.

"I'm a cop. I saw you breaking in and followed to arrest you. Now that was simple, wasn't it? Where's that den?" he asked casually, moving out into the corridor again.

The den held considerably less fascination for Duncan than it had for Max, and he saw nothing all that unusual about the living room and its collection of mismatched furniture. The music room received even less attention, eliciting nothing more than a grunt as he dismissed it without so much as even crossing the threshold.

The second floor, with the notable exception of Malcom's bedroom, impressed Duncan even less. The only thing stirring his interest in the least was Malcom's considerable wardrobe and collection of gold jewelry which Forbes couldn't resist comparing to Liberace's.

Under the pressure of Max's urgings Duncan finally abandoned the bedroom and followed her to the third floor attic.

Max frowned.

"What's wrong?"

"This door wasn't locked last night."

Duncan tried the doorknob himself. "Locked all right."

Max considered a retort but instead pulled out her tools and went to work on the door.

"Jesus fucking Chrysler," Duncan muttered as the door swung open.

Max nodded. "What did I tell you?"

Duncan poked at the debris, displaying more an attitude of disgust than curiosity. Picking his way into the midst of the crumbling pathway, he pulled a large flashlight from his pocket and switched it on. "Back this way?" he asked flashing the light further into the tunnel.

Max nodded, content to allow him to take the lead and leave her the freedom to give their surroundings a closer scrutiny. Near the area where the pathway branched off to the makeshift bedroom, Max found more and more artifacts of Meso-American art among the debris. Stooping, she picked up a small clay figurine. Turning it over in her hands, she studied the piece.

"What's that?"

"Nothing important really, but unless I miss my guess this and some of the other pieces I've seen up here could have come from the Westeridge expeditions."

"Ugly little fucker. Worth anything?"

"If it's real, maybe as much as ten or fifteen grand to the right collector. If not, maybe a hundred dollars tops."

"Must be a fake. Who would leave the real thing laying around in this rats nest?"

Who indeed, Max thought, watching him move further along the pathway. With a final look at the small piece, she set it carefully on top of a pile of old clothing and moved off after him.

The closer they came to the midpoint of the attic, the more clogged the pathway became. Several times Duncan, being taller than Max, stretched his neck to enable him to look over the top of the collected junk. "Not much further now," he said, pulling bundles of old newspapers and magazines out of the pathway and passing them back to her. "In something of a hurry last night, weren't we?" He smiled, dropping a particularly heavy bundle into her outstretched hands.

Kicking his way through the last few feet, Duncan stepped out into the opening and stopped shining his light around. Max stumbled out behind him. "Down at that end," she said, quietly pointing toward the north end of the attic. As his light turned in that direction, she stepped around him and started to move forward.

Duncan grabbed hold of her elbow. "Don't get fiesty," he warned, then pulled her behind him and took the lead.

A thick, heavy figure filled the small stool in front of the massive carving. The lower half of the figure was covered by the stuffed snakeskins forming the skirt Max had shown him in the book. A wide roll of glistening fat curled over the snake belt giving the skull buckle the appearance of peaking out at them. Two large pendulous teats rested on that roll, a large, hammered, gold amulet hanging in the deep valley between them. The woman's

face was puffy and swollen, taking on the appearance of a
bloated full moon. Two dark sockets held black eyes that
glittered in the bright light of Duncan's flash. Like a wax
figure she sat, neither blinking nor shielding her eyes
from the glare. A broad gold tiara sprouting withered
feathers covered the old woman's head.

Max took a step forward.

"Careful," Duncan warned quietly.

"Mrs. Ortega?" Max said quietly. Slowly the old
woman's eyes fixed on her. Shifting tact Max asked,
"Coatlicue, ken?" Something in her dark eyes changed,
and slowly the old woman's posture straightened. Seeing
this Max quickly added, "Coatlicue, ken. Upa cha
cumatz."

The old woman's eyes narrowed, and she cocked her
head in something similar to a listening position.

"That's got her attention. What did ya say?"

"It was either 'Lady Coatlicue, we are friends of the
sky serpent' or 'Do you have any beans, Lady Coatlicue?'
Whichever, I've only got about another five words of
Mayan."

"Wonderful," Duncan groaned. "Let's see if I have any
better luck."

Max stood there for several minutes as Duncan tried
his gutter Spanish with even less luck than she had had.
Eager to have a better look at the area, she turned,
leaving Duncan to his own devices. While poking around
in the debris pushed up against the west wall, she
inadvertently stumbled over a collection of dog-eared
books. She reached out to push them aside, but as her
fingers touched them a wave of sadness washed over her.
When she pulled her hand away the sensation vanished.
Pausing for a moment, she reached out a second time
only to have the experience repeated. Her curiosity
piqued, she pushed the bundle toward an area where
filtered light from a rooftop ventilator seeped in.

Carefully untying the bundle, she picked up the top
book and squinted at its faded cover. The book's title
was printed in Spanish. Flipping open the cover, she
found the faint stamp of a Mexican library imprinted

several times randomly over the title page. Fanning through the pages she found a number of brightly colored pictures of Aztecs in gaudy attire moving through scenes of everyday life. Max thumbed quickly through several of the other books and found similar pictures, all text in Spanish. About to abandon the collection a large book, even more worn than the others, caught her attention near the bottom of the stack.

The spine of the book was broken and several printed pages fell away as she picked it up. The cover was missing, but on the first page she could see the familiar library stamp. She ran her hands over the book and found the sensation of sadness she had gotten from some of the others lacking here. Turning it over the pages fell open to the middle of the book. The pictures were dirty and smudged yet the colors were surprisingly clear.

The double spread was a group of nobles paying homage to a woman sitting on a throne and holding an infant in her lap. Max was unable to translate the inscription below it, but one of the words had been crossed out with thick heavy lines and the name Manuel had been written in a childish scrawl over the top. Max studied the picture for a moment longer, then turned quickly back to the front of the book. On the table of contents she found what she sought—the name Manuel Ortega written in the same wavering letters. In front of the name was the word Ken, meaning Lord or Lady in Mayan.

Clutching the book Max stood quickly, turned toward Duncan's light and paused as something glinted in the air beside him. "Duncan, look out!"

Duncan's reaction to her warning was quick and predictable.

Mrs. Ortega dropped like a quarter ton of bricks and with only slightly less noise.

"She get you?" Max asked him, already looking for wounds.

"A clean miss, thanks to you," he said rubbing the knuckles of his right hand. "Old bitch had a chin like granite," he added, quickly trying to cover the awkwardness of the situation. It wasn't that he'd never hit a woman before—he'd been in too many tight spots in his career to have been spared that experience—but this was his first senior citizen. And if that weren't bad enough, it had to be Max who pulled his fat out of the fire. Well, this whole thing was getting totally out of hand.

"Look at this," Max said bending over the old woman.

"How did you see that thing from over there?" Duncan frowned down at the small dark, obsidian knife he had picked up.

"Didn't really. It was more an impression. Give me your handkerchief." Carefully Max picked up the small, heavy implement. "A knife like this could have been responsible for the wounds we found on the children's chests. Think maybe Jasper could take a squint at it for us?"

"Probably won't even have to twist his arm all that hard," Duncan said, taking the weapon out of her hands. Folding the handkerchief around it he dropped it into his pocket. "I think we've overstayed our welcome, don't you?"

"Yep."

Duncan headed quickly for the pathway. "You know we're gonna have to put our heads together on a good story if this thing turns out to be the murder weapon," he called back over his shoulder.

"Somehow I'm certain we'll be up to the task." She was about to abandon the book when she suddenly remembered the picture. Stumbling into the pathway on Forbes' heels she ripped the pages free and stuffed them into her pocket.

"My money's riding on this little beauty." Duncan grinned around a mouthful of burger and patted his pocket containing the knife.

Hungry from their adventures, they had stopped at a greasy spoon in the Eagle Rock area. Parked in the joint's back lot, their words frequently drowned out by the auto upholstery shop next door, they devoured the grease-ridden, chili-dripping concoctions and speculated on this latest turn of events.

Max swallowed a belch. "These things are awful."

"You don't want yours, pass it over."

"Touch it and die, round eyes," she snarled quickly, taking another bite. Washing it down with a long pull of watery Pepsi she continued where their discussion had left off. "Look, the kid's been an outcast his entire life. To make him feel better Mommie starts telling him about the ancient Mexicans, only she gets her facts mixed up with legends. Somewhere along the line she starts putting him into the stories, and before you know it he begins to believe he's a descendant of kings. Then he comes to America and is introduced to his real father living in what must be to him a castle. Is it any wonder the kid's a little strange by this time?"

"Shit, after seeing that mother of his, who wouldn't be? But just having a screwy mother and an identity crisis won't quite cut it with the D.A."

"Yeah, well things do get a little fuzzy at that point. It's so damn maddening. I know in my guts Westeridge is up to his little pink ears in this, but it always comes down to the same thing. Why? I'm becoming more and more comfortable with the idea that him and that crazy old lady did in the Westeridges. It all fits. There's the money, a touch of vengeance and more than a dash of Shakespearean madness just to round out the picture."

"I wish we could get the bastard on that one," Duncan grumbled, rubbing at a chili stain on his shirt front.

"Wonderful. We haven't got our plates full enough with this one and you want to tackle a forty-five year-old murder as well. Can't you just hear the D.A. now?"

"I'd do it if I thought we could put that bastard away."

"If you want to do that, help me figure out the why in all this."

"Is that really necessary? Couldn't we just tail the bastard and maybe catch him in the act?"

The two stared at one another.

"Think about what you just said," Max began slowly. "Say we get lucky, and by following Westeridge we find out he's the one responsible for snatching the kids. Say we even catch him with a kid and the knife in his hand—then what?"

"We bust the fucker, that's what!"

"The best you can get him for is one count kidnapping, possibly child endangerment. Then what? How do you prove he had anything to do with the rest of it? You can't convict him of the Golden Circle murders because he, or whoever it turns out to be, isn't technically responsible for the murders. You think you can find anyone in the D.A.'s office who can prove a human did what was done to those bodies? Bullshit. Besides, with the money Westeridge has got, he'll have the best legal minds he can buy, and I'll be willing to bet the best your boys will get for their trouble will be guilty by reason of insanity, which any smart pro would have ample evidence of. Five to seven years and he's out to start all over again. Is that what you want?"

Duncan glared out the windshield, his big hands slowly strangling the steering wheel. "Maybe he should just have an accident on the way home some night," he growled quietly.

"Hold on to that thought. If Westeridge does turn out to be the one I'll help you myself," Max said, finishing off her burger.

Duncan studied her, eyes narrowing.

"What? I got chili on my face? Where?"

"You wouldn't, would you?"

Max straightened and brushed the crumbs off her lap. "Could we get out of here now? I think I'm getting light-headed from the grease vapors."

"Answer me," he said sternly.

Max looked at him without a trace of amusement and said evenly, "I have the right to remain silent and will from this point forward, on that subject at least, keep my big mouth shut. Now, drive."

A black Mercedes glided to a stop before the gates of the Westeridge estate. Behind the wheel sat Malcom Westeridge, his thick dark face looking worn and haggard. The sight of his home did little to rejuvenate his spirits. As the gates slid open he shifted restlessly in the seat, wincing as the material of his fashionable shirt caught on the healing scabs dotting his upper chest. Pulling into the driveway he willed away the pain, soothing his feverish mind with the thoughts of the rewards this torture would soon bring him.

The tumblers clicked loudly in the aged lock of the heavy front door. He paused there on the threshold, reluctant to enter. Closing and locking the door behind him he crossed the still foyer, his head dropping forward until his chin nearly touched on his chest. Here, in this place he had called home for nearly 40 years, he displayed an image far different from the one presented to the world outside. Now, only the promise of a lifelong goal within his grasp prevented him from eradicating this last reminder of past failure from the landscape of his new, yet to be born, world.

Reaching the foot of the stairs he paused, turning his thoughts from the future to the present. His head snapped up. A seed of unreasonable irritation grew in his mind as he realized the usual quiet of the old house had been invaded by the muffled tones of tinny music. With quick purposeful strides he moved to the corridor leading to the north wing of the first floor. Here his irritation flared at the sight of light seeping out from under the door to the kitchen.

He burst through the kitchen door, sending it crashing into the wall only to rebound back against him and serve as additional fuel for his anger. Shoving the door a second time, he stepped fully into the kitchen, his black eyes narrowed and glassy. The sight greeting those snarling eyes did little to dampen the fires.

She looked up to him, a stream of milk and cornflakes dribbling over her lower lip and running down her chins.

The sour taste of nausea blossomed on the back of his palate as the smell of the old woman reached his nostrils. Her lips began to move, a gibberish of garbled words and thoughts spilling over her lips along with the last of her dinner, but his ears refused to register those words, his thoughts blinded by the loathing he experienced at the sight of the creature. Any vestige of affection—if indeed there had ever been such an ingredient in his make-up—had long since withered and died, leaving only a black, dry socket that registered only gnawing disgust at his mother.

Crossing slowly to her, he demanded to know why she was in the kitchen, his voice hissing over the brittle, gutter Spanish of his childhood. She stuttered and mumbled, tears welling up in her jaundiced, yellow eyes. Still he pressed on. Why was she in the kitchen? For the briefest of moments something sparked in the old woman's eyes, and she grunted back at him, but the defiance quickly faded as he drew back his hand in preparation of a blow.

His hand still ready to strike, he demanded to know how she had gotten out of the locked attic, warning her not to lie. At first her words were muttered and almost indistinguishable. His irritation boiled over, taking on the form of anger, an anger he took out on the senile old woman. But as more and more of her cryptic tale began to infiltrate that anger, with his repeated and stern questioning, the flames of anger began to take on a coldness.

It was not so much the woman's words. In his lifetime he had heard too many of her tales to be stirred at this late date by what he considered just another of her ramblings. No, it was not the words—this tale of messengers from Quetzalcoatl was only a slight variation of others she'd told in the past—but the opening of a door he himself had locked sharpened his curiosity. He registered the old woman's description of the white-haired woman with ice-colored eyes who had spoken to her in the language of the old ones.

He straightened, turning sharply toward the kitchen door. Without a word, he rushed out into the corridor and up the stairs to the second level. By the time he reached the third floor entrance to the attic, a coat of cold sweat bathed his body. For a moment he stood there, staring into the jumbled darkness of the room beyond, then reaching inside he slid his hand along the wall until his fingertips brushed against the old light switch.

Seemingly oblivious to the debris blocking his way, he dove into the room, fighting his way toward the distant clearing at its northern perimeter. The pathway, nearly obliterated by recent foot traffic, was further erased by his passing. Bursting out into the clearing, he lurched to a halt, his eyes bulging from their sockets. It had been nearly four years since he had last entered the attic, shortly after the old woman had taken up residence there. In the beginning he had often wondered how she spent her days; now the evidence of her occupation stared back at him with cold stone eyes.

Slowly he crossed the floor, his gaze torn between the tall carving and the disgusting display in which it played the central role. Stepping up onto the riser, he looked down at the small stool and something close to affection flitted across his face, but as he bent down and stretched his hand out to it, his nostrils breathed in the scent of filth and decay. He recoiled as if struck a physical blow.

A sound somewhere between a growl of anger and a shriek of pain ripped up out of his lungs as he bent over, snatched up the small stool and lifted it high over his head. Though small in size, the stool was carved from solid rock weighing no less than 200 pounds, but he swung it back over his head and launched it at the center of the statue again and again as if it were a toy.

When he at last returned to the kitchen, his face was a blank, unreadable mask. Only a smattering of dust and several small pinpricks of blood soiling his shirt front gave any evidence of his recent activity. If any sounds of that activity had reached the old woman's ears, she gave no sign of it having done so. Even their earlier confrontation seemed to have vanished into the chasm that served her as a mind. He crossed slowly to the sink and washed his hands, drying them on a towel hanging beside the drain board. Staring out the window at the darkness beyond, he switched off the old radio sitting on the counter. When he spoke he did so without looking at her and in a voice at once soothing and firm, all brittleness gone from his words. Speaking slowly and distinctly so that she could not help but understand his instructions, he told her to go and replace her temple finery with the oldest clothes she possessed, making certain to warn her repeatedly that they must be hers and not those of the goddess.

Looking at him, the orange she had been sucking on still clenched firmly in her hands, she questioned him, wondering why he should want her to do such a thing. Was she not beautiful and pleasing to the eyes of their god in her temple dress?

He turned to her, a warm smile already stamped upon his hard features. Crossing to her, he reached out and touched her hairy cheek, his black eyes trained on her bloated face. Indeed you are, he told her smoothly. It is because you are so that he calls you to his temple. His smile widened in proportion to hers. But you must be willing to sacrifice your old life as a mortal before you may enter his house as a true goddess. He assured her the shedding of her old clothes would serve that purpose.

She pushed back from the table, her feeble mind already busy with preparation. A part of his mind laughed at her easy acceptance of so ridiculous a tale, but then he was only using the tools she had given him. As she scuttled from the room, he warned her to be sure to wear as many of her old clothes as possible to make a more suitable offering. In reality, his mind was already picturing her dressed in several layers of filthy clothing, closely taking on the guise of a bag lady.

In the silence of the old woman's departure, he turned toward the phone, but as his hand touched the receiver he stopped. No, he would make the call from an outside phone. There must never be the slightest trace of his involvement—not that he considered the possibility of detection, not at this late stage of his plans—but caution in small matters were the mark of a great mind, and this small exercise would only serve to hone his skills for his future position.

The Mercedes pulled quietly out of the drive, moving down the street, its lights out. Leaving Hanover Drive,

Malcom switched on the lights and reminded the old woman in the back seat that it was unseemly that she show herself to those they passed. With only a coarse giggle of response, she lay back on the seat. The Mercedes entered the ramp leading onto route 210 and sped up into the foothills of La Canada.

Though traveled by thousands of tourists and natives alike, the entrance to the Angeles Crest Highway was marked only by a wooden sign similar to those found in small neighborhood parks. What few streetlights there were quickly vanished with the homes that fronted the first few turns of the narrow road.

Just below the 9000 foot level of Mt. Wilson, an area crowded with the broadcast towers of every major and several minor radio and television station and one aging observatory, there was a wide turn about. From this vantage point the entire valley floor from the mountains to the sea was visible. A glittering galaxy of shimmering, multicolored lights turned the viewer from a humble spectator looking up at the stars to a god looking down on them. A thin layer of windblown snow covered the graveled area, and the mark of at least a dozen tire tracks could be seen in its blanket. The Mercedes pulled in and drove to within a few feet of its furthest point. Making certain no other cars shared the darkened lookout and none approached up the winding road, Malcom shut off the ignition and turned around to look down on the old woman sprawled across the back seat.

Using his deep voice and the speech he had practiced during the drive, he told her she had reached the last stop before the temple and urged her to offer prayers of thanksgiving for the great honor she was about to receive. It was perhaps an elaborate device. She was, after all, an old woman possessing little strength in comparison to his, but there was a glowing warmth each time he used the power of his own greatness to make the weak bend to his will.

Moving quickly, his gaze ever vigilant for approaching intruders, he helped her from the car, and with a tenderness he had never shown the old woman before he guided her limping progress out to the edge of the precipice. For several moments they stood there together, then he stepped back as she lifted her stubby arms toward the heavens and began to chant the only prayer her toothless mouth could still manage.

Seven small pops erupted on the cold mountain winds, drifting away, lost among the clouds and starlight. Her heavy body dropped to the ground with all the grace of a felled tree. Thrusting the small .22 into the pocket of his topcoat, he squatted down and rolled the body over the edge. Without so much as a backward glance, he turned and walked back toward the car, then suddenly stopped. Pulling the gun from his pocket he returned quickly to the edge and threw it far out into the night.

The Mercedes backed out onto the road and turned slowly back toward the valley below. As he drove, a sense of elation filled his once weary body. The scars along his chest no longer pained him and his vision seemed unnaturally clear and sharp. If any part of his mind was still able to discern the depravity of his deeds, it gave no indication of having done so. Perhaps he was simply beyond the point of considering the murder of his mother a crime.

February 5th—3:10 a.m.

"BLEEDIN' WONDERFUL! DUNCAN FORBES, PRINCE OF fuckin' Darkness," Max grumbled groggily as Duncan entered the apartment. Following along behind him she continued the barrage. "If you have a home of your own why do you insist on constantly invading mine in the middle of the night?" All remaining smart remarks beat a hasty retreat when Duncan dropped onto the couch and she got a good look at the expression on his face.

"Why is it I get the feeling this isn't a social call?"

With a grunt he pulled a rumpled copy of *The Times* early edition out of his breast pocket and tossed it across to her. "They haven't found anything on the kid yet."

She nodded and set the paper aside. "I could have waited another five hours for that bulletin." Duncan opened his mouth to speak, but she held up her hand. "And please don't give me the good news/bad news routine."

He pulled the last cigarette from a crumpled pack and lit it. As he exhaled, the lines of weariness in his face seemed to deepen. "I took the knife to Jasper. He ran the tests himself."

"Good man," Max said, a quiet smile tracing her lips.

"Well, the news ain't so good."

"No blood traces, no . . ."

"Oh, there's blood, all right." Max's face began to light up, but Duncan cautioned, "Don't get crazy just yet. Jasper says the blood is old, real old. It's deep in the . . . I can't remember the word he used, but it's too deep to be traces from recent use."

"He's positive of that?"

"No, not a hundred percent, but that's not what convinced him our knife isn't the murder weapon. He called it a wide disparity in the striation patterns. It's got something to do—"

"Yeah, I know that one. Shit!" Max snarled.

"My sentiments exactly. But like you said, it was too much to hope for anyway. Nothing's gone easy so far, so how can we expect it to start now?" As he leaned forward to flick the ash from his cigarette something in Max's expression triggered a nasty feeling in his stomach. "What?"

Max looked at him and sighed deeply. "I was working on something I found in one of Dr. Osprey's books tonight. It has to do with numbers."

"Numbers?"

"I'm a little groggy so bear with me," she said, rubbing her eyes. "The Mayans, as well as most of the other cultures of that area, had a strong reverence for mathematics. Their system of worship was an extremely complicated one. Not only did their gods have different names for every day of the week, direction they faced or activity they involved themselves in, but certain numbers attached to these gods had deep religious significance as well."

"Like?"

"Like, fifty-two."

"Fifty-two."

"Yeah, fifty-two. They believed all cycles of life moved in fifty-two-year groupings. Thirteen was another, along with nine and four." She paused to stifle a yawn. "What I'm getting at is by using this information, I've formed a kind of pattern to the killings."

"What kind of pattern? You mean like, ah, every thirteen days or something like that?" Duncan asked, edging to the front of his seat.

"Easy . . ."

"Fuck easy. Show me. Show me this pattern."

"Steady. Don't get your knickers in a twist. I may be way out of line on this one."

She could see Duncan visibly trying to control his emotions. "All right, just let me see what you've got. O.K?"

Max resisted his urgings for a few minutes longer then dragged herself off the couch and upstairs to the bedroom. When she returned she was dressed in a deep green sweater, Levi's and thick white wool socks. Clutched in her arms was a collection of books, a couple of yellow legal pads and two half-used packs of cigarettes. Dropping the lot onto the couch, she turned toward the kitchen.

"Hey, where are ya goin'?"

"I'm thirsty. Is it all right with you if I get a Pepsi?"

"No, show me this stuff first. Come on," he demanded.

Reluctantly she climbed over the back of the couch and dropped down. "God, I love it when you're dominant," she said sarcastically.

"Show me," he snapped, thumping one of the yellow pads with a stiffened forefinger.

Max sorted through the material scattered around her, and when she was satisfied with the order she launched into a somewhat drawn-out explanation of her findings. Half an hour later Duncan sat frowning down at a book in his lap, open to an elaborate line drawing of what appeared to be some sort of ancient temple.

Max watched him for a moment then pushed herself up onto the back of the couch. Swinging her legs over she stepped onto the carpet.

"Come back here. We're not through yet."

"I'm getting a Pepsi. I've got a serious case of cotton mouth." Disappearing into the kitchen, her disembodied voice called, "I'm bringing you a beer, so shut up."

When she returned he seized the beer, touched it to his lips then quickly pulled it away, sniffing at the bottle.

"Drink the damned thing. It's safe. Believe me, if I had any of the mickey left I'd use it in mine," she snapped petulantly.

Tipping up the bottle he took one long swallow. Setting the bottle down he wiped his lips on the back of one hand. "I want you to go over this one more time." Max groaned and started to complain. "Only this time cut out all the scenic detours. Boil it down and give me the short version. Think you can do that?"

"I took every number of religious significance I could find mentioned for each culture."

"Why?"

"Because these murders are ritualistic in nature. Can I go on now?" He gestured for her to proceed. "I took those numbers and tried to work them into a pattern, fitting the dates for each of the murders. I was careful not to intermix any of the cultural groups."

"Why?"

Max groaned. "Because that would be cheating," she snapped. "Just trust me when I say it wouldn't be logical. I was having no luck, so I was just laying there having myself a little moan when I ran across that picture."

"This one."

"Right. I was just reading about the size of the damn thing when I found this comment about the grouping of steps leading up to the temple. Starting from the top there was one, then nine more and a break then fifteen, a break, then thirteen, a break, four, a break, and then the numbers, starting with nine, began all over again. I didn't think too much about it at the time. It seemed such an odd collection, but then it said that in all the temples they've uncovered of Mayan design consecrated to Quetzalcoatl this pattern was repeated."

"Who?"

"Quetzalcoatl was one of the supreme deities to the Mayans, and he's appeared in all the others pretty much intact—kind of like a Christ figure. Tall, fair skin and hair with light eyes—that is, when he appears as a man—otherwise he's a feathered serpent." Duncan frowned, and Max shrugged.

"And these numbers formed a pattern for our murders?"

"Almost too well. Look. The first, Worthington, was on the 27th of December. Nine days later was Paxon, January 5th. Five days later, January 9th, Dawson. Thirteen days after that, Mangrove on January 23rd, and four days later, January 27, Caldicott. Nine, fifteen, thirteen, four."

Duncan studied her chart for a long time then asked slowly, "Which leaves us where, according to this?"

"If the pattern starts from the top again that would make it nine days after Caldicott or February 5th."

"Today."

For a long time neither of them spoke. Max watched Duncan, hoping to read something in his face, but the lack of expression registered there was unnerving.

"Look," she began hesitantly, "this could all be so much blowing smoke. It could be a coincidence. A strange one, I'll admit, but one none the less. Unfortunately, the only way to be the least bit sure is to wait and see."

Duncan's head snapped up, his eyes flinty and hard. "Like hell we will."

"Duncan, don't get potty on me now."

"You really want to sit back and wait for another poor sucker to die like the others?"

"At this point I'm not sure there's much else we can do."

"The numbers fit. I'm not sure why they do but they do, and in my book that's the first encouraging news we've had on this case. Now you said something about them having to pick up the kid near where their prospective victim lived."

"No, I didn't. I said they'd have to make the sacrifice near the victim. They could pick the child up anywhere."

"But who's to say they didn't?"

"Nobody, but seeing how we don't know where the other kids were taken from, you might be a bit hard-pressed to prove that point."

"But it is possible," Duncan insisted hotly.

"In a world where carpenters die and get resurrected anything is bloody well possible, but that doesn't mean they did," Max responded with equal ire.

But her anger was lost on Duncan. "Where's that contributors list?"

"I don't know," Max groaned.

"Well, find it!"

"It's there on the table somewhere. Your arms aren't brok . . ." She bit off her words as he pulled the print out from the table's clutter and turned his attention to it. Max glared at him for another moment or two then pulled herself off the couch. Crossing to the windows, she stood there for sometime, staring out into the darkness. Reaching into the pocket of her Levi's, she pulled out the small leather pouch and held it tightly in her right hand.

Fixing her attention on the distant lights of Malibu, she called the cloak of serenity to her. Slowly the lights blurred and a soft gray fog filled her mind. With each passing moment she could feel the tightness of her muscles draining away and the heat of her anger dissipating. Patience, she warned herself mentally. Do not bend facts to meet the frame of your desires. The shape of the sphere is round. The shape of the square is square. The shape of one cannot be forced to conform with the other before it's time without great price. Patience.

After several minutes her vision slowly cleared. A small smile rippled across her mouth. Clutching the leather pouch in both hands she raised it to her lips, kissed it lightly then returned it to her pocket. In the glass she could see Duncan's reflection. As he looked up she turned slowly toward him.

"What?" she asked suspiciously.

"I think I know who the next victim will be."

11:45 a.m.

Max sighed, twisting around on the hard bench, uncrossing her legs then crossing them again. Almost three hours—what could be taking them so long? How long did it exactly take to say piss off? Starting a fresh pack of cigarettes, she noticed the collection of butts at her feet and only became more restive. Surely Duncan's long absence could only mean Diehl and the others weren't buying the theory.

With the lighter halfway to the tip of her cigarette, Max suddenly froze as an even more disturbing thought hammered its way into her mind. What if he's right? Snapping the lighter closed she broke the cigarette in half and tossed it away. Gods, she thought, what if he is? What if all of this has happened according to its own time? It was possible. But if that were true, so why did she feel so nervous? What was causing her to resist the accuracy of this strange solution when someone like Forbes took to it so easily? Chang. The name sprang into her mind with startling clarity. Could he be the root cause of her anxiety? Am I simply resistant because I'm afraid of another mistake, or did his name come to me as a warning that another was about to be made?

Her mind twisted the two-headed question round and round. Her absorption with it was so intense she flinched as if struck at Forbes' light touch.

"Come on, they want to talk to you about the numbers part," Duncan said, a small cloud of concern visible in his eyes. "Are you O.K.? I know you didn't get much sleep last night. You want some coffee or something before you go up there?"

She shook her head, her eyes losing some of their startled look. "What did they say? Do they believe us?"

"Take it easy. They're still listening, and nobody's suggested a shrink or us taking a hike. All things considered, I'd say we're way ahead of the game. Now, you just get in there and sell 'em on the numbers and I think we've got a chance."

"Duncan, look, I'm really having some serious problems."

"Problems? Like what?"

"Like . . . like I'm not sure anymore."

Grabbing her by the elbow he steered her toward a vacant phone booth. With a quick glance at the other inhabitants of the lobby, Duncan snarled through clenched teeth, "Look, don't start that shit when you get up there. I just spent the last three hours convincing a damn tough audience, and this pattern of yours is the strongest part of the theory. You start hemming and hawing now and it all goes down the crapper." Noticing her gaze aimed pointedly at his grip on her elbow, he released her and said in a less strident tone. "Look, I know you've got some reservations about this, but you got to believe me. If we blow this chance it just may mean a free pass for that bastard. If you won't do it for me, then do it for Hy. Lie if you have to, only don't let this chance get away from us. Please."

She'd been prepared to stand up to him when he pushed her, but this new Duncan with his 'please' and 'do it for Hy'—there was no strength in her spirit to fight that. "Give me a rundown on what you told them so far. No sense crossing the same road twice," she said relenting, even now fighting to ignore the fledgling rumblings of her own small voices that warned her not to relinquish her own will in the matter.

Entering the squad room, the noise level dropped to nil, and though she was aware of their stares she averted her gaze from the detectives filling that room, fixing it firmly on the door of the commander's common office.

"Ms. Morgan," Diehl said with restrained politeness, "if you'll have a seat I'd like you to explain this number pattern Forbes has been telling us about."

Copying Diehl's polite manner, Max launched into her explanation without preamble. At her side Duncan constantly added to her words, ever ready with additional embroidery or flourish, but when Liebschuetz asked for confirmation on their manner of selecting the next potential victim Max turned the floor over to Duncan.

As he repeated his logic over and over again for the benefit of the slightly befuddled Liebschuetz, Max began to realize this was where the problem lay.

Duncan's original assumption, unsteady as she still believed it to be, was that the children were not only killed within a certain proximity to the adult victim but taken from areas close-by as well. To this end he had located two members of the Golden Circle society who lived very close to the zoo, here again assuming the girl recently taken from that location was the next sacrificial offering. Both were elderly males. One was a 63-year-old realtor named Raymond Angus living almost on the border line between Hollywood and the Los Feliz area, the location of the Los Angeles Zoo; the other was a 59-year-old antique dealer in Glendale by the name of Gabriel Holt.

Max remembered clearly her misgivings at Duncan's seemingly arbitrary selection of these two men and the heated debate it had inspired. She remembered with equal clarity Duncan's passionate argument for her assistance.

Guilt—of the magnitude she had come to know since Chang's death—was a new and unwelcome experience for her. Though she doubted Duncan realized the true depths of it, he was playing heavily upon this open wound.

She had tempered her capitulation with a proviso. She would aid this conspiracy with the understanding that he would make certain both men would be part of the disclosure, even though he believed Holt to be the potential victim, and that both would be recipients of any protective action, all of which he had agreed to albeit with some additional debate. Now, however, it would appear he had forgotten that agreement, and she, whether out of guilt or fear, had become a silent accomplice to the breaking of the agreement.

As a clincher he was now informing Diehl that the Holt home, allowing for the removal of certain prime pieces of Glendale real estate, was almost within sight of the zoo. Again without so much as a hint at the possibility of a second potential victim, Forbes concentrated his arguments solely on Holt.

Max sat there, guilt and anger fighting over the last few feet of intestinal track left unknotted.

Firmly recognizing the jeopardy she placed this venture in if she made the disclosure of a second possible victim, she chose her words carefully, reentering the conversation at a convenient lull.

With a studied casualness, she led up to the core of her proposal—the inclusion of any other Society member within the area, of which, she believed, a certain Mr. Angus must be counted. With a single-mindedness of purpose, she explained to the commanders her feelings on this addition to the proposal, all the while ignoring the heated gazes and continual interruptions of Forbes. All her attention was focused on Diehl, almost as if by totally concentrating on him, she might will him to her cause.

Diehl considered the surface of the table for several minutes, then removing his glasses and rubbing the bridge of his nose, he said simply, "Ms. Morgan, would you mind having a seat outside?"

A few minutes before one, Duncan came out of the

office and sat down beside her. His smile was all she needed to see, but she did him the courtesy of at least pretending to listen to his words.

"I thought for sure you were going to blow it in there, but Diehl's filled in the chief and he's given us the go-ahead. Diehl's on the phone to the Glendale P.D. right now. They'll take care of Mr. Holt. Keep your fingers crossed, Maxie. This maybe the end of Mr. Malcom Westeridge."

Max started. She had recognized the possibility of her own failure, but she hadn't forseen the possibility of Westeridge's name being raised so prematurely. "You didn't tell them he was who we . . ." Duncan frowned. "Well, did you?"

"No, and keep your voice down."

Max sighed. She had failed to gain the addition of Mr. Angus to protective custody, a matter she would continue to attempt to correct, but at least if it all went sour they wouldn't have staked their entire hand on a single play. She had just begun to reach for her second pack of cigarettes when Diehl's voice called out.

"Forbes? You two wanta get in here?"

Max hoped for a reprieve of some sort but quickly discarded even that slim hope as she found herself explaining the procedure she believed would be used to sacrifice the child, boiling it down to only the simplest of concepts—on or near sundown but no later than moonrise, in a high place, like a high rise apartment or office building—avoiding as much as possible any mention of the magical aspects of the sacrifice.

By four o'clock Mr. Holt had been removed to protective custody in the Long Beach area and a platoon of uniform and plainclothes police had converged on the city of Glendale, each bearing an artist's sketch of the missing child and her alleged kidnapper. At the Holt home several unmarked cars and their occupants tried to make themselves as inconspicuous as possible. Max did feel a certain comfort in the knowledge that both Diehl and the Glendale commander had taken her advice about not posting anyone inside the house. She was more than a little thankful neither of them had pressed too hard as to why.

At 6:30, over an hour after sundown, the search for the little Ramos girl was all but called off. At Task Force headquarters, Max and Duncan received the news shortly after eight. As the night dragged on, Duncan drank coffee, smoked, paced and watched the clock while Max was left alone with her own thoughts.

Just after 2:00 a.m., several of the Task Force officers returned to the squad room, their fellow officers already heading home while they took up a final post to wait out the remainder of the night or until the alert had been called off. There was little in the way of conversation. Duncan and some of the men passed listless small talk, but soon the office returned to the same tight silence that had filled it most of the night.

Max rose and crossed to Duncan at the bank of windows overlooking the parking lot. "Duncan, I'm going to take advantage of that cot in the ladies room. If anything happens you will come—"

"Yeah, sure. Go on, you look like you're about ready to drop."

He watched her cross the squad room, turning back to his solitary post even before the door closed behind her.

Outside in the hallway, Max turned quickly toward the stairs, descending them two at a time. The lobby was nearly deserted and those who waited there had other things on their mind, paying her scant attention as she dashed out the doors. On the street outside she slowed her pace to a more conservative one, unwilling to garner the attention of any of the patrolmen entering or leaving the building.

Her stride lengthened as she distanced herself from the station, pausing long enough at a pay phone to locate Raymond Angus in the white pages. Carrying the page away with her, she searched the street for a cruising cab. Two blocks later she squeezed into the rear seat of one on the heels of its exiting customer. For a brief panic-stricken moment, after giving the driver the Los Feliz address, Max searched her pockets for money. Locating $83 and some change she was relatively certain of being able to afford a one way trip even in the face of inflated prices.

Nearing the house, Max slid three twenties into the cabby's peripheral vision. "Drop me off just on the other side of the house, then give me a blank receipt and you can keep the change. Deal?"

"Lady, for a fifteen dollar tip I'll park in the living room if you want me to," the driver said.

Max smiled quickly and shoved the money into his hand, felt the receipt slide into her palm and stepped out even before the cab had come to a complete stop.

Max walked slowly up to a large tree near the curb in front of the Angus house. In the stillness of the quiet residential street she could hear the sound of the taxi's engine fading into the distance, then only the sound of a light wind in the trees. The house was dark and the curtains drawn. She watched the house for several very long minutes. All right, she thought, you're here. Now what? Providing he's home, assuming he'll listen to anything you have to say, considering you're lucky enough to get him out of the house—then what? All her little voices were hammering at her at once, adding to an already overburdened state of mental confusion she was unaccustomed to.

Shutting out her mental tormentors she straightened up. I have to try, she told them. There were a number of potential options for gaining entry to the house, but she quickly abandoned them, opting instead for the front door for starters.

The button for the doorbell was a small circular disk lighted from within and old-fashioned, like the strong white house it served. Pressing it, she waited patiently. After the fifth ring she began to surrender to the realization that she may have arrived too late.

Pulling open the screen door, she used her fist against the front door. When her knuckles began to smart she abandoned the door and looked for other routes. One side of the house pressed close against its neighbor while the other faced onto a side street. A tall redwood fence blocked that side. Max groaned at the thought of clambering over yet another fence but quickly relaxed, finding the side gate not only unlatched but standing slightly ajar. She stepped inside, confident of finding no prowling canine, otherwise they would have met when she tried to batter down the front door. She smiled mentally at her quick adoption of Duncan's knack for jumping to wobbly assumptions, but as she rounded the back of the house a very strong impression killed her smile.

The tiny backyard was less dark than the sides of the house, thanks to the faint light drifting down from a second story window near the center of the house. Max looked up at the window for several minutes. The light could be some sort of deterrent for potential burglars. The house could be empty which would account for no one answering the door, or the inhabitants could be very sound sleepers. The longer she stood there looking up at that light, the more she realized a third unspoken possibility was the reality of the situation.

The house offered no handy tree or ledge upon which she could climb to reach that window. With a quick search of the small neat garage she located an aged but serviceable ladder.

Leaning the ladder up against the side of the house, she rubbed the sweat from her palms and began to climb.

The lamp that had been visible from the yard below sat on a table directly in front of the window, blocking more than a faint view of the interior, but after one glance through that window Max suddenly lost all interest in seeing further into the room. Directly in front of the lamp, facing into the room, she could see the small terra cotta rendering of the Chac Mool. Only the head and a part of the torso were visible, but she had become too familiar with the thing's shape to confuse it with anything else. Over the parts visible from her somewhat restricted view she could plainly see traces of the fine powdery white ash clinging to its surface.

Laying her forehead against the cold glass Max let the tears well up in her eyes and flood down over her cheeks.

For precisely how long she maintained this precarious position she had no idea. When no more tears remained and her mind had closed the door on the image of the strange reddish-brown thing that could have been an oddly colored, deflated football laying at the foot of the table but wasn't, she climbed slowly back down the ladder.

February 6th—6:45 a.m.

MAX PRESSED HER LAST $20 BILL INTO THE OLD MAN'S WRINkled hand. Standing at the curb, she watched as he steered the aged Chevy pickup out into the predawn traffic. She smiled a small secret smile at the sight of the single fledgling palm tree waving at her from amid the clutter of the old man's tools in the truck bed. Carefully storing away this pleasant moment she walked into the station.

The Task Force squad room was nearly deserted. Linda, the cheerleader cop, was busy behind her desk, but at the sight of Max she quickly rose and approached her.

"He went looking for you right after the call came in," she began, her voice low and breathy. Both she and Max looked to the rear of the room and the silent Forbes, sitting at his desk and toying listlessly with a Styrofoam cup. "He's taking it awfully bad. They tried to get him to go home, but he said he wanted to wait. Kept talking about something he had to say to Diehl. Ms. Morgan, do you think you . . ."

Max nodded. "It's all right."

Linda watched as Max approached Duncan. Though she couldn't understand it, she suddenly wanted to shiver. It was almost as if this strange woman radiated cold. Please God, she prayed silently, don't let her hurt Duncan any more than he's already hurting.

Max stood in front of the desk. Only then did she realize it was not the cup before him which held Duncan's attention but his gold detective's shield.

"You work better on your own, don't ya?" he said quietly, his gaze still trained on the shield. "I used to think I did, until I met Chang. It's not just that I miss him. It's like I can't do anything right without him."

"We should be going now," Max said evenly, refusing to be drawn into the dangerous emotional web Duncan's grief was weaving.

"You were right. You've probably been right all along only, I was too bullheaded to see it." He looked at her for the first time. "You know, I hated your guts from the first second I ever set eyes on you. Hy said it was 'cause we were so much alike, but he didn't have it right. It's because you were better at doin' my job than I'll ever be. I recognize that now. Don't know I hate ya any less, but at least now I know why."

Max leaned forward, resting her hands on the desk and purposely covering the shield with her left hand. "I think it's wonderful you understand why you hate me. A man should understand why he hates. Now that we've said everything on that subject which needs saying, I suggest you get up off your fat ass and come with me because we got things to do."

He smiled grimly. "You got things to do, lady. You, not me."

"Ah, Forbes doesn't want to play anymore. He fucked up and a man died, and now he wants to turn in his badge and call it quits. Is that what you're all about? Explain to me how come it's all right for you to quit and it wasn't all right for me? Excuse me, but weren't you the hardass that told me I had no right to check out? Said how I had to pay my bill and catch this fucker for Hy's sake."

"I never said that," he grumbled almost peevishly.

"Fuck you didn't. You didn't let me run when I wanted to, and now I'm not going to let you. Why don't you save us both an embarrassing scene and get up out of that chair right now?"

He looked at her through narrowed eyes. "Or what?"

"Or I'll reacquaint my right hand with your nuts."

The two glared at one another.

"That was a very funny line. One of my better ones. Go ahead and snicker a little. You'll feel better," Max said, a tight smile straining the corners of her mouth. Leaning even closer she said under her breath, "If you want to sit here until Diehl shows up and hand over your badge, make sure you tell that horse's ass he was right about you all along. Slink out of here with your tail between your legs if you want to. That's up to you, but I've wasted all the time on you I can spare. The pattern is right. Last night proved that. I'm sorry that somebody else had to die to prove it, but I'm not going to crawl up into a ball and have a lifelong moan over it. You want to call it quits, that's your providence, but we've got the scent of the bastard who's responsible for this havoc, and I mean to have him. If you want a piece of him, you can tag along. Otherwise I'm outa here." She straightened up, and with a voice that was as cold as the words she spoke, she added, "By the way, if you ever run into the Duncan Forbes who picked me up at the airport that first night, tell him I said so long and how much Chang and me would have liked to have had him with us now that the really hard part is coming up."

"You cold, fucking bitch," he bellowed. Lurching up out of the chair he growled, "Of all the smart ass, ballbreaking . . ."

Max snatched the forgotten shield off the desk. "Think I'll just hang onto this. You can never tell when another egotistical, chauvinistic, foul-mouthed Duncan Forbes is around the next corner." She dropped the badge into her pocket. As Forbes rounded the desk, a thick stream of colorful epithets embroidering his opinion of her and their precarious quasi-partnership rolled across his lips. Max began backing toward the door. "In fact, I think I see the big dumb flatfoot on the horizon now."

"You think you're pretty cute, don't you?"

Max framed an innocent look and turned it on him. "Me?"

Duncan shook his head. "You're some piece of work, Morgan."

Max grinned, purposely displaying as many teeth as possible.

"But don't get too cocky. That little dog and pony show of yours this morning don't change a thing. It's still my decision, and if I decide to call it quits I will. All you did was buy a little time, that's all." He said, his words not coming out with quite the firm resolve he might have wished for.

"Humph," Max sneered. "You are so full of shit it's a wonder your eyes are still blue."

"Oh, really? And just what makes you such—"

"Hello, hello. What's all this now?" Max interrupted, her voice and posture suddenly tight.

There are a relatively small list of sights left on this planet which will stop a conversation dead. If not holding one of the top three positions on that list, then standing at least a respectable fourth is the sight of police cars drawn around the place in which you reside.

Rolling down his window Duncan called to the nearest bluesuit, "What's up?"

The patrolman looked at him with a broad streak of authoritarian annoyance. "I'm sorry, sir, but you'll have to move along."

"Right," Duncan said, reaching into his breast pocket for his I.D. Max nudged him, his shield in her outstretched hand. With a flicker of annoyance he snatched it from her hand and flashed it in the patrolman's direction.

"We got a B & E assault."

Duncan was about to engage the officer in further conversation when he felt the passenger door open. "Hey, Max!"

Throwing the car into neutral, Duncan jumped out. "Park that thing," he called over his shoulder as he dashed into the building after her.

He caught up to her at the elevator where she was resisting the efforts of two officers trying to keep her out.

"I'm sorry, ma'am, but unless you can show me some identification, I can't let you go in."

"It's all right," Duncan cut in, holding his shield out in front of him like a crucifix in a room full of vampires. "Where's the trouble?"

"It's my apartment. I know it. Make them let me go up," Max snapped.

"Do you know this lady, sir?"

"That's Ms. Maxine Morgan. She's staying here while on assignment as a special advisor to the Butcher Task Force. I'm Detective Sergeant Forbes, also with the Task Force. Is this break-in on the penthouse level?"

"Yes sir. Look, why don't you two go up and talk to robbery?"

"Good thought," Duncan said, prodding Max into the elevator ahead of him.

Duncan looked around at the destruction, and even with his experience, he found it impressive. Whoever was responsible had been very serious about their work. Max stood in the center of the room, wearing the same expression seen on the faces of survivors of a busy Friday night in Lebanon.

"Max?" Duncan said firmly.

Slowly she turned and stared at him for a moment as if readjusting the focus on her vision. "Yeah?" she responded flatly.

"This is Detective Marley from robbery."

She nodded. "What happened here?"

"Well, about 2:15 a.m. somebody tripped the central alarm. It registered on the main console at the doorman's station. The doorman, a Mr. William Stoddard, was about to call it in when according to him he decided to check first. He said you were using the apartment while the owner, Mr. Bloom, was out of town. Stoddard figured maybe you had come in from the garage and just forgotten to remove the alarm before you opened the door. Anyway, he calls up on the house phone and gets no answer, so he comes up, finds the door unlocked and hears somebody moving around inside. He gets as far as the inside hall when somebody attacks him from the rear. Probably came out of the kitchen."

"Is he all right?" Max asked in the same flat voice.

"Sixteen stitches, possible concussion and a fractured rib, but all things considered he'll make it."

Max responded with little more than a nod. Duncan watched her as Marley ran down the standard list of questions. Without exception, she answered in a voice that might well have been a recording. It was evident to him but thankfully not to Marley that only a part of her attention was focused on the immediate problem at hand.

"Just one more question, if you don't mind, Ms. Morgan. Do you have any idea what these people were looking for?"

"No," Max snapped, almost too quickly. Flashing a significant glance in Duncan's direction she added with less vigor, "No idea whatsoever."

Duncan took over the conversation for the second time, the two men heading slowly toward a finish in the prerequisite procedure.

Then, without being too obvious about it, Forbes ushered Marley out of the apartment, promising to be in touch. Returning to the ruined living room, he found Max holding the remains of her small computer in her lap as one might an injured pet.

With a calmness more alarming than any amount of female hysteria, she told him unnecessarily, "They were looking for me. I would say Mr. Westeridge is not pleased with our visit to his home or the fact that his boys blew their earlier attempts."

"You think the old lady told him?"

"I doubt she could be that coherent. How he found out is of little importance now. He knows and is not pleased."

"Marley said they found fingerprints everywhere. He gets a match and we can tie . . ."

Max laughed softly. "You really don't understand yet, do you?"

"What I understand is that if they got in here once they can do it again. The first thing we've got to do is get you out of here. Get a few things together and I'll take you to a hotel or my place, whichever you want."

"Thank you, but no." Her rejection had the ring of finality to it.

"Fine, then I'm staying here with you." Ready for an argument, he found he had no partner for the game.

Max stood, still clinging to her ruined computer. "You can use the couch or the guest room, if anything in there is still standing. Forgive me if I don't help you get settled, but I'm afraid I need to sleep just now. My thinking is getting a bit fuzzy." Her voice had that faraway quality to it again. He watched as she picked her way over the debris and mounted the stairs. Halfway up, she paused and looked down at him. "There's a control for the curtains over there on the wall by the bar. Shut out the light if you like." She continued the climb, disappearing into the loft bedroom.

He listened for a few minutes more then pushed the couch into an upright position. Returning the cushions to their proper place, he sat down, surprised at the depth of his own fatigue. For a brief moment he considered the curtain controls on the far wall but abandoned the thought. The walk would be simply too much effort. Stretching out on his stomach, he folded his arms under his head for a pillow, and almost before his eyes closed he was fast asleep.

Upstairs, Max staggered across the cluttered floor. The bed was beyond use, the two small Japanese mattresses cut to ribbons, their strawlike stuffing scattered about the room. Tilting the remains of the bedframe up against the wall she dropped down into the cleared space. Reaching out, she dragged an undamaged pillow and a nearly whole comforter to her. Pulling the abused computer into her lap she turned it over, running her fingers over the bottom of the instrument. A soft sigh slipped over her lips and her posture relaxed. Gently laying the machine aside she tugged off her boots, dropped back onto the pillow, dragged the end of the comforter over her and fell asleep almost as quickly as Duncan had.

It didn't really sound like a phone, since few today do. Perhaps that was why it took him so long to respond to it. But when the connection was finally made, he staggered off the couch. Glaring groggily around at the debris, he tried to locate the instrument but in the end resorted to a down-on-all-fours-grope through the wreckage before finally meeting with success.

"What!" Duncan snapped, pulling a dismembered leg of the coffee table out from under his rear.

For a moment dead air was his only answer, then a familiar voice stuttered, "Is this 523-787?"

"Heep? Is that you?"

"Yes, it is. Who's this?"

"Forbes, you dimwit. What're you doin' callin' here?"

"Well, I tried calling you at home but you're not there, are you? Is something wrong?"

Forbes glanced around at the wreckage. "No, nothing's wrong."

"Then what are you doing there?"

"It's a long story. Is this a social call or was there something you wanted?"

"Well, I've got copies of the report on the Angus remains whenever you want them. And there are some things I'd like to discuss with Ms. Morgan, if I could."

"Like what. She's a little tied up right now."

"Like the fact that the damage to this body is considerably worse."

"Worse? How the hell could it be worse?"

"You want the details?"

"Thanks, but I'll pass. Look, I'll swing by and pick the report up in the next day or two. In the meantime why don't I have her give you a call?"

Duncan hung up.

"Who was that?"

"Ah, sorry, I was hoping that wouldn't wake you. That was Heep. He just wanted to tell me he's got copies of his reports if we want them. He, ah, wants to talk to you when you get the chance. Something about the body being in worse condition this time. Although I'll be damned if I know how that's possible."

"Remember how I told you these intermediate spirits are a dim lot? Well, in prolonged or more complicated rituals where they're asked to repeat a particular act over and over again they get bored. It must be close to the culmination of this ritual which is, in a way, good for us."

"How?"

"The intermediate spirit is getting progressively harder and harder to handle. Malcom—or whoever is actually performing the ritual—is having to be more careful each time he calls the spirit out. Believe me, they're having a rough time of it, and it's taking a toll. Maybe if we get real lucky they'll screw up and the spirit will turn on them."

Duncan shook his head. "You talk about this thing like it was some kind of trained monkey or something. Does it ever strike you the least bit strange that you're talking about a thing damn few people outside the local funny farm believe in?"

Max dropped down on the couch, folding her legs under her. "Do you believe in a god?"

"You mean like Christ, that sort of thing?"

"Yeah, that kind of thing."

"I guess so. Yeah, but what's that got . . ."

"Ever seen him? Ever had him talk to you? He ever answer any of your prayers or drop a minor miracle your way?"

"Well, it's not . . ."

"You and billions of people believe in a god in some form or other that they've never seen outside an artist's rendering, never gotten a message from or a prayer answered by. Wars have started over differing visions of these gods or simply opposing translations of their word. Every minute of every day somewhere in the world somebody is being injured or killed because their view of an unknown god and his directions differs with somebody else's. And you think I sound strange?"

Duncan grinned tightly. "I know an Anglican minister I'd like to sic you on someday."

Max smiled. Duncan felt the tightness in his shoulders slip away, and he smiled, too. There was something very infectious about her smiles.

"You're a wicked man, Duncan Forbes." Stretching, she took a deep breath. "If our little visitors left the stove in working order, what would you say to a bit of bacon and eggs?"

"Good, and coffee too. I could drink a ga . . ."

The phone rang, cutting off his words. For two more rings they both sat there, staring at the device as if it had scales.

"Oh, what the fuck, it could be good news. Stranger things have happened."

"Not lately," Duncan mumbled.

"Hello?"

There was a long pause. Duncan watched her, waiting to read the expression on her face as a clue, but he was getting mixed signals.

"I know and I'm sorry, but I didn't . . . I know . . . I know . . . slow down. Yes, I'm listening . . ."

There was an even longer pause this time, and Max's only expression was one of frowning concentration, the tip of her tongue caught between her front teeth. Duncan held his ground for a few minutes longer, but the urge to plead for a clue was becoming too much to bear.

"And you're telling me this Tit-a-what's-his-name is inside . . . All right, supposedly inside this thing. Right . . . right . . . So they get him out, then what? . . . I hadn't thought about . . . In the material you sent me? All right, I'll look. Would you mind repeating this story one more time?" Max leaned forward thrusting the phone at Duncan. "Listen to what Dr. Osprey's found out."

Without further explanation she shoved the phone into his hand, slid off the couch onto the floor and began digging around in the debris, searching for something. Hesitantly he put the receiver to his ear. Dividing his attention between listening to the good doctor and keeping an eye on Max's frenzied burrowing, Duncan found himself getting thoroughly confused. In an effort to minimize his confusion, he tried to concentrate on this one-sided conversation, and just when things are getting a little less murky, Max popped up from behind the couch, sprawled over it on her stomach and snatched the receiver out of his hand.

"It's right here," she grunted, pulling a large black book across the couch and dropping it open onto Duncan's lap. "If Quetzalcoatl can be brought back it will mean the return of the Mayan Empire. Thank you, doctor. Yes, I think it will be a very big help. No really. Thank you, thank you very much." Max tossed the receiver up in the air and with a gleeful yelp caught it, returning it to the cradle in one movement.

"The dummy thinks by releasing Titiacahuan he can use the priest to bring Quetzy back and restart the Mayan Empire all over again," Max announced, grinning from ear to ear.

"Huh?" Duncan frowned.

Max twisted around on the couch searching the debris. "We've got our why," she announced.

"Who does?"

"We do, dummy. There it is!" She clambered over the back of the couch and sprinted into the foyer.

Rubbing the sleep from his eyes Duncan shook his head. "I don't get any of this."

Returning to the couch Max said confidently, "Now all we have to do is figure out a way to put a very small fly in our friend's magical ointment." Over her shoulder she carried the omnipresent red tote. In her hand she held up a very old, leather-bound book. "And I think I've got just what we're looking for."

Duncan stared up at her with bloodshot eyes. "In that book?"

"Not so condescending, if you please. This is a very special book," she said, climbing over the back of the couch and taking up her former position.

"What's so special about that particular book?"

"It's full of shadows," she said slyly.

Duncan sighed dramatically. "I know I'm a little slow, but do you think we could go over this revelation one more time from the top?"

"Just bear with me a little while longer and everything will be clear as glass, I swear." She glanced around her immediate vicinity. "Find me something to write with and on."

Looking around, he located a yellow pad under the shattered coffee table. Pulling a pen from his wrinkled sports coat, he frowned at the coat's sorry condition. Handing these things over to Max, he tugged a cushion out from under the chair he'd been leaning on and sat down.

For some time he watched as Max busily searched through her book and scribbled notes before folding his arms and laying his head down. He promised himself he would only rest his eyes for a few minutes.

Finally he leaned over the couch and looked over the collection of scribbled notes and strange drawings surrounding her. "You've been busy. Any luck?"

"Some interesting possibilities." She grinned up at him.

"Okay, let's hear about it, and if you wouldn't mind, refresh my memory about how we got here. I'm a bit fuzzy on our earlier conversation."

Pushing aside her papers, Max straightened her legs and stretched. Lighting a cigarette, she offered the pack to Duncan.

"Bless you," he said, taking her up on her offer.

Exhaling slowly, she began. "According to legend, the Petan Chac Mool is said to contain the body of a once powerful priest/enchanter by the name of Titiacahuan. Now, in the sociopolitical structure of the Mayan Empire, it was not uncommon for a priest to have even greater power over the community than the king. This seems to be true in the case of Titiacahuan. The legend says he could control weather, sway battles and raise the dead. Any of this sound familiar?"

"Pagan."

Max flashed him a quick grin then pressed on. "Under the guidance of Quetzalcoatl, the Mayans rose to great power. They grew as a race, mastered the arts and sciences, trade flourished and no enemy could stand before them. But contrary to popular belief, there were factions within the Mayan Empire who were not satisfied with Quetzalcoatl's rule. Chief among these was Titiacahuan. Seems he and Quetzalcoatl were not on the best of terms. Quetzy, being a god himself, thought things like altering weather and raising the dead weren't fit hobbies for mere mortals, so he warned Titiacahuan to knock it off or suffer the consequences. You can imagine how thrilled Titiacahuan was with the news.

"Now a group of these malcontented Mayans went to Titiacahuan and convinced him to aid them in getting rid of Quetzalcoatl. How they went about it is a bit complicated, so I'll cut to the chase. Titiacahuan works up this incredible spell and succeeds in driving Quetzalcoatl from his sacred city, Tula, to wander the earth, abandoning his people. Now the malcontents are extremely pleased by this because now they can step in and take over, which they do. And their first order of business?"

"To get rid of Tit . . . the priest guy."

"Very good. Very good indeed. They know if Titiacahuan is powerful enough to run off a god like Quetzalcoatl, they'll have to act fast. See, there's a strain, physical and emotional, in doing the kind of magic we're talking about, and they know the priest is in pretty bad shape so they decide to trick him into a magical trap while he's in a weakened condition.

"They go to Titiacahuan all sweet and grateful and tell him how they plan on raising a temple in honor of him and the great service he's done the Mayan people. They show him all of these wonderful plans and bombard him with questions in the guise of seeking his advise about the proposed temple. While they keep him busy one of his own acolytes, whom the malcontents have bribed, quite literally sneaks up behind him and binds the priest with magical bonds.

"Well, now that they've got him, what do they do with him? Nobody wants to kill him because killing a wizard like this one can get you in very hot water. They can't turn him loose, and they know they can't take too long about whatever they do because he'll regain his strength and they can't take that chance—so what's to do?"

"So they bury him in that clay thing, the Chac Mool?" Duncan frowned.

"Exactly. Now this is where it gets cute. They decide it would be delicious if they build this temple and bury Titiacahuan in it. Employing all of the other priests, who were very jealous of the old man anyway, they construct this altar in the form of a man literally encasing the priest in clay. As a kind of inside joke, the priests bend the old man's body to resemble the corpses they often use as altars in certain ceremonies. That's why the Chac Mool has that offering plate across the midsection."

"Very nasty folks."

"It isn't bad enough that they encase him in the clay alive, but they quickly realize that this may not be enough. What if the old man has friends and they get him out? Or the old man manages to gain magical aid himself? Just to make sure this doesn't happen, they place the Chac Mool in the foundation and build the temple on top of it. Evidently this worked because he stayed there until some graverobbers stumbled onto the statue while looting the temple, which is another story . . ."

"No, no, let's stick with this one. So you mean after all this time Westeridge thinks he's going to wake this guy up?"

"Westeridge or whoever is handling the magic end of things for him."

"I admit I don't know a lot about this magic stuff but I'm pretty sure the old guy must have croaked by now."

"And you call yourself a Christian. Even a heathen like myself knows one of your religion's greatest tenets is the body dies but the spirit doesn't."

"So where does all this leave us?"

"Well, we know what his schedule is. We found that in

the pattern. We know what he's trying to do, which explains why he's killing off the Golden Circle Society members and—"

"We do, do we?"

"Sorry. See, religions that practice human sacrifice believed the more powerful a spirit or god you wanted to reach, the more illustrious your offering should be. The Mayans believed this, and to that end they would offer up virgins, which contrary to popular belief are quite low on the list, important political prisoners, high ranking prisoners of war and in some cases even members of their own nobility, which were of the highest importance on the sacrificial hit parade. Now there's a sad lack of those kinds of people in southern California these days so Westeridge is using the wealthy members of the Golden Circle Society. They have the money, so they have the power in today's society. Kind of makes them current day members of the nobility."

"Gotcha. So, now that we know all this, the next question is who do we get to believe us after last night?"

Max frowned. "I believe it. Do you believe it?"

"I'm sitting here, aren't I?"

"Don't hedge. Do you believe?" she asked firmly, looking hard at him.

Duncan fidgeted under her gaze. "Yeah . . . no. I mean, I believe that's what Westeridge believes and that's why he's killing off the Golden Circle crowd. I've seen the victims, and no matter how many ways I turn it I can't see how anything human could have done all that. But this magic stuff—I just don't know."

"Fair enough. Let's try it this way. Do you believe I know what I'm talking about?"

He drew in a deep breath before he spoke. "As much as it burns my ass to admit it, you got a pretty good head on ya."

"I take it that's a yes."

"Yes, you happy now?"

"Then I'm going to ask you to believe one more thing, and I beg you listen to what I say because it's the truth and we're stuck with it."

"O.K."

"It doesn't matter who else believes because we do, and we're all we've got."

"Now, wait a minute. If you're talking about some kind of vigilante bullshit I'm not . . ."

"Duncan, I can promise you that we will not lay a hand on Malcom Westeridge, nor will we break the laws of man in any way, shape or form."

Duncan frowned skeptically. "You can't go to the bathroom alone without breaking some law."

"All right, so maybe we bend them a bit."

"Say, just for fun, I believe you. Answer me this. How do you keep your promise and stop Westeridge?"

Max smiled slyly. "Ah, now that's where the fun begins."

February 7th—8:30 a.m.

57 HOURS UNTIL SUNSET . . .

Max stuck her head around the corner. Surrounded by sufficient pots, pans and discarded cartons to have been the aftermath of a banquet, Chef Forbes divided his time between the countertop range and something shrouded in paper towels working away in the microwave.

"Do you do windows as well?" She grinned mischievously, stepping up to the counter.

"That's one," he said with only a brief glance in her direction.

"Two more before I'm in trouble, right?"

"How do you like your eggs?"

"Basted."

Duncan frowned, then flipped over all the eggs.

"That's not basted," Max whined.

"So eat out. Over easy is all I do."

"Then why ask? What have you got here? Eggs, pancakes, hash browns. What's that in the microwave?"

"Move," he grumbled, bumping her aside with his hip. Reaching into the oven, he removed the tray and smiled down at a dozen dark brown strips of sizzling meat. "Just right. Get some plates."

Max gingerly picked up one of the strips and bit off a piece. "Oh, lovely. Chernobyl bacon."

"Plates," Duncan snapped, scraping at a stubborn pancake.

Thirty minutes later, sprawled amid the wreckage of their impromptu living room picnic, Max grabbed her midsection and flopped over onto the carpeting. "Now I know how a tick feels on a fat dog."

Duncan smiled tightly. "That your way of saying it was good?"

Max propped herself up on one elbow. "The man who shoots his grandmother with a rifle at three hundred yards is undeniably a good shot but not necessarily a good man."

"Huh?"

"Think about it." Max grinned, pushing herself into upright position. Glancing at her watch she sighed. "We've got some business to take care of this morning, and I'd like to get—"

"You know I had a lot of time on my hands this morning."

"I can see." Max glanced around the room at his handiwork. "It wasn't necessary, but thank you for the thought."

Duncan nodded, studying the rim of his coffee cup. Though the room would take far more than his simple rearrangement of the debris to return it to its former glory, the change made him feel better and cleared his thinking, and right now clear thinking was a vital necessity.

"Look, Max, I've been doing some thinking about the

things we talked about last night and I think we need to do some serious—"

"Things look different to you in daylight, don't they?" Max said.

"Yeah, they do."

"It always seems to work that way. Duncan, I'll answer all of your questions. I'll do my best to make you understand, and if in the end you feel you can't be a party to this undertaking . . ."

"Look, nobody's talking about getting out. All I'm saying is there are some very serious questions I need answers to—answers to fit my world, not yours."

"I'll do my best. Only if it's all the same to you, could we have this discussion on the road? No matter what you decide I've got a very tight schedule to keep." Max stood up.

"On the road to where?" Duncan frowned up at her.

"How about your place for a start?"

"What?"

"Unless you plan on living in that same sad outfit for the next three days I suggest we pick you up a few things."

"Pretty sure of yourself, aren't you?"

Max frowned. "How so?"

"We pick up clothes for me because you're certain no matter what questions I have you'll be able to clear them up, therefore I'll need other clothes because I'll be going along with your plan."

"Actually, I figure that whether you're on the bus or off I'm stuck with you for the duration, and I'm really getting tired of seeing that same, sad, rumpled, old sports coat and those tired old slacks. Don't you own a pair of jeans?"

Duncan ground his teeth but pushed his protesting body into a standing position. "God? You wanta make me happy? Turn her into a man for about half an hour and look the other way."

10:15 a.m.—55 hours, 15 minutes until sunset . . .

The living room was small, gently worn at the edges but neat in the extreme. A soft smile clung tenaciously to Max's face as she moved around the room. Crossing behind a faded blue wing chair, her mind could detect the quiet scent of lilacs and the impression of a small, dark-haired woman with great smiling blue eyes. It was a pleasant room, and the impressions of many happy hours echoed across the wallpaper and over the furnishings, clinging to every article within the room, but the impressions were not recent. In recent times sadness plagued this room. She found this impression most persistent when standing near the large brown recliner whose deep sagging cushions and worn armrests gave no doubt as to its owner's identity.

"O.K., I think that about does it," Duncan announced.

Max bit back a smile. Forbes had resurrected his running suit, and the image of him in it, a sports bag hanging from one shoulder, was quite a jaunty one save for the ominous bulge at the ankle of his right leg.

"What's wrong now?" Duncan grumbled, locking the front door.

"Nothing," Max said, walking out the front door. "Only with that lump around your ankle you look like an escapee from a La Costa chain gang."

"You want I should leave it at home?" he asked sarcastically, tossing his bag into the rear seat.

"Never leave home without it," Max snickered. His only response was an arching of one eyebrow. "Why is it," she asked, "I get this picture of you losing a serve, whipping out your gun and blowing away the tennis pro?"

"'Cause you are one very sick puppy," he answered, dropping the gearshift into reverse and lurching down the driveway.

A few blocks away from the house Duncan picked up the threat of an earlier, more serious conversation. "One thing I don't get. If this guy is able to get this spirit thing to do what he wants, how come he just didn't send it after us? How come the direct approach?"

"First thing to remember is we're not dealing with ifs. Malcom can, has and so far does control the spirit."

"And you're certain now it's Malcom we're after?"

"Yes."

"You were still hedging on that point last night."

"I'm as certain as I can afford to be—means, motive and opportunity. He's the only one I can give a full score to."

"Suits me. Now back to my original question. Why not send the spook after us?" Duncan asked doggedly.

"Ritual magic comes in several degrees or levels of difficulty. On a scale of one to ten, the kind of stuff our boy is dealing with is about a ten plus. It's both physically and emotionally demanding. During the ritual itself he is in constant physical danger. By one wrong word or a misplaced gesture or missed timing, dead is the least he could get. We're not just talking about fixing a race or—"

"You can do that with this stuff?"

Max groaned, then picked up where she had left off. "Or causing it to rain. This man is not only trying to raise the dead, and we're not just talking dead here. We're talking dead, at the very least, nearly two thousand years. On top of this not only is his chosen subject a man who legend says did this kind of thing before breakfast, but our boy has to overcome the enchantment of an unknown adept, free his subject and then control him once he's out. And then, just to make things interesting, he's got to force the old man into bringing his worse enemy—a bleedin' god, for pity's sake—back to life. Offhand I'd say our boy's dance card is all full up."

Duncan looked at her for several seconds then said, "Is there a short version to all that?"

Max shrugged. "We're just too unimportant for him to go to that much bother."

"Why didn't you say that in the first place? Christ, you rattle on."

Max nodded at the appropriate places, all the while relieved she did not have to tell Duncan just how much trouble they could find themselves in if Malcom took objection to her future actions and did attempt such a feat. She hoped she would never have to, but in the same breath she reminded herself to keep a sharp eye out, just in case.

"I still don't see what we need this guy for," Duncan grumbled.

"I'm not about to go over it all again. We need him and that's that."

"For what? We can rent a limo, at least you can. You're the one with the money. I pick up Holt and get him to the airport."

"I'm getting out of the car now. You have the grocery list." Digging into her pocket she dug out $50 and handed it across to him. "That's for my share, and try to buy at least a few items whose main ingredients don't consist chiefly of saturated fat, sugar and preservatives."

"Nag, nag, nag," he grumbled under his breath.

Closing the door she bent down, speaking through the window, "Say hello to Jasper for me, and I'll see you back here in about two hours, O.K.?"

"Yeah, yeah, yeah."

Even at this early hour of the day, several professional drinkers were perched at the bar getting a leg up on tomorrow's hangover. Riley, camped at the head of the bar behind a pile of last night's receipts and a pot of coffee, waved her over.

"Making money, are we?" Max asked, peeking at the ledger while helping herself to the coffee.

"Don't be rude. It's too early," Riley clipped, closing his book over the receipts. "Bring your cup," he ordered, climbing off his stool and leading the way to a more private corner booth.

Once they were comfortably settled, Riley opened the floor to discussion with a simple statement of his position. "Let's get somethin' right before things go any further. There's damn little I'd be denyin' you if you really needed it, but if it's all the same to you, could you be makin your requests during civilized hours and save the late night calls for someone else?"

Max tried not to smile and failed. "You want I should schedule any future emergencies between nine and five?"

"Cheeky baggage."

"Thank you." Max grinned.

"Come along, get on with it. I'm a busy man."

By the time each had started on a third cup of coffee Max had laid out the plan, hiding nothing from him including the possible danger from sources other than the norm in such ventures. Riley considered this, appearing relatively assured Max could handle that end of things. His only problem was one more centered on the personnel involved in the proposed plan—namely Duncan Forbes.

"Now let me get this straight. The crusher—"

"Duncan. His name is Duncan."

"Maybe to you, but to me he's the crusher."

"I understand how you feel about police in general, but believe me, Forbes is a decent man and not unlike you in a number of ways."

"You'll forgive me if I don't ask him round for tea."

"Ratbag."

"Well then, as for Mr. Holt I think I'll put that in Sean's capable hands. As for the other, what's it to be then? A straight away haul?"

"Right."

"By tradition?"

Max laughed. "By tradition, what I don't see I can't stop."

"Right enough."

"But that's not the end to it. I'll be needing a bit more."

Riley's gaze shifted away from the table then quickly back again. "No doubt you will, but perhaps another time would be best."

Before Max could do more than frown Riley's face split into a broad smile as he boomed, "Well, if it isn't Mr. Duncan Forbes, himself."

There was no arching of backs nor spitting, but if you listened very carefully you could catch the hint of hissing just under the cautiously polite greetings the two men passed.

2:15 p.m.—51 hours, 15 minutes until sunset . . .

Max surveyed the den once more then returned to the living room and her biggest concern.

She sat down on the arm of the couch. After one too many at Riley's, Duncan lay on his back, the steady rise and fall of his chest attesting to the fact that he yet lived despite his earlier assertions to the contrary. It went without saying that he'd wake, sooner or later, with one hell of a hangover, but she had a much more pressing concern.

For the next several hours, possibly longer, she would need every bit of her concentration for the things that she must do. There would be no margin for division of her efforts which meant Duncan must be kept occupied —but how? Should she wake him now and explain that she must not under any circumstances be disturbed, or simply leave him be and hope he slept through the remainder of the night? Either way, things could get sticky. She considered her dilemma a few minutes longer before finally settling on a compromise.

Once more in the den, Max again wished the door had a lock. For a moment she considered jamming a chair up under the knob but quickly abandoned the thought, realizing that a knock could be equally as disruptive as Duncan opening it and just walking in. Moving into the center of the room, she sat down and emptied the contents from the first of several packages clumped on the floor near her. This completed, she removed a small screwdriver from her pocket and turned to the remains of her ruined computer laying beside her.

Exposing the bottom of the machine, she quickly went to work on a panel held in place by four screws, not part of the original design. Placing the screws to one side, she pried open the panel, revealing the guts of the machine. After her discovery of the damage recently done to the machine she had seized the first private opportunity to determine the safety of its hidden contents.

Flat black metal, its surface worn and bearing numerous scuffs and dents, it slipped from the opening, its total size no larger than a child's shoebox. Max placed it on the floor directly in front of her, then quickly cleared the computer debris aside. Even under the most determined of inspections, the box appeared to have been constructed of a single piece of metal without openings, seams or latching devices readily visible. Moving her hands over the box's surface, she smiled, feeling the familiar ridges under her fingertips. Exerting very little pressure on those ridges, the top of the box popped up.

Setting the top aside, Max removed its black, plastic-wrapped contents. Peeling aside the plastic and a blue silk scarf beneath it, she lifted out a small bundle wrapped in a silvery white rabbit pelt. Spreading the scarf over the carpet before her, she opened the fur, displaying a silver chalice, a bronze disc inscribed on one side with strange designs and a mirror on the other, a small Mycenaean dagger and a fat white candle. Placing these items on the scarf, she shook out the fur pelt and lay it in the center of the scarf, fur side down, exposing the lettering and richly detailed drawings that covered its worn surface.

When the placement of these curious artifacts met with her satisfaction she pulled the leather pouch from her pocket and added its contents to the collection. With a final quick appraisal of the arrangement she turned to the items clustered around her—a two liter Pepsi bottle now containing sea water, a bag of beach sand, another containing sea salt, a five pound block of brown modeling clay and a plastic bowl she relocated to a position on her right side. The remaining objects she pushed behind her, unwilling to bring them into the field of play before necessary.

Making one final check of her equipment, Max opened the Pepsi bottle containing the sea water. Carefully she poured a small amount over the fingers of her right hand and then her left. Holding the bottle between her legs she quickly rubbed both hands together in a washing motion. This completed, she resealed the bottle and set it aside. Dipping two fingers of her right hand into the bowl containing the overflow she marked a broad swipe across her forehead, one down both left and right cheeks and, closing her eyes, repeated the gesture with a single digit over each closed lid. Returning to the bowl once more, she dipped the fingertips of both hands into the water and raised them to her ears, briefly covering each appendage with a cupped hand, then lowered her fingertips to her lips. Finally she brought them to rest in the middle of her forehead and held them there, the palms of her hands covering her face.

For nearly half an hour she sat in this position, hands covering her face, mind turned inward. By this gentle ritual she disassociated herself from the world beyond the fragile barrier of the ceremony. Slowly opening her eyes, she moistened her index finger and touched it to the tip of her tongue.

"For clearing my sight so that I might see the many forms of the light, for freeing my ears that I might hear the many voices of the light, and for cleansing my mind that I may understand and recognize the light, I thank you, brother Gabriel."

In the manner prescribed, Max moved through this ancient ritual, entering deeper into a world few living today remembered and even fewer sought entry to. Three times she repeated these gestures of entrance, moving her hands through the flame of the candle for Michael, Guardian of Fire, through the sand for Ariel, Guardian of Earth, and finally making the appropriate gestures saluting Raphael, Guardian of the Air.

Eyes fixed on the center of the flame Max opened the doorway and stepped across the threshold, sending on ahead this ancient entreaty. "By the black ravens of thought and memory, the double polarity of the astral light and the creatures who dwell in the two houses therein, the fluid phantoms of ether and sea, the mortal spirits of the elementals, protectors of shadow and reflection and those yet born transmutations, hear me for I am the seeker."

As always the challenge came—not in the clumsy vowels and syllables of human speech but in the rushing of the wind, moving of the ocean, sighing of the stars, flickering of the flame and muffled keening of the Earth. "What do you wish?"

Covering her eyes a second time Max said quietly, "To see the light."

And the response came. "Open to the light, and the light will open unto you."

Max lowered her hands, her eyelids remaining closed. Within a few heartbeats the rising and falling of her chest slowed until the movement all but disappeared. Her pulse rate fell to a dangerous level, and though her eyelids slowly opened the visions her brain recorded held little recognizable comparison for the modern mind of man.

All speech converted to the faster language of thought, she placed her dilemma before her hosts. "You who see all things know why I have come. Though the terms of good and evil as recognized by the inhabitants of my plane have no equal meaning for you, I must stop he who moves before me for he has brought great evil upon innocents. I lack the power and the understanding to stop him alone. I ask your aid, as one who has never given harm nor offense to you, against him who has dishonored your presence and who will defile the laws no living thing may disobey. I ask only you guide my hand in this work and know I offer no offense to you by my efforts."

4:30 p.m.—49 hours until sunset . . .

"Give me that, idiot," Malcom snarled, snatching the broom out of the man's hand. Looking around at the small group of observers, he snapped, "Haven't you seen sand before? Go on, all of you, and get back to your work!" When all but the timid janitor had shuffled away, Malcom turned his attention back to the problem at hand.

It was a simple thing—no more than a minor

annoyance—or at least that's all it should have been. Malcom glared down at it, and with almost humorous arrogance it glittered back at him. A single, slender, line of sand, no wider than a child's jump rope, circled the huge Chac Mool and the platform it rested upon, forming a complete circle.

"I tried, I swear, but it wouldn't go away," the janitor said timidly.

"Shut up!"

"As quickly as I'd brush it away it came back."

"Be quiet!"

"Five times, I swear it, five times."

"Fool!" Malcom hissed, slamming the head of the broom down across the back of the glittering chain. With quick, brittle movements he flicked the broom back and forth, scattering the soft sand. He had nearly completed the circle when suddenly the janitor shouted.

"See, look there, it returns," he cried, his voice trembling over the words.

Malcom spun around at the man's cry. The breath in his lungs grew cold as he watched the slender rope slowly reform itself.

"Sweet Jesus," the janitor muttered.

As the sand rope neared the tip of his shoe Malcom unconsciously stepped back as it moved doggedly forward to rejoin with its broken half.

"Oh, God!" the man wailed, rushing out of the hall.

"Come back here! You fool, come back here!" When it became apparent the man had no intentions of honoring his request Malcom snarled, "then get out, you idiot. It's nothing, nothing."

Alone, Malcom slowly turned back to the problem, his confidence considerably lessened. He attacked the sand rope again, this time removing all but a small fraction of its length before it once more began to replace itself. A third and fourth time he confronted the thing, the fury of his attack increasing geometrically only to have victory stubbornly snatched from him as the rope patiently regrew itself each time.

Again and again he tried to banish the glittering noose,

his strength gradually waning, his frustration growing to unbearable proportions. All patterns of cohesive thought were driven from his mind until he became little more than a slowly dwindling force moving the broom. Sweat dripped from his face and hair, the skin of his hands were bruised and sore from the force of his swing, his knees buckled and he sank slowly to the floor, his glazed eyes watching the sand reform itself yet again as another element was added to the equation.

It came down out of the high dark places at the top of the museum, swooping across the chamber and filling the great cavern with the sound of its movement. The work curtain shivered and then billowed as the wind increased. Malcom stumbled to his feet, his eyes wide as the huge curtain lashed as the full brunt of the wind struck its surface. For but a few heartbeats that unnatural wind howled around his head and then, like a train in the night, faded away into the darkness.

The broom slipped from his hands, dropping to the floor with a clatter that echoed eerily in the silence following the gale. Slowly, Malcom turned and crossed between the now-still partitions of the work curtain. Moving to the elevator, he stepped inside. He felt no compulsion to remain near the statue any longer, for one brief glance had told his befuddled mind more than he wished to know.

Across town, Max knew through senses keener than the human kind, that the messenger of sand had done its work, then vanished with the wind.

7:26 p.m.—46 hours, 4 minutes until sunset . . .

Several things occurred to Duncan all at once. He was not blind as he feared upon first waking, but simply looking out into a very dark room. Nothing had crawled into his mouth and died while he slept. What he tasted he could now put name and source to, and the sharp pressure he was now experiencing in the small of his back was nothing more than his kidneys begging for relief.

His first attempt to stand met with failure, but faring far better with his second effort he leapt on to bigger challenges. Feeling his way along the couch, he managed the greater distance to the hallway and the guest bathroom.

After relieving himself, he stared into the mirror and was surprised to discover he did not look as bad as he felt. But a greater surprise came in the discovery of a piece of crisp, white notepaper pinned to the jacket of his warm-up suit.

The note was short and simple. It was Max's way of assuring him she had not ducked out again and was in fact closeted in the den, working on something for which she begged his patience. She would, she told him, explain when she had finished. There was food in the kitchen, the bed was made up in the guest room and if neither of those alternatives suited him she had several items she needed researched and had listed them on the note. The last line again asked that he please not disturb her under any circumstances. The last three words were heavily underlined.

He considered the note in general and the last line in particular for a few minutes longer. His mind hung itself up on that last line. What kind of work, he wondered, was she so totally involved with that she could not be disturbed? His naturally suspicious nature began hoisting the idea that this note might be another of Max's ruses, and should he look inside the den he would find it empty and his car keys gone as well.

Stuffing the note into his pocket, he pulled himself up with the aid of the sink and when his head stopped spinning stepped out into the hall. As he reached in to switch off the bathroom light, he found his gaze directed at the door to the den a few feet away. On the edge of a dilemma, he stood there, torn between checking to see if Max was really in there or finding his way back to the kitchen and making a pot of very strong black coffee in hopes of clearing away the cobwebs. He soon realized the decision was not so difficult a one. He knew sooner or later the cop in him would resurface and he'd look in the den. Besides, he didn't need to kick the door in, just open it a crack, and if she was in there he could close it quietly without her knowing and just go away. If she wasn't he could save his strength for something else that needed kicking a whole lot more.

Switching off the light, he staggered across the hall to his goal. Pausing for a moment, he listened, hoping to catch some hint of sound coming from the other side. Hearing nothing, he reached for the doorknob and a tiny spark jumped from the knob to his fingertip. Damn wool carpets, he thought, reaching out a second time. This time several sparks, visible in the dark hallway, jumped across to his hand, shocking him even harder.

Angered and more than a little bit annoyed by the shocks, he rushed the knob, locking his hand around it before the sparks had a chance to attack him, and as a reward for the effort an entire army of little blue/white sparks danced over his hand. As they started a spearhead action up his arm the sparks weren't the only thing that jumped. Duncan lurched away from the door, his entire right arm tingling from the encounter.

Stifling a curse, he rubbed his arm and glared in the general direction of the offending hardware. Pacing in a small tight circle he considered a second rush when a better option sped across his mind. Feeling his way back to the bathroom he switched on the lights, wincing at the glare but unswayed from his quest. Searching the small room, he located a pair of worn yellow rubber gloves in the cabinet under the sink, and he returned to his target with renewed confidence.

Reaching out, he flicked a finger against the knob, and when no sparks appeared he stepped forward and took a firm hold on it. Turning the knob slowly, taking care not to make any further unnecessary noise, he could feel the catch disengage. Slowly he released the knob and gently pushed the door open a crack. In the narrow space afforded him he could see a number of the same tiny blue sparks that had attacked his arm. Edging forward, his toes pushed the door open further.

The darkness of the room was rent by thousands of the

same tiny blue sparks that had appeared on his hand. The very air was alive with them, and in the midst of the maelstrom of shifting, darting light sat Max. The sparks flitted over her clothing and raced through her hair, causing it to crackle and move in the wind of their passing. Overlaying all this was the strange, brittle odor of ozone.

For precisely how long he stood there watching the bizarre light show he did not know, but when he finally stirred himself to move his concern was no longer with stealth but speed. Turning back into the hallway he found a considerable number of the small lights had attached themselves to him. He made several spastic attempts to brush them away but in doing so only seemed to increase their number. Adding to a rapidly building sense of panic, he now began to feel the hairs on his arms and the back of his neck stand on end. Abandoning all efforts at ridding himself of the things, he moved to take flight only to falter. There, little more than a few feet in front of him, stood a large dark figure, outlined by the same glittering lights that now covered his own body. Acting more out of instinct than coherent thought he lashed out wildly with a hard right in the general direction of the figure's head.

Several events then occurred at once. There was the sound of breaking glass, a pair of screams, one loud popping noise that drowned out all other sounds, a blinding flash of blue/white light, and a power surge that blanked out the lights over two-thirds of Marina Del Ray.

The lights were still flickering intermittently when Max finally opened her eyes. Duncan, visible relief washing over him, smiled wearily and murmured, "Thank God."

Max blinked, looking around as if the living room were an alien landscape. "How did I get back in here?" She frowned, speaking more to herself than to him.

"I brought you in here when the explosion—"

"What explosion?"

"The one that knocked the lights out."

"When?"

"I don't know. A while ago. Look, why don't you just lay back. You don't look so good," he said, trying to push her back onto the couch.

Max kept looking around, a frown now permanently engraved on her face. "Leave me alone," she snapped, brushing his hands away. "What explosion?"

"The one that knocked the lights out. I just told you that a minute ago. Did you hit your head or something?" It was Duncan's turn to frown.

Max sat up clinging to the back of the couch for support. "Knocked what lights out? They're on now."

"Of course they are. I didn't say they stayed out. Look, are you sure—"

"What the bleedin' hell happened?" Max snarled, the leading edge of hysteria creeping into her voice.

"Well, I was kinda figurin' you could fill us in on that."

"Why me?"

"Well, I wasn't the one sitting in a dark room with all those sparky things."

"What?" Max's eyes narrowed to mere slits.

"Don't you remember? You were sitting in the den in the dark with all these—"

"How do you know that?"

"I saw you when I opened the door," Duncan said.

"You opened the door?" Max snapped.

"I just said that. Are you sure you're all right?"

"Did you get my note?"

"Sure."

"And you read it?"

"How else would I have—"

"You read the note, and you opened the door anyway?"

"I said that."

Max's eyes had lost their squint and had now gone all wide and glassy. "You read the bleedin' note and opened the door anyway? After I asked you not to?"

"Why do you keep repeating everything? I think you better lay down. You're not right in the head." He reached out, trying to push her down onto the couch again, but all he got for his trouble was a shot to the chest that surprised more than hurt him.

"Get away from me! Back off," Max snarled, pushing her way up onto the back of the couch where, taking a parting swing in his general direction, she toppled over backwards, landing with a thump on the carpet. Apparently the fall did her little injury for she was on her feet almost instantly, a string of curses issuing from her mouth that could light the city if the power failed again.

At first, Duncan was stunned, more by the vehemence of her words than their content. But at the first opportunity he got his tongue in the door. "Shut up!" he barked, rattling the windows with the command. "You scared the shit out of me. When I saw you laying in there like some kind a broken toy, I thought for sure you were dead, you silly bitch!"

There was a small catch in his voice in those last few words, and that catch penetrated Max's anger. He was scared, perhaps almost as frightened as she. "You could have killed me, you great daft penguin," she said, a pouting note in her voice.

"What?" he asked, his voice sounding as if coming from down a deep well.

"By opening that door, or whatever it was you did, you could have killed me." There was no anger in her voice now, only the flat, even tone of one stating a simple fact.

Duncan stared at her for the longest time, his lips occasionally twitching, but no recognizable words came out. Lowering himself onto the couch he shook his head slowly, his face a mask of confusion and anguish. "I didn't know. What you were doing? I didn't know . . ." His head dropped forward into his hands, the muffled words continuing over and over again.

Max looked up at the ceiling. A part of her wanted to remain angry, but a number of her little voices informed her that she was indeed being a shit.

Crossing slowly to him, she dropped down on the floor at his feet, crossing her legs under her. For a long minute she sat there, unable to do more than toy with his pant leg. "I guess I should have found a better way of handling this," she began softly, her words more for her own benefit than his. "I'm not real sure just what might have been a better way, but the note definitely wasn't it. It's just that I'm not used to . . . ahh, shit! Duncan, look at me," she said pushing against his forehead with her index finger. "I'm sorry. I should have prepared you."

"What was all that in there?"

"Don't interrupt," she said gently. "You've had a nasty shock." She shrugged, a tight grin pulling at the corners of her lips. "We've both had a nasty shock, but that's done with. I promise when this is over I'll explain about what you saw in there, but for now you have to promise me you won't come into that room again when I'm in there. For both our sakes, promise me."

A look of utter disbelief twisted up Duncan's features. "No."

"What?"

"I'm not going to promise you anything of the kind."

"I don't have time for this, Duncan," she stammered, unfurling her legs in preparation to stand.

"Make time," Duncan grumbled.

"Later, when it's finished."

Before she could stand he took a firm grip on her arm. "When what's finished? Were you responsible for those things? Was that you? What's going on in there?"

"I'll answer your question when you let go of my arm."

"Talk first," Duncan demanded irritably.

Max refolded her legs and said calmly, "Then we'll sit here. I can use the break." She then promptly closed her eyes, sighing contentedly.

Duncan wanted desperately to call her bluff, but patience was not a quality he possessed in vast quantities. After less then five minutes he freed her arm, grumbling, "So talk."

Max opened her eyes slowly but not before thanking a number of deities she'd been coaxing for a speedy release. "What exactly do you want to know?"

"Exactly? How about everything, exactly? What were you doing in there, exactly? Did you have something to do with that explosion, exactly? And—"

"All right, I get the picture." Max sighed. Quickly sorting through the information she considered safe to expose and separating it from the more lethal aspects of the situation, she began haltingly. "This isn't going to be easy."

"Try."

Tossing a frown in his direction she was about to return to her explanation when her nimble mind stumbled onto a possible out. "Actually, I'm keeping Malcom occupied." Duncan frowned. "Really."

"You're trying to tell me that all that stuff I saw in the den is supposed to keep Malcom occupied? How?" Duncan asked. "Better yet, why?"

"This is not working," Max said, rubbing her tired eyes. "Duncan, forget what I just said."

"You haven't said anything yet, but you're going to, aren't you?"

Ignoring the implied threat she said, "I'm giving our friend a small dose of his own magic medicine, so to speak. What you inadvertently stumbled into was one of the small doses I have planned for him, although I'm not sure that last one went very far."

"You made those things appear?" he asked slowly, each word pronounced with a measured cadence.

Max frowned, considering all the possible correct answers to that seemingly simple question and in the end was left with a lame but accurate answer. "In a manner of speaking."

"Ahhh," he groaned. "You either did or you didn't. That's not a hard question, is it?"

"Yes, as a matter of fact, it bloody well is." Ignoring his second groan she continued, "If you mean did I create the phenomena you saw, no. If you mean did I cause it to appear, to collect—yes, I did."

"How?"

"Neither of us has long enough for that. Look, Duncan, I said I'd answer your questions and I will, but if you think I'm going to waste valuable time trying to explain something to you I've spent damn near my entire life trying to grasp, I won't. Not that I could even if I wanted to. If it makes things any clearer for you to say I was responsible for what you saw in there then go with that."

"You did that by magic?"

It was Max's turn to groan. "Duncan, we're gonna spend years going round and round over this thing, and the biggest problem we're gonna have is one of semantics. When you say magic you think card tricks and rabbits out of hats. That's what magic means to you and most other people on this planet, but that is not nor will it ever be the only or even the real meaning of the word. Your kind of magic means a guy pulling a rabbit out of a hat because he put it in there in the first place, not because he created it."

"And your kind does?"

"In a way. When Malcom calls the spirit forth that kills, he is employing a kind of magic."

"A kind? Not like the rabbit or what you do?"

"No, not like the rabbit, but in a way something like what you saw. Trust me, Duncan. The only off-ramps on the freeway of this discussion lead to other freeways. In the magic I deal with, there are thousands of levels, some so old and arcane we don't even have records of their existence any more. The only time we find out they still exist is when some poor sucker bumps into one on his way somewhere else. More importantly for you to remember is that all of these levels are divided into just two categories. The words may not be the same, but they all boil down to good and evil. I don't have to tell you which side Malcom and his lot is mucking about with."

"And your kind is good."

"Semantics again. Technically, yes."

"Well, that part at least wasn't hard, was it?"

"Bet me," she mumbled. More clearly she continued, "By means of this magic it's my hope to keep Malcom on edge and off guard. The busier he is with my little pokes, the less likely he is to get wind of anything we're about." This was the tricky part of the half-truth she was telling Duncan. While keeping Malcom on edge and off guard was a part of her goal, it certainly wasn't the sum total.

"Isn't there an easier way of doing that?"

"Possibly—but this is faster, neater and in a language he understands."

"Not to mention dangerous. That explosion—things like that happen often?"

"Not usually, although they can. What I gather happened is that something you did in either entering or leaving the room broke my concentration, and before I could correct the breakage everything just got away from me. What exactly did you do?"

"Everything happened so fast I couldn't tell you." It was Duncan's turn to lie. To further cover his trail he slowly folded his arms over his chest, burrowing his right hand deep in his armpit and hiding the cuts and scrapes on his knuckles.

"Well, whatever it was, something broke my concentration, and that's when it all went sour." Max repositioned her legs. "Does that answer your questions?" she asked hopefully.

"No, but I'm not sure I want the rest answered."

Max smiled. "Well, I'll give you credit. You took it better than I figured you would."

"Humph."

"Look, why don't you just take the rest of the evening easy. I only need a couple more hours," Max said.

"To do what?"

"To finish what you ruined."

"No, uh uh, no more."

"I beg your pardon, but that is not your decision to make."

"Think again," Duncan said stubbornly.

Max shook her head. Climbing up onto her knees, she rested her elbows on his thighs and looked him hard in the eyes. "You're a stubborn man, Duncan Forbes. It's one of the things I like about you, and believe it or not I do like you in a warped kind of way. But you can save the stubborn routine for another time because I'm going to finish what I started, and there is nothing you can do about it. Oh, I know you could do something silly like handcuff me to the piano or some such nonsense, but you can't stop this," and she pointed to her head, "and this is where the magic starts and ends. Granted, you can slow me down, delay me even, but you can't stop me and that, dear Duncan, is the complete and unalterable truth of the situation. I truly wish there had been some way of keeping you away from this part of me, but what's done is done." Leaning back on her heels, she asked, "So what's it to be?"

For several minutes the pair stared at one another, then Max stood up. "Thank you," she said softly, turning away.

"Maybe I should just get out of here and leave you alone. All I ever seem to do is screw things up."

Max's soft underside cringed. "That's not true, and you know it. Besides you can't leave now. You're needed."

"For what? You've got your friend Riley for the heavy work, and from what I've seen you can handle the rest with your eyes closed. No, I think I'll just go on home and leave the work to the professionals." With this he stood up and made all the motions of a man about to pack it in.

"Hang about. Where do you think you're off to? You're not leaving me in the middle of all this."

"No, you don't need me. You'll be better off."

Max, startled by this sudden reversal, moved closer. "You can't leave now. Who'd keep me honest? You can't go like this. I won't let you!"

"All right, I'll stay, but if I'm in for a pinch I'm in for a pound," he said quickly, more than a trace of smile in his voice.

Max's eyes narrowed. "Why, you little louse."

"You want to proceed with your hocus-pocus uninterrupted? Fine, but let me in on the act."

"What?"

"I want to see this magic of yours."

"You've bleedin' well seen all—"

"Look at it this way. You can either let me in or leave me out here getting up to God knows what. And believe me, I'll be less bother in there than I will out here. So what's it to be, hey?"

Max considered him for several seconds, then snarled, "Remember when I said I liked you? I lied."

"Good. I was afraid for a minute this wouldn't hurt." He grinned.

Moving into the hallway, Duncan close on her heels, Max warned, "This is not a spectator sport. If there was ever a time in your life you managed to keep that big mouth of yours shut, this had better be it."

"Are those spark things coming back again?"

"No, I think we'll give electricity a rest for tonight." Pausing, Max frowned at the broken mirror littering the floor across the hall from the den. "Jesus, did I do that?"

"Guess so." Duncan shrugged, seeing no reason to burden her with the story of his phantom attacker.

The den, epicenter of the explosion, showed little evidence of being so, a fact which appeared to come as a surprise only to Duncan. Max stepped into a cleared space around which an odd collection of items was gathered. At the top of the circle was an area covered by a square of blue material, a piece of leather with a kind of writing on it and several other objects of which he could only recognize a thick white candle.

"Sit over there against the wall," Max said pointing to a place across from her.

Duncan crossed to the head of the cleared area, his eyes busily scanning the odd assortment. "What the hell is that?" he asked pointing to a glob of clay that vaguely resembled a man laying on his back.

"You wanted to watch, then watch. Questions are out." Max was turning around in tight little circles within the cleared area, moving some of the items to new locations. When the new arrangement was to her satisfaction, she turned back to the cloth-covered area and said, "You might as well sit on the floor. This is going to take awhile." When he had settled himself she sat down cross-legged and continued. "From this time forward I cannot impress this upon you strongly enough! Under no circumstances must you move about the room, particularly in my direction. Neither must you speak nor make any sound. You've seen what can happen when my concentration is broken. Trust me when I tell you we were both very lucky the last time. I'm not looking for any repetition of that experience, so if you don't think you can do as I ask, leave now."

"What's going to happen?"

"In the beginning, not very much. In fact you'll probably find it rather dull. Later things may become a bit . . ." Max paused, searching for just the right word.

"Weird?"

"Semantics again, but I suppose that one will work as well as the next. The only thing I must demand is that you do not interfere. Think you can do that?"

There was a very long pause.

"Well?"

"I'm thinking," he snapped.

"Well, think about this. You cause me to screw up in any way and we could both wind up dead. Get the picture?"

"Yeah, I get it."

"Well?"

"No matter what? What if you're in trouble? What am I suppose to do? Sit on my hands?"

"Hands, tongue, anything that could get in the way. Besides, if I get in trouble there's only one person who can get me out—and trust me, love, it isn't you."

Duncan didn't like that answer, her attitude, or much of anything else right at that moment, but he'd dealt himself in and unless he wanted to fold he knew he'd have to tough it out. "All right, get on with it and don't worry about me."

Easier said than done, she thought. "Briefly, what I'm going to do is prepare myself for the ritual, try to repair the damage from that last little dust up and then, if my apology takes, I'll seek entrance once again. Assuming everything is all right that's when things will start to get a bit strange. Please, remember—"

"Not a word, I know. You've made your point," he grumbled, crossing his arms over his chest.

For well over an hour Duncan watched the nearly silent ritual, his mood shifting from skeptical curiosity to cramped boredom and all the other stops along the route. About the half-way point, he found his ass falling asleep and even with the minor adjustments he'd been able to make in his posture, his legs had rapidly followed suit. For several minutes he'd been dividing his time between staring at the light patterns the candle's flame made on the ceiling and listening to the embarrassingly loud rumblings of his stomach. Just as his mind had turned to creating food pictures his eyes registered a subtle shifting of the patterns. It also appeared as if the room had grown a bit lighter. Turning his gaze in Max's direction, his grumbling stomach was quickly forgotten.

In the center of the blue cloth sat the thick white candle. Up until this moment, its small flame had been behaving in prescribed fashion, but now the flame was changing and mutating. As he watched, a second flame, seemingly attached to the single wick, was slowly separating itself from the first, larger flame. Though half the size of its brother, this second flame had an intensity far beyond that of the first, an intensity that increased with each flicker of its birth throes though its size remained the same.

For several minutes longer the flame's strange contortions continued and then, with a fragile sound like that of a twig snapping, it separated itself from the wick and shot up into the air. Rising to a height of several inches above the candle, the infant flame hovered there, seemingly content for a few moments more, then it began to change again.

Slowly the rich golden light of the flame began to shift in hue. From deep within its center a blue/white brilliance began to form until, after several minutes, the gold had all but vanished save for a very small area at the tip of the flame. The remainder of its small body was a series of ever lightening colors of paler light until at the very center it was a pure white, the likes of which Duncan was certain he had never seen before.

Watching this glowing curiosity with open-mouthed intensity, he flinched when the small flame darted forward, coming to a halt a few inches short of Max's impassive face. He watched the flame sit there as if studying her and then, with the same quick, darting movements, it scrutinized her, not unlike a curious animal would a stranger entering its domain. This bizarre scrutiny continued until the small flame had made a complete circle around Max. It appeared to sniff, if a flame can be said to do such a thing, at her clothing and hair before returning to its original position in front of her face.

Slowly Max raised her left hand and extended it, palm up, toward the flame. In response to this gesture, the small flame darted back just out of reach and sat there for several minutes. Then it moved cautiously up to the tip of her fingers, sat there a few moments longer, then slowly glided over her outstretched fingers, coming to rest in the palm of her hand.

For the next several minutes Max balanced the small flame in the center of her palm. Then, with her right hand, she held something over the flame and released it. Almost instantly the flame flickered with a kind of animalistic anger. Duncan could smell the faint odor of burnt hair. Then the flickering stopped. Everything seemed to stop. It was as if the very air currents within the room froze.

Abruptly, with a sound like a microscopic jet plane, the small flame shot up out of Max's hand and through the ceiling, vanishing from sight.

February 8th—12:56 a.m.

40 hours, 34 minutes until sunset . . .

IT WAS A SMALL THING, NO MORE THAN A TICKLING OF HIS consciousness, yet it woke him.

Malcom's eyes flashed open, and for the first few seconds he moved no further, allowing his senses to probe the thick darkness beyond his bed. His eyes registered a subtle variation in the darkness. His ears detected a fragile crackling sound. A trembling in the pit of his stomach told him that which had sent the rope of sand was moving against him once more.

Malcom pulled himself into a seated position, almost immediately confronting this newest harbinger of things to come.

Like the sounds that proceeded it, this latest specter was small in size, no larger than the flame of a candle on a child's birthday cake, yet different. Though diminutive in size, the light glowing from its tiny heart was equal to flames of a much larger variety. So harmless in appearance, so charming in its movements, so unthreatening in its presence was the miniature flicker that Malcom experienced a lifting of his previous dread.

He still firmly believed the rope of sand had been sent as a warning from some lesser godhead jealous of his growing powers, but surely this undersized wraith was nothing more than a shy tribute to his future glory—perhaps a herald of the return of the great god of light, a return for which he would be responsible.

Buoyed by these arrogant notions, a condescending smile curled up the corners of his thick lips. "Why is it you have come to me at this hour, my astral one?" His voice was rich with the arrogance of his own convictions. "Speak to me that which you have come so far to deliver. Speak it to me and then be gone, for it is late and you disturb my rest, littlest brother."

Malcom's speech appeared to have little effect on the small flame before uttering the words "littlest brother," but at their sounding the flame began to shiver, flickering wildly as if angered.

Malcom watched the miniature flame as it began to move down off the foot of his bed and onto the shimmering surface of the black satin comforter that covered him. With growing alarm he watched as it moved toward him, leaving a fiery wake in its passing. When it mounted his foot and slid down to his ankle, Malcom abandoned his arrogance and lashed out at the spreading flames, but rather than smothering their number, his actions only seemed to increase them.

Still certain in his own mind that the little flame was a good omen, Malcom could not bring his hands to strike it as it continued its course over his body. The comforter began to smolder around him as the child flames of this diminutive parent grew in size with each inch of cloth they devoured until they had surrounded his body like a frame, leaving a broad black shimmering pathway over him upon which only the tiny flame moved.

Driven back against the headboard, his gaze was riveted on the hypnotic movements of the miniature flame, not unlike the gaze of the white doves his mother's pet used to devour. As he watched, the small flame moved nearer until it settled on the back of his left hand.

At its touch the skin under the flame registered a sensation of extreme cold, and a bit of Malcom's fear retreated once again until the flame began to move and his gaze fell on the blackened trail left in the flame's wake. Jerking his hand up toward his face, the flame skittering away, his eyes widened to impossible widths as he watched his skin begin to wither and crack open, exposing the very bone beneath. A cry was strangled in his throat as the crack continued to widen until the skin and all layers beneath it slipped over the sides of his hand, leaving only a skeletal appendage behind.

The flame shot forward attacking his arm a second time. In its wake, the skin of his arm cracked, peeling open to the bone.

All thoughts of godly heralds vanished, his arrogance thrown aside, Malcom rolled away, trying vainly to escape the small monster, only to be brought up short by the very real and tangible heat of the flames holding him prisoner in the center of the bed. Again and again he tried to beat his way through the ringlet of flames, only to be driven back by the intensity of their heat. A series of whimpers worked their way up out of his clogged larynx as, unable to retreat, he was forced to confront his tormentor.

He began to formulate one last effort to gain sway. When the words were clearly formed in his mind he made to speak.

Like a projectile launched from the muzzle of a gun, the small flame shot forward at the same instant his lips began to part, slicing through the partially opened fleshy barrier. Piercing even his white teeth, it ripped down the length of his tongue, slamming off the back of his throat. At this concussion it split its tiny self into two separate entities, one racing down his throat while the other cut through the spongy material above, drilling its way into his brain. Arriving there, it exploded.

Malcom abruptly sat up, the sound of his scream still reverberating through the house. Slack-jawed, wild-eyed, his hair plastered wetly against his sweating forehead, he gulped great gasping breaths of air. The hammering of his heart pounded in his ears. Fighting his way free of the covers, he stumbled off the bed and lurched into the center of the darkened room, his bulging eyes raking the darkness for the diminutive demon of his dream. Dream! Abruptly his search skittered to a halt as that simple word penetrated his brain.

A dream, nothing more than a dream. A small bubble

of hysterical laughter slipped out of him. Leaning against the bed, he breathed deeply, the sound of that breathing nearly, but not quite, swallowing up a new sound, no more than a tickling at his consciousness yet . . .

The sounds of Malcom's screams at the sight of the shriveled and burnt replica of himself on the bed shattered the still of the great house once again, their report lost to the outside world, but not to Max who acknowledged their passing—and by that passing the completion of the flame's task and its return to that place between worlds it called home.

For an instant she thought to include Duncan in this triumph but desisted. Glancing down the darkened hallway to the closed door of the guest bedroom she wished him peaceful rest.

Pushing herself up from the couch she swayed there for a moment, the full depth of her fatigue weighing heavily on her. Willing her aching legs to cross the living room, she mounted the stairs, then paused. Turning her bleary glaze to the huge windows, she focused on the face of the swollen moon.

"Walk close with me, great mother," she said softly. "Do not desert your child now as she faces the tide." With a small bowing of her head Max continued the climb, her mind already turning to the greatest of her tasks.

Settling onto her makeshift bed on the floor, she immediately reminded herself to make a mental note to finish preparations with Riley first thing in the morning. Then, pushing sleep from her weary mind, she centered on more demanding needs.

Perhaps almost from the first days of her involvement on this case she had known this hour would come. The monster responsible for this chaos must be utterly destroyed. The fact that the directing force of this terror was a human being gave her no pause. There was no guilt, no remorse, no emotions common to humans finding themselves in similar positions, perhaps save for a tiny, burning morsel of vengeance. But where none of these saving emotions registered on her conscious mind, they did so on another part of her being, and with that registry her already aged soul grew older still.

Several courses of action immediately presented themselves to her and were immediately abandoned. While a bullet in Malcom Westeridge's deserving brain had a certain savage appeal it was not an option holding a prominent position at the top of the list. The employment of forces such as those he used were also not a prime selection. Where as the bullet had a more immediate physical punishment, this second option had one equally dire if not as immediate, a fact Malcom had apparently overlooked. Or was he too much of a novice to understand? Max considered this possibility for some time.

Westeridge could be nothing more than a skilled novice in the realm of magic and this his maiden venture into the hidden sciences.

Westeridge was, trusting the accuracy of her impressions, an educated savage wrapping himself in the mantle of a sophisticated man while harboring in his heart the primitive heritage of his ancestors. He had access to literature on the subject and, thanks to the indoctrination of his childhood, a firmly entrenched belief system. All of the necessary elements were in place. Max's own introduction to the art had been far less fluid. So it was not so very far a reach to believe Malcom, a gifted amateur, was overreaching his abilities with potentially fatal consequences. Stunning evidence of his lack of mastery lay in the animal savagery of the spirit's attack on it's victims. A true adept would have had more control over the creature, guiding its killing, not simply allowing it to run wild. No, the more Max thought on it the more convinced she became of Malcom as a novice. In that knowledge lay the key.

Because of his ego, Westeridge had stepped across the threshold and, not content to play the part of neophyte, launched himself into the role of master against forces his meager understanding could not remotely comprehend. Was there a way in which Max might insinuate herself between Malcom and the spirit, thereby turning the creature against him without actually calling it out in her own behest? Where Malcom did not understand the payment required by such acts Max did, and the alternative of allowing Westeridge to pay that debt was by far the most appealing.

11:44 a.m.—29 hours, 46 minutes until sunset . . .

Malcom shoved the fragile pages of the ancient manuscript away from him, causing several of the lower sheets to fragment and crumble into dust. Mentally he conjured pleasant images of the thief who had procured the pages for him, suffering numerous delicious torments for having served his master so poorly. Never did he consider that the work had been incomplete before the theft and that, even had all the pages been intact, the information he now thought to seek would not have appeared on them. All that filled his fevered mind now was the desperate search for the reasons behind these recent attacks on his person.

For the briefest of moments he had considered the possibility that in his rush to resurrect his god, he had insulted other deities, but he had quickly abandoned such a notion. Certainly he was protected by his god and therefore immune to such attacks. Besides, he reasoned, if he had erred in some way he would not now control the most powerful of the lower gods, the mighty Lord of the Night Hammer. No, these assaults were not the results of his own actions but some outside force. But who?

Who could wield such power and have remained hidden from him? Quickly he eliminated his own associates. Their low birth and peasantlike ignorance ruled out such a possibility. With equal quickness he ruled out the possibility of these acts having been prompted by his mother's vengeful spirit, knowing, by virtue of his own chauvinism, females incapable of such power, dead or alive. He had run the gambit of possible suspects when, quite unbidden, the faces of the two detectives, the annoying Anglo and the mutant Oriental, flashed into his mind. Orientals were a sly race, not unschooled in their own brand of magic, he thought. It might be possible the Chinaman's spirit was seeking retribution against the man who had directed his killer.

He considered this possibility for some time, then abandoned it. The Chinaman was not the target of the assassin. It was no fault of Malcom's that the stupid man had simply gotten in the way. Besides, he assured himself, Orientals were a subservient race, unlike his own warrior ancestors, and even their ancient gods would not lift a hand to the future master of such a powerful race. The Anglo he dismissed even quicker, certain that the race's adoration of their anemic Christ immediately ruled them incapable of such feats. Who was this power moving against him?

3:00 p.m. — 26 hours, 30 minutes until sunset . . .

Malcom stretched out in his chair resting his head against its high, worn back. Slowly turning the chair toward the window, he gazed out at the gardens below and the Pacific beyond, only a part of his mind occupied with the conversation. As the woman's nasal voice droned on in his ear, he cradled the phone between cheek and shoulder, dropping his hands to the arms of the chair. Suppressing a sigh, he willed the irritation from his voice, softly crooning, "Of course, Samantha, I'm absolutely certain you'll manage the affair with your usual aplomb. You are, after all, our guiding light in such areas." All the while he fervently wished Samantha would suffer a stroke, leaving him to more urgent matters.

Swinging back to the desk he pulled another of the volumes he had removed from the museum's research lab and began thumbing through its contents. Even as his eyes scanned the worn pages, he knew he would find nothing relevant to his current situation, still . . .

"Really, Samantha, I'm sure whatever you think on the matter will be correct. As for the menu, I'm certain the caterers will—" He broke off in midsentence as his words became lost behind an annoying blockage in his throat. Covering the receiver, he coughed once and then again, and the blockage vanished. Uncovering the receiver he continued, "I'm sorry, Samantha, but—"

Suddenly his posture became tense, the phone forgotten on his shoulder. He tried to swallow but suddenly seemed unable to. Opening his mouth he tried to cough, the air passing through unhindered as if nothing blocked its way. Then something tickled at the back of his throat, and he bent forward abruptly. The phone slipped to the floor as he gagged.

He gagged for several minutes until his face was red from the effort and his throat was raw, but nothing emerged. Gradually the discomfort in his throat was replaced by a new sensation. At first it was so strange a sensation his mind could put no name to it. Annoyed and a bit frightened by this nameless thing he stuck his finger into his mouth and touched the back of his tongue where the sensation had begun. He found nothing, yet the feeling persisted.

Frantically he pulled open the bottom desk drawer and snatched out the mirror he kept there. He craned his neck, trying to see into his mouth. Swinging the chair around into the light of the open window, he twisted first one way then another, unable to gain a clear view of the area in question. He was about to abandon the clumsy mirror when a tiny glimmer of movement caught his attention.

Frozen, he sat there, helplessly watching as the tiny horror slowly finished its journey. For nearly a full minute the wasp sat, perched on his lower lip, its rounded, triangular-shaped head turning from side to side in typical insect fashion. Slowly, and with extreme caution, he pulled his tongue back, curling it painfully toward the roof of mouth, fearing an accidental collision with the creature's tail. He redirected his breath to his nostrils, afraid to disturb the insect, and swallowed down a whimper as it turned around to reenter.

He lost track of all else as the creature crawled over his teeth, stepping down onto the soft, wet underbelly of his tongue. The scraping of its tiny feet drove him near to madness with their touch. When its wings began to move he could feel the breeze they created against the soft flesh there, yet he dared not react. Suddenly it flew out of his mouth, and such a wave of relief washed over him that his bladder involuntarily released itself.

He became aware of the clinging wetness between his legs, and at the sight of his disgrace the urge for revenge reared it's head.

He searched the air for the wasp and found, to his delight, that the creature sat upon one of the books on his desk. Carefully, he removed one of the heavy volumes, taking special caution not to disturb the insect. As he raised the book, he had the strange feeling the wasp was watching him, but if so it gave no evidence of fear.

Slamming the volume down atop the creature, a twisted smile turned up one side of his face. For good measure he bore down on it to crush the small insect more fully. Dropping down into his chair a flicker of irritation raced across his face as he came in contact with it's wet surface, but that sensation was soon erased by the overwhelming relief flooding his being. For a few brief moments he sat there oblivious to all else when gradually he became aware of a persistent humming.

As his ears centered on that sound a moment of panic flashed through him, vanishing as his gaze drifted to the phone, its receiver dangling at the end of it's cord. He returned it to its cradle and the humming ceased—at least most of it did.

Glaring at the phone, he jiggled the receiver, making certain it was in its proper place. Still the sound persisted. Slowly his gaze turned toward the two books sitting in the center of the desk. Watching them closely he frowned, his mind telling him it wasn't possible, but even as that thought lanced through his brain his hand was already moving toward them. Once, then again, he slammed his balled fist down violently against the top book.

That part of his mind that lived in the civilized world told him an insect that size could not possibly have survived such a blow. At the same time, his more primitive half reminded him where the creature had originated from. Both halves of the man warred against one another, one half demanding he remove the top book and see the evidence for himself, the other urging him to flee.

In the end the primitive half won out, and without a backward glance Malcom left. Although his eyes did not verify it that primitive half of his mind told him the creature yet lived, something he could have seen for himself had he waited but a few moments longer.

6:43 p.m. — 22 hours, 47 minutes until sunset . . .

Hanging up the receiver Max rotated her head in a circle, wincing at the soreness this caused. The small chime on her watch sounded. Five o'clock. Time for a break, she thought. Walking into the living room she sat down on the arm of the couch and glanced at Duncan. "I don't know about you, but I'm starved. All you've had is coffee since you got up. What would you say to a good meal out, my treat?"

After a moment's pause, he slowly lowered his newspaper and glanced in her direction. "You look tired."

"Well, that's a start. You realize that's the longest sentence you've spoken to me all day?"

He glanced at her a second time, then looked away almost as if he could not bear to look at her. "You were busy. I didn't get up until late . . ." His words trailed off.

Max slid down onto the couch. "Bullshit. You want to talk about it or shall we—"

"If it's all the same to you, I'd like to forget about last night." The anger was thick in his voice.

"If that's what you want," she said quietly.

"What I want is to forget you, this case and the last month of my life. That's what I really want."

"Okay, now that you're mad at me again, how's your appetite?"

"I'm not mad at you, damn it," he growled, "and get that cute look off your face. You'll just have to overlook it if I seem a bit off to you, but I'm not real used to having everything I believe in torn up in front of my eyes and thrown in my face."

"I offered to buy you dinner."

"Don't you ever take anything seriously? Is that all this is to you, some kind of fucking joke?"

"You're too bright a man to believe anything that stupid."

"Well, forgive me I'm a bit thick right at this minute 'cause that's how it looks to me," he snapped, shoving the paper on his lap off onto the floor.

"You know you don't have to hide your fear from me." Duncan's head snapped around at that remark, but whatever he might have said was lost as he saw the expression on Max's face. "Because I'm every bit as scared by all this as you are."

"Then why do it?" he challenged, some of the heat gone out of his voice.

"For the same reason you've spent—what? Fifteen, twenty years?"

"Twenty," he answered evenly.

"Twenty years doing what you do. This is my job. I chose it, or maybe it chose me. Either way, it's what I do, and even if some parts of the job aren't to my liking, they go with the territory."

He considered her point for a moment, then said, "You could get out. It's not like you need the money."

She laughed abruptly. "When was the last time you showed up just for the check?"

He tried to answer but only shrugged, shaking his head. "It's not the same."

"Fuck it isn't. It's exactly the same. You have pimps and pushers and guys who blow their old ladies away for the sport of it. Me, I got poltergeists and things that go bump in the night."

After a short silence during which they both seemed to sigh mentally, Duncan said, "There's an envelope for you on that little table in the hallway. It came while you were . . ." He made a vague gesture toward the den.

"Oh yeah?"

He watched her go, trying in his mind to imagine her being afraid of anything. Even though this was the second time she'd admitted her fear to him, it was still a fuzzy concept.

She plopped down on the couch.

"What's up?"

"It's from Riley. Just a little note to let me know things are well in hand on his end, and these . . ." She held up a set of keys.

"Which are?"

"The keys to our new transport. I thought something a bit more substantial might be called for so Riley arranged it. It's in the parking lot now."

"How very efficient," he grumbled.

"You eating, Forbes?"

"You paying, Morgan?"

"So who else?"

"Then I'm eating, smart ass," he replied with mock sternness. As they stood up to go, he felt a strange urge to hug her, but he shook off the urge, certain she would not welcome the gesture.

In the hallway he paused in front of the mirror, ran his fingers through his hair then tugged his clothing into place. When he turned and smiled at her like a small boy seeking approval of his appearance, Max found herself biting back an urge to hug the big cop. Instead she flung open the door.

"Come on, Beau Brummel."

9:36 p.m.—19 hours, 54 minutes until sunset . . .

The Mercedes moved slowly up the drive.

It wasn't that Malcom was drunk, though he'd consumed enough to accomplish the task, but the edges of his focus were a bit on the fuzzy side. As he switched off the ignition his gaze turned to the darkened house, and for a moment he took pleasure in the fact that the usual anxiety it normally caused him was absent. This, he felt, was to the credit of the liquor he'd consumed, and a small part of his brain wondered why he hadn't seeked this refuge sooner.

The afternoon had been pure misery for him. Under normal circumstances the museum had always been his single refuge, a place to lose himself in the things he held most dear, but now even this had been torn away, driving him out into the real world and the only solace he could find.

Forgetting to lock the Mercedes for the first time in years, he climbed the stairs to the front door with slow, plodding steps. Standing there in the dark, fumbling with his keys, it was several minutes before his clouded mind registered the sounds his ears perceived.

At first it was no more than the gentle sounds of the wind, a rustling in the trees, a whispering in the grass—and then a piece of that gentleness dropped away.

He stared out into the darkness behind him, his ears no longer having to strain to capture the sound. Stepping further out onto the porch he squinted, confusion filling his mind as he looked at the trees and shrubs and found, though the sound of the wind was strong, that their branches did not move in the growing wind. Nothing moved, yet he heard movement.

Turning away, he located his missing key and quickly opened the door. Reaching inside, he flipped on the switches for the porch and ground lights, blinking at the glare that shone down from above his head. For several minutes he stood there, blearily squinting out into the night while the sound of the rushing wind pressed in around him.

Dust devils were not an uncommon phenomenon. They were common enough in the land of his birth, but those miniature tornadoes had come in the daylight—on days when the wind slithered through the tall grass and brushed against the hard branches of the few, draught-ravaged trees that dotted the landscape—not in the dark of night. Yet there one stood in the darkness, its shifting outline marked only by the debris filling its swirling core.

As he watched, the whirling spout of wind began to expand, drawing in the dried leaves edging the drive as well as bits of gravel, the small white pellets swarming in the thing's belly. His hand was reaching for the light, ready to return the abhorrent wind creature to the darkness when something began to take shape inside that small funnel. He stood there drawn by the revolving formation, trying to make sense of what his eyes sought to recognize.

Pulled out onto the edge of the porch by his own curiosity, tried to define the shifting shape. His attention was so wrapped in curiosity that at first he had not realized the wind dervish had moved closer to him until several of the small pellets flew off and struck him sharply.

Taking several steps backward, he realized the thing was moving toward him. Without awaiting further evidence of its bizarre behavior, he quickly backed over the threshold, his hand clamping onto the door, ready to close it if the thing pursued him. It did not.

Over a period of several more minutes his eyes gradually began to adjust to the moving texture of the thing, making him realize that within the swirling mass a face was slowly beginning to take shape. Consumed with the desire to capture the image, he strained his vision, small beads of perspiration glittering on his upper lip with the effort. Just as the face within the thing became clear to him, the situation altered drastically.

Despite the alcohol in his system, he managed to slam the door one second before the suddenly maddened dervish reached the porch. He swallowed a cry as the thing slammed into the wooden door, shaking it on its hinges. He lurched away, glaring at the trembling wood as the wind demon spent its fury, slowly dying away.

That which would not so quickly die away was the glimpse of the face that had fully formed within the whirling demon.

His own.

February 9th — 3:24a.m.

14 hours, 6 minutes until sunset . . .

THE SHEER VOLUME OF THE SCREAM FILLED THE HOUSE, setting the fragile crystal sconces in the dining room a tremble with its painful tones.

Malcom's head jerked up even before the first sound had been pushed aside by its twin. Pulling himself away from the desk, he stumbled to the doors and threw them open. The jarring cries echoed even louder in the hallway outside.

Pushed forward by dread, he staggered toward the source of the noise. Throughout the long hours of the night, his fear at each new occurrence had turned now to anger. Reaching the foyer, a dim recognition of the shrill shrieks and whines had begun to form in his mind, causing him to abandon the living room as its source with little more than a glance. Malcom fixed his attention on the closed doors of the long abandoned music room. Almost boldly, he flung them open, wincing at the wall of strident noise pelting out at him. Even before his hand reached out to the dimmer switch he knew the source of the racket, but as the lights flared he flinched at the sight he beheld.

Like some fragile, wounded thing, the great old harp trembled on it's narrow base. A tall floor candelabra had penetrated the heart of the instrument, the ruptured strings surrounding the wound writhing in the air like blunted serpents. The candelabra, flung there during one of Malcom's tantrums, flexed its trunk, its heavy metal base banging against the floor again and again, keeping a strange kind of cadence with the music of the angered strings. Its movements worked in concert with the instrument as it also labored to free itself and thereby its victim.

"Stop it!" he screamed.

As if the insanity had been controlled by a single switch, the writhing of the strings, the spasms of the candelabra and the trembling of the harp ceased as one, taking the riotous sounds with them. However their departure was just a small retreat, not a rout. Before the last sounds of conflict had vanished, they began again as the instrument and its tormentor continued their struggle.

Emboldened by the sound of his own words and his victory, however brief, he crossed toward the struggling pair, his posture taking on the air of a man on the attack. Almost as if recognizing the alteration in their audience, the harp and candelabra's efforts redoubled until with a barely audible twanging noise the candelabra dislodged itself, the suddenly freed strings launching it like a spear across the room.

Malcom twisted aside, the projectile slipping past him and slamming into the surface of the nearest door with sufficient force to bury itself into the wood.

The strings of the wounded instrument continued to writhe but now in an even more purposeful manner. Like severed worms the broken ends sought out their mates, intertwining until the rent formed by the candelabra had been healed. This done, the great old harp was silent and inanimate once more.

Forty miles away, Max smiled softly. Closing her eyes she turned her gaze inward, directing her thoughts to another. "Soon it will be your turn, old one. Hear my words and know them for the truth they are. The time of your imprisonment is near an end. I swear it." For several minutes she lay there in the dark, fearful that her words had not reached their goal when a sliver of ice raced through her body and then disappeared. A sigh of relief filled her as she pulled the covers tight around her, and she turned herself over to the drug of sleep, confident her message had been received.

9:21 a.m. — 8 hours, 9 minutes until sunset . . .

His body was stiff and sore, his eyes red and ringed by dark circles, every fiber of his being an open, tender sore. Shedding his soiled clothing, Malcom kicked them into the corner of the immaculate bathroom, taking no solace from the gleaming black tiles this morning.

Stepping into the midst of the steaming shower, he alternated between wincing as the hot water pummeled his body and groaning contentedly as the pummeling gradually became a caress. Eager to wash away the filth of his fatigue he soaped his thick, heavy body once, twice and then a third time. Each successive washing gave him a growing feeling of regaining control. Reluctant to leave this pleasant cocoon, he slowly lathered his hair as time ceased its forward progression, allowing him the luxury of gaining a slippery grasp of his own sanity once again.

His movements pleasantly lethargic, he pushed open the glass shower stall doors and reached out into the mist-filled room. Reaching out for a towel, his fingers registered the touch of the bare metal rack. Mildly annoyed by this inconvenience, he stepped out onto the tiles, his heavy-lidded eyes blinking slowly in a vain effort to pierce the mist. Locating a dark lump at the base of the wall below the rack he bent down and picked up the slightly dampened towel, then frowned as the thick cloth seemed to come away in his hand and fall in two halves to the floor.

Because of the thick steam several things slipped past him, hidden by the fog, but when something wet and cloying wrapped itself around his face he knew the contours of his reality had been altered once more.

He jerked open the bathroom door, releasing the moistened air into the bedroom beyond.

Slowly, as the mist slipped away, the true condition of the once-pristine bathroom became jarringly evident. A thick collection of cobwebs festooned the ceiling draping down onto wall and lighting fixtures. A thick layer of dust, bearing the indelible print of his wet feet on its surface, covered the floor and the pile of discarded clothing. The once shining black tiles that covered the walls were streaked with dust and grime, many having broken away and fallen to the floor.

In the spaces where a large number of the tiles had fallen away, exposing the yellowing white plaster behind them were drawings of great flowing figures. To anyone else those drawings would have been unrecognizable, but to him they were all too clear. Carefully drawn in the ancient language of the Mayan, the message said simply, "Go no further."

He read those three simple words over several times. He stood before them visibly shaking, but this time not from fear. Throwing his head back, he glared up at the ceiling and screamed out his defiance.

"No! No!" he bellowed. Wheeling, he strode from the ruined room into the comparative order of his bedroom. "No, you will not stop me!" he screamed to the room in general. "You will not stop me. You cannot. I am too powerful now. I am one of you now. I am the god you must fear. I am the god!"

12:00 p.m. — 5 hours until sunset . . .

Frank Martinez was proud of his small daughter Gina. With a fatherly pride he would have found embarrassing to display in front of his male friends, he straightened the ruffled skirt of the new dress his ex-wife had dressed the child in for her monthly visit with her grandparents.

Gently, he told Gina to be a good girl and to stay in the car and that daddy would be right back. Then he rushed into the market for the beer his father had come to expect with each of these visits. The lines were not particularly long, nor was he gone more than a few minutes, but when he returned to the car he would discover that a very large piece of his heart had been stolen. His daughter was missing.

3:00 p.m. — 2 hours, 30 minutes until sunset . . .

"Lawrence, are you sure this looks all right?"

"Gabby, you're getting on my nerves, sweety."

"But does it look all right?" Gabriel Holt pleaded, glaring at his image in the mirror.

"Wonderful, marvelous. Now give it a rest, will you, swee . . . Well, well, well, aren't we impressive."

Holt turned abruptly with a broad smile on his face that quickly faded to a pout as he realized Lawrence was looking out the front window and not at him.

Pulling into the driveway, a bright silver Mercedes stretch limo complete with liveried driver rolled to a stop at the front door. Both Gabby and Lawrence, noses pressed to the living room window, watched eagerly as a tall blonde giant got out from the driver's side and moved up the walk to the front door.

"Please God, can we keep him?" Lawrence whispered softly as Gabby rushed to open the door.

If either men noticed the driver's hesitant delivery or slightly nervous appearance, that was buried under their appreciation of the way he filled out the uniform and his absolutely charming Irish accent.

Wrapped in the comfort of the Mercedes spacious rear seat, imported champagne in hand and excited beyond words at the prospect of a flight on a private jet to San Francisco and a night at the opera, Gabby and Lawrence were certain God was in his heaven and all was right with the world. After all the nonsense of the past week with the police, neither was too eager to look this gift horse in the mouth. The first prize in a contest they knew nothing about from a store they had never been in was just one of those wonderful things that happened to people like themselves.

"There they are. Very nice, Conna. Right on time as

well," Max smiled broadly as the limo passed, catching Conna's subtle nod. Starting the engine, she looked to Duncan. "Showtime."

"I really hate this shit," he grumbled, folding his arms across his chest. "You said we weren't going to break the law. What do you call this?"

"My, my, but we've gotten fastidious of late, haven't we? Need I refresh your memory about a certain climbing expedition in the hills of Pasadena?"

"That was different."

"Like hell," Max snapped, turning into the Holt driveway. "You know what I think your problem is?"

"No, and I don't care. Just get out there and do what you have to and don't get caught."

Balancing a large basket of flowers in front of her, Max grinned back over her shoulder. "I thought you had that possibility covered after the Pasadena gig?"

"Will you get the fuck on with it," he snarled.

Max smiled innocently and headed for the front door.

With a furtive glance over her shoulder to check for nosy neighbors, she held the basket in one hand like a shield while employing the other with the lock.

Duncan twisted nervously, his eyes scanning the street for any potential interruption. Checking the front door he felt a certain relief to find Max inside and the door closed. Halfway home, he told himself, but 15 minutes later that sentiment had worn a bit thin. Checking his watch, he ground his teeth silently, cursing Max one moment while pleading for her speedy return the next. Trying vainly to calm his already frazzled nerves, he made a survey of the van's luxurious appointments, finding momentary interest in the cellular phone, but when his eyes drifted over to the instrument's digital clock what little patience he had retained vanished.

No longer caring about nosy neighbors, he climbed out of the van, rushed up the walk and into the house. "Max? Max?" He called in a loud whisper.

"What?"

Locating her at the head of a long flight of stairs he rushed part way up. "What's taking so damn—"

"Stop whispering, dummy. We're the only people here!"

"I said, what the fuck's taking so long?" Duncan yelled.

"No need to shout. I can't find the bloody thing."

"What do you mean you can't find it? It has to be here. You said everybody got one."

"Well, you and I know that, but that doesn't alter the fact that I can't find the bleedin' thing, does it?" she grumbled, coming downstairs.

"Well, get up there and look again. I'll check down here."

"What the fuck do you think I've been doing? I've looked and it's not there, so it has to be down here."

"Are you sure we really need it?"

"Do you think I'm doing this for practice? Of course we need it. I'll take the back of the house, you take the front, and sing out if you find it. I've already seen more of this place than I ever wanted to."

Max disappeared into the back recesses of the house, leaving Duncan to his own devices in the front. With anxiety rumbling in his belly, he moved into the sterile modern expanse of the living room.

"What the fuck are you doing in there?" Max snarled upon returning to the living room minutes later and finding Duncan in the hall closet.

"Looking, that's what."

Slamming the door he marched over to the couch and sat down. "I don't know where the ugly little fucker could be."

"Wonderful." Max sighed, perching on the arm of a convenient chair.

"Now what?"

"I'm thinking."

"This is no time to try something new."

"Piss off." Looking around quickly, her eyes narrowed as she concentrated on the problem. "They obviously spent a lot of money getting this place to look this way, and it sure as shit doesn't go with the decor in here. But it is an award, and I don't recall seeing any others in the house. Now where would I put an award so that everybody who comes into the house would see it, but it wouldn't ruin my decor or seem too pushy?" Max pondered this for a moment longer then grinned broadly and rushed from the room.

Less than a minute later she returned with the trophy in hand.

"Where'd you find it?" Duncan frowned.

"Where's the one place everybody always goes with nothing else to do but study the wallpaper?"

"Where?"

"Think about it. It'll come to you."

In the van, Max tied the last strands of Malcom's hair from her stash around the sculpture's neck. As Duncan backed down the drive she considered the small sculpture, repeating mentally the precarious permutations she must follow precisely in the coming hours. Flicking a bead of sweat from her forehead she glanced in Duncan's direction, relieved to find him absorbed in his driving and not witness to the trembling of the sculpture as it sat in her hands.

3:45 p.m. — 1 hour, 45 minutes until sunset . . .

A chilly northwesterly breeze was rapidly becoming a wind heavy with the smell of rain. A few dark clouds were beginning to roll up over the western horizon, and beachfront residents along Pacific Coast Highway were beginning to fill sand bags in defiance of local television weathermen who were predicting a warming trend.

Max turned up the collar of her jacket and glanced worriedly at the western horizon.

"Get down. There he goes now," she hissed.

Duncan hugged the damp ground, lifting his head just high enough to see the guard at the rear door come out onto the dock and begin his rounds. In the stillness he could hear the old-fashioned key marker slide into the round clock the guard carried to record his rounds.

"We've got ten minutes before the museum closes and another ten to get back to the van before Westeridge can leave at the earliest."

"What if you can't get it in the trunk?"

Max wiggled a flat silver key between her fingers. "Why do you think we went to all that trouble getting a Benz limo? There he goes," she said quietly as the guard reentered the museum. "Here goes nothing." She grinned then crawled forward on all fours through the shrubbery.

For a minute or two Duncan lost sight of her as she worked her way along the lot to the space nearest the door where Westeridge's Mercedes was parked.

Hunkering down behind the car, she glanced around quickly, then put the key in the lock. Max turned the key, fully expecting the trunk to pop open, and when it didn't she found herself suddenly wishing she'd heeded Duncan's warning. Several more times she twisted the key, each attempt meeting with an equal lack of success.

"Now what!"

Max bit her tongue to keep from screaming. "Damn you, don't you ever—"

"Give me that thing and keep watch."

Duncan tried jiggling the key, pressing and turning and even pulling it out and shoving it back in again, but nothing worked.

"Let me," Max hissed, trying to elbow him aside.

"Look out," he growled and twisted the key as hard as he could. The trunk lid popped open, and Max thrust the small Chac Mool inside. It wasn't until they were safely back in the van that Duncan held up the half of the trunk key that had come away in his hand.

4:15 p.m.—1 hour, 15 minutes until sunset . . .

Malcom Westeridge stepped out of the aging elevator and crossed the central hall toward the great terra cotta figure. As he drew near, he looked at the floor below it. He smiled a small, arrogant smile as he realized the annoying chain of sand had not returned. Lifting his gaze to the Chac Mool's cold face he said quietly, "Soon, my brother, soon."

As he started to turn away something glinted on the face of the statue, catching his attention.

Standing there, he watched helplessly as tiny rivulets of clear liquid sprung up across the statue's surface, running down onto the floor. He blinked once and then a second time, thinking his vision was at fault, but the rivulets remained with new arrivals appearing with each passing second.

Rushing forward, he reached up to the statue and attempted to staunch the strange flowing liquid with his hands. It was then the smell reached his nostrils. Sniffing at his wet fingertips, he quickly recognized the tang of salt water.

"No," he shouted. "No, I will not allow this."

Despite his words, several of the small rivulets merged into one larger spring, and as they did, the ancient clay beneath their watery flow began to crumble. Frantically he pushed at the discomposing earth in a vain effort to halt its destruction, but more and more of the statue began to crumble and fall away.

Staggering back from the decaying statue he cried out and covered his face with his hands.

"Sir?"

Malcom swung around glaring into the face of the guard. "Go away," he shouted, his normally deep voice reaching an almost feminine pitch. "What are you doing here?"

"I heard you. I thought I heard—"

"You heard nothing. Get out, imbecile. Get out!"

The guard slowly backed away, then turned and fled from the hall. Malcom's fevered gaze followed his departure, and when he was certain he was alone once more, he looked quickly down at his hands. A small sob caught in his throat as their dry, clean surface greeted his gaze. His head swung around, and he looked at the statue. Slowly, his mind began to grasp the root of this deception, and a deeper fear gripped his mind. Nothing must harm the great figure now. Not this close. Nothing must allow Titiachhuan to escape his control. Backing away, he spun around and rushed out. Behind him the Chac

Mool sat unchanged and patient as it had for nearly two thousand years.

He stabbed the key into the lock and climbed quickly into the Mercedes. Slowly, he willed the vision of the crumbling statue out of his mind. "So close. I must concentrate. Nothing must mar my concentration. Not now, not this close."

Breathing deeply, he turned his thoughts to the ritual and the rewards that lay just beyond his reach. Filling his mind with this, he smiled quietly. I am too powerful to be stopped now, he thought, smiling all the more. He put the car in reverse then reached up to adjust the rearview mirror.

Perhaps it was because the windows were up, or possibly it was the gradually rising wind that prevented the sounds of his screams from being heard—screams at the sight of the wet clay clinging to his cheek.

"We can't be out of cigarettes now," Duncan moaned.

"Just keep your eyes open for Westeridge. We lose him now, and you can kiss this whole thing off."

"I'm watching. Quit being such a pissant and look for my smokes."

Max climbed into the rear of the van and pulled out a large black satchel. She had just found a pack of Duncan's brand when she heard him exclaim, "Jesus Christ!" and then the van lurched out from under her.

Fighting her way forward, she felt gravity slipping away from her again as Duncan banked the van around a corner, crossing the intersection and running a red light in the process.

"What in fucking hell are you doing?" she snarled, slamming herself down into the seat and grabbing hold of the dash.

"You see that black dot up there moving like a bat outa hell? Well, that's our boy. Come on, you silly bitch, move!" he swore at the motorist in front of them.

Max squinted, trying to pick out Malcom's Mercedes from the other cars starting to clog Pacific Coast Highway in the Friday night rush for home. Pulling her seat belt around her, Max shook her head. "I think you can forget my little lecture about tailing him subtly."

The van lurched into the right lane and managed to gain another three car lengths before skidding back to a five mile an hour crawl.

"Well, that was wonderful," Duncan said.

"We're in the same lane as him, aren't we?"

"Yeah, only about forty cars back."

"Look, where's that silly bastard going now?"

Duncan watched Westeridge slide into the exit lane and moved up toward 3rd St. "I think I know." Duncan craned his neck trying to see out the side mirror. "Fat lot a good it's gonna do us. Nothing's moving."

"Hold on. I think I can fix that," Max said, flinging off her seat belt and dashing into the back of the van. A few seconds later she scrambled back, hugging a red plastic bubble dome and trailing black wires. Rolling down the window she slapped the dome on the roof and connected two wires to something inside the glove compartment. As the line of drivers in front of them began to edge nervously away from the flashing light and wailing siren she grinned. "I thought it might come in handy."

Wasting little time Duncan squeezed the van hard up against the dividing rail and worked his way toward the exit. When they slid into the off-ramp lane, Max reached out and pulled the dome off the roof.

The view at the top of the overpass was not encouraging. Westeridge's car was nowhere in sight. "Don't tell me we lost the bastard," Max groaned.

Ignoring oncoming traffic, Duncan spun the wheel left and roared out onto the overpass. "Where are you going?" she asked.

"If we're right about Holt being the next victim he's got to be heading for Glendale, right? There's a shortcut through the barrio. My guess is that's where the bastard's gone."

They continued, pausing at each cross street and looking up toward the beckoning hills. Max saw the sun beginning to drop toward the horizon, but made no mention of their need to find their quarry quickly, both well aware of the price of a tardy arrival. Approaching a broad intersection only a few blocks from the Holt house, Duncan turned to the right.

"Where are you going?"

"You said he needed to be up high. Well, what about up there?" He pointed up into the mountains and the homes that crawled up toward the top.

The Mercedes turned into a broad street, passing a brightly colored sign announcing the future location of Mountain View homes and directing prospective buyers to models located on Seaview Avenue. Moving past the deserted model, the Mercedes continued up to a nameless street where the signs of construction bordered the broad street. Driving to the end of that street, Malcom turned into the driveway at the last house in the row, a two story colonial with a bright red "Sold" sign out front. With little more than a quick glance over his shoulder, he crossed quickly to the house and entered.

"He could be up here in any one of these houses and we'd never know," Duncan said flatly.

Max looked at the homes around them, sharing Duncan's dejection, when a small blue sign caught her attention. Sliding forward in her seat, she looked up to the top of the hill. "Let's take a look up there."

"Where?"

"Up there. Mountain View."

"Why bother? Look at the sun."

Max didn't need to look. "It's not sunset, not yet, but it will be if you don't move your ass."

The two glared at one another for a moment, then Duncan, grumbling under his breath, turned in the direction indicated on the sign. Five minutes later they had both forgotten their anger.

"Look at that. Parked in the driveway."

"Cheeky bastard. Don't get too close in case he's got somebody watching out front."

Parking the van two houses away behind a small backhoe, they wasted little time scrambling up to the house.

Inside the colonial, what one day would be a living room for some unsuspecting family had been converted to an arena for spectacle. The west-facing floor-to-ceiling windows framed the setting sun that flooded the room with its light. Malcom turned slowly, his arms outstretched, his mind firmly fixed on his part of the ceremony, arrogantly ignoring the ministrations of his attendants as they fitted him with the accoutrements of his role. As the heavy gold headpiece settled onto his brow, the attendants backed away, their eyes reverently lowered.

Duncan pressed his face close to Max's ear. "That opening there, you figure that's where they're at?"

Max nodded, her attention riveted on the area in question.

"I'll go first," Duncan whispered.

Before he could take more than half a step toward his goal Max latched onto his arm and tugged him back to her.

"What?"

"Remember, no matter what you see or hear, you must not move until I give you the signal."

"I know, I know," he hissed irritably.

"I know you know. I just want to make sure you do it. One wrong move here and we are right and truly screwed to the wood."

Duncan gave her a withering look, then pulled free of her hold. Crouching down, he sprinted across the opening between the two houses. Drawing his service revolver, he looked to Max, gesturing her forward.

Malcom took up his position before the blackened stone altar raising his arms above his head. Using all the power of his deep melodious voice he began the invocation, the strange harmonics of the Mayan language mixing hypnotically with the soft undercurrent of the flute. His dark eyes, the pupils so condensed as to make them all but invisible, gazed into the fiery orb in concentration so fixed as to render him oblivious to all else.

Duncan frowned at the sound of the strange words and eerie music that drifted away on the rising wind. Out of the corner of his eye he noted the presence of a clump of small dark clouds roiling down over the mountaintop above them but gave them little heed. Looking to Max, he tried to gain her attention but her gaze was directed not to him but to the slowly disappearing sun.

Eyes reduced to mere slits, Max stared into the sun, her concentration fixed firmly on the words of the invocation. Slowly and with infinite care she recorded the words within her mind then rapidly repeated each phrase and sentence backwards, mimicking as closely as possible the placement of each inflection and rolling consonances.

Slowly lowering his arms, Malcom retrieved the small, heavy stone knife from its resting place on the altar and held it out to catch the last glowing radiance of the rapidly vanishing sun, chanting over it all the while. When the sun had vanished below the horizon, he drew the blade back to him, pressing its cool surface first to his forehead and then to his lips. Stooping quickly, he likewise touched his forehead and lips to the altar. Behind him the music rose in volume.

Taking up a position behind the altar, Malcom took up the conch shell and, raising it to his lips, blew into it. Almost as if having sprung into life at the bequest of the shell's single note, the flames in two braziers, placed on either side of the altar, glowed into life, filling the room with a pale imitation of the sun's glory. At the third sounding, he lowered the horn from his lips and turned his gaze to the small girl. In response to that gaze, not unlike the dancing flames, she lurched into the ancient dance, her small body moving flawlessly to the strains of the music.

The faint rumble of thunder echoed away against the high peaks above the house. Max took a deep breath and closed her eyes, willing all her concentration on the words drifting out from the room above.

Malcom turned his attention to the swaying child before him. Slowly he spread his arms in a welcoming gesture, and her rhythmic movements stuttered to a halt. Looking up at him through glazed eyes, she moved forward, clambering clumsily up on to the altar, and spread herself out upon its surface.

Max looked quickly to Duncan, then eased her head to eye level with the floor above. Though his back was to her and the long feathered cape blocked much of his actions from her view, Max registered the sharp upward swing of one arm and without further hesitance gestured Duncan into action.

Raising the dagger above his head Malcom prepared for the downward stroke when something solid collided with his calves, causing him to pitch backwards. Straining to regain his balance, he fell forward over the altar and the drugged child lying there.

"Get away from that kid," Duncan snarled, jerking Malcom back from the altar.

While Duncan centered his attentions on Malcom, Max turned hers to the three remaining men, surreptitiously dropping the remaining stash from Malcom's bathroom into the brazier as she passed. Dividing her focus between the two musicians to the left of the altar and the acolyte on the right, she made certain each saw the gun in her hand. "Let's not get nervous, gentlemen. Don't do anything rash and nobody will get hurt."

But instead of heeding her warning, the acolyte made a threatening move in her direction. With the fluid motions of a machine, Max swung the gun into the man's path and fired, putting a bloody cavity through the instep of his right foot.

Duncan glanced in the wounded man's direction, then pushed Malcom ahead of him. "Very nice."

Malcom, his gaze riveted on Max, stumbled, resisting Duncan's insistent pressure to move.

"Get over there with your friends, Westeridge, or I just might let the lady get in a little additional target practice."

Malcom whirled, his eyes narrowing to slits, the

golden head piece tumbling from his head. "Fool! I have rights you would not dare to violate."

Duncan grinned. "Try me."

"He knows we're not the one he has to fear, don't you, Malcom?" Max purred, moving closer.

A sneer fixed itself over his hard features, but giving lie to his confident veneer was a small tic pulling at the corner of his thick lips.

Seeing this chink in his armor Max allowed herself a tiny gloat. "We have yet to hear from Yohual-i-Tepuztli, don't we?"

The tic stopped abruptly and his eyes went wide, hearing the name of the dark god on the lips of the white bitch. "You foul his name with your mouth."

Duncan, keeping part of his attention on the group, looked down at the silent child. Placing his fingers just below the jaw line, he searched for a pulse. Turning back to the group he said urgently, "We better get a move on. There's almost no pulse."

Max nodded, her attention focused on the men. "You get the kid out of here. Adventist's Hospital's at the bottom of the hill."

"Wait a minute. You didn't say anything—"

"I changed my mind," Max snapped, hoping Forbes would buy the lie. "I never counted on the kid being drugged."

"I'll call from the van."

"No time. Get her out of here now. This lot will stay here with me until the cavalry arrives." Outside, thunder rumbled, causing Max to add quietly, "Which shouldn't be long now." More loudly she snapped, "Go on, get her out of here now."

Out of the corner of her eye, Max registered the nervous glances Malcom directed out the open window.

Duncan made a half-hearted protest, but his concern for the child overruled anything else. "I'll get her down, then come right back. Westeridge and I have some things to discuss." He returned his gun to its holster.

"Don't worry, me and the boys will find something to occupy ourselves with," Max said flatly, knowing if things moved according to plan, Westeridge would be far beyond conversation long before Duncan could return.

Lightning flickered outside the window, drawing the attention of everyone in the room. Almost before its light had vanished, Malcom suddenly came to life.

Max flinched, turning her head just enough to cause the blow to glance off her shoulder even before she fully realized she was under attack, but this small gesture did not save her completely. Malcom's fist slammed into her collar bone, driving her backward. As she tried to recover, she found herself toppling over the crippled acolyte huddled on the floor.

Duncan registered but a part of the attack, his mind already guiding his hand to the gun at his side. Pivoting toward Malcom, he shouted, "Hold it, motherfucker!"

Before he could pull the revolver free, Malcom flung a dark object at his head.

Max scrambled free of the acolyte, gaining her feet in time to see Duncan sway backward, clutching his forehead, and Malcom wheeling toward the doorway.

Staggered, Duncan pulled his gun, taking shaky aim at the fleeing Westeridge.

"No!" Max screamed, her cry washed away by the roar of the gun.

White dust showered into the air a few inches above the space Westeridge's darting form had vacated.

Knees buckling, Duncan slipped heavily to the floor.

Max took a hesitant step in his direction, torn between pursuing Westeridge and aiding Forbes.

"Get that bastard," Duncan groaned, settling her indecision.

Max sprinted out of the room.

Slamming against the doorjamb, Max staggered out onto the front porch. Regaining her stride she ran down the driveway toward the Mercedes which was momentarily stalled in the middle of the street as Malcom shifted out of reverse.

A cloud of smoke billowed from the rear wheel wells as the small Mercedes dug in and suddenly lurched forward. The tires were still screaming as Max stepped into the midst of the fresh trail they had left behind and, taking careful aim, clipped off three shots in rapid succession. The first shot pulled just to the left, wasting itself against the front of a small backhoe, the second whined off the cement but the third smashed into the Mercedes' rear window.

Max raced after the car, as she saw the window explode, heard the brake lock and saw the car slide sideways into the curve leading out into the street. No, she cried silently, don't die now, you bastard.

The Mercedes straightened out and swung down the street, heading away from the development.

Racing to the van she snatched open the door and leapt into the driver's seat. Max steered with one hand and tapped the 911 sequence into the cellular phone, cradling it against her cheek with her shoulder.

She heard the call connect as she maneuvered the lumbering van through the first tight curve ahead. Barely allowing the operator to finish her opening spiel, Max snapped, "I'm calling from a mobile phone in the new home construction area of Mountain View. Officer down, shots fired, send a car, ambulance needed. Hurry, please." Without waiting for the all too predictable questions that follow such a request, she broke the connection, tossing the phone into the seat beside her. Ahead, she caught a glimpse of Malcom's taillights entering the next curve.

Malcom looked in the rearview mirror, then looked back again quickly. As he saw the lights of the approaching van he had little doubt as to his pursuer's identity.

Getting a firm grip on the wheel, Max redoubled her efforts to catch the fleeing Westeridge.

The two vehicles, sometimes separated by less than a few feet, roared down through the quiet dim streets. Oncoming traffic, seemingly sensing the approaching hazard, pulled over and allowed the two combatants to pass. But as Max pressed the Mercedes across a second side street she suddenly slammed on the brakes and turned off. "You've gone just about far enough Westeridge," she grinned, turning into the next street over.

Max's sudden departure was not lost on Westeridge. Squinting into the rearview, he waited for her to return, even twisting around in the seat to look out the shattered rear window. Careening down the first block and then the second without further sight of his pursuer, Westeridge's hopes were beginning to rise when ahead, at the intersection still nearly half a block ahead, a vehicle pulled into the middle of the road and came to a complete stop.

Max watched the Mercedes swerve when Malcom slammed on the brakes, then it straightened out and rolled to a stop. For several minutes the pair sat there, neither moving.

"That's right, asshole. Just sit there and let old Night Hammer get your rotten little scent."

Almost as if he had heard her challenge the Mercedes began very slowly to back away. Matching his speed, Max rolled the van forward. As the Mercedes accelerated so did Max. As the Mercedes screeched into a backward turn the van leaped forward, closing the distance between the two with alarming speed. Horn blaring, Max slammed on the brakes and nudged the Mercedes left rear flank as it completed the turn. Before Malcom could coordinate his actions, she bumped a second then a third time, removing one taillight and a good deal of chrome from his rear bumper.

The pair raced down the narrow hillside roads, dodging slower traffic. Swooping into the edges of Glendale's mushrooming business district, they darted in and out of traffic, oblivious to signals and oncoming vehicles. A glowering sky descended on the area, in defiance of the meteorological forecast, punctuating its presence with booming thunder and a strange white/green lightning.

Malcom careened onto the Ventura Freeway with Max not too far behind.

Max strained to make out the location of the Mercedes in the sea of cars crawling along ahead of her when suddenly the sky flared an eerie greenish white and the sound of thunder rumbled down, shaking the very concrete beneath them. Blinking against the flare, she frowned as a sea of red lights erupted ahead of her, stretching as far as she could see. Max gasped as the rear end of the Ford ahead of her came rushing toward the van with alarming speed. She slammed on the brakes with both feet, managing to stop barely a hair's-breadth from the Ford's square little bottom.

A cyclone of sounds assaulted her as she rolled down the window and stuck out her head, straining to see ahead. Blasts of wind screamed around the van—then, as if turned off by a switch, it was gone. Around her other drivers, confused and disorientated, looked about, a number of them getting out of their cars.

Climbing down from the van, Max cut a path through the milling drivers, working her way toward the front of the pack and the position where she had last seen Westeridge's Mercedes. As she neared her destination she noted traffic on the eastbound lanes had stopped as well, a number of drivers likewise exiting their cars and moving in the same direction as she.

Nearly 30 vehicles, bearing various degrees of damage, sat sprawled across all six lanes of the freeway. Clumped in groups ranging from twos and threes to as many as eight, the cars sat motionless.

Separated from the other vehicles sat the Mercedes. The only outward signs of damage to the vehicle were those Max could easily account for. Approaching the car cautiously, she stopped several feet back from it. Even in the gray half-light of the overcast, the spattered blood on the remaining car windows gave ample evidence that Yohaul-i-Tepuztli had sated his hunger.

"You all right, lady?"

Max looked into the face of the bearded youth who had suddenly appeared at her side.

"Are you all right?" he asked a second time more loudly.

"Fine," she said quietly.

"Danny. Jesus Christ, take a look at this," another youth called out, staring into the ruined interior of the Mercedes.

Max glanced in the direction of the caller, vaguely

aware of the growing collection of curious gawkers closing on the Mercedes. No longer concerned with the spectacle she turned and walked slowly back to the van.

Climbing inside she dropped her head in her hands and closed her eyes. Halfway home, she thought wearily, halfway home.

Max turned slowly into the street, pleasantly surprised to see Duncan, a white bandage around his head, sitting at the curb beside a single black and white. After three hours spent sitting in traffic and another 45 minutes creeping along to the nearest exit ramp, she wasn't sure he'd still be here.

He climbed into the front seat of the van and settled back without saying a word. Max waved as the black and white glided past, then she turned the van around and began moving back down the mountain in a much more leisurely pace then her last trip.

Neither spoke for a long time, both immersed in private thought. At the bottom of the foothills Max turned away from the freeway and broke the silence, saying quietly, "Freeway's closed along here, so I guess I'll have—"

"That bastard got away, didn't he?" Duncan said wearily.

"Malcom Westeridge is dead. What he tried to summon came back for its payment," she said calmly.

Duncan watched her for several minutes, then turned his gaze out the windshield. After a few minutes he asked quietly, "You knew it would happen that way all along, didn't you?"

Max didn't answer.

"Good. I'm glad the bastard's dead," he said firmly. "That only leaves the Chac Mool. What do we do about that thing? You know they'll never allow it to be destroyed." The leading edge of hysteria was slipping into his voice. "They're too worried about lawsuits and public opinion to do anything. You know they're never gonna let anybody know what really happened here. Nobody but us is ever going to know."

"Duncan," Max interrupted, "If I told you it was over, would you believe me?"

Duncan studied her for a long minute then looked out at the traffic around them as they crossed the intersection.

"It's over. It will never happen again, I promise."

"But you said . . ."

"Never again. And you can forget that dribble about nobody ever knowing. Neither of us gives a flying rat's ass who knows and who doesn't. It's over, we won, and that's all that bloody well counts."

Duncan looked at her. "You're sure? It's really over?"

"It's over."

They drove along silently for several miles before Duncan spoke again. "I figured out where it was, you know."

Max smiled at him. "Where what was?"

"The little statue. It was in the bathroom."

Max grinned and nodded. "Not bad, detective."

She dropped him off in front of his house. For several embarrassing moments they both danced around what each knew would most certainly be their last parting.

"You get a good night's sleep for a change and I'll call you tomorrow."

"You're not going back to the apartment, are you?"

"No," Max said. "Fact is I'll be spending the night with Riley and his family," she added, smiling mentally at the half-truth.

"Oh."

"Have a good night, and I'll call you tomorrow first thing."

"Not too early," he said, backing away toward the walk.

"Not too early." She smiled and started the van.

"Drive careful," he called as she pulled away from the curb. He stood there watching the van move down the street until it turned the corner and disappeared. Walking slowly up to the front door he put his key in the lock, thinking that she wouldn't call and suddenly realizing the thought of not seeing Max Morgan again wasn't nearly as pleasant a one as he would have believed such a short time ago.

Waiting for traffic to clear, Max reached for the phone and punched in a number.

On the second ring a deep voice with a thick Irish accent answered.

"Showtime," Max said evenly then broke the connection, returning the receiver to its cradle.

3:19 a.m.

The moon flitted between high scudding, white clouds, its reflection glittering brightly on the restless ocean below.

Like a funeral cortege, there were four black vehicles, the van in the lead followed by a large truck and two smaller cars. They crossed the bridge above the piers of San Pedro. Following the circuitous route down to the dock area, they passed row after row of wharfs, warehouses and rusting cargo ships. Turning into a gated area reserved for the slowly vanishing private fleets of independent fishermen, they were guided by other dark figures to a waiting shrimper.

Riley jumped out of the van and moved quickly back toward the truck where several sturdy-looking men were gathering. In a voice soft enough not to draw attention but loud enough to reach the waiting men he ordered, "All right, you lot, get to it. We haven't got all night."

Max smiled quietly as the door on the drivers side of the van opened and she found Sean McCall smiling in at her. Gallantly, but unnecessarily, he helped her down. "You got everything?"

"My luggage is in the back."

"I'll see it gets on board. Don't worry about the van. The boys will take care of it."

"You've got the keys to the apartment."

He patted his pocket. "Da gave 'em to me. Not to worry. Things'll be shipshape before your friend gets back home."

"And the check? If you have any trouble cashing it, you call . . ."

"Don't give it a second thought, and if there's change I'll see it's sent to ya."

"Thank you," she said softly, her voice heavy with fatigue.

"Not necessary," he said solemnly. "We owe you a lot more."

She held up her hand, stopping his words. "Old proverb. Debts of friendship are repaid in the thought not the deed—or some such foolishness." She tossed him a quick grin then turned, crossing quickly toward the truck and the approaching forklift.

Riley put his arm around her shoulders as she came up along side of him. "Well, it's over now, love. Why don't you get on board. The lads'll see to this."

"We're not completely out of the woods yet. Can't afford for things to go sour now."

"Nonsense. They'll not disturb the old blighter. Come along. Da knows what'll do ya."

The diesel engines of the old ship purred contentedly, vibrating underfoot with a comforting rhythm. Max stepped onto the deck, trying not to smile at the clattering sound of ill-gotten gains from Riley's bulging pockets as he jumped aboard. Inside the weathered bridge, Max was too weary to register surprise at the amazing array of state of the art technology crammed into its small confines. Cupping her hands around a thick mug filled with steaming tea, she sipped at the rich brew, welcoming its warming embrace.

Gliding out of the harbor, they passed within speaking distance of three large Coast Guard ships resting at anchor, even waving nonchalantly to the officer of the watch. Breaking free of the harbor, the small shrimper headed out into the channel.

"The channel here, between Catalina and the coast, is particularly deep," Riley said tapping a large map spread out before him. "Will somewhere in there do ya, or would you fancy someplace else? You know we could run you down the coast to Mexico if you've a mind to take the old thing home."

"No, the channel will do nicely."

"Right you are. Out to the channel and over the side with himself, is that how it's to be?"

"There's something I have to do first. Once that's completed, then let the boys finish the job, but make certain every piece, no matter how small, goes over the side."

"If that's how you want it, love, that's how it'll go. Why don't I warm up that tea?"

Slightly over a half hour later the engines stopped, and the shrimper drifted on the swells somewhere in the middle of the Catalina channel. Max stepped out onto the deck and watched as Conna and several other men pulled away the dark tarp covering the great Peten Chac Mool.

As Max approached the statue, the men crowded back, opening a pathway for her. Climbing up onto it, she straddled its midsection. Riley stepped forward and handed her a small sledge-hammer. Laying it across her lap, she reached out, placing her hands on the figure's broad head.

Almost before her eyes could close she could feel his presence. A kind of darkness closed around her, but this time the center of the darkness was broken by a softer grayness.

The time has come, old one, she thought. You will be free once more, but your time here is gone. Only memories mark your home now. The others have all gone on ahead of you. The stars are different here now, and the earth too old and worn for your presence. Climb away. You know the path. Climb away to where the others wait. Go to that place where time is of no importance and the old ways still exist. Climb away, old one. Your place is prepared.

Opening her eyes she whispered, "Climb away. The old stars await you."

Taking a firm hold on the hammer, she swung it back over her shoulder, bringing it down with all her might onto the statue's crown. She struck once, then again and again, and with the fourth blow a wide crack snaked across the statue's face. With one last blow the face split in two, and as the two halves fell apart there was a smell of virgin land and vegetation—and the faint laughter of strange music rippled away across the water. Max swayed backward, crying out as a cold wind passed through her heart. Tears sprang to her eyes, her body trembling at the flicker of brightly colored images that paraded across her mind.

"Easy," Riley shouted. He and Conna quickly reached out to her.

She came down, accepting their aid without protest, and while the men turned to the destruction of the old wizard's coffin, only Max, her misted vision turned toward the heavens, saw the shooting star pass overhead.

February 15th

800 miles north of Los Angeles.

MAX SMILED, WATCHING THE ANTICS OF THE SMALL PERSIAN kitten as it raced back and forth and chased the seagulls feeding on the balcony outside the window. Suddenly the kitten stopped and crouched down as one of the gulls strayed too near the glass. With a crisp yelp it launched its small body toward the glass, colliding against it with a soft thump.

"Oh, Pumpkin," Max crooned, a small giggle in her voice. "Come here, baby."

The small animal sat down, licked at its paw for a moment, then turned, its bushy tail flicking angrily, and marched across the office and through the door.

The phone beside her rang.

"Hello."

For several seconds she heard only the static rush so common with long distance calls.

"Hello? Are you there? Hello?"

Slowly Max cradled the phone against her shoulder and laid her head back against the chair. Smiling softly, she said, "You're welcome, Duncan."

A moment passed, then she heard a click on the other end as the line went dead. Slowly she returned the receiver to its cradle, a picture of a smiling Duncan Forbes clearly etched in her mind's eye.